MW00436993

BLUE SKY ADAM

A Novel

ANTHONY MCDONALD

Anchor Mill Publishing

Anthony McDonald

Anchor Mill Publishing

4/04 Anchor Mill

Paisley PA1 1JR

SCOTLAND

anchormillpublishing@gmail.com

First published by BIGfib Books

Blue Sky Adam

For Tony as Always

Anthony McDonald

Acknowledgements

The author would like to thank Barry Creasy, Olivier Cuperlier, Steve Gee, Yves Le Juen and Alexandra Rativeau. Also Bryan Kelly and John Newberry, in whose millstream garden at Sourreau the seeds of this story began to grow.

ONE

Adam felt guilty about not attending Georges Pincemin's funeral, although he'd had the perfect excuse. It had clashed with the cello recital that was the most important element of his music finals exam. Nevertheless, he felt ashamed of the relief that the coincidence gave him. He was not a fan of funerals – even if his roommate Michael did remind him that the anagram of funeral was *real fun*.

But in the couple of weeks that followed, images of Georges and memories of the unlikely weekend he'd spent with him at the big rambling house among the vines kept flooding into his mind. Adam told himself that was only to be expected when his feelings were in the yoyo-like state that every student experiences between taking a major examination and learning the result.

Another symptom of that condition was his tendency feverishly to tear open every letter that arrived, especially any that he had to sign for. He did this with one smart white envelope to find that it came from a Chancery Lane solicitors' firm of whom he had never heard. He noticed this with feelings of mixed relief and disappointment, then got on with reading the letter itself. Which told him that he was a beneficiary under the terms of the will of the late M. Georges Pincemin. He would receive what the letter described as a legacy. Adam stopped reading. How very good and kind Georges had been, to think of adding a detail like this to his will during his final illness. Adam felt himself go hot with shame at having even occasionally resented the time and effort he had spent on those hospital visits. A mere six or seven trips to Hammersmith. They had cost him nothing except his time: he had a student travelcard for the underground. He read on, almost casually because after the humbling discovery that Georges had wanted to do something for him the details hardly mattered. What the legacy might consist of – a treasured watch perhaps? A couple of hundred pounds towards his overdraft? – was hardly the point. Then his thoughts were stopped, like his eyes, in their tracks.

'...the property known as Le Grand Moulin de Pressac in the Commune of St-Genès-de-Castillon, Gironde, France, including the attached dwelling known as Le Petit Moulin at the same address, together with all land and other buildings at present constituting the said property, including the parcel of vineyard which forms that part of the Château L'Orangerie estate belonging to the late M. Pincemin at the time of his decease.'

He saw the place now, as he had seen it first: the autumn vineyards turning to bright lemon yellow, with here and there among them a maverick vine that had gone a blazing cherry red; the valley bottoms filled with dark copses; the trees, not yet starting to turn colour themselves, looking almost black beyond the luminous yellow of the slopes; the flinty track diving downhill to where a huddle of roof ridges and gables appeared teasingly among the trees.

Adam could only make sense of a few odd words after that. '...*awaiting precise and up to date valuation of the said property ... obtaining probate ... take some time ... estate in more than one country...* '

Adam could take no more of it in. Nor could he begin to think through to any of the implications it might have. He held on to only one, extraordinary, undreamt-of-before-this-morning, thought. He was the owner of a property, substantial as well as picturesque, in a ravishingly beautiful part of France. Professional cellist he might or might not be when his results came through in a few more days. But right now he was a landowner and a winegrower, a *vigneron*. He was not quite twenty-two.

Being a *vigneron*, or the thought of being one, kept Adam's thoughts and feelings in a balloon-like state of suspension for a good thirty minutes. He found himself flying at a considerable height above the hills and valleys of everyday emotional experience – even the intense highs and lows that are lived through by someone awaiting the result of the most important exam in his life. He regretted that he was alone in the flat: Michael was not there to share the news with and, furthermore, he could not be phoned because he was at that moment sitting an important university exam himself, and something similar went for Sean also. There was no-one else he would have wanted to phone just yet: not before he had put his thoughts into some kind of order. Other friends, parents. They would all have to wait. Yet he felt he must do something to celebrate the moment. He jumped in the air once, with an inarticulate shout, letter still in hand, then felt rather foolish, despite, or perhaps because of, there being no-one in the flat to witness his display of euphoria. He looked around him. There was nothing to drink in living room or kitchen. Not because it was a teetotal place; rather the opposite in fact: bottles of alcohol seldom lived to see the morning after the day of their purchase. He thought for a moment, then, feeling rather self-conscious because it was only ten minutes past eleven in the morning, he walked out and round the corner to the Cornet of Horse, where he bought himself a pint of Grolsch and sat nursing it in the empty bar, in a grubby armchair under a window in whose shaft of morning sunshine the dust motes swam randomly up and down, keeping company with his thoughts.

He tried to make sense of what had happened. He and Michael had met Georges first in Paris on Adam's seventeenth birthday. Next morning they had heard about the watermill for the first time. 'Hundreds of years old,' Georges had boasted, 'and very picturesque. In my grand-parents' day there was a whole wine estate as well, but it was split up after they died and most of the vines sold. I still hang onto a little bit though.' His blue eyes had twinkled mischievously as he said that. Georges, half French, half Irish, had been about sixty even then, but the gravitas that went along with the silver hair was still underpinned by something boyish.

'Do you make your own wine?' Michael had asked him.

'It would be fun, wouldn't it? But it wouldn't really be economical – or very practical for me. People don't expect you to give harpsichord recitals with blue-stained fingers. No, the grapes are sold, still on the vine, to the owners of the rest of the estate – Château L'Orangerie. They do the pressing and have all the headaches.' It was then that he had looked carefully at each of the two boys in turn before adding, 'You must come and visit me there sometime.'

'Be careful, Georges,' Gary had cautioned. 'These two are only too likely to take you up on an invitation like that.' He had smiled. 'As I know to my cost.' They were drinking Gary's coffee at the time. In Gary's kitchen. And Adam and Michael had for two weeks been occupying the spare bedroom of his elegant flat.

'I don't mind if they do,' Georges had said calmly, again looking at the two boys with his strong blue eyes. 'The invitation was meant.'

The phone in Adam's pocket chirruped for attention. It was Michael. His exam was over. It was ten past twelve. Everyone was in The Jeremy Bentham. And where was Adam?

'I'm coming over,' Adam said.

'Where are you?'

'Still in Clapham. At the Cornet of Horse.'

'Jesus, what are you doing there? We'll all be bladdered before you get up here,' said Michael.

'Then meet halfway. Somewhere ... say ... say the Bell and Compass at Charing Cross.'

'The where?'

'It's in Villiers Street. Imagine you're coming out of Heaven and turning left. It's right there.'

'Nobody we know goes there.'

'That's why we're meeting there. There's something important. Something you need to know. But without an audience. Be there.'

Adam had met Georges again just as he was beginning his new life – the one that was now ending – at the Royal Academy of Music. Georges Pincemin had been billed to do a harpsichord recital, to be recorded by the BBC, in the Duke's Hall. Adam persuaded Michael, starting his law studies a few blocks away at UCL and already sharing the room with him in Clapham, to join him. Adam and Michael were among the small number of people who 'went back' after the recital was over, to pay their respects to the artist in the band room. 'You're not expected to remember us,' Adam had begun diffidently, unaware then that a person of Georges's age and sexual temperament would be no more likely to forget meeting a pair of teenagers like Adam and Michael than forget how to ride a bicycle.

'Of course I remember you,' Georges said. 'And I haven't forgotten my invitation to come and visit me in the Gironde, even if we did lose touch for a while.' Then, after the shortest of pauses, 'What about next weekend?'

Later, on their way home to Clapham in a taxi, Michael said, 'You can't possibly be serious about taking him up on it.'

'I don't see why not,' Adam objected. 'You took him up on his offer of dinner just now, and he turned out to be a very generous host. And a gentleman,' he added, removing Michael's invading hand from his crotch, where it was in danger of becoming visible in the driver's mirror. He put the hand to his mouth and gently bit it, like someone training a puppy. 'Wait till we're home.'

Michael wouldn't be able to go anyway, they had realised later: he'd committed himself to a weekend coursework project. He suggested Adam invite Sean along as a substitute if he was really going to take the invitation up. Adam thought this would probably be a non-starter but he called Sean anyway.

'Yeah, OK, cool,' Sean had answered from his hall of residence in Newcastle, where he was just embarked on his own long university course, studying architecture, far from home and friends. 'But you know, if someone invites two guys – as a pair of friends, he's going to get a bit pissed off if a different pair turn up. Besides, have you any idea how long it takes to get from Newcastle to Stansted?'

A pair of friends was Sean's phrase back then and Adam had to admit that even now it still applied. Adam-and-Michael was one pair of friends, Adam-and-Sean another. The complexity of their triangle, going back as it did to pre-teen days, was such that Adam didn't even try to get his head round it on a day-to-day basis. Sometimes he focused, deliberately, on one of the most superficial aspects of the thing to save himself time. His shorthand-thought was this. Adam and Michael came over as a very presentable couple, both of them nice-looking, though in quite a regular way – cute rather than either pretty or beautiful. And by common consent, including his own, Adam was the cuter of the two. Which was nice for Adam. On the other hand, when he was being half of Adam-and-Sean, although still registering as cute, he was mightily eclipsed by the hunky blond beauty, just a year older than himself, who was Sean. It was to Sean that all eyes, male or female, gravitated first when they were out together and when those eyes later rested on Adam, they were admiring him perhaps less for his own physical charms as for whatever power it was that had enabled him to capture the friendship of a beautiful creature like Sean in the first place. As a compliment to Adam it tasted bittersweet. As far as any Michael-Sean pairing went ... well it didn't go all that far.

It had finally been agreed that Adam would travel on his own to spend a *fin de semaine hermétique* with Georges in his rural fastness in France. The others would cross their fingers for him. Their legs too if necessary.

Adam's tube train jolted to a halt at Embankment station and his thoughts came back to the present with a similar bump. What was going to happen to him now? Being a man of property in another country was going to change forever his relationships with his two closest friends. Whatever they might do to convince themselves that nothing was any different, he would be the one who owned a place in France and they the two who didn't. He could hardly expect to export them, like furniture or luggage, and imagine life going on as before. So, would he keep his room on in London, in the flat in Clapham … for the sake of Michael's rent bill? Whichever way he looked, Adam now saw only negatives, his windfall coming between him and his family, tearing him apart from his friends. He would have to sell the place, he suddenly thought. Take the money and run. But then he realised that – quite apart from the fact that this was clearly not Georges's intention – nothing at all would be solved. What would he do with all that money? Buy a big house somewhere else? Live on it in a style his friends couldn't possibly aspire to? Get shot of it completely? He began to understand now what had made Saint Francis give the whole of his inheritance to the poor – plus the clothes he stood up in. Adam made his way out of the station and towards the Bell and Compass.

He and Michael were still there a couple of hours later, Michael listening patiently to Adam's increasingly maudlin account of the drawbacks to inheriting a valuable property in France. He had been as astonished at hearing Adam's news as Adam had been himself. There had been one awkward moment when it dawned on them both that the invitation to visit the Moulin de Pressac had been made to the pair of them and that it was almost a matter of chance that Adam had gone alone; it could have been the other way round. 'Except it wouldn't have been,' Michael conceded graciously. 'I wouldn't have gone on my own, the way you did. I said so, I remember.' He gave Adam a mischievous smile. 'Of course I might have done if I'd thought I stood a chance of inheriting the place, but there it is. Anyway, I'm not a musician and you are.'

Once they'd got that out of the way it was clearly easier for Michael to take a more objective view of the situation than for Adam. Although buying Adam pints to cheer him up after coming into so much property did strike Michael as ironic to a rather extreme degree, it gave him the time to make two key observations. The first was that the end of Adam's studies were upon him and that the same went for himself: Michael would shortly be leaving university life behind him and starting his one-year legal practice course at law school. Everything was about to change anyway, that was Michael's point; it was something neither of them had faced yet; life wasn't going to go on as before, with the two of them rooming in Clapham for ever. Adam's news didn't necessarily herald a greater seismic shift in the pattern of their lives than was going to happen anyway.

The second thing was easier to put simply. 'You'd be on the same land-mass as Sylvain at any rate. You can think about that.'

By the end of the afternoon Adam had clearly had enough of both thinking and drinking, and Michael, not too steady on his own feet either by now, was only just able to steer him out through the door before he was sick on the pavement among the rush-hour crowds in Villiers Street. 'Now I understand why you wanted to go somewhere nobody knew us,' Michael said as, propping each other up, they stumbled towards Embankment station.

Sylvain. Michael had brought the name up. They didn't often discuss him. It must have been the beer – or the occasion. Though Georges had broached the subject of Sylvain, to Adam's surprise, during that awkward, if interesting – and now it seemed, consequential – weekend at the Moulin de Pressac.

It had been awkward only in that one sixty-year-old gay man had found himself alone with one extremely young one when he had expected the easier presence of two. They were both conscious of it, and Georges had dealt with the situation by keeping them both in a state of perpetual brisk activity. A walk around the domain, a rendezvous with neighbours' dogs, Georges cooking supper with some panache while Adam laid the table following his host's instructions. After supper, a tour of the house, which was two houses in fact. The working part of the old mill – the Petit Moulin – was now a separate dwelling, let out to holidaymakers in the summer months. Where the stream ran below the building the wooden mill wheel remained in place, though permanently out of gear. You could see it behind a glass partition in the hallway of the rental accommodation and, when you switched a certain light on, you could also see the water tumbling below.

Georges had shown Adam his prize possessions: two harpsichords from the eighteenth century, which elegantly filled one end of the big living room. One was by the great English maker, Kirkman; it was seven feet long, oak-cased, veneered in Cuban-curl mahogany and with shiny brass hinges on the lid. The other was French, by Taskin. Lighter in appearance and style, it was painted a pastel green. Inside the lid there was a design of flowers and cherubs painted on the soundboard beneath the harp of golden strings. Georges had played a short piece on each instrument. To show off the French one he had selected a piece by Rameau: *Les Niais de Sologne*, the Simpletons. It began with an air of nursery-like simplicity, yet opened out into a peacock's tail of richness in its variations. The lightweight instrument seemed to grow in size and power as the piece progressed, and Adam imagined that it shimmered and glowed like some device used in sorcery and magic. He had found himself strangely affected.

In the morning, a short drive to the little town that was the focal point of all the billowing hectares of vines: St-Emilion. Nestling against the hillside, in a natural hollow which had roughly the shape of an oyster shell, it still retained its medieval outline as well as its crowning church spire. The town was entirely contained within its ancient honey-coloured stone walls where fig trees rambled against the crumbling masonry, while on the outside the sea of yellow-green vines began directly. There were no outskirts: no factories or car repair yards, no housing estates or shopping sprawls; the value of the land for wine production saw to that. Georges took Adam on a voyage of exploration of the steep cobbled lanes and stone staircases, they peered into cloisters of old convents, visited temples of wine, then Georges bought them lunch on the Place du Clocher, into which small square sprang the tall church spire, rising surreally up through the ground from the monolithic church that was hewn out of the bedrock below. Over the parapet they could peer down at the orange-tiled rooftops of the lower town all spread out beneath them, while the Dordogne ran through the further distance in its broad valley, snaking towards Bordeaux and the unseen sea.

In the evening they dined at a neighbour's. A neighbour in that sea of vines was, usually, someone who lived a kilometre's drive away at least. By which standard this one was pretty close. So Adam found himself meeting a family of *vignerons*: a couple in their fifties, an elderly grandfather, and two young people of about Adam's age, Françoise, who was perhaps a year his senior, and – more interestingly from Adam's point of view – the slightly younger Stéphane.

Adam had been determined to keep his end up in the conversation over the roast lamb. 'And is the whole of this wine region St-Emilion?' he asked.

His hosts laughed self-deprecatingly, to indicate that they would all be far richer if it were. Georges explained that they were now in the Côtes de Castillon. It was, like St-Emilion, very much a part of the Bordeaux *vignoble* – claret country still, not Bergerac – but the fact remained that Côtes de Castillon wine, excellent as it was, did not command the prices or carry the international reputation of the St-Emilion châteaux. So where did the boundary lie, Adam wanted to know?

The boy, Stéphane, took it upon himself to answer. 'The line is a little tributary of the river Lacaret: it's the millstream which runs right through Georges's garden.' He raised his eyebrows – a little camply, Adam thought. 'You must have seen it.'

Adam turned to Georges. 'Then is your patch of vines part of St-Emilion or Côtes de Castillon?'

'Côtes de Castillon,' Georges answered, 'like my friends' here, and nothing wrong with that.'

'Couldn't you grow vines on the other side – the other side of the stream, I mean?' Adam's innocent inquiry had his hosts smiling and nodding to each other and saying, in French, things that meant roughly, 'We've got a right one here.'

Georges had put Adam wise. 'First I'd have to cut down all the trees; they're an ancient spinney and they shelter the vines on the other side. People would have a lot to say about that. Then, the area permitted for growing wine as St-Emilion *Appellation Controlée* is very strictly controlled by law. And third, the area is so tiny – half my lawn and the little wood. You wouldn't want me to plough up my lawn, would you? It's hardly worth thinking about anyway.' He helped himself to another chunk of baguette.

After the meal Stéphane said he would show Adam around outside: the winery, *les chais*, and so on. His parents protested half-heartedly that it was dark. But there were arc lights in the yard, Stéphane argued, and besides, there were stars to see by and they could listen to the owls.

Adam read between the lines quite easily, or hoped he did, and was only too happy to go. Stéphane was slim and wiry, with spiky blond hair and a longish face, but he had nice brown eyes.

The night air was heavy with a scent that, Adam guessed, could only be fermenting wine: part sulphurous and farty, part spirituous – like raw brandy – and part the wholesome smell of rising bread. 'It's the yeast,' said Stéphane. They did the briefest tour of the yard and buildings, listened under the pine trees for the resident owl – which duly called in shivering funnels of sound as it arrived, unseen and otherwise silently, overhead.

'I need to piss,' Adam said. He unzipped and did so, without turning away from Stéphane who, a few seconds later, obligingly followed Adam's example. It was a quick and easy way, Adam had discovered, of gauging the nature and extent of another boy's interest in your company. Under Adam's gaze, Stéphane's jutting penis began to metamorphose into an up-curving slender horn, while his own stouter organ swiftly mirrored the transformation. A quick glance at the other's shy smile was all that was required for confirmation. Then they were clinched together, with jeans halfway down their thighs, and, in a rough and businesslike way, at work on each other's cocks. It was less than a minute before, almost simultaneously, they both released their harpoon-threads of semen, turning slightly aside in a practised last-second twist to avoid compromising each other's clothes. As they zipped up afterwards Adam gave Stéphane a quick peck on the cheek. It had become a trademark of his over the past year. It was meant to signify: *the end*.

'How did you get on with Stéphane?' Georges had asked next morning. They were eating a kind of brunch. It was a very un-French thing to do, but in view of the time of Adam's flight back from Bergerac it had been the most sensible option.

'You knew?' Adam had blurted, then tried to bury the unguarded response with a sulky, 'I suppose you arranged that we'd meet on purpose.'

'I know nothing at all,' Georges said very sweetly, while debating with himself whether to offer Adam a third cup of coffee or to shock him by uncorking an eleven a.m. bottle of champagne. 'However, I do remember what I was like at your age, and I had a hunch, of sorts, about young Stéphane. So, yes, perhaps I did engineer the evening on purpose – but only in the most general way.' He decided on the champagne and stood up to go and get it. 'And now,' he turned back to Adam from halfway to the fridge, 'I don't want to know anything more about the two of you.'

Georges had been an excellent host, Adam thought, as he accepted the early morning *coupe* with as much surprise as pleasure. He could have interrogated Adam about his progress at college – since Georges was an occasional tutor of harpsichord in the very building on the Marylebone Road where Adam studied the cello – but didn't. He could have fussed him with questions about his love life – as a gay man forty years his senior – but he hadn't done that either. He had led the conversation only when it rambled around inconsequential subjects and only shared his thoughts on important matters like life and music when Adam himself introduced them. Adam was conscious of all this and respected Georges for it. Perhaps that was why the next thing he'd said was, 'Maybe you're wondering about Michael. I mean, about me and him.' He hadn't waited for Georges to try to answer. 'Well, it's not an exclusive thing with us. In case you're thinking that last night was some sort of cheating on my part. It doesn't work like that with us. We're friends who love each other, rather than actual lovers, if you can understand that.'

Georges had no difficulty with the concept.

'And anyway,' Adam went on, 'there's a third person in the triangle.' He mumbled a bit inarticulately about Sean, intimated rather than stated that Sean and he occasionally slept together; emphatically did not say that he, Adam, was besotted with Sean but that Sean was something of a floating voter when it came to *a)* sexual orientation and *b)* relationships in general. But Georges nevertheless got the picture pretty precisely.

Then Georges at last broke his own rules of engagement and fired a direct question at Adam. 'Gary told me – perhaps he had no business to, but so be it – about someone else. A young Frenchman from the Plateau de Langres. I don't remember the name. Is he still a part of the big picture?'

'Sylvain. His name's Sylvain.' Adam heard his own voice faltering and diffident like a child's. He pulled himself together. 'We weren't supposed to contact each other after the court case – that's well over a year ago now; I suppose Gary told you all about it – but of course we have.' He didn't elaborate on the means or the nature of their contacts, though he did add, 'Only we haven't actually managed to see each other.'

'But you'd like to?' Georges pursued gently.

'Of course,' said Adam. 'Of course we both want to. But, you know, people can change a lot – or develop at any rate – in the course of a year. Especially when they're young. We might find we'd grown apart. It would be a bit crushing to discover that. Anyway, he's in France, I'm in England. So... I don't know. I think I'd like us to meet, but it scares me.' He was silent for a moment. Then he said, 'And it wasn't a particularly easy relationship anyway.' He didn't volunteer any more than that and Georges did not press him.

Instead, Georges had walked Adam out of the house (they were still, rather preciously, carrying champagne flutes) past the spinney that bounded the garden and up a little way into the vines: the steep slope of vineyard that was Georges Pincemin's share of Château L'Orangerie. After only a few, if somewhat vertical, paces they were looking over and beyond the roofs of the mill house, down the steep valley of the Lacaret, across to the parish church of Ste-Colombe on the opposite hill, then on across the Dordogne floodplain to the distant hills of the Entre-Deux-Mers on the south side. It was a serene landscape of green and early autumn yellows, with only a few brisk dark cypresses standing to attention in distant château gardens to challenge the general softness. Adam had looked intently around him, at and into the depths of the view, drinking in its loveliness, but assuming that he would never stand here again. Then he had drained his glass of champagne in one quick impulsive gulp.

TWO

Adam decided to deal with the problem of telling his parents that he'd come into property by not telling them anything at all.

'You can't do that!' Sean had almost never raised his voice at Adam in all the years he'd known him, but he did on this occasion. 'That's copping out of things mega. It's also incredibly selfish. And anyway, they're going to find out sooner or later.'

'Who from?' asked Adam.

Michael answered. 'You can't go and live in a big house in France for the rest of your life without your parents noticing at some stage – however unobservant they may have been about you in the past.' The three of them were sprawled around the living room of the flat in Clapham; nobody else was in. 'Besides, they'll hear it from my parents soon enough.'

'So you told your bloody parents before I've told mine,' Adam grumbled.

'I'd no reason not to. I had no cause to think you'd be mad enough to try to keep the thing a secret.'

'And mine know too,' added Sean. 'And for the same reason. I agree with Michael for once.'

'Anyway,' said Michael, 'if you want to keep quiet about it for ever and ever it'll be a waste of a whole bloody summer. And I don't know about Sean but I'm counting on a good long holiday down there myself.' He grinned at Adam. 'And if you don't want to come, I'll steal the key and go by myself.'

'You can't,' said Adam. 'Call yourself a lawyer? You've forgotten probate. The solicitors said it would take ages.'

'Actually, where is the key?' Sean asked.

'It's with a *notaire* – that's French for solicitor – in St-Emilion. Though there's a couple of copies with neighbours.' As he spoke, Adam wondered suddenly, which neighbours? He remembered again his encounter with Stéphane in the dark among the trees at the back of the wine sheds.

'Probate, forget probate,' said Michael. 'You can get the key and have a holiday there, I'd have thought, provided you clear it with the executors. They'll only want to be sure you don't try to sell the place or pull it down or something stupid.'

'I hadn't thought of that,' said Adam. 'I suppose it's worth a try. Anyway you're right, of course. I can't just ignore the place. Only don't you go thinking of it as a holiday home, because I certainly can't. Not at this stage in my life. Unless I win the lottery as well, of course, but I'm not counting on that. It's either got to be the place I live and work from, or pay its way some other way, or be sold.' Adam looked suitably grave as he said this.

'So when are we going?' Michael asked.

Adam pounced on him and wrestled with him on the sofa for a moment, then they both spilled off it onto the floor. 'It's OK for you. You've got your near future mapped out. Law school. Sean goes on with his architecture studies in Newcastle. But I'm out in the world now with a living to earn and no idea how I'm going to earn it.'

Sean made a violin-playing gesture while Michael, whose arms were still pinioned by Adam, joined in the sound effects. 'You sound like a chorus of cats,' observed Adam.

Sean too had met Georges on a few occasions. From time to time Georges had invited Adam out to dinner or even, with other company, to his Holland Park flat. Sometimes Michael had got himself invited too, and once, because he had been at a Duke's Hall concert with Adam when one such invitation was being made, Sean had been included also: he had had the same effect on Georges as he did on practically everybody else.

And then Sean was there when, just before the start of Adam's final term at college, he had got the call from Gary Blake in Paris telling him that Georges was ill and that no doubt Adam would want to know.

Sean, who had been used to spending quite big chunks of vacation time staying with Adam in Clapham – as well as a good few weekends in term-time – was lying on Michael's bed, shirtless and sockless, though still clad in jeans, when the call came.

'What's he got?' Sean asked, pulling himself to a sitting position on the side of Michael's bed. A sense of propriety so deep-rooted in Sean as to be unconscious made him feel uncomfortable discussing a friend's illness in too languidly sensual a posture.

'They're not quite sure, according to Gary.' Adam caught a look on Sean's face. 'But they know it isn't that. He's in hospital here in London. At the Charing Cross. Which is not at Charing Cross at all but at Hammersmith – I can't think why. It's about seventy-two light-years away from here. I suppose I'd better go and see him anyway, though. Come with me?'

Sean had said he would, and after that, his conscience clear now that duty had been decided upon, he lay back down on Michael's bed, where Adam quickly joined him; then, more slowly, they began to undo each other's jeans.

Adam had gone to see Georges almost every week. Having made what he thought was a one-off duty call during a short illness he had felt committed to keeping up the visits, however reluctantly. Georges so clearly enjoyed Adam's visits that, much as Adam might inwardly curse the inroads they made into his time, he was never tempted to suspend them. Then in early June

Adam had gone along as usual to see Georges, to be met with the gentle-toned announcement that he was dead. To his dismay he'd found that his first reaction was one of relief: at last the tiresome trips to Hammersmith could stop. It was a reaction that he felt even worse about now. And he was no nearer to knowing why Georges had given him the Moulin de Pressac.

THREE

Adam's final results were published. He had passed. Of course he had. He wondered now why on earth he had ever worried about the outcome. He was Adam Wheeler, B. Mus., LRAM. Licentiate of the Royal Academy of Music. As he had always been destined to be.

Within a week he had sent his details, with a covering letter, to every top-rank professional orchestra in the United Kingdom. Within another week they had nearly all replied, in the stamped addressed envelope he had courteously provided, with a polite 'No'. A week after that Adam set off for France. With him went Michael and Sean but not the cello. Adam reckoned they deserved a break from each other.

Adam did tell his parents of course. He phoned them to say he was going to spend a fortnight or three weeks with his friends in an old mill house in the French countryside. His mother asked where on earth the money was going to come from. He told her they had got cheap flights to Bergerac, and that they didn't have to pay rent when they got there. He'd been left the mill house in someone's will. She remembered Georges Pincemin? Adam had told her he'd died, hadn't he? Well, he'd left Adam his house, that was all. In the stunned silence that ensued, Adam said that he would ring again as soon as he got there, then put the phone down.

They stepped off the plane at Bergerac into baking summer heat. The low hills of Monbazillac, half wooded, half vine-carpeted, shimmered in the distant haze. They had chipped in together to rent a car for the first week. What they would do after that they didn't know. No doubt it would become clearer when the time came.

Adam drove them away from the airport, a little apprehensively in the unfamiliar vehicle. He wasn't sure if he would remember the way after nearly four years, but at least he – unlike the others – might recognise the place once they got there. And, again unlike the others, he had actually driven a car in France, albeit briefly, all those years ago, unlicensed and under age, with Sylvain. It wasn't a very auspicious memory given that they had both been carted away by the police minutes after the end of their ride, with Sylvain under arrest.

To his surprise Adam remembered the way, the little back roads that Georges had shown him, perfectly well: meandering lanes through the low hills that edged the Dordogne valley. At first they drove through hamlets of pinky-white stone where all the houses gave the impression of having roses round the door – even the ones that hadn't. A few miles later and the houses were of a yellower stone, and roofed with orange or red canal tiles, with vineyards tumbling downhill from them on every side. Standing next to the walls of some of the houses were huge shiny steel fermentation *cuves* – where other people might have had gas cylinders or oil tanks. At last they found themselves passing the village of St-Genès-de-Castillon, then turning out of the lane and down the steep rough track towards – Adam felt his heart knock a couple of times at the thought – Adam's house. The Moulin de Pressac. There it was, set in a deep combe: the big, roughly L-shaped stone building that comprised the 'Grand' and 'Petit' Moulins, shielded from the omnipresent vines by trees on two sides. They stopped the car and got out. At first nobody could think what to say. They stood and stared at the reed-fringed millstream winding its way around and under the house. And at the two ponds, the still, mirror-placid one above the weir and the turbid, foaming one below into which the overflow tumbled with a ceaseless, muted roar. Then they pulled themselves together and realised they must drive back up the track to collect the keys from the neighbour, one Madame Leduc, who lived just across the road from the top. That had been arranged. Madame Leduc also gave them a basket of groceries, which had not. Then, quite suddenly they were on their own, the three of them, in a totally new situation, in the depths of the countryside, in a great stone house where – as Adam realised the moment they entered the cool hallway and the others looked expectantly at him – he was the proprietor and was expected, for the first time in his life, to be in charge of whatever happened next. With a slight sinking feeling he realised that, apart from anything else, it would be up to him to make some sort of suggestion about where everyone slept.

Briefly they explored the ground floor rooms with their beamed ceilings and solid chestnut furniture. All was much as Adam remembered it except that the two harpsichords had gone. He noticed this with a momentary frisson of memory and regret. There was a piano in the living room though, which rather surprised Adam. Just an ordinary workhorse of an upright, but a piano all the same. Adam supposed he hadn't noticed it on his first visit because the two harpsichords had so brightly outshone it.

Adam remembered dimly that there was a big wine cellar but couldn't remember where. It was Michael who found it. It was not underground, which made sense, given that the ground floor was only a foot or two above the level of the streams and lower pond at the front of the house, and some way below the top of the weir at the back. Instead, it was housed in a stone-walled cool room behind the kitchen. It was impressively well stocked. 'Remember this for later,' Michael said as they closed the door.

They trooped upstairs. 'We can have a room each,' Adam said a bit uncertainly, 'if that's what we want.' And each of them then laid claim to a separate bedroom by dumping his backpack in one, in a sort of mad race, like schoolchildren commandeering desks and lockers at the start of term. Then, significantly, nobody unpacked anything at all but headed straight back downstairs. The next thing to do now became obvious as their eyes wandered round the big hall for the second time, and homed in at once on the door to the wine cellar. Adam uncorked a bottle, Sean found glasses, Michael got a cloth and wiped down garden chairs. Two minutes later they were seated on the lawn above the millstream, basking in the still hot rays of the evening sun. With the comforting splashy rumble of the weir as background, with Sean and Michael for company, and with a glass of glowing red Château L'Orangerie in his hand, Adam managed, for a short time at least, to forget the awesome extent of his new responsibilities and indulge himself with the feeling that life could not possibly be better. Ever.

Later, after the sun had gone and the colour, deep and luminous as a gas flame, had faded from the sky, Michael volunteered to cobble together some sort of supper with pasta and tuna chunks. They ate out of doors, with garden floodlighting and mosquitoes, though they were too high on wine and wonder to be concerned by the latter.

They stayed up till four, still outside, still talking, still drinking. Their conversation came round again and again, as if on a pre-set loop, to the property they were holidaying at and to what Adam was going to do with it. As the hours passed, the helpful proposals made by Michael and Sean became more and more far-fetched, till the word helpful no longer seemed to apply. Turn the place into a conference centre. A conservatoire of music.

A finishing school for young ladies. For young laddies. Young squaddies. Young paddies... An oenological research centre. Gynaecological institute... And that small section of the rational, thinking Adam that was still functioning became more and more convinced that, sadly, once they had all enjoyed a holiday or two here, the only possible thing to do was to sell it. *It gives one position but prevents one from keeping it up; that is all that one can say about land,* Michael quoted, in what was meant to be the voice of Edith Evans playing Lady Bracknell. He also went on at some length about assets and liabilities, and how the difference between them was not always as clear-cut as was often supposed, some time between three and four in the morning, over the umpteenth bottle of red wine. They were still aware of the colour of the wine, though they had given up trying to read the labels some time earlier.

A little after that, Sean took exception to something that Michael said – nobody would remember in the morning what it was – and floundered crossly off to bed in the room he had put his backpack in nearly twelve hours before. It took him a little while to find it. Not much later, Adam and Michael, for their part, did finally end up cosily under the same, not very well aired, duvet together. But they went out like lights as soon as their bodies hit the horizontal. Which answered the question that each one of them had privately asked himself during the previous day: namely, who would be having sex with whom that night? In the event, nobody had any sex, of any kind, with anyone at all.

In the morning they all had serious hangovers, serious mosquito bites and, in Adam's case, a serious meeting with the *notaire* in St-Emilion. Adam only just managed to phone the *notaire*, to invent a flimsy excuse and put off the appointment till the following day. The hangovers and mosquito bites were more than enough to deal with for the present.

They explored no further that day than the big Leclerc supermarket at St-Magne, outside Castillon. They also had a thorough look round the house. It was well furnished in a heavy but still attractive French country style. There was a library of books and another one of music; there were even some quite nice suits hanging in a wardrobe in one of the bedrooms, including what appeared to have been Georges's concert outfit: tailcoat and an assortment of both black and white bow ties. They left them where they were.

That evening something happened that was very new indeed. Adam put one hand on Michael's shoulder and the other one on Sean's and said, 'I'd like both of you to sleep with me tonight. The three of us together. Even if it's only just the once.'

Since Adam had been having sex regularly with Michael since they were both fourteen and with Sean – although much less often – since he was sixteen and Sean seventeen, it might be wondered that this neat closing of the circle had not been mooted before. The biggest reason that it had not was probably the fact that, although Michael fancied Sean – for who didn't? – Sean was much less attracted, at the physical level, by Michael. Sean wasn't always sure he even fancied Adam. He simply knew that he loved him. Whatever he meant by that. However, for some years now it had seemed to Sean a perfectly good enough reason for going to bed with Adam from time to time and having sex with him.

Adam would never have had the nerve to make such a proposal before, even if, before now, he had really wanted such a threesome. If someone had said no, no thank you, it would have been both mortifying and also difficult to decide what to do or say next. But Adam was in a new situation now. At least while they were at the Grand Moulin, he was host, master of ceremonies and king of his little court. It was quite a new sensation for him and he was beginning to suspect that it was affecting, even if only very slightly, the way he behaved and thought and spoke. He didn't imagine for a moment that he now had the power to command his two lovers' presence together in his bedchamber. Nevertheless, he found it had emboldened him first to want and then to suggest it.

There was a split second's frisson before anyone spoke, as if everyone's heart had skipped a beat at the same time. Then Sean broke the tension with a grin and a shrug, and said, 'Yeah, why not? First time for everything.'

'Who says we're going to do everything?' said Michael. Once Sean had counted himself in, there had been no likelihood that Michael might say no, but he didn't manage to make his voice sound as jokey as his words. Choked would have been nearer the mark.

They did not in fact, try to do everything, which perhaps saved the experiment from being an embarrassing disaster. Once they had managed to undress each other while standing in a close circle, and each was reassured by finding himself and the others aroused to an almost unprecedented degree, everything went ahead most naturally and happily, everyone exploring the new situation and one another's bodies with hands and mouths, until everyone had climaxed in an orderly fashion: first Sean, then Adam, and finally Michael – to the unspoken surprise of the other two, who had both privately assumed that Michael would be the first.

They stayed the night together, all three of them in Adam's bed: Sean in the middle and Michael and Adam cuddling up against him one on either side. This double thermal input made Sean rather hotter than he would have liked to be on an August night but he stayed where he was, partly to savour the novelty of an experience which might not happen to him very often again, and partly to spare the feelings of the others – which he felt might be hurt if he were to get out of bed and leave them.

Adam showed off the town of St-Emilion to his friends as if it too had been left to him in someone's will. They spent the early morning exploring its three-dimensional labyrinth of alleys and cobbled steps. Then it was time for Adam's appointment with the *notaire*. He left the others to do a circuit of the ramparts and to locate a cheap bar for them to have lunch at.

The *notaire* had really only wanted to meet Adam in order to put a face to the name. Permission to use the Moulin for the holiday had been given quite readily, as Michael had predicted, and arrangements made, in the course of a couple of phone-calls. But now Adam was here in St-Emilion it had seemed only natural that the heir and the lawyer should meet. The *notaire* talked about probate's being expected in about another four months, and then spelled out a few mundane details concerning title deeds and other documents. They discussed the arrangements for the harvesting of the grapes in September; it could all be left safely to the owners of Château L'Orangerie proper, though perhaps Adam ought to pay them a courtesy call and introduce himself. Adam handed over a couple of bills which he had found inside the letterbox on his arrival. They included one from the Leducs for the mowing of the lawns. 'I'll deal with those,' the *notaire* said matter-of-factly. 'It's not only the hair and fingernails of dead men that go on growing. The same goes for their gardens too.' But then he said, 'There is something else that may perhaps interest you,' and reached inside a file. 'A couple of items which go with the property but which weren't actually specified in the letter you originally received: namely two bank accounts held at the Crédit Agricole here in St-Emilion. They're now both yours.' He handed two bank statements across the desk. 'The current account, Georges appears to have used for paying the Leducs for cleaning and grass cutting, plus a few odd payments to others. It doesn't amount to a fortune, I'm afraid.' Adam looked. The balance stood at eighty-seven euros.

'And then there's this one. A high interest savings account, which seems to have been a reserve fund for repairs and other major outlay. You may find it a little more interesting.' The current balance was shown as one hundred and twelve thousand, two hundred and forty-seven euros and thirty-six cents. Adam estimated it quickly at somewhere between sixty and seventy thousand pounds. He was silent for a moment, then he looked up at the *notaire* and said,

'*Bonne nouvelle, quoi?*'

The *notaire* looked back at him with a smile that was quite human.

Sean and Michael were waiting for him outside. They had discovered a feature of St-Emilion that is common to all great wine towns: although well supplied with expensive restaurants and opportunities to enjoy its upmarket vinous products, it had less to offer the visitor whose business in the town was more mundane, or whose pocket was less deep, and who only wanted a beer and a sandwich. It was Michael who had insisted on persevering. He had reasoned that there must be at least a few people in the town who did ordinary jobs and who wanted to relax over a *pastis*, a cigarette and a go on the one-armed bandit at the end of a working day, and that there must be a place for them to do so. And he had been right. They had finally located what Michael insisted on calling the 'Spanish' bar, a little way down the Rue Guadet, the steep hill that the traffic came winding up, near the Auberge de la Commanderie.

'Did the *notaire* have anything interesting to say?' Sean asked, as they began to wander downhill from the Place du Clocher.

'One or two things,' said Adam a bit guardedly. 'No explanation of why Georges left the place to me, of course. Actually, there was one good bit of news. Georges kept some money for repairs and so on in a special bank account.' He noticed that they were just walking past the Crédit Agricole on the corner of the Rue des Girondins as he said this. 'And that it'll be mine in due course, after probate. So maybe I won't have to sell the place quite yet.'

'Wa-hey!' said Michael, 'that's great. How much is it?'

'I don't think you've any business to be asking him that,' said Sean, with uncharacteristic sharpness. Adam had detected a slight awkwardness between Sean and Michael this morning.

'I don't see why not,' Michael came back with similar heat. 'Since we've more or less lived together for three years. And if he doesn't want to tell me, he can say so himself.'

'Well,' said Adam, 'I'd rather we just forgot about it if you don't mind. But it isn't going to make me specially rich if that's what you're wondering.' He was silently grateful to Sean for saying what he himself felt but would have found difficult to come out with, but he was even more conscious of the chill in the air between the other two. He wondered whether that was his fault for persuading them both to share his bed last night and in the process to have sex with each other. Perhaps threesomes weren't such a bright idea after all.

Fortunately the moment of awkwardness was brought to a natural end by their arrival at the door of the Spanish bar. They went in, found an empty table and sat down at it. A young waiter appeared beside them almost at once and Adam was momentarily tongue-tied by the shock of recognition. The waiter was quite cute, in a thin and gangly sort of way, with short-cut hair that had once been blond and still wanted to be spiky given half a chance. He had a face that was a bit too long to be considered conventionally handsome but which was redeemed by a beautiful, friendly pair of chestnut brown eyes. Although he was four years older than when Adam had first met him, he was unmistakeably the same boy. Recovering himself, Adam addressed him. 'Stéphane?'

Stéphane looked at him for a moment and glanced quickly at his two companions, taking in their age, sex and appearance: all three of them relaxed and boyish in T-shirts and shorts. Then his face relaxed into a grin and he said, 'We met. *Ah oui. Et ben oui.* I don't remember your name. You stayed at the Grand Moulin with Georges. Now that Georges is dead, people say … that it's you who...' He tailed off, a little confused, not wanting to come out with the wrong thing.

'I'm going to be living there. *Ouais.* And it's Adam, by the way. We're having a holiday there just now.'

'*Ça se voit,*' said Stéphane. So I see.

Adam gestured briskly towards the others. 'Sean, Michael, Stéphane.' There were brisk French-style handshakes. 'Come and see us there. A drink, a meal or something.'

'Oh … right.' Stéphane was a bit thrown by the sudden encounter. He tapped his order pad with his pencil. 'You want to order something? This is a holiday job,' he was suddenly anxious to let them know. 'I'm really studying in Bordeaux.'

Beers and *rillette* sandwiches were eventually ordered and consumed and then, before they left the bar, it was arranged that Stéphane would join them at lunchtime at the Moulin in two days' time: that being his next day off. Adam knew, when he made the invitation that that was the moment for Stéphane to say, could he bring his girlfriend? – if he had one. But he didn't say that. So Adam concluded that he didn't have a girlfriend, or at any rate, not a local one. Of course Bordeaux might be another matter.

FOUR

The grapes ripening in the heat on the slope behind the house had been a major source of interest to the three young men since their arrival. Already on their first evening, in between sipping glasses of the vineyard's fermented product on the lawn – and while they were still able to walk without stumbling – they had taken an exploratory stroll among the rows of vines, splashing across the stream to do so, in preference to going the longer way round by way of the plank bridge. The grapes, which would be purple-black in a month's time, now hung in amber pendant bunches low down on the vines; and the rows were themselves trimmed low – about a metre and a half in height – like hedges.

The morning after their visit to St-Emilion, Adam took the *notaire*'s advice and went, with his two lieutenants, to introduce himself to the owner of Château L'Orangerie. The handsome yellow stone buildings of the château were visible across the sea of vines once you had climbed to the top end of Adam's patch and so, rather than drive the long way round by road, they decided to trek through the vineyard. No fence but only a metre strip of bare earth separated Adam's vineyard plot from the much larger area of vines that was the territory of Château L'Orangerie proper. All they had to do was wade along between the leafy rows until they reached the house. Some of the rows were punctuated by single rose bushes in bloom; it was an attractive sight – though Adam guessed that it served some obscure viticultural purpose rather than a merely decorative one.

Arriving this way seemed to Adam a friendly, neighbourly thing to do but his idea was not shared by the bull-mastiff that leapt up barking from the patch of tawny sun in the middle of the yard. Mercifully the beast was on a chain, though the chain was attached to some ten metres of rope: enough to prevent the visitors from gaining unchallenged access to any of the surrounding buildings. A male figure appeared from somewhere: grey-haired, stone-faced, in blue overalls and Wellingtons. *'Qui êtes vous? Que faites vous ici ? '*

Adam found himself absurdly remembering the story of the boy King Richard II facing down the Peasants' Revolt as he announced, a bit tremulously, *'Je m'appelle Adam Wheeler. Je suis l'héritier de Monsieur Georges Pincemin.'*

Still stony-faced the figure shouted back at them, 'You should have phoned and said you were coming. *Quand-même...*' He softened suddenly. 'You're here now. And very welcome. *Soyez les bienvenus.* Don't worry about the dog. He's an old softie. *Pourri-gâté...* Come this way.'

That was one of the endearing things about France, Adam thought. One minute you were an outsider: out, very out; the next minute you were very in.

'This is the *millésime* of ninety-eight,' their host was saying as he handed round small tasting glasses. They had made it into the house – the farmhouse, the château itself – had kicked off their shoes in the bright kitchen and penetrated to the inner sanctum, the holy of holies that was the salon, where they sat in their socks – and their host in his boiler suit – on brittle Second Empire chairs. 'The two thousand was even better, and the two thousand five's coming on nicely too, though you've probably discovered that for yourselves down at the Moulin – that is, if Monsieur Georges didn't empty his cellars before he died. A shame, that was. Very sad.' He shook his head and observed a two seconds' silence before raising his glass with a cheery *Santé*. He was the sole owner of Château L'Orangerie – except for the small parcel of vineyard that belonged now to Adam. His name was Philippe Martinville and he was, just at

34

that hour, alone in the house. His wife was out shopping at Leclerc, he explained, his children grown-up and living away, and his cellar-man and other château staff were all on holiday. In the winegrowers' year August was the lull before the storm: the harvest, or *vendange*, of September.

Philippe told Adam about the *vendange*. As far as this year's went, Adam wouldn't have to worry about a thing. The grapes would be picked by Philippe's staff using a machine – a towering yellow monster of a harvester that straddled the rows of vines and plucked off the bunches with two slowly revolving Archimedes' screws; Philippe would show them the contraption when they went on a tour of inspection presently. Adam's grapes would be separately weighed in Adam's presence, or if he wasn't there he could nominate someone to verify the figures in his place. There was an agreed price, set each year by the Association of Winegrowers of the Côtes de Castillon – of which body Adam himself would in due course be eligible to become a member. Set against the resulting sum would be the detailed bill for the cultivation, pruning, spraying and so forth of Adam's plot during the year. The balance would be paid over to Adam, or to Georges's estate if probate had not been granted by that time. Philippe stopped and gave Adam a long hard stare. Perhaps Adam would prefer the payment to be deferred until after probate and Adam was in full financial charge. *'Qu'est-ce que tu en penses?'*

Adam looked steadily back at Philippe, registering the familiar *tu*, and realised that he was for the first time in his life discussing matters of financial moment with a business partner. He had no idea whether Philippe's suggestion would be in his own interest or not. 'Yes,' he said, striving to convey an impression of savoir faire. 'Perhaps that might be a good idea.'

Madame Martinville's arrival back from her shopping trip was loudly heralded by the mastiff in the yard, and the presentation to her of Adam and his two friends became the excuse for a second glass of wine – for everyone except herself: time didn't stand still; there was shopping to unpack. A tour of the outbuildings followed. They saw the huge yellow harvest monster, the hydraulic press and the grape crusher, then the *chais* and the bottle cellar. The *chais* were the long sheds where the last two vintages still slumbered in wooden casks – *barriques* – prior to being bottled during the winter months, while the bottle cellar was everything it ought to have been with its comforting, musty smell and respectable accumulation of dust and cobwebs. It contained bottles of L'Orangerie, and a few of its neighbours' wines, dating back, though in diminishing numbers, all the way to the Second World War. But by now it was getting near lunchtime and Sean, who was sensitive in these matters, suggested it was time they left their host in peace and so they took their leave and went plodding back home again through the vines, the way they had come.

That afternoon and evening they talked of nothing but vines and vineyards. Michael began to scribble figures on a scrap of paper. 'At least we know you're going to have some sort of an income now. Plus the fact that you'll be renting out the Petit Moulin.' He gestured towards that other half of the big house. 'Say two hundred and fifty pounds a week from lettings in May and June and September, and double that in July and August. That's, er, seven thousand pounds for you already. And you're going to be selling those grapes for – what? Another couple of thousand pounds at least.'

'That's nice, but it's still not a living. Income isn't the same as profit.' Adam wasn't as quick with figures as

Michael, nor did they play as prominent a part in his thoughts, but he did at least know that.

'Yes, I know,' Michael defended himself, 'but at least I'm making you think about financial possibilities. You wouldn't have got round to it for another fortnight – you'd have buried yourself in music and learnt two cello sonatas first.' Which was probably true.

Michael's 'couple of thousand' was very much a guess. He had tried, unsuccessfully, to calculate the number of vines in Adam's plot during the walk back from the château. He chided Adam for not asking for this information from either Philippe or the *notaire*. Sean reproved him. 'You might as well say he should have asked Georges himself. You're always thinking about money these days, and Adam's money at that. Anyway, you can't possibly work it out. You don't know how many kilos a single vine's supposed to produce, nor the price per kilo.'

'Neither,' Adam added, 'do we know how much Philippe's going to charge for a year's cultivation of the Moulin's vines.' He was still too shy to say to them, *my* vines. 'I didn't think to ask him that either. There may be very little left in it for me in the end.'

But Michael's next idea found more general favour. 'OK, so Philippe's done all the work this year. But next year you could think about keeping his counter-charges down by doing some of it yourself. That is, if you're planning on spending much of your time down here. Better than twiddling your thumbs.'

On my own, thought Adam. Me down here on my own. He couldn't quite get his head round the idea. It distressed him to think that Michael apparently could.

'What does it entail?' Sean asked. 'Philippe mentioned pruning and spraying. Sounds routine enough if a bit boring. What else is there?'

'I don't know,' said Adam. 'But we know someone who does.'

Stéphane turned up punctually at twelve the next day, arriving on the kind of small motorbike, popular in the Latin countries of Europe, whose engine generates noise in inverse ratio to its output of motive power. So his hosts were aware of his impending approach some considerable time before he actually turned into the yard, as he bounced along the track down from the road, in a whirlwind of dust, and making enough noise for a battery of machine guns, at a steady four miles an hour. He finally rounded the corner of the mill building, crossed the bridge over the stream that ran beneath it, and dismounted at the main door, to find Adam, Michael and Sean lined up and awaiting him like a guard of honour receiving a visiting head of state. Stéphane had taken his cue as to sartorial style from his first sight of the other three together two days ago and, like them, he was wearing shorts, T-shirt and trainers and nothing else – certainly not a crash helmet.

He was welcomed with the pop of a champagne cork, not because Adam thought of him as in any way special, nor because he felt especially rich, but because he was conscious of being one of the winegrowers of the area, even if one of the smallest and youngest, and that was the sort of thing – he knew – that one did. The gesture was well received at any rate.

Over lunch, which was a selection of quiches and charcuterie from the supermarket with salad, cheese and fruit to follow, Stéphane paid for his welcome in useful information and practical help. He told them that Philippe would probably charge him about ten thousand euros for looking after his vines for the previous year. That the grapes would fetch somewhere between twelve and fifteen thousand, leaving him with a potential net

gain of something between two and five thousand.
'Depends on the year, of course. Other factors too. If
there's a glut...' He shook his head, then smiled
reassuringly. 'Don't worry too much. This year looks
like being OK.'

Stéphane told them which local shops sold what and
which ones were open on a Sunday, and that their
nearest café-bar was in St-Genès. He told them about
interesting places to visit in the region. For instance, had
they seen the medieval *bastide* towns towards the
southeast: Beaumont, Monpazier, Monflanquin? They
were tourist spots, true, but so beautiful they just had to
be seen: it was like stepping into the fourteenth century.
If they wanted to go there – or anywhere else for that
matter – and it was one of his days off, he'd be only too
happy to come along as their guide. And, once he was
sure he had picked up the right vibes from Michael and
Sean (Adam he already knew about of course), he told
them about a particular nightclub in Bordeaux that they
might like. They could take the train if they didn't want
to drive, and friends of his would give them a floor to
crash on.

The lunch party went extraordinarily well, two bottles
of Château L'Orangerie playing their part in its success,
and the late afternoon found them all sprawled shirtless
on the sunlit lawn between the front of the house and the
millstream – although Sean took care to arrange himself
on the dappled edge of the bright arena for the sake of
his fair complexion – exchanging somewhat carefully
selected fragments of their autobiographies to date.
Stéphane, who told them with pride that he was doing a
course in viticulture and oenology at an institute in
Bordeaux, was being admitted to the pack. And with
very open arms indeed it presently appeared, when
Michael, judging the moment and the omens right, rolled
over on top of Stéphane and kissed him playfully on the

nose. Stéphane did not try to push him off but gave him a tentative return kiss on the mouth. A minute later the two of them were getting on so well that Sean was moved to say to Adam, in the world-weary tones of honorary elder brother, 'We don't really want to watch these exhibitionists shagging, do we? Let's move somewhere else.' He got to his feet and pulled Adam to his, then kept hold of his hand while he led him down the bank towards the stream at a point where some low shrubs above them provided a partial screen between themselves and the activity on the lawn. Adam knew, from years of knowing Sean, what this leading him by the hand indicated, and made no protest.

Making love with Sean was always a gentler, sweeter, business than it was with Michael. No doubt because Sean was himself a gentler, sweeter-natured person than Michael was – or Adam too, come to that. Adam shared with both of them the same repertoire of activities, the same roughly fifty-fifty ratio of active to passive role playing, the same variety of positions. Perhaps most people did; Adam wasn't sure; he didn't have limitless experience to draw on for comparison. Other than with Michael and Sean, his sexual encounters during his student years had not been that numerous and had been brief and functional in the extreme – as in the case of Stéphane four years before. There was Sylvain of course, but he was not admissible in the comparison stakes. Sylvain was long ago, but not only that, he was quite different. A case apart. A different life, almost. There was no comparing Sylvain, Adam realised, with anything else that had happened to him or, probably, that ever would. But Sean and Michael... Inevitably Adam compared the two. Michael was impulsive and hard-edged in sex, making it clear what he wanted to do on any given occasion, forcing Adam to choose quickly whether he wanted the same or to indicate clearly if he did not. Sean, however, would feel his way towards whatever was going to happen between them by reading Adam's body language, his breathing and his eyes. Things took a bit longer to get going when he was with Sean, but in the main Adam preferred it.

And so it was today. Neither of them, they discovered in the course of a minute or two, was in the mood to fuck or suck the other; they simply lay together, belly to belly, shorts pushed below their knees, and let things take their course. And when things had taken their course, the two of them were left afterwards looking a little like an advertisement for a reassuringly expensive brand of ice cream – were you to imagine one that had been made exclusively for the gay segment of the market.

It was while they were still lying together, and waiting for the sun to dry their tummies, that Adam's feelings for Sean as he experienced them at that moment came bubbling up to the surface just as his physical excitement had overflowed in a minor tidal wave a few moments earlier. 'You know,' he said, 'what I would like to do most of all with this place – the mill here I mean – would be to make it mine and yours. D'you understand me? I mean for us to live here, just the two of us. You and me. Us two together. You and me for keeps.' Adam clasped one of Sean's hands tightly. He didn't dare to look into his face.

It was a declaration and a half. A proposal of marriage in effect, and Sean knew that it was nothing less. He didn't reply at once but caressed Adam with the hand that Adam wasn't holding, running it over his cheek and down the side of his neck, over his collarbone and ribcage, down to his still wet belly. 'Oh dear,' he said at last. 'My God, Adam, what you've asked me! I couldn't imagine a more beautiful place to live, or a more wonderful guy to share it with, if only I was really gay.

If only I was. If only. I've often thought that and never more so than now. But I'm not gay, Adam. I'm not and we both know it.' He paused for a half-second, then finished softly, 'If only life wasn't such a bloody muddle.'

'We've been through all this before,' said Adam in a voice that sounded suddenly tired. This was true, and that fact enabled Adam to deal with Sean's rebuff and to continue the conversation with more equanimity than might otherwise have been expected. 'But if you're really not gay, then it's hard for me to make sense of all this.' He squeezed Sean's sturdy penis.

'And I don't understand myself,' said Sean resignedly. 'I don't know if there's a label for people like me. For a straight guy who loves one other guy, just one, and likes to fuck and do all the rest of it with him. I don't even know if there's anyone else like me, with or without a label. It's easy if you've got a label. Straight. Gay. Bisexual. You kind of know what's expected of you, and so does everybody else.' He tailed off.

Adam was well able to think of a label for Sean: it was 'gay but in denial'. However he had said this to him so often over the years that he saw no benefit to be gained from repeating it yet again. Instead he lay back patiently and waited for Sean to say something more. Which, a minute or two later, he did.

'I'm sorry I answered you the way I did. I know I've hurt you horribly. If you want to know, I felt incredibly flattered by what you said. More than by anything else that anyone's said to me in my life. But I don't suppose that's much of a consolation.'

It wasn't. 'It was just a suggestion,' said Adam in a prim voice. 'Forget I said it.'

'Hardly just a suggestion,' said Sean, half sitting up. 'It was a proposal – in every sense of the word. We both know that. But it was made to the wrong man. I've always believed, and I still do, that when the time came – when the time comes – it'll be me doing the proposing, and not to a man but to a woman. I haven't met the right one yet, that's all. But I don't want to box myself into a corner before I do.'

Adam wasn't sure that Sean had ever slept with a woman. He rather doubted it. He himself had not, and he knew that Michael hadn't either, but Sean had always been evasive on the subject. He had talked vaguely of girlfriends in Newcastle, mentioned names occasionally, but had never brought anybody to London with him, or shown them off when Adam had gone north to visit him.

'If you're thinking of settling down here with someone,' Sean set off on a slightly new tack, 'then why not Michael? He's been your real boyfriend all these years, after all. He loves you – even if he has a funny way of showing it at times – and he's as loyal as a dog.'

'He has a funny way of showing that too,' said Adam, gesturing up the stream bank and towards the shrubs that masked their view of Michael at that precise moment, 'having his way with Stéphane in full view on the lawn.'

'Pots and kettles,' said Sean. 'Pots and bloody kettles, Adam. You're hardly the greatest pillar of monotony yourself. I... I mean ... monogamy.'

This spectacular Freudian slip successfully dispelled all the awkwardness that had come into being between the two of them since Adam had made his modest proposal. They both began to laugh, awkwardly at first and then uproariously as the tension drained out of them, and then they fell back into each other's arms once again. So that was how Michael and Stéphane found them – clasped together and naked but for the shorts that still snagged around their ankles – when they came to look for them a few minutes later. Michael and Stéphane had abandoned their own clothes entirely at some point in their exploratory grapplings and appeared now to

Adam and Sean, when the arrival of their shadows across them made them look up, like two slender statues, brazen and resplendent in the sun.

For Adam, that last half hour – the all too perfect lovemaking with Sean, Sean's subsequent crushing rejection of his idea that they might spend the rest of their lives together, the neat punctuation afforded by the arrival of an admiring and transfigured Michael and Stéphane – was to be the defining moment of the holiday, the turning point. One of the big turning points of his life. It held within it the same paradox that defines the summer solstice: the midsummer day each year that announces the arrival of summer's heat and joy, but from which same moment begins the inexorable countdown, in the shortening of the days' length – at first imperceptible but then headlong – towards the darkness of winter.

On the good side, a pattern for the remainder of the holiday had emerged that was almost too happy to believe. Stéphane became one of them. He was a lovely boy. He took more and more days off from his work in the Spanish bar and spent all of those days with them. In the car with them as they drove here and there Stéphane was their expert guide. He showed them walks along the streambeds, and how to catch and cook crayfish. Sometimes the three of them simply lazed in the sun on the lawns between the mill house and the millstream, overlooked only by the billowing acres of sun-drenched vines. At night Stéphane stayed with them too, sharing a bed with Michael, while Sean – painfully conscious of having wounded Adam deeply by his rejection, and wanting to make such reparation as he could – slept every night in Adam's arms. He was even more gentle now in bed than he had ever been and – despite being bigger and stronger in every way than the other three, with his solid frame and chunky muscles – somehow softer than Michael. If Adam imagined Michael in bed these days, curled up with Stéphane, then he imagined by contrast a hard and urgent physicality and a pair of bodies as lithe and tense as greyhounds.

There were no more threesomes, nor – even though, when they were together in the garden of the mill they all went unselfconsciously naked – was there ever any move towards experimenting with sex *à quatre*. They would be two couples for the duration.

For the duration. That was the downside. Once the holiday had ticked away to its end there would be no more sleeping with Sean, at least not on any regular basis. Adam would not be sharing his future with Sean. Nor, he thought, with Michael. Michael and he were not as compatible as Sean comforted himself by trying to believe. At the end of the holiday Adam still had no job to go to. Just a wonderful house – five hundred miles from the places he still thought of as home – that would cost an arm and a leg to run. And a future alone.

Adam experienced the remaining days of that holiday with an intensity of sensual awareness that made the days themselves seem almost tangible: he imagined them like a string of jewels of transcendent beauty; saw them running sparkling and precious as the last drops of a priceless wine.

When their rented car had to be surrendered at the end of the first week it was Stéphane who came to the rescue with the loan of an old banger of a Renault 4 from the farm. His parents' address was actually the Château Beaurepaire, but the reality was better conveyed to non-locals by the word 'farm'. Not that that stopped Stéphane from grandly announcing, *Je téléphone au château, Je rentre au château*, and suchlike whenever the occasion arose.

They entered the medieval world of the *bastide* towns on the upland between the rivers Dordogne and Lot:

fortified and cloistered village squares where Edward III and the Black Prince had shed the blood of thousands in the cause of keeping the two halves of their Angevin kingdom – cold northern England and sunny southern Gascony – together. Then they re-engaged with modern life on an evening in Bordeaux. They caught the little blue and silver diesel train which – rather after the manner of Stéphane's motorbike – roared through the vineyards as it made its slow way alongside the Dordogne river, and saw the waterway broaden into the crescent-moon harbour of the great city. They had drinks at the Café de la Victoire near the university, dinner with friends of Stéphane in the rue Rue Sainte Cathérine, then danced the rest of the night away at Le Grand Polux before collapsing on the hard floor at the apartment of Stéphane's friends – which he himself shared during term-time – somewhere off the Cours de la Marne. They took the train back late the next day, to find Stéphane's old banger safe and sound in the station yard at St-Emilion.

They were invited to lunch one Sunday by Stéphane's parents, whom Adam remembered from four years ago. They seemed no older now than then – of course it was the teenagers who had been growing up fast, not the parents – and asked the boys to call them Marc and Béatrice. Perhaps they wouldn't have done if Adam hadn't just become their neighbour and, as a landowner in his own right, in some sense their social equal. Stéphane's sister, Françoise, no longer lived at home. She had recently qualified in accountancy and gone to a job in Périgueux, forty miles away, where she lived with her boyfriend. Stéphane showed them a recent picture of her instead.

Finally it was time to go. Keys were returned to the Leducs. (*'Je serai de retour très bientôt'*. Adam would be back very soon.) Stéphane received his goodbye kisses from all three of them when he deposited them back at Bergerac airport – and especially from Michael. The parting words of the two of them were meant to be private but Adam did overhear Michael copying his own French: something at any rate would be *très bientôt*. The small twin-jet whisked them up, across the winding silver rivers of Aquitaine and Charente-Maritime. Michael spent most of the flight with his face glued to the window in uncharacteristic silence. Sean and Adam didn't manage much in the way of conversation either, though Sean did take Adam's hand and give it a squeeze from time to time, not caring whether anybody was looking or not. Adam couldn't decide whether he found this comforting or, in the circumstances, merely mildly irritating.

The day after his return to England, Adam wrote to the human resources department of Eurostar UK Ltd. asking for a job as a steward on the trains that plied between Britain and France.

FIVE

It was the middle of September. Adam was beginning a letter to Sylvain.

Sylvain, mon Sylvain...

That would hardly do. There was an echo of Captain, my Captain, about it – not that Sylvain would recognise that – but Adam really did not feel he had the right any more to call Sylvain his, not after all this time and after all that had come about to separate them. He tried again.

Mon cher Sylvain...

Too formal by half.

Copain... Simply copain.

Copain,

Comme il fait longtemps depuis qu'on ne s'est pas contacté... What a long time since we've been in touch. So much has happened to me. (Maybe to you too, but how should I know?) I'm a professional cellist now. I passed my exams and recital, just as you said I would...

In his last letter. Last Christmas. The Christmas letter.

...Only I don't get to play the thing. Can you imagine? No-one wants professional cellists – least of all orchestras! And who wants to be a school music teacher? Shades of my mother...

Why was he pouring all this out to Sylvain? Did he really want Sylvain to have to struggle through all these words? Words weren't Sylvain's big thing, after all. At least, not the written sort. He could talk beautifully enough in his own unique, off-the-wall way. But even that wasn't the main thing about Sylvain. He had paid Adam the compliment of falling in love with him more deeply, more dangerously, than anyone before or since. More than five years ago, when Adam was still only sixteen and Sylvain – in the world's eyes – a threatening twenty-two. Afraid of losing Adam, Sylvain had abducted him – or had they run away together? Adam still wasn't sure – and he had ended up in a secure psychiatric unit for his trouble, with strict instructions, handed down by a French court, never to contact Adam again.

...But more interesting than all that is that I may be going (he crossed out *going* and wrote *coming*, the more positive word from Sylvain's point of view) *coming to live in France. In fact I'm halfway there already. I've got a job as a steward with Eurostar (that's the Channel Tunnel train company)* ... He could hear the injured tone in Sylvain's response: 'I do know what Eurostar is. We're peasants, not yokels, right? *Paysans oui, ploucs non.*'

...Anyway, I started earlier this month. I'm going to be living partly in London, keeping a sort of base camp in Michael's place in Clapham, and part of the time in Paris. Gary, the concert pianist...

'Oui, oui, je sais bien qui c'est, Gary...' Adam heard Sylvain's voice as clearly as if he were in the room with him.

As clearly as he remembered Sylvain's first letter. A letter from Sylvain wasn't the same as a letter from anybody else. Even five years ago emails and the mobile phone had made letters virtually redundant, so to receive one from anybody at all was a rare enough event. But to get a letter from Sylvain, who had never written one before in his life; who had left school at twelve and never put pen to paper except to garble a phone message at home on his parents' small holding... To say nothing of the address.

Abbaye de Notre-Dame-de-Cîteaux,
Saint-Nicolas-les-Cîteaux,
Côte-d'Or,
France

Mon Adam,

Me voici est toi autrepart est je t'aime tousjours... I'm here, you somewhere else and I still love you. *Je te reverré unjour, ben sur. Ecris-moi.* I'll see you again one day, that's for sure. Write me. *Je t'aime. Sylvain.*

The words had etched themselves on Adam's heart for ever, misspellings and all; it was not the kind of letter a seventeen-year-old would forget, coming from the lover who had been forbidden to contact him. But what was Sylvain doing in a monastery? How had he got hold of Adam's parents' address in England? Those questions had been answered in time over the following year as normal contact began to be resumed between Adam and his old French school-friends. From them he had learnt of the psychologist who had reckoned that a move back to his parents' home immediately after his release from confinement would do Sylvain more harm than good. No, Sylvain had not become a Trappist monk, Adam was relieved to hear, but had been found a job – the official title was monastery servant – in the ancient abbey near Dijon.

So that was the genesis of Sylvain's first letter. Sylvain had worked on the abbey farm, tending the gardens, making cheese and managing bees for nearly two years, and during that time his letter-writing skills had improved considerably, thanks to the patient help of his employers and mentors, the monks. He now made only about the same number of mistakes in written French as Adam did. It had to be said, though, that Adam still made quite a lot.

Neither of them wrote frequently – they had only exchanged letters twice since Sylvain had gone back to his parents' farm. But when they did it was Adam who tended to write at soul-baring length while Sylvain's letters continued to be brief and hermetic. The day when he would write a whole book about blue sky – as he had once told an impressionable young Adam that he wanted to – was apparently still some way distant. Adam's old friends Céline and Christophe were able to fill in a few bits of background from time to time when they phoned or emailed him, and with those half-glimpses of the sun whose radiance had once filled his own sky and warmed his world Adam had to be content. He had never plucked up the courage to go back alone to France, to the village on the plateau, and to knock at the peeling front door among the chickens and dogs.

...It's not intended that the Eurostar job should last for ever. It's just a stopgap while my future sorts itself out. You see, I've been left a big house (you may not find this easy to believe but it's true) on the border of the Gironde and the Dordogne, with vines and stuff. I want to find a way to live down there full time, if I can. Not so easy though. But I mean, who knows what life has in store for them? ...

Who was all this for: Sylvain or himself? Adam made himself a promise as he at last posted the comprehensive annual report that his letter had become. If Sylvain answered it, he would go and find him. He was not a timid schoolboy now. On one of his stopovers in Paris he would take the train from the Gare de l'Est up to Langres, screw his courage up and knock on that familiar shabby front door. And the rest of his life could take its chances in the fallout from that moment. If Sylvain replied to his letter.

If.

But Sylvain did not.

Starting work as a steward for Eurostar, Adam had found himself back in the classroom again, at the company's training centre in Wimbledon. He had done role-plays in a mock-up of a section of a tunnel train, which Adam, but nobody else among his fellow trainees, called the flight simulator, had attended lectures on Health and Safety, had done first aid. They were sent down to Kent and driven into the tunnel itself where they learnt to find their way around the escape routes. It was not going to be a job for claustrophobes.

Within a couple of weeks Adam had started work on the trains themselves. For the first few days he was under the tutelage of a 'buddy'. His was a young Frenchman with a cheeky grin, who was called Nicolas. They worked four days on, three days off. Some days they went to Paris and back, on other days it was a roundtrip to Brussels. When you were very busy you sometimes didn't notice the undersea crossing, even in daylight. But then, when you had a moment to breathe and glance out of the window, you were never in any doubt about which side of the water you were on. There was no mistaking the miniature meadows and unthreatening hillsides of Kent for the seamless undulating prairies of the Pas de Calais, nor confusing the brick and half-timbered farmhouses of the English countryside with the brown stone and slate roofs that characterised their Picardy counterparts.

Working in two languages was a novelty, though Adam's experience of living in France came in handy. After a while, he found, you developed a sixth sense that told you as customers approached you – or, in first class, as you approached them – which language they were going to address you in. Sometimes Adam got it wrong, but not often. Fortunately the Flemish-speaking Belgians invariably spoke to you in English; for political reasons they preferred to avoid compromising themselves by speaking French.

He only had one real run-in with a customer during his first few days. An order of 'lager and tomato juice' prompted a surprised Adam to pour the two liquids into the same glass together. 'You stupid pillock,' his customer said.

'There's no need for that,' Adam protested. 'You should have said *a* lager and *a* tomato juice.'

'And you should have used your brain,' the other told him. 'Call yourself a steward? Nobody drinks tomato juice and beer together, anywhere in the world.'

'All the same…'

Fortunately Nicolas arrived at that moment and took over. Later he took Adam aside. 'When that happens, just throw the bloody mess away, say sorry, and start again. Never argue with them. It isn't worth.'

Adam was about to draw Nicolas's attention to the missing *it* on the end of his last sentence but stopped himself just in time.

On his turnarounds in Paris and Brussels Adam had a little time – anything from half an hour to three hours, it depended on his shift pattern – to spend in the foreign city, and an allocation of *tickets-restaurant* to exchange for food. He usually went off for his meal breaks with Nicolas or some of the other stewards. Before starting his new job he had had the idea of contacting Gary Blake, the only person he knew in Paris, to see if they could have lunch together some time. But when Adam phoned him, Gary had replied that he was going to be out of Paris for the next week. However, if Adam's schedules ever necessitated his staying overnight in Paris, he was more than welcome to use his flat as a base. Which Adam thought was more than generous.

With his frequent early morning starts and late returns, Adam found himself spending less time at the flat in Clapham, and seeing less of Michael when he did so. It was not surprising. Michael had just started his one-year Legal Practice course at the College of Law. He had new colleagues and a new social life to go with it. Adam found himself having sex with Michael only occasionally: not regularly, as before.

After returning from the Moulin in August, Michael had exchanged emails and phone-calls with Stéphane. Adam had seen the pleasure that this had given Michael at first. But then, as the weeks passed, he had grown aware that Michael's feelings for his new friend were cooling off. Michael confided in Adam on one of the increasingly rare evenings that they were spending together: 'I'm not so sure about going on with this. He's started using the L-word – and not just at the ends of his emails. I mean, a holiday romance is one thing but… I'd never imagined he was going to get clingy.'

Adam was not altogether sympathetic. 'Well maybe you should have. Should have imagined, I mean – before you started in with him so strongly. He's a whole year younger than us. Maybe you took advantage, just a little bit, perhaps? Which wasn't very fair on him. But if you are going to dump him, at least do it gently. Try not to break his little heart.'

Presumably Michael did end it with Stéphane soon after that. But he didn't volunteer any further information to Adam on the subject, and Adam didn't ask.

It was company policy at Eurostar to return stewards each night to the city they were based in. So Adam was surprised to hear it announced at the morning briefing one day that, for the next couple of months at least, they were looking for a steward who was able to be flexible and to end and start some of his shifts in Paris. It chimed with his present mood, given the gradual withdrawal of Michael from his life in London, and also with Gary's kind offer to allow him to stay, rent-free, at his Paris flat. He phoned Gary again, and later the same day accepted

Eurostar's offer – to be the only steward that he was aware of who would be working out of two capital cities.

He paid one of his increasingly infrequent visits to his parents around this time. They naturally wanted to hear, not only all about his new job, but also about his holiday the previous month at the Grand Moulin. He gave them a very full account of the first, but a very heavily edited one of the second. 'Of course we very much want to see the place ourselves,' Jennifer said.

'Indeed we do,' Hugh agreed. 'But let's be practical about this. You don't really want to have to take us there. On the other hand, we haven't had a proper holiday this year. A holiday would cost us money wherever we went. So why don't we come to a commercial arrangement that benefits us all? We simply rent the Moulin from you for a fortnight. That way we get our holiday, we get to see your place without being under your feet, and you get some money, which you could no doubt do with. We thought of doing it quite soon, actually, while the weather down there lasts.'

'Well thanks, that's great,' said Adam. 'And if I got a Paris weekend off while you were there I could pop down from Paris and visit you.'

'There's just one thing we'd need to insist on,' Hugh added.

Adam felt his heart sinking. 'What's that?'

'A clearly drawn map of how to find the place, coming from the airport.'

'I think I could manage that,' said Adam with some relief.

SIX

Approaching Gary's home in the Rue de Florence, Adam experienced a strange sensation as he realised that everything was completely unchanged. There was no reason why it should be any different, he told himself. Haussmann's buildings had been put there to last and Paris had suffered no large-scale bombings or remodelling since he had first been there. Yet so much had happened to Adam in the intervening years – all those things that filled the huge gulf between being seventeen and being twenty-two – that he felt it almost an affront that the same café was on the corner, with the same chairs out on the pavement in the autumn sunshine, and that the entry phone made exactly the same familiar sound when Gary buzzed him in.

Adam thought it was extremely kind of Gary to let him use his elegant second-floor apartment (architect: J.J. Depras, 1892) as a temporary pied-à-terre while he worked on the tunnel trains. Gary for his part, exactly eighteen years older than Adam, had felt more flattered than put out when Adam had phoned and made the initial contact.

But their opening conversation was not the cosy chat over a coffee that Adam might have been expecting. Other people would have sat him down and said casually, 'How's the cello going?' without meaning very much by it. Not Gary. When he began a conversation in this way it was not just small talk.

'Well,' Adam answered, feeling a little uncomfortable at being put on the spot quite so quickly (they had got as far as the living room, but not so far as Gary inviting Adam to sit down in it), 'as you can see, I'm not making a living from it right now.'

'But you must,' Gary said, knitting his brow. 'I mean, very soon you must.' This obliged Adam to recite in self defence a litany of all the orchestras he had written to and who had turned him down. 'And what about the music colleges? What about schools?'

'I did try one or two of the colleges. They all said I needed more experience as a performer. As for schools, I just do not want to teach in a school and that's that.'

'Don't knock teaching,' Gary warned him. 'I do it. We all do it.'

'What you do is different. You've never taught in schools, working with brats all day.' Adam looked around him. The room was comfortingly the same: the big Steinway at one end, the great gilded mirror over the fireplace. All the same, that coffee would be welcome – or better still, something stronger.

'Perhaps I was lucky,' said Gary, 'perhaps not. But most musicians teach in school. Think how much you owe to the people who taught you the cello – not so long ago – when you were a brat yourself. Anyway, leave that aside for a moment. Now you've got this travelling job, how are you managing to practise? What are you working on?'

'I'm not,' said Adam, and tried to sound blasé. 'I haven't done any real practice since I passed my recital exam.'

The colour drained from Gary's cheeks. Adam had never seen him look angry before. 'You're not practising? Adam, that's awful. Practice is what musicians are for. That's why we're put on this earth. You can't just not do it.'

'Well it seems that's what I am doing,' Adam said huffily. But he felt himself turning red.

'It isn't bloody good enough,' said Gary. 'And you know it. All the efforts you've made, that other people have made for you: you don't have the right to throw that away. You do not have that right.' Gary flicked his hair back from his forehead. 'Come with me. We're going out.'

'Can't I just...?' Adam hadn't even put his bag in the spare bedroom. He needed to pee.

'Yes, OK. Do all that. But we're not going far. Just round the corner to Eschig's in the Rue de Rome. We're going to hire a cello for you. And whenever you're here with me in Paris you're going to bloody well practise it.'

Gary was not a relative nor had he been one of Adam's teachers. But he had been at music college with his mother and was an old family friend – he had smoothed things over with Adam's parents when he and Michael had run off to Paris together five years before, and on that occasion introduced him to Georges Pincemin. He was also now letting Adam use his flat for nothing. So Adam couldn't manage to feel as angry with him as he might have liked to. But an even bigger reason for this was the fact that he knew that Gary was absolutely right.

'To make it a bit less of a penance,' Gary said when Adam had re-emerged from the loo, 'I'll play your accompaniments for you.' He stopped for a moment. His tone had softened and the familiar twinkle was back in his eyes. 'I guess we'll have to borrow a few scores as well – for this time. In future, bring your own.'

There was no arguing. The man whose CD of the Chopin Ballades had just arrived in the shops to a fanfare of good reviews was now offering meekly to play Adam's piano accompaniments while he practised. 'You're very good to me,' Adam said in a subdued voice. Gary planted a light kiss on his forehead.

Back at work behind his two-hundred-mile-an-hour serving counter, when his colleagues asked him what he had been doing with his time in Paris, it wasn't very easy to find things to say. 'Oh, I spent most of the time playing the cello with the pianist Gary Blake. You know.

He's the one who's just had the new Chopin CD
released. But we mostly did Beethoven.' That wasn't
really possible. So, 'This and that, you know, the sort of
things you do in Paris,' had to do instead. It was the
same with the question of where he lived. He had told
people, 'A friend of mine lets me stay with him when
I'm in London; he shares a flat in Clapham. And in Paris
I kind of do the same with another friend.' So that he
came over as rather sad and homeless. He couldn't really
claim that he lived with 'my boyfriend Michael' when
that wasn't really the case now, if it ever had been. The
reality was so much more complicated. To have said,
'Actually I'm the owner of a mill house and part of a
wine estate near St-Emilion,' would have sounded more
than just boastful or lying; it would have sounded mad.

It was a couple of weeks later that Adam's parents
began their holiday at the Grand Moulin. Adam drew
them a road map, phoned the Leducs to let them know
they were coming and left them to it. But he did arrange
to take some time off work so that he could travel down
and spend a couple of days with them towards the end of
their fortnight.

His father met him off the TGV at Libourne station in
bright sunshine. Grapes were being picked on both sides
of the road as they made the short drive through the
vineyards of Pomerol and St-Emilion. 'Yours are already
picked,' Hugh told his son. 'Though not by hand like
that.' He gestured through the car window where a
classic scene was unrolling as they passed: stooping
figures among the vines, shoulder-borne panniers full of
black bunches being tipped into carts that waited at the
ends of the rows. 'Your Monsieur Martinville sent in a
great yellow machine that stripped the vines in no time.
Very beautiful the fruit looked as it came off the stems.
We went up to see the crop being weighed at the
château. Where we met a young friend of yours –

Stéphane? – who was apparently there as your designated observer to see there was no foul play. Did you know he was going to do that?' Adam did. 'He was hoping to see you, but I don't think he'll be able to. He had to go back to Bordeaux last night. Seems a nice chap.'

That was Hugh's invariable verdict when meeting one of Adam's friends. Seems a nice chap. He must have been able to calculate that, since Adam was gay, most of his male friends might be expected to be gay also, but at another level he seemed to be unable to make that particular logical connection. Perhaps it was a case of the left side of the brain not knowing what the right side was doing.

They skimmed past the top end of the town of St-Emilion, past its familiar landmark spire, and the crouching Collegiate Church, then the romantically ruined Gothic arches, tall and marooned amid the lapping yellow-green tide of vines. 'He had several messages for you,' Hugh went on. 'This Stéphane I mean. One was, that next time you come down on your own you could borrow the old Renault again. Apparently you all used it when you were down here last month. I must say I thought that was awfully decent of him.'

'You haven't seen the car,' Adam said archly. But he too thought it was 'awfully decent' of Stéphane, especially since he had had the brush-off from Michael, which must have hurt. None of this could be conveyed to his father however.

'He also said that if you wanted to work your bit of vineyard yourself in future years and avoid having to hand back most of the proceeds from it to Philippe Martinville, he would do all he could to help you.'

Adam requested a clarification. 'When he said *help* did he mean he'd simply tell me how to go about things, or that he'd be physically humping fertiliser sacks with me and wielding secateurs?'

'A bit of both I would think,' his father answered, 'though you'd better ask him yourself if you want to be sure. But he mentioned lending you some special kind of plough from his father's place. He owns another château, isn't that right?'

'Château Beaurepaire. It's sort of next door but one. Which, round here, means about a mile in the car.'

'Then the last thing he said, which is probably the most important, is that if you decide to go it alone you're going to have to take the bull by the horns with Monsieur Martinville and tell him pretty soon.'

'I see,' said Adam. His heart sank. He did not relish the thought of going to see his neighbour, a man more than thirty years older than himself and whose family had owned Château L'Orangerie for generations, and telling him that he, Adam, had made a decision that would effectively cut his income by some ten thousand euros a year. 'Then I suppose that's what I'll have to do.' He paused for a second. 'That is, if I decide to go for that option.'

'Quite so,' said his father. They were slowing down now, passing the Leducs' house, preparing to turn onto the stony track that led down the escarpment to the Grand Moulin. It all looked so familiar, so vivid. The landscape radiated that urgent September brightness that Adam remembered from his first visit all those years ago with Georges. 'Quite so. It might be something that you'd want to talk over with your mother and me before rushing into.'

Adam knew what that meant. It meant that his mother was not happy with the idea of her musician son getting too involved with all the physical work of grape farming and had already voiced her concern to her husband.

She voiced it again that evening. 'It's not your musicianship I'm worried about you losing, or any of your mental alacrity and discipline. It's simply your hands and fingers. If you damaged them...'

'Or if I lost one altogether.' Adam could not resist winding his mother up.

'Heaven forbid. Don't... don't even think about that. But it's... It's not only that. I try to think of you, living alone down here – so far away from us. And I can't really manage to imagine it. It's so different from anything I might have expected until two months ago. That's all.'

Much of what his mother said found a pretty strong echo among Adam's own thoughts and feelings. He also still found it difficult to believe that he might one day be living here *all by himself.* Making his living God knew how. Earning a little bit of money growing grapes, a little bit more by being a holiday landlord, doing a spot of cello teaching? His future being dictated in effect by the house he had so unexpectedly come to inherit. Had Georges Pincemin had any idea at all of what he was doing when he made that will?

'Not that it isn't a most beautiful place,' Jennifer went on. 'A perfect house in a dream setting. We've had the most wonderful holiday. And the Leducs have been so... Well, you know them. And the lovely little church. Not that I imagine you've given a thought to looking for that.' It was true: he hadn't. His mother was a Catholic, his father not. As far as he was concerned, and despite his forced baptism when a baby, neither was he. His mother continued, 'But have you given any thought to what it would be like in the winter?'

'Yes I have. Of course I have.' Adam felt torn. Living 'so far from us' as his mother had said, was not one of the place's drawbacks in Adam's eyes, though he was polite or prudent enough not to say so. But the other points she had raised – together with others that he had tussled with in his own mind – certainly were. The winters. The impracticality of it all, with high running costs and no real income. Taking on the kind of responsibilities that usually come with middle age when you were only twenty-two. Above all, and unthinkable to someone of Adam's age and temperament, the idea of living quite alone.

There was no way that Michael would have even considered dropping his life and the beginning of a promising career in London and coming to share Adam's solitude with him. He would have thought Adam had gone crazy had he even raised the question. And, for his part, Adam could not honestly say that he would have wanted to spend the rest of his life buried in the depths of the countryside and closeted with Michael. Whereas with Sean... Adam had found it only too easy to imagine himself living out his days with Sean in this tranquil spot, in beatific harmony, waking to see that handsome head on the pillow beside him every morning of the rest of his life. That fantasy had been so compelling that he had actually set it before Sean, had imprudently blurted it out in a moment of post-coital euphoria. And Sean had so crushingly, so memorably, turned him down.

Alone then. Alone it would have to be – if he took the plunge. A small voice inside his head whispered to Adam: *It still isn't too late to sell the place; get out before you get sucked too far in.* Adam realised that he had lapsed into silence and that his parents were waiting for what he would say next.

But then his mother broke the silence herself. 'Yet I suppose it can't be as isolated as all that. All these people living here in their châteaux. People must see each other. The young people getting married among each other. There would be daughters. Of your age. There'd be – opportunities.'

Really, Adam thought. Talk about hope triumphing over experience. Some people just would not be told. Show them the earth from space and still they'd want to believe it flat. He felt suddenly angry. 'OK,' he heard himself say, 'I'll do it.'

'Do what?' Hugh asked.

'Tell Philippe Martinville that I'm going to look after the grapes myself from now on.'

Jennifer looked momentarily taken aback. Hugh exhaled slowly. 'Are you sure,' he asked, measuring out his words carefully, 'that he'll still want to buy them if you do?'

Adam was stopped for a second in his tracks. He had not thought of that. Then he recovered his resolve. 'I'll just have to ask him then, won't I?'

From that point on, now that the Rubicon had been crossed, Adam's parents were full of support. It was a discovery that surprised him. His father first offered to be with his son at the crucial meeting and then, when Adam said, no, he would rather handle it on his own, agreed that Adam was quite right to do so and that he, Hugh, was proud of him. Hugh also said that Adam must not think of going over to Philippe's house to tell him of his decision but should invite him to come and meet him on his own home turf. 'Over a drink or two,' he advised, in man-to-man tones. And Jennifer said she would make some really stylish pastry canapés for the occasion.

Philippe arrived on foot, the way Adam had gone to call on him a few weeks earlier, striding down between the rows of brightly yellowing vines. Feeling rather self-conscious, Adam invited him to be seated at a table on the lawn on which a wine bottle and two glasses (not forgetting his mother's canapés) rather ostentatiously sat.

'I expect you'd like to take a look at this,' Philippe said, taking a piece of paper from his pocket. On it was a handwritten account of his expenses in maintaining Adam's vineyard plot alongside the sum that the sale of the grapes back to Philippe had realised. Taking one from the other showed a net balance in Adam's favour of some three thousand euros. Stéphane's prediction had been correct.

'I'll type it up and date it just as soon as your probate comes through, then I'll give you – or post you – a cheque on the same day. As we agreed.'

Adam supposed this was OK. He poured them both a glass of wine, though it was only ten thirty in the morning. One could get used to this, he thought. Then, bull by the horns, he thought.

'I guess it won't surprise you, what I want to tell you next,' Adam began. 'I'm planning to take on the care of my bit of vineyard myself for the coming year. I fully expect to be able to offer you a crop next year that's just as good as any that Georges's plot has produced up till now. Of course, if you decide for any reason not to buy the grapes, that's your right ... and I'll have to see what I can get for them elsewhere.'

There. He had done it. Philippe looked thunderstruck, and God only knew what he was going to say next, but at least Adam had fired his bolt without flinching. He blessed his father for warning him that Philippe might not want to buy his produce. Forewarned had been forearmed.

Philippe leaned across the table towards him. 'Well, it's your right too, of course, to do as you please with your own grapes. But I have to tell you that you should think very carefully before putting a plan like that into action. First class grapes don't just produce themselves, you know. They need professional care and attention. With all due respect, you have no experience, no background. *En plus*, you don't have a picking machine. A plot the size of yours would never support the purchase of expensive kit like that, and you can forget trying to hire one in September. It might be different if you had grapes that ripened in January.'

'I plan to learn quickly,' Adam answered. 'And not without help. Stéphane from Beaurepaire has agreed to be my guru.' A bit rashly, since nothing had been agreed except in the vaguest terms, he added, 'He'll be with me every step of the way. As for picking, well, I thought I might dragoon my entire cohort of friends.' He tried optimistically to imagine Sean and Michael, heads down among the rows. But it didn't seem a very probable scenario, especially where Michael was concerned.

Nevertheless, to Adam's surprise, Philippe seemed a little bit impressed. Sufficiently so as to take a sip of wine at least. 'Stéphane's a funny kid,' he said. 'His parents had no end of trouble with him when he was younger. But he's taken to the business, I'll give him that. Doing a course in Bordeaux now. Who'd have thought of such a thing when I was his age? Maybe, maybe if he really was with you every step of the way, you might just about manage. If you're not afraid of tough physical work yourself, that is.' Philippe scrutinised him carefully. 'You've got a good strong pair of forearms, I'll give you that at least.'

Now was not the moment, Adam thought, to announce that he had got those muscles playing the cello.

Philippe took another sip of wine. 'I suppose it might work out. Mind you, I'm not promising you here and now that I'd buy the grapes. I'd need to come and inspect them first. You'd still let me have access, I suppose?'

'Of course,' said Adam. 'After all, I might want to walk up between the rows to your place sometimes to bum a glass of wine off you.' He wondered if this time he had gone too far with his very senior next-door neighbour.

To Adam's relief, Philippe laughed. 'And I might want to do the same. To tell the truth, your plan might not suit me so badly after all. There's an old fellow who works for me part-time. He's due to retire next spring. I'd been wondering whether to replace him or not. Maybe, just maybe, you've helped me to make that decision.'

At that point it was Adam's turn to take a sip of wine. Quite a large one actually.

Paris London, London Brussels, Brussels London, London Paris ... and suddenly it was Christmas. The Grand Moulin was shuttered, locked and unvisited, save by the Leducs who had been programmed for years to watch for burst water pipes. The vines surrounding it were dry tangles of branches, dormant and bare of leaves; they were the forest of thorns that encircled the Sleeping Beauty's castle. Adam had not decided when he would visit the place again.

He was spending Christmas itself in the small town, a hundred miles from London, where his parents lived, and where he had been brought up. It was also where Sean's and Michael's parents lived. The three young men had decided on a practical show of solidarity this Christmas. If they *all* went back to their parental homes but still arranged to spend as much time as possible together, they reasoned, then everyone's filial duty could be done with minimum personal cost. The responsibility of being a good son weighed slightly more heavily on Sean than on the others. He was an only child whose father had died three years previously. Adam too was an only child but he did at least have two parents to support each other. Michael was the only one of them with brothers and sisters.

Christmas was a time-honoured occasion for family bombshells, they all knew, and they were, up to a point, braced to withstand them. But this Christmas the bombshell was dropped by Michael in the local pub on Boxing Day among the silvered decorations and the pints of Carlsberg, and it fell squarely on Adam and Sean.

'I've been putting this off for days,' Michael said, 'but it's time you knew. I'm moving out of Clapham for good in the new year.'

'Why?' asked Adam. Clapham without Michael made no sense.

'It's someone I've met.' He stopped.

'Boy,' enquired Sean, in a very careful voice, 'or girl?'

'Neither,' said Michael. 'She's a woman of thirty. Melissa. Divorced. She's asked me to move in.'

There was quite a long silence while Sean and Adam tried to take this in. Finally Adam said, 'Has she any idea what ... what you're like?'

'She knows all my relationships to date have been with men if that's what you mean. That's not a problem for her.'

Sean said, 'But do you ... I mean ... have you...?'

'Once,' said Michael. 'And it all worked like clockwork in case you're wondering.'

I've been too far away from him, Adam was thinking. *Not to have noticed that something was going on. My lovely friend's gone mad.* 'Don't do it,' he blurted out. 'It isn't you. Have sex with women if you want to. Experiment. Try everything. But don't go and get involved with − move in with − a woman of thirty. It's not you.'

'Excuse me,' said Michael, 'but shouldn't I be the judge of who I am and what I do? Look.' He found a conciliatory tone. 'I knew you might take it badly. I know you love me, and I love you too. But there are different ways of loving, and there are different ways of living together. It's just that something new's happened for me and, well...' He broke off with a shrug.

Sean and Adam exchanged a look that went way beyond astonished. 'Have you told your parents?' Sean finally asked.

'Not yet,' Michael answered. He managed a rueful smile. 'I thought I'd see how it went down with you two first.'

Adam's mind was still in a state of numbed shock, his brain incapable of any intelligent decision when, back at Clapham two days later, he received three letters from France: one from the lawyers, announcing the settlement of Georges Pincemin's estate on both sides of the Channel with the granting of probate; the second enclosing Philippe Martinville's cheque, in euros, for the sale of his last year's crop of grapes; and the third from the lycée in Castillon.

'Which is Castillon?' Sean asked. There were just the two of them in the flat, waiting about, rather emptily, for the start of Sean's university term to part them in a few days' time.

'The town with the supermarket on the outskirts – you know, Leclerc at St-Magne.' Somehow the fact of pronouncing the words made him feel better already, even before he had digested the contents of the letter. 'They – they've got four cello pupils for me. They want me to start in February. There may be more. Hey, listen to this.' He translated into English for Sean's benefit, '...honoured at being able to profit from the arrival in the district of a cellist with such a distinguished profile...'

'Did you apply to them?' Sean asked, surprised.

'Gary made me,' said Adam. 'He got me to write to all the secondary schools within driving distance of the mill, one Paris weekend. The carrot was a signed testimonial from him.'

'And the school at Castillon's bought it? They must be mad.' Sean ruffled Adam's hair. 'Or else Gary's been telling them the biggest load of porkies ever invented.'

'It's meant,' said Adam, still peering into the letter and feeling something like wonder. 'It's clearly meant to happen. Michael moving out, Clapham coming to an end, getting probate at last, and now this. I've obviously got to finish at Eurostar and go.'

'Maybe you have,' said Sean. He did not sound very enthusiastic.

Adam took a deep breath. Sean was only half surprised to see that there were tears in his eyes. 'I'll have one last crack at this, Sean. I really mean this. Will you, as I asked you before but you... Look, will you come with me? We share whatever life throws at us together?'

Sean shook his head. There were tears in his own eyes now. 'You know the score. I've got my course in Newcastle to finish. And I'm not looking for a young man to spend the rest of my life with. I've told you. Not even you.'

'But it would be me if you were,' said Adam flatly. 'OK, I hear you. And I think... I think ... right now I need a drink.'

'Not first of all,' Sean said. Then he did what he was good at and took Adam in his arms. A few minutes later they were on Adam's bed and making love with an intensity that, on Adam's side at least, as he plunged himself into his friend, bordered almost on anger.

SEVEN

Thus Adam found himself boarding a Brittany Ferries ship, the Normandie, in Portsmouth one early February afternoon. A grey sky was letting loose a light fall of snow which danced on a northerly breeze. He threw his suitcase and backpack into the racks of the foot passengers' left-luggage room with a mixture of trust and fatalism, then headed for the bar. He drank a pint of beer slowly, as he thought, but when, having finished it, he looked at his watch he saw that sailing time was still ten minutes away. Rather than abandon himself to total incapability – for there would be no one to prop him up when he arrived at the other end – he went up on deck among the dancing snow.

In the berth next to the Normandie a P&O ferry, the Pride of Portsmouth, was also making ready to depart. She would be sailing for Le Havre. Adam knew this because the on-board announcements were floating up from her decks and getting entangled with the announcements of the Normandie's own imminent departure for Caen. In the event the Normandie left her berth first but had to turn round in the harbour before heading out to sea. During this stately but exacting manoeuvre the Pride of Portsmouth, her bow already pointing in the right direction, slipped smoothly away from her own berth and set off towards the harbour mouth. So that when the Normandie at last got under way she found herself meekly following in the wake kicked up by the departing P&O ship, and at a prudent distance of a mile or so astern. Their farewell siren blasts echoed in mournful antiphony across the grey water. Still in procession the two ships filed out through the narrow harbour entrance and turned westward into Spithead, as indeed they had to. Directly ahead of them lay the solid mass of the Isle of Wight.

The dismal afternoon was merging imperceptibly with dusk and to Adam's eyes the lights of the ship ahead of him grew brighter in the surrounding gloom. For another half hour the Normandie remained in convoy with the Pride of Portsmouth, their path marked out for them by the coastline of the Isle of Wight to starboard and a succession of marker buoys to port. But then, as they passed the sharp angled cliffs of Bembridge Point and the line of buoys came to an end, the open sea was all before them. Freed from their enforced companionship, the P&O vessel turned almost imperceptibly to the left and the Normandie to the right, as if the two ships had scented their different destinations on the air. Little by little their diverging roads grew wider apart. After ten minutes there were several miles between them and soon after that the lights of the Pride of Portsmouth, which Adam had, without realising it, grown attached to, come to think of as a comforting presence, a guide or companion on his lonely journey, had disappeared for good behind the curtain of snow still softly blowing in the dark.

A wave of desolation broke over Adam at that moment. His ship was alone on the vast sea and he, alone of all its passengers, stood stupidly on deck in dark and cold. He was alone at the beginning of his new life. He shivered and went below. That second pint seemed more than merely tempting.

Just three hundred miles south of Caen where he disembarked, St-Emilion presented a different world to him when, next morning, he finally got off the last of the three trains on which he had spent an uncomfortable but economical night. The difference could be summed up in four words: warm, sunny, spring-like and Stéphane. Stéphane had brought the old Renault 4 they had all used back last summer; he would take him to the Grand

Moulin in it; then it would be on extended loan to Adam until either he sorted out something more permanent or it fell apart – whichever happened first.

On the short journey through the vineyards to the mill, Adam was shocked, though most pleasurably, at the alacrity with which spring was arriving here. It had not been like this when he had lived on the Plateau de Langres in his teens. There, in upland, north-eastern Haute-Marne, the snow had lain deep on the fields till early March. But here, celandines already made the hedge banks butter-yellow, magnolia trees wore enveloping crowns of fat white flowers, and the glossy green cushions of camellia bushes were studded with blooms in clashing shades of red, as if colour-blind staff in a sofa factory had mixed up the boxes of upholstery buttons. The sky was a friendly blue.

'I'd like to stay and help you settle in,' Stéphane said once they'd greeted each other and exchanged their first few inconsequential words. 'But I've got to get back to Bordeaux this afternoon.'

'What about the weekend?' asked Adam, already disappointed that the promising start to this re-encounter with Stéphane looked about to be cut short.

'Weekend's fine. We could spend some time together – if you'd like that.' Stéphane began confidently but then sounded uncertain. He was not quite sure how far his friendship with Adam went.

'I'd like that. There's so many things I'll need to know, and that if you don't help me with them, God knows who will. Besides, we all need friends.' That last bit sounded a bit uncool, Adam thought, in whatever language. But it had just slipped out. Anyway, it couldn't be unsaid.

Stéphane didn't seem fazed by it, fortunately. He just said, casually, *'Bon bien. On se voit, on se téléphone.'* We'll be in touch.

There was just time for the briefest look around the Grand Moulin before Adam had to run Stéphane back to the station to get his own train to Bordeaux. And then, for the first time in his life, Adam was truly alone, the master of a sizeable house and grounds for which no-one was responsible but he.

Resisting the (surprisingly strong) temptation immediately to crack open a bottle of wine and drink the lot, Adam took a proprietorial walk around the outdoor part of his domain. He looked for fish in the fast flowing streams and the millponds but saw none; perhaps the light was wrong. He saw, without looking particularly hard, that several roof tiles had fallen from one of the outhouses and that a hinge on one of the garage doors had nearly rusted through.

He walked around the vineyard on the slope above the stream at the back of the house. In some of the neighbouring vineyards the pruning had already been done, so that the vines were reduced to twisted black stumps sticking about a foot out of the ground with, on each one, a single thin woody cane tied down to the lowest wire, while the upper wires ran through the vineyards like unused tramway cables. His own plot looked slightly different. A tangle of old dry canes hung twisted and straggling among the wires. Only the memory of what it had looked like last summer and the knowledge that it would do so again prevented the spectacle from being depressing.

Indoors again, Adam unpacked quickly and then, giving way to a sudden panicky desire for company, drove into St-Emilion and treated himself to a beer and a sandwich at the Spanish bar. It was nice to find that one or two of the regular customers remembered him from the previous summer and spoke to him. They asked him about his friends and about Stéphane and he was guarded in his replies. It was too soon to decide who was friend and who was not. Yes, he was living at Pressac now, he told them if they asked. And yes, it was at the Grand Moulin, if they asked that too. And alone? At the moment yes, he said with a smile and without elaboration. Had the weather been mild like this all the winter, he asked? Pretty much, they all said. The area was blessed with an exceptionally favourable microclimate, they all said, that was famous throughout France. But he knew that people said that everywhere.

He drank two beers more than he'd intended to and drove back. Back ... back ... back home. There. He'd said it for the first time. Home. *Chez moi*. But when he reached it he found he didn't want to be indoors and so he took a walk up the track and along the road. Couldn't do that too often, he told himself. People would take him for the local loony. He thought of Sylvain when he first knew him. Have to get a dog.

It got dark. He drove out one more time: to the supermarket at St-Magne now, to get some provisions for the evening and next day. The things you had to remember when you were on your own. Loo-paper, pepper, rubbish-sacks, tea.

Then finally there was just him and the house, the big old house, with the Petit Moulin adjoining, not so small itself, and empty, locked and dark. In his own Grand Moulin he put on all the lights, downstairs and up. He remembered the bedrooms as he had last seen them, occupied and, er, used, last summer. He wished he could re-people them now.

The cello would be coming with the remainder of his things in a few days. That had made good sense at the planning stage but he missed its company now. He made do with the upright piano instead and strummed some Mozart and Scott Joplin for a while. But when he stopped, the silence and emptiness were worse. *Alone.*

He phoned his parents and, after some argument with himself, Michael and Sean as well. They seemed a bit unreal, just then, spotlighted by a phone-call in their different worlds. And so he too seemed to them.

He cooked a chicken breast and sautéed potatoes with it, had fruit and cheese. And yes, in the end he did uncork that bottle of wine. Surprisingly soon he had polished it all off, watching absurdly meaningless things on TV. He had some trouble following. Surely his French wasn't still rusty after four months on Eurostar? It must be the wine. But at last, when he looked at his watch, it was no longer too early to go to bed. And everything would look better in the morning.

Adam awoke, with the lights still on in his bedroom and throughout the house, to the sight and sound of pouring rain. He spent the morning waiting until it stopped. But it didn't. There were so many things he'd planned to do – see the *notaire*, go to the bank, get in touch with the school, talk to the Leducs – but he knew deep down inside that they would all go badly if he tried to do them on a morning like today. A morning, then an afternoon. He didn't go out all day. At least there were books to read. Books. A slightly out-of-tune piano. TV. A bottle of wine. So this was what living alone was like.

The following day brought no relief. The rain had continued throughout the night and now the millstream was not just tumbling over the weir when you watched it from the kitchen window but shooting horizontally over the top and crashing like a ski jumper far out into the middle of the lower pond. The water had risen to within three feet of the sill and Adam noticed for the first time that there were slots carved in the stone window surround for the placing of wooden flood guards. When he went and inspected the doors he found that the doorposts were furnished with them too. Somewhere he had the number of Stéphane's mobile. Today was Friday. They had sort of said the weekend.

Stéphane arrived at about five, splashing down the track, the feeble headlight of his motorbike just visible in the gloom but its engine inaudible this time against the thunderous roar of the weir and the interminable downrush of the rain. 'You're soaked to the bones,' Adam said, when they had got the bike under cover and Stéphane indoors. *'Tu es trempé jusqu'aux os.'*

'Yes but I've brought some *marc* to keep the cold out.' Stéphane had reached some things out of his saddlebag in the garage. He held them out for inspection: a bottle of local brandy and another of Château Beaurepaire. Adam embraced him, ran a hand through his sopping hair – it had grown again since the summer – and tried to give him a kiss. But he didn't get as far as the kiss, instead he broke down in an uncontrollable storm of crying, his face cushioned on Stéphane's wet coat collar and his arms around his neck.

'T'en fais pas, mon vieux,' said Stéphane gently. 'Don't worry about it, mate. Nothing you do could possibly make me wetter.' Then, when Adam's convulsions had died away to something like silence, he said gently, 'Why don't we just go upstairs?'

And upstairs, together in Adam's large bed, was where they spent the greater part of the next twenty-four hours.

So Adam found himself in the middle of an affair. Not at the beginning of an affair but right in the middle of one. Was that perhaps the nature of 'affairs'? That they didn't have beginnings but you were plunged immediately into the middle? What did this word mean, this word 'affair' that first drifted into his mind during the stillness of that first Monday morning, after Stéphane had ridden off ear-splittingly some time before dawn to catch the early train to Bordeaux? It had to refer, he decided, to something that was intense and passionate and powerful but which was of its essence finite. Affairs came with sell-by dates. Affairs were fun while they lasted, but they always ended. Didn't they?

The sun was shining again. The weir still cascaded in a furious fortissimo of sound and white water, and the lower pond had invaded half of the lawn, but the heady sensation of spring-in-February had returned. It was the three-day spell of unbroken torrential rain that had turned out, mercifully, to be the aberration, not the gentle warmth that both preceded and followed it. Adam was under no illusion about himself and Stéphane. They would not go striding off down life's road and into the eventual sunset together. This was a temporary thing that had had happened. A very nice thing, but temporary. A gap had opened in Adam's life where home had been, and where England had been, and where Sean and Michael had been. And into this hole in Adam's existence young Stéphane had unexpectedly but conveniently tumbled.

The same thing went for Stéphane as it happened, which was just as well for both of them. Adam had learnt this during the wonderful, unscripted, weekend they had just shared: a weekend of laughing and talking and crying, of hugging and kissing and fucking, of exploring and discovering and sharing; a weekend when the rain didn't matter, and the world outside and beyond the mill could go hang, and Adam didn't even remember to phone his parents on Sunday night. Yes, Stéphane was also a boy with a vacuum in his life, one into which Adam had been blown as if on a lucky wind. Stéphane had allowed himself to get too serious about Michael, he told Adam now. It had only been a little holiday fling after all; both Stéphane and Michael knew that at the time, so Stéphane had had no business to go on thinking about it afterwards, magnifying it into something it was never meant to be, getting it out of proportion, getting hurt. On the rebound, Stéphane had rather too quickly let himself get involved with a fellow student in Bordeaux – only to realise he was very definitely *pas du tout son genre*: not his type at all. How wonderful it was for Stéphane that Adam had turned up, himself feeling bruised and lonely – and needing *him*. Adam who was already a friend. Known, safe, trusted. All this Stéphane shared with Adam while they fondled each other, sometimes gently, sometimes fiercely, needily, under the warm duvet.

Both of them felt immeasurably stronger now than before the weekend: totally confident and ready to cope with life. They would spend the next weekend together at the Moulin. They had said so. They would spend all their weekends together for the foreseeable future. They didn't actually say this, but neither of them could at that moment imagine it being otherwise. Meanwhile Adam would go into Bordeaux on either Tuesday or Wednesday and stop over with Stéphane. He would never need to be alone at the Moulin for more than a couple of nights at a time if he didn't want to be. It was a bolstering thought.

Adam had discovered that becoming a landowner at the age of twenty-two had marked him out as being different from most other people no less surely than the fact of his being gay. As far as his recent workmates, the stewards at Eurostar, were concerned he might as well have announced that he lived on Neptune. With Stéphane, however, no such difficulty existed. Stéphane did not find him in any way odd or different just because he owned part of a wine estate. He himself would one day become the owner of a whole one. Well, he and his sister would in theory become joint owners when their parents died; but Stéphane was pretty sure that Françoise wouldn't want a stake in it and that he would end up buying her out. This too he told Adam under the duvet. Stéphane thought it would be wonderful that there would be two of them, two gay boys, owning estates in the Côtes de Castillon. It had been a bit isolating, before Adam arrived on the scene, to think that in this land of family châteaux and intermarrying dynasties he would be the only *petit frère. Un pédale sans vélo.* Their land almost adjoined; did Adam realise that? Where Adam's parcel of vineyard narrowed to a point as it climbed towards the road, there on the other side of the road was the boundary of Stéphane's parents' property, Château Beaurepaire. Together they pored over the large-scale map. 'Do you realise,' Stéphane said, 'that if the two of us were to buy up the rest of Château l'Orangerie, we'd own this whole solid block of vineyard?' He ran his forefinger round a largish square area of the map.

'Jesus, what are you saying?' Adam answered, laughing. 'I've been here less than a week. I don't have two euros to rub together and you're talking about the two of us buying a château! Oh yes, and buying up your sister's share of yours.'

Stéphane laughed too, and shrugged. 'Just a thought. Just a dream. *On peut rêver quand-même, quoi?'*

In bed Stéphane fluctuated between being cuddly-soft, and hard, energetic and agile. Adam found he really liked it. *'On est bien assortis, toi et moi, tu penses pas?'* Stéphane said at one point. We go together well. Then, *'Comme deux lévriers,'* which gave Adam a start. For that was exactly how he had himself imagined Stéphane in bed together with Michael back in the summer: like two greyhounds.

Stéphane had an idiosyncracy that first surprised Adam, then amused him and that he finally found endearing. His long tapering cock had such an upward curve, such a back-curve to it as to make pissing when he had a hard-on something of a hazardous operation.

His solution, the first morning they awoke together, was to stride across the room naked, fling open the casement and empty his bladder upwards out of the window. 'Which is all very well,' Adam said, 'down here where no-one can see you. But you won't be able to do that when there's paying guests in the Petit Moulin. And you surely don't do it at your parents' house or in the centre of Bordeaux?'

'You're right,' Stéphane said. 'I have to use the shower – or stand up one end of the bath.' They both guffawed. By the end of that first weekend Adam was following Stéphane's example – not with regard to the bath, but with the early dawn trip to the bedroom window. It was set to become one of their shared daily rituals, part of their bonding.

This Monday Adam had more to do than merely shop and tidy the house. He took the dark suit that he'd brought from England out of the wardrobe where he had hung it in the hope that its latest set of travel creases would drop out without assistance, and put it on. He checked himself in the mirror as he did so. White shirt and silver tie. With his dark hair and eyes the effect was terrific. He was over-dressed, perhaps, for a visit to a school, but – who cared? He wasn't going to turn up like this too often, so let them see him looking his smartest just for once. He combed his hair and drove the six miles to Castillon, parking the ancient Renault at some distance from the school where he was hoping to make an impression. The car, had anyone seen it, would have rather cancelled out the suit.

'Some have cellos provided by the school, others bring them from home.' The head of music was showing him round the lycée. She pushed open a door. *'La salle des profs.'* Incredible. Just five years ago Adam had been a pupil in a French lycée. From next week he would be a *prof.*

He told Stéphane how strange an idea this seemed to him when he related his adventures to him and his student friends in Bordeaux on Tuesday night. 'Other big news,' he added. 'My things have come. Pickford's lorry arrived this morning. Computer, sound system, cello – especially cello, since I'm going to be teaching the thing next week – clothes and books.' He stopped. Stéphane looked at him expectantly. Adam laughed. 'Elephants? Lions and tigers? No. That's it. I don't own anything else.'

'I've got a couple more books for you,' Stéphane said. 'On looking after vines. You need to read the chapters on pruning before the weekend. Then I'll give you a practical demo. And there's your next six weeks taken care of.'

'In between everything else – and teaching, and cello practice.' Any previous ideas that he might find himself at a loose end all by himself at the mill now seemed wildly at variance with the emerging reality. 'People keep arriving,' Adam went on, 'now the rain's stopped. A man turned up with a truckload of shingle and a small motor roller and said he'd fill in the potholes in the yard for six hundred euros. Fortunately Monsieur Leduc was there and told him to get lost.'

'Quite right,' said Stéphane, nodding sagely. 'That's Pépin the Mad. Have nothing to do with him.'

'And somebody else turned up who had a sort of cherry-picking machine that would root weeds out of the high gutters. I told him I'd think about it.'

'*Bon*. That might be useful. I've noticed that you've got quite a little forest of baby ash trees on the back roof. They'll do damage under the tiles if they're left and it won't be easy to get at them otherwise.'

'It's just the money I keep thinking about.' Adam had told Stéphane about the hundred thousand euros in Georges's old bank account; it had seemed easy –

natural – to share this with Stéphane, his fellow *vigneron*. 'I just hate letting it trickle away when there's nothing coming in from anywhere.'

'Yeah, but it has to be done. Think of the money you're going to save by doing your own pruning.'

'I fully intend to. I imagine that focusing on that thought is the only thing that'll stop me going stark staring mad while I'm doing it.'

It was a bizarre novelty for Stéphane to arrive at the Moulin on Friday night and find his dinner being cooked by an English boyfriend – it would have seemed bizarre to most Frenchmen. But it was the thought, rather than the actual cooking, that counted, and Stéphane fully appreciated that. He also had to admit that Adam's cooking was not in fact as bad as his upbringing had conditioned him to believe that English cooking would have to be. Nevertheless, there was still room for improvement: Adam's cooking could do with becoming just a little more French for a start (kedgeree was the dish of the day this Friday evening) and Stéphane decided to make this desirable transformation one of his longer-term missions during the weeks ahead.

'What are your parents going to make of your spending all your time here and not going to see them at weekends?' Adam asked Stéphane. They had lit a blazing log fire in the great chimney and were sprawled on the floor in front of it. There was a bottle of wine not too far away.

'I forgot to tell you,' Stéphane said. 'We're going there for Sunday lunch next weekend.'

'What, like a couple?'

'No, not exactly.' Stéphane looked uncomfortable for a second. 'They see us as – well, just as two *mecs*, two mates.'

'They're going to see through you at some point,' said Adam. 'Are you going to have to go on pretending to them for the rest of their lives?' A new thought struck him. 'Am I?'

'It's all very well for you,' Stéphane said, 'but it's not like London here. It's not like Paris. People like us leave places like this and go to Paris – or London – for that very reason. But what should I do? Walk away from the château and lose the lot? And you're in the same boat too, now that you're no longer a holidaymaker but have come here to live. *Dans la même galère, dans le même bain.* You're in the same boat whether you like it or not.'

People were just so wrong about 'coming out', Adam thought. As if it was a great big once-for-all crossing the line ceremony with liberation on the other side of it. But it was not like that at all: you were never through with doing it. It was like the early feminists burning their bras. How did they manage to keep letting new people know that they'd done it? They must have mostly had to go back to work on the Monday morning afterwards. So what had they done then? Kept the ashes in little boxes on their desk tops?

'It wasn't in Paris or London that I came out to my parents,' Adam tried gamely. 'It was in a little *village paumé* in the Haute-Marne.'

'Yes, but that's only because your lover Sylvain tried to run away with you and you both got caught. Sorry, but Michael did tell me that.'

It had not crossed Adam's mind before this moment that Stéphane might have learnt vastly more about Adam from Michael during their brief fling together than Adam had yet told Stéphane. 'Yes, of course,' he said. 'You're absolutely right. I'm sorry. You can tell your parents whatever you like. Tell them I'm teaching you the cello. Tell them I'm helping you with your English for all I care.' He thrust his head towards Stéphane and kissed him, then Stéphane caught him in an embrace and they began to tussle together on the carpet.

Stéphane had brought two pieces of equipment with him in addition to his viticultural know-how. One was a power-assisted pair of secateurs. 'Don't laugh,' he said when Adam did just that. 'You've got about eight thousand vines to do. My old man would take about four weeks to do that many, but it'll take you about six as it's your first time. You wear the power-pack on a belt round your waist.' Stéphane demonstrated. Adam stopped laughing and remembered that he would still need to be able to use his fingers for playing the cello. The second item was a pistol. It would be used to tie the vines' remaining branches down to the horizontal wires along which they had to be trained. You aimed at the tying point and a tiny wire shot out and instantly coiled itself around both branch and supporting wire.

They went outside and among the vines. It was sunny but a wicked wind was licking down the slopes from the north. Stéphane showed Adam how to select the most promising of last year's fruiting stems and to bend it down to the bottom wire and then tie it. All the other branches were then pruned off. Once Adam had done a few it was quite easy to see the pattern. The first one took him about five minutes, but soon he got it down to three. It was quite satisfying to look back at the twenty or so vines they had tidied up in this way during the first half hour. But when Adam straightened up and looked around him at the seven thousand nine hundred and eighty bushes that still awaited his attention his heart sank.

'My father says you should never do that,' said Stéphane. 'I mean, to look around you at everything that's still waiting to be done.'

'That's probably a good tip for life as a whole,' said Adam.

Later and back indoors, Adam was surprised to hear Stéphane strumming on the piano. He did not play at all like the professionals and students that he had been used to hearing at the Academy. The notes were put down deliberately, ploddingly, in the way of someone conscientiously remembering as an adult a piece he has been taught as a child. Adam recognised the piece, though at first he couldn't place it. But it stirred his memory strongly and caused the hairs on the back of his neck to rise. 'What's that piece you're playing?' he called out.

'Les Niais de Sologne,' Stéphane said. 'I think it's by Rameau.'

It came back to Adam suddenly. The Simpletons of Sologne. Georges Pincemin had played it to him on one of his golden-tongued harpsichords in this very room. It had made him think of Sylvain. It had nearly made him cry. Now it had nearly done so again.

'All French kids learn it when they begin learning the piano,' said Stéphane. 'Only the first bit though. I can't play the end of it. It gets difficult.'

'I know,' said Adam. Then, 'Can you read music? You wouldn't like to try and play some of my accompaniments for me sometimes?'

Stéphane stopped abruptly. His chestnut eyes had opened very wide and his jaw had dropped by the time he was turned to face Adam. 'You are joking! Me, accompany a professional cellist? I think not.'

'I didn't mean accompany me professionally. Just here – just sometimes. There'd be no-one to hear you. Even if you only did the right hand – and even then you could miss out the fast bits. Even just one note at the beginning of a bar would be something. Please.'

'No way. I'd get totally lost. I can't sight-read. I could never find my way through the simplest piece after all this time.'

'Please give it a go. Even just once. For me. A very special favour. I could help you – you know, show you myself how the music went. It's only that I can't play the piano and the cello at the same time.' A thought struck him and made him giggle. 'You know what? You'd be able to tell your parents I was your piano teacher.'

EIGHT

Béatrice sat everyone down in the big homely farmhouse room that did double duty as salon and dining room. She was a comfortable-looking woman, at ease with herself – *at ease in her skin*, as the French say. She had a round, smiley face that was almost unlined, and wore her long chestnut hair, which was only just beginning to grey, swept back and tied in a thick bunch. 'You should have called round before,' she told Adam. 'Not waited for an invitation from dreamy-one here.' She nodded in the direction of her son.

'On the contrary,' said her husband with exaggerated courtesy, pouring Adam a generous measure of Monbazillac, 'we were remiss in not calling on you.' Marc was a thin, wiry man like his son, and his face wore his wife's share of lines in addition to his own.

It was a pleasantly informal Sunday lunch; though, since this was France after all, that did not prevent it from being both substantial and elaborate and involving some three and a half hours at the table. Françoise was also there. Adam had not seen her since their first meeting four years before. She had the same deep chestnut eyes as her brother, but they were set in a more conventionally attractive face. She was also intelligent and vivacious, with a keen sense of humour. Adam remembered being told, last summer, that Françoise was working in Périgueux as an accountant and living there with a boyfriend. Partly that was still true, only the boyfriend and she had split up and she now shared a flat there with two other young women.

They all talked about Adam's arrival in France and then, almost inevitably, about the influx of so many of his compatriots in the shape of second home owners among the hills and valleys of the Dordogne.

'You'll have seen the plaque down by the river,' Marc said. 'The one celebrating the final eviction of the English from the region in 1453.'

'The Battle of Castillon.' Adam felt obliged to show off the little he knew. 'The end of the Hundred Years' War.'

'How little they realised,' Marc continued, 'those people who inscribed the monument, that the English would have the last laugh. Re-conquering Gascony half a millennium later without firing a shot.'

'I'm not so sure about that,' said Adam. 'About the English having the last laugh, I mean. The second home owners have handed over a hell of a lot of cash in the process. Think of all those peasant farmers who had a tumbledown dovecote or cowshed on their land they never thought to find a use for. They've been laughing all the way to the bank.' Adam had been little more than a child when he had first sat at this table with Stéphane's parents. Now they were treating him on equal terms as a fellow adult and landowner.

'You are like one of the Angevins, then,' Françoise suggested, 'like Henri Plantagenet or Richard Coeur de Lion. Inheriting an empire on both sides of the Channel. King in England and Duke in France.'

Adam made his face into a pantomime mask of surprise. 'I hardly see myself as the ruler of an empire,' he said. Then he had second thoughts. 'All the same, to have a little kingdom, to be a little king, does have rather a nice sound to it.'

Le Royaume d'Adam,' said Béatrice. 'Adam's Kingdom. We'll have to find you a Queen Eve.'

The conversation had taken a squirm-inducing turn. Adam took a gulp of wine and exchanged a look and a conspiratorially raised eyebrow with Stéphane across the table. Adam and Eve, he thought, or Adam and Steve? – and then realised for the first time that Adam and Steve

already existed in the coupling of his name with
Stéphane's. He wondered that he had never thought of
this before and had to stifle a sudden urge to giggle. He
didn't risk catching Stéphane's eye again. He would
have to explain another time.

Stéphane needed to return to Bordeaux that evening
and Adam offered to run him to the station by way of
engineering his own departure from the lunch party at
the same time. He explained the Adam and Steve joke
on the way to the station, which made Stéphane laugh,
but they did not pursue it any further in case it led them
into places they were not yet willing to explore. All the
same, Adam waited with Stéphane on the ankle-high
platform of St-Emilion station till his train came in, and
when it did, they parted with a butch but fairly public
kiss.

Back at the Moulin, while Adam was getting things
together for the morning, the phone rang and gave him
the voice – and the minor culture shock – of Sean. They
had only spoken once since Adam's arrival in France
and that was on Adam's first evening, before anything
much had happened, before even his baptism by three
days of torrential rain.

Sean was sorry he hadn't been back in touch before.
He had rather imagined that Adam would phone him
again when he'd had a day or two to settle in; that was
why he hadn't rung. He felt bad, he said now, especially
in view of things that had been said between the two of
them, and was unhappy at the thought of Adam being
lonely, all by himself in that big house, in the winter. Of
course he realised that Stéphane...

Adam had to cut him off. 'Stéphane – actually you
don't have to worry too much. You see, Sté has sort of,
in a kind of way, moved in.' There was a clear sense of
shocked silence coming down the phone line; it was as if
the electric current that powered it had suddenly run

cold. It was the first time that Adam had referred to Stéphane as Sté when talking to anyone except Stéphane himself. 'I mean, I'm actually alone in the house tonight, but Sté has spent the last three weekends here with me. It sort of – uh – just happened that way.'

'I see,' said Sean. 'Well, I suppose that's good, isn't it? I mean I won't have to worry and feel guilty about leaving you on your own.' There was another pause, though less frozen this time. 'But maybe I'm getting the wrong end of the stick. I mean, are you – do you – are you actually...?'

'He keeps his condoms under my pillow, if that's what you mean.'

'Well I'm very glad you're both being safe – if that's what you're trying to tell me. But – sorry I'm not being too coherent – it's just that you've taken me a little by surprise.'

The English end of his kingdom, Adam couldn't stop himself thinking. Unworthy thought. That Sean was jealous. Didn't want Adam for himself – had spurned his offer of a life together – but was now clearly put out because Adam was getting cosy and domestic with someone else. 'Sorry,' Adam said. 'It was an even bigger surprise for me. And for Stéphane too, I think. But if it makes you feel any less ... surprised, I don't feel that it's going to be the big Once-for-Ever thing. At least, that's not how I see it right now.'

'And Sté... Stéphane? How does he see it?'

'I can't say for certain. But neither of us has said anything stupid to the other. I haven't offered him to be co-owner of the Moulin or anything.'

'Ouch,' said Sean. 'Unkind. Though I can't pretend I don't deserve it.'

But once all that was out of the way their conversation steered into smoother waters and continued for some considerable time. As for Michael, Sean had spoken to

Anthony McDonald

him once by phone briefly but Michael had been uncharacteristically unforthcoming. 'That's what shacking up with a woman does to you, I suppose,' Sean commented. 'At least you're still happy to chat. Maybe boys are better in that respect. Not cutting you off from your old friends, I mean.'

When Adam put the phone down at last he realised, with a feeling of satisfaction – and people didn't call it *a glow of satisfaction* for nothing, he thought – that, whatever might have happened, Sean still loved him and – rather more to his surprise – that he still loved Sean.

What Adam had always told himself – that he did not play the piano – was not strictly true. When he had presented himself for his first lesson in his 'second study' at the Academy and said, no, he had not had lessons before, his teacher, a well-known lieder accompanist, had raised an eyebrow. 'Well, OK,' Adam had amended, 'we had an instrument at home. My mother teaches piano.' His teacher had nodded; he was used to this from second-study pupils. 'She taught me my notes.' They all said this too. 'And I taught myself to pick out one or two things.' When his mother was not around, of course. He had soon grasped the twin nettles of playing with two hands together and reading two clefs at the same time, and long before going to music college had reached the stage of being able to have a reasonable stab at almost anything that wasn't too fast or virtuosic. It was only his own consciousness of the world of difference between his professional approach to the cello and the way he dabbled with the keyboard instrument that caused him to say, whenever people asked him, that, no, he didn't play the piano.

But now there would be no getting away from it. Teaching the cello or any other orchestral instrument in school meant sitting down at the piano – as all his own teachers had had to do – and, for better or worse, hammering out his pupils' accompaniments during lessons. It was this, the prospect of having to play unfamiliar piano music at sight, rather than any anxieties about his capacity to deliver quality teaching, or about the characters and attitudes of his students, that gave rise to the flock of butterflies that fluttered below his diaphragm as he parked his battered, borrowed Renault discreetly out of sight of the school buildings and made his way round to the main entrance.

Indeed, once the head of music had settled him into the bare, rather chilly room in which he was to teach, he was so focused on the challenge presented by the piano accompaniment that his first pupil placed in front of him – it was an arrangement of Tchaikovsky's *Chanson Triste* – that it was not until the piece was finished that he realised that, beyond making sure that the two of them were playing in time together, he had totally neglected his main task – of applying a critical ear to the details of his pupil's cello playing. For a moment he was aghast, but then a simple solution presented itself. 'Not at all bad,' he said brightly to his young charge, a stolid and bespectacled girl of thirteen. 'Wouldn't you like to play it again?'

By the time he had given his four lessons Adam was mentally exhausted but beginning to get the hang of things. He was relieved to find that all four pupils were bright and conscientious and willing to accept correction from someone who was not that much older, in three cases, than themselves and who still spoke French with a light but unmistakeable English accent. He was mildly disappointed, but not unduly upset, to find, when he visited the *salle des profs* during his short break in search of coffee, that his arrival was of no interest whatsoever to any of the full-time teachers, despite the head of music's friendly effort in introducing him

93

around the room. Peripatetic music teachers were clearly the lowest form of humanity. He remembered how his mother had uncomplainingly taught in the schools around Langres during that year when they had all lived in the Haute-Marne – and, six years too late, felt a pang of sympathy. Had she had the same experience back then? At any rate she had had her husband to come home to. And in this respect, at least for tonight, Adam would be lucky too. Stéphane had exceptionally arranged to travel back from Bordeaux that evening to spend the night with Adam. He hadn't wanted Adam to go home to an empty house at the end of his first day in a new job, a new profession.

Arriving home, Adam got out of the car to check the letterbox at the end of the drive. And the one letter that lay inside it immediately had the whole of his attention. The envelope, readdressed from his parents' home in England, was handwritten and in a script which, though he could not immediately identify it, was somehow achingly familiar and important. The postmark was hard to read, but it looked like *Côte d'Or*. Adam tore the envelope open, trying not to jump to a wishful conclusion about the letter's authorship. He knew that when you did that you were always disappointed. Expect disappointment, he had learned, and then you might – though even then, only might – be rewarded with a pleasant surprise.

Or a surprise at any rate. The letter was indeed from Sylvain. It bore the same address as Sylvain's first letter to him: the abbey of Cîteaux.

Excuse-moi d'avoir pas répondu à ta belle lettre... I didn't get your letter – the one that you wrote in September – until just now. It wasn't easy living at home and working for my father, so I came back here last summer. The monks were agreeable to take me back. Now I work in the gardens as before, but also I work as a supervisor on a work-experience programme for young offenders that the abbey is involved in...

The letter was almost as long as the one Adam had written to Sylvain back in the autumn. He stood reading it, completely caught up, standing between the open letterbox and the car, whose door stood open, engine still running. It was hard to imagine Sylvain stamping his authority on a bunch of delinquent teenagers – and yet, maybe not. In his own way he had managed to be quite assertive with Adam, when he wanted to be, back when Adam himself had been a teenager. Adam felt a reflex twinge of jealousy. Now that he was twenty-two Sylvain might not necessarily feel the same about him, especially since he was now apparently at the centre of a more youthful, albeit delinquent, coterie. Adam wondered if Sylvain behaved himself with his young charges or whether... But he couldn't bear to pursue this line of thought.

You don't say where exactly is your place in the Gironde. So I have no address for you there but must write 'aux bons soins' of your parents. Can I come and visit you down there?

'Of course, of course you can.' Adam discovered that he had said the words out loud. His hands were trembling by the time he had read to the end *(Je t'aime – Sylvain),* had refolded the letter back into its envelope and got back into the car.

But it was much easier to refold the letter than to recompose himself in the half hour that was left to him before he had to set out again for St-Emilion to meet Stéphane off the train. It was not until much later in the evening that Adam got round to the subject of Sylvain's letter. They tended not to sit on the furniture after dinner on those winter evenings but on the floor in front of the big fire, using the front of the settee as a back rest and draught excluder, and alternately chatting, roasting

95

chestnuts and tussling each other semi-excitedly on the hearthrug in varying states of half-undress, while the occasional sound of a distant train chuntering along the river valley made comforting echoes in the chimney. Only then did Adam tell Stéphane about the letter he had received.

'I thought you were a bit wound up when I got here,' Sté said. 'I'd put it down to your adventures in the classroom today.'

'He wants to come and see me,' Adam told him, in as neutral a tone as he could manage. They were sitting close together on the floor, each with his hands clasped around his own knees. 'I'm not sure how I feel about it.' He had known how he felt, reading the letter, all alone at the top of the drive. It wasn't so simple now, though, feeling the warm pressure of Stéphane through his clothes where their shoulders softly touched. 'He doesn't know about you for a start.'

'Well,' said Stéphane, proceeding with caution, 'we're not actually married, are we?' This was tricky ground for both of them. They both knew it. 'And actually, I was meaning to tell you, after next weekend I've got to be away for the next two. It's sort of two extended weekend field trips. Up into the Médoc, and down to the Sauternes.' Sté unclasped his hands and ruffled Adam's hair. 'You'd be on your own for a bit. So, if you wanted to have some company, well, that's up to you.' He gave a small shrug. 'It's your house after all. What you tell Sylvain about me – or what you don't tell him – that's up to you, I guess.'

'You're amazing, Sté.' Adam started to cuddle him like an overgrown puppy. He had almost literally to bite his tongue in order to stop it adding an involuntary 'I love you'. He had said that too often in his life already, and he knew that it would complicate things no end if he came out with it now.

Adam had plenty of time to reflect on this over the next few days. His one day a week of cello teaching over, he had now to get down to the solid work of pruning his vines. He knew that he must accomplish this within the next six weeks: before the dormant buds awoke with spring and broke into the thrusting growth of a myriad green shoots. It was essential for a good crop that he leave no more than a dozen buds upon each vine. The idea of days spent in the open air with the sounds of mistle thrush, wren and robin for company had a certain appeal to one side of Adam's nature: to the side of him that had enjoyed the escapades that he had shared with Sylvain on the Plateau de Langres. But this time the outdoor days were clouded to some extent by the thought that this was real work, that it had to be done to a strict timetable, and that all this physical effort in March would not be rewarded financially until September or October. There was also the gruelling nature of the task itself. Pruning one vine with electrically powered secateurs was one thing but eight thousand of the things were another matter entirely. In the evenings his forearms and battered fingers ached and his wrists stung with scratches. Plus there was the weather itself. One moment the sun would be fully out – it was really hot at this latitude for all that it was still only the beginning of March – and then he would dump the oilskin jacket in which he worked. But the next moment he would be running, stumbling along between the rows to retrieve it as a sudden cloud arrived overhead with a trumpet blast of icy wind and let fly a battering of rain and hailstones that seemed as sharp and painful as the arrows of a medieval battle scene.

And also, there was too much time for thought. Yes, he wanted to see Sylvain again. At times even longed to, yet he was terrified that things would go terribly wrong in some way if he did. You should never revisit your past, everyone agreed. People changed, developed, moved on; you could not simply go back to how they had been – how you had been – years before. Besides, although he certainly wasn't married to Stéphane in anyone's understanding of the word, they did have a very good thing going together now; everything had clicked into place so well between them since that weekend (was it really only three weeks ago?) of the unceasing rain. Whatever Stéphane might say, the arrival of Sylvain at the Moulin could not but unsettle things between them. Sté was too young to know this, for all his generous broad-mindedness. The fact was, they were not teenagers any more. Just. The time when you could sleep around among your best friends without offending any of them too disastrously was probably drawing to a close.

Adam thought of inviting Sylvain down during Stéphane's absence in the Médoc without telling him of Sté's existence but dismissed the idea at once. He had lied to Sylvain on that earlier occasion, like a child, and had grown up a little as he discovered the bitter consequences. He would not lie to Sylvain again; it would demean them both. To say nothing of the impracticality of trying to keep such a secret. There were signs of Stéphane's presence all over the house. And who else would have taught him how to prune a vineyard?

Adam put all these thoughts to one side once the weekend came and Stéphane returned from Bordeaux. He went into the vineyard at once and inspected the result of Adam's labour. 'You're doing it very correctly,' was his verdict. 'I mean the way you're doing each vine. But you're not nearly up to speed yet.'

'Merde,' said Adam. 'I was out here eight hours yesterday and Wednesday. I didn't even have a lunch stop.'

'Yeah, but you'll still need to get a lot quicker. Otherwise you'll still be at it in April and the buds'll be breaking. Besides, there'll be the ploughing to be done.'

Adam groaned theatrically. 'Dear God, what have I taken on?'

They spent the whole of Saturday and most of Sunday working together among the vines and the hail showers: Adam with the power-clippers and Stéphane selflessly working away with a blister-making pair of garden secateurs. On Saturday night they were even too tired for sex but fell sound asleep as their two heads flopped onto their pillows soon after nine o'clock.

On Sunday evening Adam put Stéphane back on the train to Bordeaux. They said, 'See you in three weeks,' and then – though both of them had assiduously avoided any mention of Sylvain during the whole weekend – Stéphane added, 'If you see Sylvain, say hallo from me.' Which left Adam as undecided as ever.

Monday was Adam's cello teaching day. His fingers were so battered that he had difficulty playing the piano. As for doing any serious cello practice, that would have been physically impossible, while his suggestion to Stéphane, just ten days ago, that they might make music together with Stéphane picking out Adam's accompaniments on the upright piano, seemed a laughable irrelevance.

Tuesday was another punishing eight hours in the vineyard. The endless sea of gnarled and twisted vine-stocks had become transformed in Adam's fevered brain into a three-acre crown of thorns which he must wear forever. By the end of the day his mind was made up. There was no phone number on Sylvain's letter. He could have tried directory enquiries, but his courage failed him at the prospect of cold-calling a Trappist monastery to enquire, in French, about his lover of six years ago. Time was not on his side, so the easier option of writing a letter could not be considered. There was only one thing to be done. Adam spent the tail end of the evening looking up train routes and timetables on the internet.

NINE

Before it was light, Adam drove his rusting Renault to the main line station at Libourne. There existed an interesting route to Dijon via Limoges, Montluçon and Nevers (that last name particularly apt, Adam thought) that would have taken till nightfall. He opted instead to take the TGV Atlantique up to Paris and then catch another TGV down into Burgundy. That way he might arrive by early afternoon.

'Do you have a reservation?'

'Unfortunately no.'

'Then unfortunately I can not sell you a ticket. The train will be here in five minutes and, as always at this time of the morning, she's booked solid.'

Adam had not known at the time why he had grabbed his old Eurostar *carte d'identité* at the last minute, along with his wallet, before leaving the Moulin. But he knew now. 'SNCF,' he said, producing the card with a flourish. 'French Railways staff.'

'You should have said straightaway.'

'Sorry.' Adam paid for a single through to Dijon. 'Thank you very much.'

Soon Adam had left his home region of vines and warm orange roof tiles. His TGV snaked its way beneath the perched towns of Angoulême and Poitiers with their brown stone, black-slated houses; traversed the flatter lands of Tourraine and its elegant townscapes of cold white chiselled stone; then crossed the Loire and flew like an arrow into the heart of Paris, reaching the Gare Montparnasse through an ear-popping series of high-speed tunnels. A couple of changes on the Metro RER and he was boarding the flame-orange TGV Sud at the Gare de Lyon. He arrived at Dijon in just over an hour. There was a bus that passed the Abbey of Cîteaux: the number forty-three. So far so good, and swift, Adam thought. Eagerly he peered at the timetable. The bus would be departing the Gare Routière in three hours' time.

An alternative, someone suggested, might be to take a different, earlier bus to Nuits St-Georges on another road out of town, where he could find a taxi for the last few kilometres across country, or hitch a lift, or walk. The idea of catching buses to towns that sounded like wine bottles appealed to Adam, so that was what he did. The road signs he passed along the way read like a very smart *carte des vins* indeed: Gevrey-Chambertin, Chambolle-Musigny, Vosne-Romanée... On both sides of the road stretched a now familiar landscape of bare, pruned vine-stumps: gently hilly to the right, flatter to the left. But it was colder here; there was no sign of the early Atlantic spring he had been enjoying in the Gironde; he regretted not thinking to bring gloves.

And Nuits St-Georges, though as pretty and prosperous looking a wine town as anyone could wish, was notably under-endowed when it came to taxis. Adam followed the signposts out of town and set off on foot. He waved his thumb, not very hopefully, at passing cars and was pleasantly surprised when, after only a couple of minutes, one stopped. A grey-haired woman let down the window of a four-wheel-drive and asked him where he was going. 'Cîteaux,' he said.

'St-Nicolas?'

'Is that the abbey?'

'No, the village. That's as far as I'm going. But get in anyway.'

By the time Adam had charmed his lady driver with his story – though he strongly doubted that she believed any of it: that he owned a small parcel of vines in the Bordelais and was on his way to seek help from a friend who was temporarily working for the monks at Cîteaux

– she was ready to go the extra couple of miles with him and deliver him at the abbey's front door. But he didn't have to take up the offer. As they arrived among the clutch of barns and houses that comprised St-Nicolas-les-Cîteaux, Adam called out: 'Stop. You can drop me here.' His attention had been caught by the back view of a figure, just ahead of them, on the other side of the road, walking on the grass verge between the tarmac and the open country beyond. It was a perfectly ordinary back view: of a young man dressed in jeans and working boots, with a shabby leather jacket whose collar was pulled up around his ears against the cold; he had an untidy mop of thick dark hair, and was of the same trim build and medium height as Adam himself. Nevertheless Adam would have recognised Sylvain anywhere. 'Thank you very much for the lift. But, believe it or not, that *type* over there is the person I've come all this way to see.'

Adam jumped down and the car drove off. They had met almost no traffic on their rural way but now, as luck would have it, going in the other direction, a tractor was bumbling past. Eight other vehicles followed the tractor, at an infuriating snail's pace. 'Sylvain!' Adam shouted. 'Over here! It's me.' And between the crawling vehicles Adam caught a series of glimpses of Sylvain against the backdrop of rolling fields – as if in a sequence of time-lapse photographs: first turning, then looking, next expressing doubt, then wonder, disbelief, and then amazement and, at last, pure joy. They met in the middle of the suddenly empty little road. Too surprised, too overcome to hug or kiss, they just clasped hands.

You could imagine that they had both been carrying an unsafe quantity of treasures and keepsakes beneath their arms; imagine how, when they extended their arms towards each other, those precious things would have fallen and crashed in confusion about the road. So it was that their memories of things shared together came suddenly unfastened, as each took the other's hand, and came tumbling in disorder into their conscious minds: not only memories of high exalted moments, but everything together, all mixed up.

You are the man, the very same, into whose pockets I used to put my hand – how I remember those ripped and bottomless pockets – to caress your handsome cock as we walked side by side among the fields.

Voici les dents – les mêmes – que je t'ai cassé... Those teeth of yours I accidentally chipped.

Damson brandy beneath the floorboards and a smell of hay.

C'était tout d'abord les jonquils... the daffodils that started everything.

It took no time at all, all that. There was no silence waiting to be broken. Sylvain simply spoke next. 'I dreamed you'd come. Last night I dreamed you'd come.' He sounded very choked. 'I thought this morning it was just a wishing dream. But now ... now you're here.' He yanked Adam back across to the side of the road. 'Safer here.'

'And now I don't know what to say.' Adam's voice sounded thinner, like the uncertain, youthful one that had been his on the day he'd first met Sylvain and said *bonjour m'sieur*, as he dropped out of a tree into his path among the woods, and then been shown the daffodils – and other things besides.

Sylvain took Adam down the only turning off the main road that aspired to the condition of a side street. A minute later they were seated at a table in a rough and ready café-bar. The clientele was pretty rough and ready too – though it wasn't really all that different from the 'Spanish' bar in St-Emilion – and Adam was quite relieved to find that they were pretty much left alone. He wasn't in the mood to be thrust, shaking hands all round, into a throng of people who might all have been acquaintances of Sylvain. But the people here didn't seem to know him. Perhaps he still tended to be a loner. They ordered two espressos.

'Show me your hand again,' Sylvain said. Adam had been struck by the hardness of the skin on Sylvain's palms and fingers when he had taken his hand a few minutes before. It was something he must have forgotten; either that or the younger Sylvain's hands had been softer. But Sylvain had clearly noticed something too. 'How did you get those blisters?' he asked, gently exploring with a forefinger the little water-filled domes at the base of Adam's fingers and on his palms. 'Your hands are like bubble-wrap.'

'Pruning vines,' Adam explained. He told the whole story. It was good to have something concrete to discuss, a definite problem to share, rather than to try, at such a moment, to find words to express the complex cut and thrust of emotions he was, quite physically, feeling. Among all the things he noticed, among all the visual and sensual impressions of Sylvain that he was absorbing in an experience dizzying in its intensity, the one that struck him most forcefully was the fact of Sylvain's looking rather smaller than he remembered him. This should not have been surprising; after all, it was Adam who had grown during the intervening years in the normal course of events. But they were now almost exactly the same size, Adam guessed, both in height and build, and probably would have evenly balanced a set of scales. Sylvain's face looked slightly older, though the rest of him didn't. Perhaps it was just the fact of being twenty-eight.

'Your front teeth,' Sylvain suddenly said, which made Adam wonder if he had been listening to his story quite as attentively as he would have wished. 'They don't look so jagged as they did when they first got chipped. Just slightly shorter than other people's. *Je peux?'* He extended a finger and explored the edges of Adam's top incisors while Adam submissively opened his mouth and curled back his upper lip. 'All smooth now,' Sylvain said. And then, 'You're still beautiful.'

'So are you.' No-one in the bar heard or heeded this intimate exchange.

'If you're wondering why I'm telling you all this boring story right now,' Adam suddenly blurted, 'about the vines, it's because I'm all behind and – well, you've seen the state of my hands – and I desperately need help from someone. I could only think of you.' He stopped. He had seen something darken in Sylvain's face.

Sylvain laid his hands on the table, palms down and fingers spread. It was a gesture Adam had never seen him make before. *'Qu'est-ce que tu me dis?'* Sylvain sounded sad and hurt. That was less of a novelty. 'Are you saying – that after nearly six years when you haven't come to see me – that you've only come to me now because you want me to prune some vines for you – and that that's because you can't get anybody else?' He looked down at the table, traced the rim of his saucer with one finger.

'Hey, it's not like that. You make it sound like...' Adam tailed off.

'There was me thinking – hoping – when I saw you across the road just now – right after my dream last night – that you'd come for some bigger reason. Or at least a better one than that. Now I see I was wrong. It was just a wishing dream after all.'

Adam's eyes felt the sudden prick of tears, but he was cross with Sylvain too. 'Don't be like that. Not when we're just meeting again – just starting, trying, to get to know each other again – after such a long time. And anyway, you didn't try to come to find me either.'

'And how would I have done that, Adam? I was forbidden to contact you again, if you remember, by the court. But I still wrote, even when I hardly knew how to. But could you have imagined me turning up at your parents' house? I hardly think so. And you never invited me to your student place in London. You didn't expect me to just turn up there, did you? With no money to my name and not speaking a word of English.'

And vulnerable and epileptic. The scenario was too painful to contemplate. Ashamed, Adam put out a hand and placed it over one of Sylvain's on the table. 'Please, please stop. We can not, must not, start like this. I'm sorry, really sorry. *Je disais des bêtises.* I was talking stupidly. Insensitive. I didn't mean... Look, I'm here because of you. Forget the bloody vines. The vines don't matter. They were just the catalyst, the thing that tipped the scales. I'd been wanting to come for ages. But I was scared. *Tu sais?* I know you understand that, because you must have been scared yourself. What would I be like, you must have asked yourself? How much would I have changed? Would you still...? Let's just forget the vines. Either you can help me with them or you can't. It really doesn't matter. And your dream wasn't wrong. I'm here because – because I love you. I don't know if your dream told you that.'

'I think perhaps it was trying to.' Sylvain's eyes too were glistening with tears. 'But when I woke up I didn't dare to think about it too much. But then I heard you – actually heard you – just a few hours later, and saw you, calling across the road between the cars...'

It hurt to be sitting at a table in a public place, not to be able to embrace and cry together as they had done in the past when making up after a row. But they had weathered their first ten minutes together after years apart. The signs so far were good. Better than Adam could have imagined. But then, with a jolt to his system so violent that it made him feel for a second that he was going to be sick, he remembered Stéphane: that he hadn't yet mentioned Ste's existence to Sylvain, and that at some point he would have to.

But not right now. Adam pulled himself together, and then another thought struck him. 'Shouldn't you be at work or something?'

'Shouldn't you?' answered Sylvain.

'How do you mean?'

'I mean pruning your vines.' Sylvain smiled, a bit self-consciously. Adam surmised that his sense of humour – not Sylvain's strongest suit when they first knew each other – had developed just a little.

'You're right.' Adam said. 'But I happen to be self-employed. If I take too much time off I might go bankrupt but I wouldn't get the sack.'

'You may be surprised – but it's a bit like that for me. I don't exactly get a salary, you see. Board, lodging – no bills to pay – and I get a little money each week. Pocket money really. But it's not so different from when I was working with my dad. Anyway, this afternoon there wasn't much to do, so I came out for a wander.'

Just like the old Sylvain, Adam thought. 'But what about the boys you're supposed to be in charge of?'

'That's not all the time. This month there's nobody on the programme. That's why it's a bit quiet. The bees don't need much attention this time of year.' He gave Adam a mischievous look. 'And we finished pruning our few vines last week. If you wanted me to help you for a week or two I could probably get away.'

'Who do you have to ask?'

'The bursar.'

'You can talk to him? And he to you?'

'*Et ben oui.* I know you think – Cîteaux, Cistercians of the Strict Observance of La Trappe. But the ones who deal with the outside world have to be allowed to speak in order to do their jobs. The abbot, the prior and so on. I can prove it.' He started looking around the café for a phone. But Adam pre-empted him.

'Here, use this.' He pulled his mobile from his pocket and handed it to Sylvain. Sylvain looked slightly baffled. 'No. Here. Press this. Then dial.' A little distrustfully Sylvain tapped out a number and put the little instrument to his ear.

A few seconds later he was explaining Adam's situation and saying he needed a couple of weeks away. And yes, Adam could faintly hear a buzz of answer at the other end; he was listening to the voice of a Trappist monk, for the first time in his life, via a mobile phone.

'That's all OK then,' Sylvain said, a minute or two later, handing the phone back to Adam. 'I can come back with you. I just need to get a few things from my room at the abbey.'

Adam hadn't thought through to the journey back. The meeting with Sylvain had preoccupied him in the same way that the high peak ahead of him preoccupies a mountain walker: he had not concerned himself with what might lie beyond; had not considered whether he would be travelling back to the Gironde today or tomorrow, whether with Sylvain or on his own. But now it suddenly seemed that everything was possible. Compared to Sylvain he felt rich, rich as he had never felt before. Only yesterday he had been panicking at the thought that he was – quite literally – eating Georges's capital fund away. But now that lump of capital seemed wonderfully solid and substantial. Meeting Sylvain had changed everything. He felt as if he could spend the whole of it with Sylvain in one glorious spree, because after this moment nothing else could possibly matter any more. 'We could spend the night in Dijon,' he heard himself saying. 'A good dinner and everything. Or in

Paris. I've got money.' He thought: *We could stay at the fucking Ritz.*

As a more modest first step, they ordered a glass of beer. Then, after they had drunk it, they set off on foot towards the Abbey of Notre Dame de Cîteaux – Sylvain's improbable temporary home. It was about two kilometres, a walk of half an hour or so, though that hardly mattered, and anyway Sylvain knew a short cut across the fields. They were still shy of intimate physical contact – not ready quite yet to abandon themselves to needy lovemaking in the open fields as had once been their custom, and made do instead with momentary, exploratory throws of arms around necks, and pecks on cheeks. Then soon they saw the monastery buildings ahead of them, across a little river, on a gentle rise in the ground: the barns and workshops, the squat modern abbey church, the long ranges of its living quarters.

'We could have asked to stay the night, I suppose,' said Sylvain as they climbed the little slope towards the buildings, 'but I'm not sure I'd have felt comfortable about it. Either with you in a separate guest room or … well, eyebrows would have been raised. I know I'm not a monk, and the block I sleep in isn't even part of the enclosure, it's the guest wing, but even so.'

'That's how I feel too. You're right. We'll get your things and get out.'

Adam went with Sylvain into his bedroom – his cell. The few white-hooded monks they had passed on their way in had greeted them with nods of the head and incurious half smiles. Inside – although, as Sylvain had said, it was only the guest wing – there was an atmosphere of cool, quiet and calm. A smell of beeswax polish, and Adam was suddenly transported back to the *maison de repos* at Auberive where he had been sent to recover after his breakdown, after … after he and Sylvain had been forcibly parted by parents and the law.

Once inside Sylvain's room (white walls, a single bed, a small plain crucifix upon the wall), *'Embrasse-moi,'* Sylvain said, and they kissed properly, intensely but still not with total abandon, and not moving on to anything else; their immediate surroundings as well as their years of absence from each other still seemed to exert a restraining influence on their natural desires. Then Sylvain delved in a wardrobe for a rucksack, threw half the contents of his locker and chest of drawers into it. He didn't appear to possess many more clothes now than he had done in earlier times, though Adam noticed that he was careful to pack an alarming-looking assortment of prescribed medications. Then they were on their way.

'I suppose,' Adam said as they passed the abbey church, 'I might as well look inside while I'm here. I probably won't...' He left the sentence unfinished. He could not imagine himself coming here again, or if he ever did, in what conceivable circumstances that might be.

They stood in the bright interior in silence for a minute or two. The church was empty and still. It was also the plainest, least ornate of churches Adam had seen. The clear glass windows and the arches were square, not round or pointed, and the unadorned walls were of bare cement. The altar, a block of grey stone, stood at the centre of the crossing on a little dais, also of grey stone. 'I haven't been inside a church for quite a while,' said Adam as they came back out into the bright cold sunshine.

'Neither had I before I first came here. Hey – there's our minibus just going out. If it's going in to Dijon...' They ran to catch it up.

On the TGV to Paris they sat opposite each other, both too amazed to find themselves where they were, in space and time – to find themselves arrived at this conjuncture in their lives – to manage to say very much. Instead, they spent most of the time when they were not looking at the fleeting, racing landscape, simply gazing into each other's eyes as if to reassure themselves that this previously unimagined situation was an objective reality and not just a shared continuation of Sylvain's last night's dream. Then, as if they needed further, more tactile, evidence of this, they gradually stretched their legs towards each other and interlocked them around calves and ankles, each hesitantly rediscovering and enjoying the other's animal warmth. If any of their fellow passengers wanted to take offence they were welcome to. None of them did.

Adam had never been happier, he thought. When you were unhappy you felt only unhappiness and nothing else. It was like walking or driving in rain and cloud; you saw nothing but cloud and dark around you; you had no way of knowing whether they were confined to a small area from which you would soon break free, or if the conditions blanketed thousands of square miles. But when you were happy you could never feel only happiness, happiness without reservation or limit; it was always hedged about with something else. Journeying under the bluest of blue skies you always saw, however distantly, some lines of cloud on your horizon. For Adam, at this moment, that line of cloud was represented by the eventual return of Stéphane into his life sometime in the next two weeks and the necessity to alert Sylvain, at some point, to his existence. How could you ever be happy when you knew that your happiness was fated to be bound up with the happiness of one other person and the crushing disappointment of someone else? And at a more mundane level, how on earth was he going to handle the irreconcilability of his own warring wishes, let alone deal with the conflicting claims on him, the innocent expectations, of both Stéphane and Sylvain?

The speed of the TGV, as great as a small aircraft's, brought the rolling countryside of Burgundy to within a few minutes of the gates of Paris, which they reached at sunset. Had Sylvain ever been to Paris? There was so much they had shared together, but so much more that they hadn't. Never been on a train together before today, never walked together among city streets, never... The list was endless.

'*Et ben oui.* Of course I've been to Paris. Well, I went there once. I saw a doctor. And I saw Montmartre and Place Pigalle, Notre Dame and the Quartier Latin.'

Perhaps that was just as well, Adam thought. It had crossed his mind that, if Sylvain had never visited the capital he might be so blown away by the experience of seeing it for the first time with the person he was in love with that he would want to stay there for a week and see it all.

Adam hadn't seriously entertained the idea of staying at the Ritz. More sensibly he had telephoned Gary from the train and asked if they could stay the night at his flat. 'Of course,' said Gary. 'And I don't have to tell you how curious I am to meet Sylvain. Though curious is hardly the word. Agog would be more like it. But I'm going out later in the evening, so you'll have to make your own arrangements for dinner. No doubt that'll suit you better, though.'

'Since we're not staying at the Ritz,' Adam announced to Sylvain when they disembarked at the Gare de Lyon, 'we can at least run to a taxi.' Another first. Dusk had turned to night, and they shared the sight of the lights of the Rue de Rivoli, of the floodlit distant towers of Notre Dame, the Place de la Concorde, the Madeleine...

They threw their scant luggage into Gary's spare bedroom and collapsed into each other's arms upon the bed.

'Après, après,' they both said – 'Later,' – giggling, trying not to be too noisy through the half-closed door. 'It wouldn't be fair to Gary.' Reluctantly they scrambled to their feet and ran fingers through their hair, rejoined Gary in his elegant, mirrored, salon. He was pouring glasses of kir.

'One aperitif and then I have to go.' Gary turned to Sylvain. 'Adam knows all the restaurants near here. He'll show you somewhere good.'

'I've seen you before, monsieur,' said Sylvain.

'Are you sure? And it's Gary, by the way, and *tu* and *toi*. No more *monsieur*.'

'It was at Adam's parents' place in Courcelles,' said Sylvain, staring rather. 'You were there the day my family came to take a swarm of bees and it pissed with rain all day.'

Gary laughed. '*Mon Dieu!* I do remember. Not a day to forget, was it? The dreadful weather. And the mess! Your whole family turned up, I think, including dogs. So that was you. I remember you very clearly. The dreamy boy with the poet's face, I thought at the time. A bit sentimentally, I must admit. Adam had told me there was someone. You. But I never made the connection before now. It's good to meet you properly at last.'

It was weird to see Sylvain sipping kir beneath Gary's crystal chandelier. Adam remembered the time he had entertained him in the house in Courcelles when his parents were out. They had drunk beer out of cans and Sylvain had insisted Adam play the cello to him.

'That's a beautiful piano you've got,' Sylvain said now, taking a step towards Gary's shiny black concert grand. Adam was relieved that he didn't ask Gary to play something on it and then was cross with himself for having had such a condescending thought. Sylvain had very finely tuned social antennae, he already knew. Where had he got them from, coming as he did from a peasant small holding in the middle of nowhere? Maybe from his mother. Adam's memory retained just a few fading snapshots of her: plodding among the beehives on the farm; dealing in a spirit of calm fortitude with the infestation at his parents' temporary home and stoically accepting the two or three stings she took in the process; then, the last time he had seen her, in her own living room, checking solicitously that her son was taking his medication and was all right for money. Adam wondered why he had not thought more about her, been more curious, more interested.

Adam and Sylvain had dinner together at the restaurant Clos St-André. It sounds ordinary enough, put like that. But nothing was in any way ordinary on this momentous day in both their lives. Adam wasn't even sure if Sylvain had eaten in a restaurant before. Though once they were inside the restaurant, and had been seated and Sylvain, unfazed, was studying the *menu du jour*, Adam decided that he probably had. They settled, without much difficulty, on a starter of Puy lentils, anchovies and preserved peppers and limes, followed by duck legs braised in a wine sauce. The young waiters, who knew Adam slightly, seemed to be quietly sharing his pleasure in bringing a handsome, slightly older young man out to dinner with him. On the other hand, they might have simply been pleased to have an extra customer.

Sylvain insisted on choosing the wine, and Adam made a bet with himself that he would choose whichever one on the list hailed from the nearest point to Cîteaux. Adam was right: Sylvain chose a bottle of Hautes Côtes de Nuits; you could see those vine-crested hills from the front gate of the abbey.

Slightly more surprising was the fact that Sylvain wanted to talk, and hear, about Adam's musical career, about his progress with the cello. But Adam drew some comfort from this unexpected turn that their conversation was taking. Nowhere did it come too close to the thorny issue of Stéphane.

On the way back to Gary's flat, which was only just around the corner, Adam steered Sylvain into the Bar Florence – to have a small beer before bed, he said. But he also wanted – even if not quite consciously – to show off his prize, his capture, and to mark this moment in public. He knew the Bar Florence well now. It was small and bright, occupying a street-corner site as narrow as a wedge of cheese. The same friendly Algerian *patron* and his staff had run it all these years. They gave Sylvain as uncomplicated and warm a welcome as they had always extended to Adam; all bought each other drinks to celebrate this unexpected visit. How easy it was to be two young men and go to bars together in metropolitan Paris or London. How differently he felt about going with Stéphane into village bars around the vineyards of St-Emilion and Castillon: how much more wary and circumspect they had to be. It would be the same – worse in fact – if he started parading Sylvain around the same rural spots. He remembered how carefully Sylvain had chosen the bars they used to frequent on the Plateau de Langres. But now he was running ahead of himself and looking uncomfortably closely at those clouds on his horizon. *If* he went to his village bars with Sylvain. *If* with Stéphane. He had no idea what was going to happen once he arrived back in the Gironde with Sylvain in tow. There were big bridges to be crossed tomorrow and in the days that followed, and the problem of dealing with local gossip and rough country boys in bars was hardly among the biggest of them.

Gary had not returned by the time they got back to the flat: finally the two young men were alone. 'I don't imagine he expected us to wait up,' said Adam, turning on the lights.

'It's such a beautiful apartment,' Sylvain said, resuming his inspection of the salon, exploring, appraising. 'I couldn't have imagined, this morning... Oh, but I could, remember? I had my dream.'

'Take off your pullover,' said Adam quietly. The words had a familiar, ritual sound. Sylvain obeyed, and Adam copied his action exactly.

Sylvain laughed softly, remembering. *'Toi maintenant. Ta chemise.'* And Adam obediently removed his shirt. *'Comme avant.'*

Slowly they undressed, alternately leading, then following: stripping off item after item and revealing piece by piece the contours of their two physiques, the two warm naked bodies that had once been their shared domain and playground and that tonight would become so again. At last they stood unclothed, and massively erect, facing each other and looking each other up and down for that very short space of time that remained before each would feel compelled to clasp the other to him with the irresistible force of magnetic poles. 'There's a few hairs on your chest now,' Adam just had time to notice, 'where there weren't before.' But he remembered well the pattern of pubic hair that bushed up from around Sylvain's sex to finish in a little tapering curl at his navel like a Van Gogh cypress tree. That was just the same.

'And you've grown a forest,' Sylvain replied, 'on your chest and down below – where you had next to nothing before. But all of you has grown – you've got good muscles now – to say nothing of *that*.' It was true. In terms of *that* they were now equally matched, both formidably equipped. They closed together, hugged, kissed, pressed forward with their hips until their cocks nuzzled.

'You're very wet.' Adam smiled.

'Are you surprised? It's been a long evening and afternoon with nothing to do but look at you and think about this moment. Anyway, so are you.'

Neither of them heard Gary's key turn in the lock. They only sprang apart in startled embarrassment at the pantomime noise of throat clearing that he made as he entered the room.

'Well, well. Though I shouldn't have been surprised, I dare say. Only I did provide you with a bedroom for privacy – mine as well as yours. It's lucky I didn't bring back some unsuspecting female colleague from the conservatoire for coffee. You both look very lovely, I have to say, but now please go to bed, the pair of you, before you give me too much to think about.'

The two young men, frozen into immobility for a shocked second or two, now came quickly back to life and, with laughing apologies, but still with unabashed erections, scuttled towards their bedroom door.

'Hey,' Gary called after them, now laughing with them himself. 'Take your bloody clothes with you. You make the place look like a charity shop.' He stooped to pick up the discarded garments and threw them at the two lovers who caught them, laughing.

TEN

Adam had been wrong in imagining that Sylvain would be alerted to the existence of Stéphane as soon as he arrived at the Grand Moulin. Everything here was new and astonishing for Sylvain: the simple fact of his being reunited with Adam again, the gobsmackingly big and beautiful house that was Adam's new home, the strange story of how he came to possess it. Even the weather came as a surprise: the Atlantic mildness of the Gironde presented Sylvain with an agreeable shock after the chill of inland, more northerly Burgundy. Against such a background, the question of whether anyone else had been sharing Adam's bed before Sylvain got there was hardly going to loom large as an immediate preoccupation.

Despite the energetic and nearly sleepless night they had spent at Gary's flat, they were ready for sex again the moment they were through the front door. The morning's train journey had been much longer than the previous day's, and once more they had been able to do little more than look at each other and intertwine their legs between their facing seats while their fellow passengers pretended not to notice. Then they had stroked each other's thighs across the gear lever during the whole of the short car ride from Libourne station, Sylvain only twice breaking off his caresses for a few seconds: on his first glimpse of the ancient spires and towers of St-Emilion rising surreally from among the vineyard slopes, and again when he had his first sight from the top of the drive of the roofs of Adam's home, below them in the valley among the trees. But as soon as they stood in the privacy of the cool entrance hall, their jeans were unbelted and falling round their ankles while they brought each other off, still standing, bespattering the flagstones with pearly drops. Quick and businesslike, as so often back in teenage days.

But, very quickly, it was down to business of another sort. After the obligatory tour of the house and gardens, Sylvain insisted on getting out into the vineyard and setting to with the electric clippers. He knew all about power-secateurs; he had recently been using them at Cîteaux. He wouldn't let Adam do any more pruning himself just yet. 'Give your hands a couple of days to heal. Then you can work alongside me as hard as you want. For now just keep me company. We can talk and...' He grinned. 'Well, you know.'

Sylvain noticed that the vines were trained differently here, in contrast to the way things were done in Burgundy. Here only one stem from the previous year's growth was allowed to survive the pruning, to be bent down along the bottom wire and to produce all the coming year's new shoots. In Burgundy they kept two; there, the newly pruned vines were roughly T-shaped, here they made an inverted L. Adam had a moment's anxiety, based on prior knowledge of him, that Sylvain would energetically denounce the Bordelais system and unilaterally try to impose the ways of the Bourgogne upon Adam's small plot. Mercifully this didn't happen; Sylvain quickly adapted to the local procedure, unwittingly following the pattern set by Stéphane, and was soon snipping away at the same speed as Stéphane had done – and nearly twice as fast as Adam had yet managed.

And they did talk. In spite of the fact that Sylvain's narrative style, in speech as in his letters, could be frustratingly concise and elliptic, he did manage to convey to Adam some idea of what his life was like at Cîteaux. He told him about the early morning starts, about the work, either in the open air or in one of the farm buildings: hoeing among the crops, bottling honey, racking wine. Meals were simple but wholesome, eaten in the monastery kitchen. You were allowed to talk in there. The monks ate more formally in the big refectory, in silence, while one of their number read aloud at a lectern from scripture or some theological work. How did Sylvain know this? Had he been invited? Oh yes, many times. There was a mime you had to do when you wanted the water passed to you, another one for bread. It was a good and healthy life, if a simple one. But of course you missed certain things. He looked knowingly at Adam. Between them hung the question – the Pandora's box – of each other's recent sexual exploits, if any. But it was as if they had an unspoken agreement not to open up that subject yet.

And for the first few days they managed not to. Still no occasion arose on which Sylvain was forced to confront the existence of Stéphane, and it crossed Adam's mind that the very situation he had promised himself would not arise – that of himself failing to bring up the subject of Stéphane and thereby lying to Sylvain by omission – might still come about by default. They would sail through the next fortnight avoiding all stormy weather and Sylvain would return to Cîteaux in blissful ignorance that anyone else had a claim on Adam's affections. It was a tempting prospect but not one that Adam could feel comfortable with, even now.

Adam's hands healed surprisingly quickly. Soon he was working away at Sylvain's side, the two of them taking turns to use the powered and the un-powered clippers. Their trips out during the first two days had been limited to a visit to the supermarket at St-Magne and one quick beer at the roadside café in St-Genès-de-Castillon. They cooked together in the evenings and had big fires. All their wants were, at that particular juncture in their lives, entirely supplied by each other, and it would have seemed to both of them a waste of precious time and energy to focus their attention on anything beyond.

But once that first couple of days was past, they ceased to live quite so much like hermits. Though Sylvain was happy to leave the exploration of the regional capital, Bordeaux, for another time, he was curious about the more immediate neighbourhood, and asked, at the end of their second full day's labouring in the vineyard, to be shown St-Emilion, of which he had had only a tantalising glimpse from the car.

In the course of their tour of the cobbled streets, aromatic with baking almond cakes, it was impossible not to visit the 'Spanish' bar, though Adam guided Sylvain towards Stéphane's former place of work with some apprehension. Once inside, Adam's heart sank to find one particular regular customer propping up the bar: a rough-looking character, about ten years older than Adam, called René. Adam knew him only slightly but today, as luck would have it, he seemed only too eager to involve them in conversation. Perhaps the other occupants of the bar, sitting in twos and threes at tables, had already tired of him. But since the tables were now all occupied, Adam and Sylvain had no choice but to share their space with him as they ordered their beers and stood at the bar to drink them.

'Where's Stéphane these days?' was René's opening shot, ostensibly addressed to Adam but delivered at the same time as a quick insolent glare at Sylvain. Adam answered, in one brief sentence which he hoped would close the subject, that he was away on a college field trip in the Médoc.

'Pissed out of his skull all day, no doubt,' said René. 'And this is your new friend, then?' There was only the faintest hint of innuendo in the way he said it, but Sylvain could not have failed to pick it up.

'Sylvain's a very old friend, in fact,' Adam answered, trying to keep his voice steady, his tone neutral. He introduced them with the bare minimum requirement of courtesy: 'Sylvain, René.' They shook hands without warmth. Then René did change the subject. Adam would have preferred him to drop dead but this was better than nothing.

'You sell your crop of grapes to the Orangerie, *n'est-ce pas*? To Philippe Martinville.'

'That's right,' said Adam. 'They're actually part of the Orangerie estate. But it got split up in some inheritance tangle two generations ago.'

René nodded. He knew that, of course. Everybody here knew the geography and proprietorships of the *vignobles* of St-Emilion and Castillon like the backs of their hands. René went on. 'You don't have to sell to Philippe, you know.'

'What do you mean by that?' Adam asked warily.

'Think about it, kid. Philippe's plot adjoins yours on one side. But who's on the other? Armand Pigache at Château Lafontaine, and old Ducros at La Carelle. You could sell to them instead.'

'You've got to be joking. They're on the other side of the river. They're St-Emilion châteaux. L'Orangerie is Côtes de Castillon.'

'I know that, don't I? And that's why you don't get the price for your grapes from Philippe Martinville that you'd get on this side of the river. Not even a river. A little millstream that you can jump over. Think about it.'

Sylvain came in at this point. 'That would be crazy. Somebody tried to pull that one in my part of the world last year. Had a patch of vines just the wrong side of the railway line that runs past Nuits St-Georges. Somehow managed to get a few lorry-loads of his grapes mixed up with the real thing. Got two years inside for his trouble.'

'Then he was a fool for getting caught.' René looked at Sylvain with undisguised contempt. 'Think of the hundreds that do it and don't get caught. But if you don't know about that, then maybe you're not so bright yourself.'

For a moment Adam thought that Sylvain was going to punch René. To avoid such a development he leapt in himself with a less potentially dangerous response. 'But your suggestion wasn't too bright either, René. Even if I wanted to pass my crop off as St-Emilion, just imagine me, a young newcomer, a foreigner with an English accent, walking up to the front door of Châteaux La Carelle or Lafontaine and offering them grapes for sale. No, I don't think so. And what would Philippe Martinville say when he found I had no fruit to sell him?'

René shrugged. 'Other people find ways. Anyway, the suggestion was free. *Tu la prends ou tu la laisses.*'

'Let's go,' said Sylvain. He turned to René and shook his hand again. 'Nice to have met you,' he said, with what might have been irony – not a quality Adam had associated with Sylvain in the old days. They downed their beers and left.

'Who's Stéphane?' Sylvain asked as soon as they were outside the door.

'He's a friend and neighbour,' Adam said. 'His parents own the estate on the other side of the road from us.' Us? Adam heard himself using the word and wondered to whom he was unconsciously referring. To Sylvain and himself? 'He's helped me to settle in. It was he who showed me how to prune the vines.'

'I guessed someone must have done. You never mentioned this Stéphane till now.' There was a pause. Adam waited with glum resignation for what he knew was coming next. 'Is Stéphane gay?'

'Yes,' said Adam.

'Ah bon,' Sylvain said, and let the matter drop. But Adam knew that this was not the end, only the beginning.

The car was parked at the top of the town, under the old stone wall that guarded the vines of Clos Fourtet. On the climb back up to it they paused in the Place du Clocher and went to look over the parapet, down at the lower town square beneath them. The lights were already on in the houses below, but there was still enough natural light to paint the spread of Roman-tiled roofs in dull reds and browns.

'Pittoresque, non?' said Sylvain. And as they stood by the parapet, admiring the view below and beyond, even as the rolling vineyards and the distant river were being swallowed by the oncoming dusk, he took Adam in his arms and gave him a kiss, heedless of the two or three late tourists who were crossing the other end of the Place du Clocher behind them. 'That's the sort of thing lovers are supposed to do in this sort of place, right?' he said. Then his expression changed and he looked hard into Adam's eyes. 'We are lovers, aren't we?'

'Yes,' said Adam. 'Of course we are.' He stopped. He had really meant that. He also meant what he said next. 'You'll want to know, of course – and I have to be honest and tell you – that, yes, I have slept with Stéphane. But that was before I came looking for you. Now I'd like it to be us. You and me from now on. I don't know if...'

'That's what I want too,' said Sylvain, still holding Adam loosely. But his voice sounded a bit doubtful, a bit sullen.

'You wouldn't have expected me to spend nearly six years of total celibacy,' Adam pointed out reasonably. 'I haven't been kidding myself that *you* would have.'

'No,' said Sylvain. 'I may have spent a few months in a monastery, but I haven't gone completely without sex for years either.' He didn't elaborate on this, but went on, 'And I didn't imagine you would have done. You've told me about student life in London, and about Sean and Michael, and I'm easy with that. They're part of your past and that's fine. But this Stéphane character does sound ... kind of ... recent.'

'Recent but finished,' said Adam with conviction. He still really meant it, but he felt a hole opening up in the floor of his existence, an all too familiar sensation: the one he had experienced years ago when he betrayed Sylvain by sleeping with Michael and Sean. Now he was betraying Stéphane – or possibly both of them together. What in the world was he going to say to Stéphane when next they met?

'Tout cela est bien joli,' said Sylvain. 'That's all very well. But what are you going to tell Stéphane?'

Adam winced, then pulled away from Sylvain and turned his back to the parapet and the view beyond it. 'I don't know. *Allez, viens.* Let's go home.'

Adam lay awake, pressed up against the sleeping Sylvain's back and stroking his downy balls. Earlier they had made love tenderly and comprehensively. But Adam had a sense that the best part of Sylvain's visit was over. Sylvain hadn't exactly shown anger on discovering Stéphane's existence, rather he seemed apprehensive as to what would happen next. Inevitably, after spending three days lost in the ecstasy of simply being together, they were going to have to come back down to earth.

They had agreed that they were lovers. But what did that mean? It gave Adam the right to be in bed with Sylvain now, stroking his private parts while he slept. That stood for a kind of mutual entitlement to each other's bodies, to the sharing of emotions, to a window on each other's private thoughts. They had got to this point before. Back then it had also entailed the idea of exclusivity. That had been tested by Adam almost to destruction and he had learnt in the process that Sylvain did not view exclusivity as mere vague theory. He was not going to be prepared now to share Adam with Stéphane in the relaxed and casual way that Sean had shared Adam with Michael.

So what now? Should he make a declaration to Sylvain tomorrow morning, the way he had done with Sean: stay with me here for ever? At this point reality intervened as if with a blunt and heavy instrument. They could not both live out their lives here on an unpredictable twelve or thirteen thousand euros a year. And if they did try to stay on here as a couple, living on God knew what, and Stéphane had to be shown the door by a regretful Adam ('Sorry, Sté, but that's the way the cookie crumbles,') was it likely that he would still be keen to lend them the plough he'd promised, the spraying equipment they'd talked about, the use of his wiry little muscles at harvest time, and the general expertise and savoir faire that would help persuade Philippe to buy Adam's crop of grapes? Stéphane was as generous and understanding a person as Adam had ever met, but everyone had their sticking point.

Sylvain stirred in his sleep, then rolled around, still asleep, till he faced Adam. He nuzzled his forehead and threw an arm approximately over Adam's shoulder. They hadn't mentioned Stéphane again since Adam's moment of candour in St-Emilion, but the fact of his existence had somehow managed to colour everything that had happened since. Sylvain had cooked chicken legs with garlic and parsley, and afterwards they had strolled out onto the dark lawn – it was a mild night – to listen to the croaking of the frogs and the rush and tumble of the weir. Then, in bed, Sylvain had been softer and gentler than he had been on the previous few nights. Making love with Sylvain now seemed very different from the wild rough sex they had once enjoyed together in the forests and fields of the Haute-Marne. They had only ever spent two nights together in a bed back then – and on one of those Adam had passed out cold following an excessive intake of alcohol. So… Adam's thoughts did a kind of somersault. Wasn't this new feeling something to be treasured, however impossible the future might seem? Was not this new kind of night together a happiness to be clutched at, savoured … precious? Adam started to stroke Sylvain's thick hair. Precious … precious. Movement stopped. Precious. Adam was asleep.

ELEVEN

They were winning the battle with the vines. Six hours a day, not eight, was quite enough now. There was time left, and his hands were sufficiently healed, for Adam to resume his acquaintance with his cello – even if only for a few minutes a day. And he would be able to do his Monday afternoon's teaching in Castillon with a clear conscience, leaving Sylvain patiently, indefatigably, working his way along the rows of vines. There was time to visit the bars of Castillon, St-Emilion and St-Genès; time to relax beside the water, watching for the kingfisher to materialise then disappear along the stream: first his whistle and then his trademark flash of blue, exotic as a darting, fluorescent, tropical fish.

One afternoon, as they were both working among the vines, a figure came striding down between the rows towards them. It was Philippe Martinville. *'Salut les copains,'* he said. Then, to Adam, 'Oh, I thought it was Stéphane working here with you.' Adam introduced Sylvain. 'I've been a bad neighbour,' Philippe said. 'Done nothing to welcome you or mark your arrival in any way. The fact is, I had a spell in hospital after Christmas – nothing life-threatening – but it laid me low for a bit and I'm only just beginning to get out and about again.'

Adam went hot with embarrassment. Clearly it was he, not Philippe, who had been the bad neighbour. Stéphane had told him, right back during their first weekend together, that Philippe was ill but Adam had been too preoccupied with the sudden upturn in his sexual fortunes to take much notice. Now it dawned on him that he had social responsibilities that he had never had to consider before, a network of tiny obligations that Stéphane, for example, had not yet had to think about. When Stéphane's neighbour was in hospital it was his parents, not he, who would have sent the get-well card (*Prompte guérison*, or, as his old French schoolmates had liked to transform it, *Prompte hérisson*); it was Stéphane's parents who would have phoned Philippe's wife to see if she needed any help with anything. But Adam was not in Stéphane's position, coming and going as he pleased at his parents' house. Adam was Philippe's neighbour in his own right; there was no responsible adult to maintain his place in the social network on his behalf. With a further jolt he realised that he had seen nothing of the Leducs since he arrived in February. He should have gone to see them straightaway: those first few days of rain did not excuse him the weeks that had passed since. Had he been imagining that M. Leduc would simply appear, like the swallows, when the grass began to grow in another week or two, and unquestioningly cut it? He would call on them this afternoon.

Meanwhile, Philippe was, without fuss, inviting Sylvain and Adam to have a bite of lunch with himself and his wife at the château – say, in one hour's time, at twelve o'clock? Humbled by his neighbour's kindness, Adam said a grateful, 'Thank you, yes.'

They kicked their boots off in the back hall and sat down to eat at the big table in Philippe's kitchen. It was sunny and warm and the door stayed open. Madame Martinville served a thick cabbage soup, then a fresh baked tart filled with leeks, cream and cheese, followed by salad and fruit.

'It's good to see you with friends,' Philippe said to Adam between mouthfuls of *flamiche aux poireaux* and red wine, 'and not rattling about down there on your own. With Sylvain here and with Stéphane to look after you. Stéphane's his other great mate, I suppose you know.' Philippe added the last bit in an aside to Sylvain,

which mortified Adam. He was almost relieved when
Philippe went on to say that no doubt they'd all be
seeing more of the two charming Englishmen who had
come over with Adam last summer, but less so when
Madame joined in with, 'But what he really needs is to
find a nice girlfriend. What do you think, Sylvain?'

'Well…' Sylvain almost choked on his wine but then
recovered himself sufficiently to manage the following.
'Well maybe. Unless of course we find out that he's
married already.'

Adam thought this rather clever of Sylvain, as it not
only made the Martinvilles laugh but also appeared to
close down the rather uncomfortable topic that had been
opened up. Then it occurred to him that Sylvain might
have been covertly identifying either Stéphane or
himself as the person Adam was married to, and he felt
less happy about it. He decided to change the subject –
and, flailing about in an effort to find one, caught at the
first thing that came to mind. It might not have been a
happy choice.

'What would you say,' he addressed Philippe a little
desperately, 'if I were to tell you – this September or
next – that I had no grapes to sell you because I'd
flogged them to Lafontaine or La Carelle?'

Sylvain looked horrified, but Philippe's reaction was
to burst out laughing. 'I'd say you'd been very lucky not
to have been turned over to the police. But on the other
hand that you were not a great credit to Her Britannic
Majesty.'

'Why to her, particularly?' Sylvain wanted to know.

'As the representative of his compatriots in general.
The *Appellation Contrôlée* laws exist to protect the
customer – our export market as well as the domestic
consumer. Great Britain happens to be just about the
biggest overseas market for red Bordeaux. I'm sure the
British public would be unhappy to know that their

claret was being mucked about with by one of their own citizens. On the other hand, I might just say good luck to him.'

'I see,' said Sylvain. 'But he's not going to do it, I promise you. It's just that we met some *plouc* in a bar who thought he ought to.'

'*Ah bon.*' Philippe snorted. 'We do have a few of those.' Then he changed the subject. 'Do you shoot?'

Sylvain said yes, and Adam no. They looked at each other. It was a subject that they had never discussed. Adam had seen Sylvain raise a shotgun towards a policeman – while he was in what had been charitably described to the court as 'a state of diminished responsibility'. But that had been the last time he'd seen him, save only for a few seconds at the *palais de justice* in Chaumont. They hadn't discussed firearms then or since.

'You'll have to teach him,' said Philippe to Sylvain.

'Perhaps I will,' said Sylvain. 'Provided he wants to learn.'

'We'll see,' said Adam. 'Right now I think I'm going to be quite busy enough.'

They returned from their lunch with a second pair of battery-powered secateurs – which Philippe pressed on them, having seen them that morning making do with one. ('You should have come and asked before.') As they walked back into Adam's piece of vineyard from the top end it was plain to see now that more than half the pruning was already done; the back of the job was well broken and the remainder of the task would be accomplished in plenty of time before the buds burst. Adam would be able to finish the work at a more leisurely pace within the first couple of weeks after Sylvain's departure. Sylvain's departure. That was not something that either of them wanted to think about.

And following that, Stéphane's return. The same went for that too. In spades.

Later that day Adam presented himself to the Leducs, and apologised for his rudeness in not calling on them before. He had been so busy. That was no excuse, he knew. There had been so much to think about. Would they care to call in for a glass of wine some time the following day? *Volontiers*, they said. They would love to. And might they bring their daughter too? She would be staying the weekend with them, would be arriving tomorrow. She was nearly twenty-five, they said. And unmarried.

'You're going to get a lot of that,' Sylvain said sagely, as they sat, sipping an early evening beer in the sunshine outside the café in St- Genès.

'People throwing their daughters at me, you mean?'

'Of course. People round here must consider you quite a catch. I mean people who don't know any better.'

'Yeah, but there must be loads of richer boys than me, tucked away in the châteaux of St-Emilion and around – with big inheritances in the offing, and proven heterosexual credentials into the bargain.'

'With bigger cocks too, for all we know, though I doubt it,' said Sylvain. 'But an inheritance is just an inheritance. The château kids of your age aren't proprietors yet. They probably won't be for another thirty years. So you see, you are the bigger catch.'

Sitting in the sun at their pavement table outside the only café in the village they were pretty conspicuous. Indeed, someone in a passing car apparently recognised them, or one of them, because the car braked and drew up a few metres further along the road. A young woman in smart jeans and a fresh white blouse got out and walked towards them. It was Stéphane's sister, Françoise.

If Stéphane's existence had been almost magically hidden from Sylvain at the beginning of his stay, the situation now seemed to have reversed itself, with Sylvain metaphorically having his nose rubbed in Stéphane wherever he went. To his own discomfiture and Adam's.

'I thought it was you,' Françoise said brightly as she came up to their table. *'Adam Coeur de Lion.'* She interrogated Sylvain with a look, but clearly liked what she saw. 'Are you going to introduce us?'

Adam did. 'He's come all the way from Cîteaux Abbey to help me prune the vines. I was getting behind.'

'Without Sté to help you. Yes of course.' She'd been bound to say that, however innocently. 'From Cîteaux Abbey? Are you a monk?'

'Do I look like one?' Sylvain countered.

'With that fine head of hair, no,' Françoise conceded.

Adam gestured to Françoise to take a seat with them, summoned the waiter and asked what Françoise would have to drink.

'I can't stay long. I'm on my way to the parents for the weekend – expected for dinner. But a coffee would be nice.'

'I was working for the monks,' said Sylvain disconnectedly. He had a disconcerting time-lapse way of answering questions sometimes.

'Everyone seems to be visiting their parents this weekend,' Adam said, an idea forming in his mind.

'Everyone except Stéphane,' Françoise said. (Did she have to?)

'I've got myself into a bit of a corner with the Leducs,' Adam told her. 'I invited them in for a drink tomorrow, and they've insisted on bringing their daughter as well. For what purpose I can only guess. With a bit of a sinking feeling.'

'*Oh là,*' said Françoise, and then, '*Merci.*' Her coffee had just arrived. 'She cuts hair in a salon in Libourne. Would it make life any easier if I was there as well?'

'That would be brilliant.' Adam thought: what a great elder sister Françoise would make. If you had to have an elder sister. Then: did she know they were all gay? Did she know about her brother?

Françoise drank her coffee and got on her way, with a renewed promise to be on hand when the Leduc trio arrived the next day.

'Why does she call you Adam the Lion-heart?' Sylvain asked after she had gone.

'After Richard Coeur de Lion. Heard of him?' Sylvain nodded. 'It's a sort of joke. She says I'm like the Plantagenet kings – with half an empire in France and the other half in England.'

'I didn't know that,' said Sylvain innocently. The monks had made great strides with his delayed education but there were still a few gaps.

'She's a beautiful girl,' Sylvain went on. 'Does her brother look like her?'

Adam hadn't been a hundred percent sure that Sylvain had worked out what her connection with Stéphane was. Clearly he had. '*En quelque sorte,*' he answered, half reluctantly. 'He does a bit.'

'I notice you've had your gutters cleared,' said M. Leduc by way of a conversational opener, accepting his glass of Château L'Orangerie 2005 with a nod of the head.

'I had those people with the cherry-picker round,' said Adam. 'Stéphane recommended them. They made short work of the ash seedlings that were growing up there.'

'A good thing too,' opined M. Leduc. 'Another year and you'd be having problems with the tiles.'

'I had another visit from Pépin the Mad,' said Adam. 'This time it was did I want a load of crazy paving.'

'You told him to get lost again, I hope.'

'Taking my cue from you, thank you, yes I did.'

'Next thing you'll need to worry about is frost,' said M. Leduc cheerfully. 'It's in the late spring you can expect a problem though, not now. It's no problem at the moment. Vines all dormant. Course I don't need to tell either of you this.' He nodded his grey head first towards Françoise and then Sylvain, to indicate that he wouldn't dream of trying to teach his compatriots anything about wine growing. 'But young Adam needs to know. It's in late April and in May that he wants to watch out. With the buds breaking, that's when they're most vulnerable. He could lose the lot.' He swallowed a mouthful of wine with grim relish.

'We've had some bad years down here,' his wife picked up the baton. 'Nineteen-fifty-six was a real disaster. The whole region was under snow. Minus twenty-four in February.'

'It can happen any time,' her husband said. 'One year the vines were frozen into the ground just up the road here at St-Genès.' He waved towards the wall of the living room to indicate the general direction.

'Wow,' said Adam. 'What year was that?'

'Thirteen-fifty-four,' said M.Leduc.

'I see,' said Adam. 'You do have long memories. Are there any precautions I can take?'

'In Burgundy,' Sylvain offered, 'they fly helicopters round the top-rank vineyards on cold spring nights. I think the movement of the air is supposed to stop frost forming or something.'

'They do it in the top estates in the Médoc and Pomerol too,' said Françoise.

'It must cost a fortune.'

'Which is why the rest of us don't do it,' said Françoise.

The Leducs' daughter, Amélie, had said little up to this point. Dressed in a voluminous pink dress that gave her something of the shape as well as the colour of a strawberry, she had contented herself with gazing wonderingly at both Adam and Sylvain as if trying to make up her mind which of the two she was supposed to flirt with when the moment came. But now she spoke. 'Some people round here stay up all night keeping braziers going in the vineyard. Feeding them with vine prunings. It's supposed to raise the temperature just enough to prevent frost.'

'It sounds a bit hit and miss,' said Adam.

'It is,' said M. Leduc.

'But if you decided to do that,' Amélie said slowly, and to general astonishment, 'I wouldn't mind staying up with you and helping to keep the braziers going. Provided it was at a weekend, of course.'

'I'm sure that won't be necessary,' said her mother very quickly.

Amélie was uncrushed. 'There were one or two occasions in the past when I saw Georges's son doing that, on a late spring night. Sitting up with the braziers until dawn.'

'Georges's son?' Adam wasn't sure if he'd heard that bit correctly. 'Georges Pincemin had a son?'

'Oh yes,' said Madame Leduc. 'Such a handsome young lad he was.' Something suddenly struck her. 'Looked quite a bit like you, actually. You or your friend here,' she added, as if to make the compliment more even-handed.

'But if he had a son...' Adam's brain was whirling.

Françoise stepped in. 'Alain died fifteen years ago. I just about remember him. Of course I wouldn't remember him staying up tending braziers.' She turned to Sylvain. 'Do they have those machines in Burgundy that spray freezing water over the vines? You know, when the water freezes and the ice protects the vines from frost?'

Sylvain said that they did. Adam thought it perverse of Françoise to want to steer the conversation back to vineyard practices just when it had taken an interesting turn, but maybe she had some reason for not wanting to talk about the hitherto unsuspected Alain Pincemin – or perhaps not wanting to discuss him in present company. Adam decided he would tackle her on the subject some other time. For the moment he would go along with her change of topic. 'What about people like me?' he asked. 'People with just a few vines, no helicopter and no expensive spraying equipment. Apart from staying up all night, what do they do?'

'They hope for the best,' said M. Leduc.

Conversation turned to Adam's garden. Largely ignored by him during January and early February it was now exchanging its carpet of snowdrops and bright yellow aconites for the lemony primroses and early violets which bloomed along the stream banks. Soon the flower borders and lawns would require attention. Vegetable seed would have to be sown. And though the fruit trees could be left to themselves, the same did not go for the cane fruits or the asparagus beds. Adam bowed to the inevitable and, privately wondering where on earth the money was going to come from, asked M. Leduc if he would start putting in a few hours for him every week, for the same rate of pay that he had had in Georges's time.

During the remaining days of Sylvain's stay with Adam a measure of equilibrium was restored to their relationship – somewhere between the unsustainable high on which they had floated through the first couple of days after their reunion and the inevitable let-down that followed Sylvain's discovery of Stéphane's existence: the serpent in his Garden of Eden. Now it was more like it had been in the old days, and the similarity of those two states of being was reflected in their lifestyle, the nearly identical routines that they unconsciously fell back into after a gap of six years. Now that their social duties were discharged, and that Françoise had returned to Perigueux – without Adam having had a chance to question her as yet on the mystery of Georges Pincemin's son – their two lives once again revolved entirely around each other. They still had to work among the vines, but for shorter periods each day, and in their free time they walked together along the streams, among the kingfishers and dabchicks, the burrowing crickets and swimming water voles, the early butterflies – brimstones, marbled whites and speckled woods. And, just as when they had been younger, they would stop suddenly in the middle of their rambles, impulsively undo each other's belts and trousers and make love where they found themselves, deciding who would do what to whom as casually as if they had flipped a coin.

They drove into St-Emilion sometimes; they explored the arcaded medieval squares of Libourne and Ste-Foy la Grande. And on one such trip, near Libourne, just where the St-Emilion *vignoble* gave way to that of the Pomerol, Sylvain pointed to a pair of dark brown birds of prey quartering the ground about ten metres overhead the omnipresent vines. Adam said, 'Kites,' very quickly: he was driving and had only caught a glimpse. 'No,' said Sylvain. 'No forked tails. Look again.'

'Harriers?' Adam guessed. *Busards?*

'Two hen birds,' said Sylvain. 'There'll be a male somewhere about, this time of year. You wait till you clap your eyes on him. He's nearly snow-white with golden eyes and beak and claws. *Spectaculeux, hein?*'

They looked out for the male bird as they continued on their journey; they looked out for him on other days. But he was never to be seen.

Normally Adam and Stéphane would telephone each other two or three times in the course of a week when Sté was away in Bordeaux. But all during Sylvain's visit no calls, not even a text message, had come from Stéphane. Perhaps more understandably, Adam had not tried to contact him either. But the time was approaching for his probable return. Friday. Adam would be putting Sylvain on the early morning train from Libourne to Paris then, in principle at least, meeting Stéphane off the Bordeaux train at St-Emilion in the evening. For the second time in less than three weeks Adam could not imagine how one particular day could possibly turn out. Eventually Sylvain's departure had to be talked about. Adam broached the subject. 'Do you really have to go on Friday?'

'I'm expected back. I said I'd go. There's a new batch of young troublemakers coming in, starting a programme on Monday. I told you about that. I can't just run away.'

'But you'll come back soon?'

'If you invite me soon. Depends a bit on Stéphane though, doesn't it? I guess he's expecting to spend this weekend with you. *Non?*'

With some difficulty, Adam said, 'As a friend, yes. Not as a lover.'

'But he doesn't know that yet. And you're going to tell him that when he gets off his train on Friday night?'

'Somehow, yes.'

'You'd better tell me,' said Sylvain, in a not very optimistic tone of voice, 'how it goes.'

And that was how matters stood when Adam drove Sylvain to Libourne station in the pre-dawn chill of Friday.

On the drive back from the station Adam felt numb, all feeling spent. Ahead of him the sun was feeling its way among the indentations of the low hills. And then, beside the road, perched on a low wire fence, an arrestingly handsome bird, nearly as big as a buzzard, was sitting perched. It was pearl-white all over, except for its black wing tips, but the sun's first rays were lighting it with a faintly pink reflection of the blazing dawn. Its beak and legs were brilliant yellow. It stared at him with fierce gold eyes. It was the male harrier hawk that Sylvain and he had been searching for. But Sylvain was not there. His train was already bearing him away, leaving behind the Bordelais vineyards as it passed the Lalandes de Pomerol. Adam didn't know how easily Sylvain would find his way across Paris, what kind of sandwich he would have for lunch. He wanted to shout, across the growing kilometres that separated them, 'I've found the *busard*. It's more beautiful than anything I could have imagined!' But no shout of his could ever be loud enough; there was no way to share this moment that so importantly cried out to be shared. A deep pain of longing caught him just below the diaphragm and he gasped aloud with the shock of it. The beautiful bird continued to stare at him; he saw it in his mirror, looking back after he had passed. It was a bird of omen, he thought, set on fire now by the risen sun: something in a fable or a myth, a prophet bird come to tell him the simple, monumental truth – which, nevertheless, he already knew: that he had never felt more deeply for anyone than he did for Sylvain now – not even when they'd first fallen in love in what seemed another world.

TWELVE

Adam busied himself in the vineyard for the rest of the day. It was good to have something physical, something constructive, to do. And now, at last, pruning the vines no longer seemed a hopeless, endless task. A few days would see it finished, and bud-burst was still some weeks away. The vines – for now at any rate – had ceased to be a problem. His problem now was love. Or rather, life.

Or trying to make the two fit. For all those straight wine estate heirs, those rich young men whose parents owned the neighbouring châteaux, the two things would come together – all being well – in dynastic love matches. In fact it did for most straight people. A family was a business. The gaining of a son-in-law was a new step forward, advancing the family's fortunes. Not every son-in-law could be expected to bring a château or a vineyard with him, but there was always something. If he were a plumber he might have access to supplies of materials that would help his father-in-law's building business to keep its costs down. If he were a lawyer he might have expertise that would be invaluable to his new family in their ongoing battle with the local council. And families were prepared to shunt their funds around between heterosexual member and heterosexual member. They might not always like doing it but they usually did.

Somehow gay people missed out on all of that. There would be no father-in-law to bail Adam out if things went wrong for him. His parents had been great in paying him rent when they holidayed at the Grand Moulin last autumn. And they would probably do the same again. But that was all there would be. Inevitably the parents of gay children saw their offspring as dead ends; it was not unreasonable. Any money that went in their direction was seen as money spent or money lost. It was never an investment that could deliver a return – if not necessarily a return to the parents themselves, then to the family as a whole: to the business as a going concern, with grandchildren and all. All sorts of people, politicians, churchmen, talked about family values. Yet what they usually meant, without even realising it, was commercial, business values.

All of which left someone like Adam rather out on a limb, alone with his grapevines on a sunlit hillside in springtime. Alone as Sylvain would be tonight in his monastery. And it was only a matter of time before Stéphane would be in the same boat. He hadn't yet crossed that Rubicon of letting his family know that he didn't quite belong to it. One day soon he would have to.

So what was Adam to do? Build an alternative setup by creating the first gay wine-growing dynasty on the Côtes de Castillon? And do so by choosing Sylvain as a partner for life? Sylvain, with whom he was now totally in love, but who had neither dowry nor much potential as a money earner. Together they would run out of cash, the property go to rack and ruin, themselves become beggars on the streets of Bordeaux. Or by choosing his friend Stéphane for a more practical dynastic union that would at some point in the future bring together the châteaux of L'Orangerie and Beaurepaire? Stéphane with whom he was not in love, yet for whom he also felt love in a quieter way.

He had twice embarked on a new adventure in the past two months, first with Stéphane, and second in his rediscovery of Sylvain. If you lived in London or Paris, or even Bordeaux, you could probably go on at that rate for years – at least while your looks and luck and youth all lasted. But that was not an option in this rural area; the limited supply of potential partners saw to that, no matter how well-favoured you might be in the looks department. It seemed as if he had to make a choice. One that could not be put off. Later today he was going to have to go back to St-Emilion and meet Stéphane off his train from Bordeaux. He needed advice from someone; he needed help. He felt he could hardly consult Sean. In the middle of the afternoon he called up Michael.

A woman's voice answered.

'Hallo,' said Adam. 'Is Michael there? It's Adam.'

'Adam Wheeler? Oh, I've heard such a lot about you. Hold on, I'll just get him.'

His first contact with Melissa. He wondered what she looked like.

Michael's voice. 'Adam, *quelle surprise*. How are you, man? Why haven't you been in touch? What have you been doing?'

'Come on. Why haven't you been in touch, more like? Look, I need your advice. I'm kind of in a situation. I don't know what to do.'

'Situation with the law? Or with sex? If it's the first, I'm not yet qualified, remember.'

'But if it's the second, you are, right?' Adam briefly outlined the predicament in which he found himself.

'I see,' said Michael. 'Same old Adam. You don't half believe in making life difficult for yourself. But it seems to me that you've two different questions to deal with. The long-term one is which of these two guys you want to settle down for the long haul with. The short-term one is how you deal with Stéphane when you meet him this evening. I think it's important you don't get the two questions mixed up. I can't actually answer the long-term thing for you at all. Except – has it occurred to you that you might not really want to spend the rest of your life with either? Life's a big sea and there's lots more fish in it.'

'That might be true for you in London – I mean for people in general in London,' he added hastily, 'but it's hardly the case here in the commune of St-Genès. Anyway, I don't feel in the least like giving up the two of them. If anything, my problem lies in wanting them both.'

'Well, I don't know,' Michael said doubtfully. 'I can't tell you who to fall in love with. And as for the short-term thing, handling Stéphane, I'm not really sure I can say anything useful about that either. What is he expecting from you?'

'I haven't made him any rash promises or mentioned the L-word, if that's what you mean.'

'I'm glad to hear that. But you may find it's not enough not to have said things. As I found out for myself last year. He's quite capable of reading between the lines of what you *have* said, and of what you've done together, and finding things you never meant. I know that to my cost. He's like a woman in that way.'

'Er – are you sure you should be …?'

'It's OK, she's in the other room.'

In the other room. How mysterious were the geographies of other people's flats – those that you hadn't visited – and how mysterious the lives of people you had once been intimate with but no longer were.

'I don't know what to say,' Michael went on. 'Except that you need to be gentle with Stéphane. He bruises easily. But you know that, of course. You gave the same warning to me when I was going to break up with him last year. And anyway, you're much more sensitive in your dealings with other people than I am.' Adam almost thought he heard a sigh at the other end, but perhaps it was just his imagination. 'Sometimes I wish I was more like you in that. Mind you,' Michael's usual bantering tone returned, 'not all that often. Look, couldn't you just stall Stéphane for a bit? Until you've had more time to decide what it is you really want.'

'Yeah, but I've told you, he'll be wanting us to sleep together tonight – and so will I once he gets here and looks at me with those spaniel eyes – and I've promised Sylvain I'll tell him we can't. That's just hours away. Not exactly a lot of thinking time. Anyway, it wasn't fair of me to expect you to sort it all out. Though going through it with you has probably helped me as much as anything. And you were right to point out that it's two issues, not one.'

'Well …'

'And it's been good to hear your voice again. How is… how's life, I mean. Assuming she's still in the other room.'

'Pretty good, pretty good,' Michael answered. A little defensively, Adam thought. 'And the sex is – well – surprising.'

In what way surprising, Adam wanted to know? Did he mean surprisingly good? He found himself unable to ask, and felt twin pangs of jealousy and sexual arousal as he put the phone down.

Adam parked outside St-Emilion station and watched Stéphane's train grow slowly, as it puttered along the track towards him, from a distant buzzing insect to a massive, roaring blue and silver metal box on wheels. A box that contained Stéphane. Assuming he was on board.

He was. 'I wasn't sure you'd be here,' Stéphane said. He looked uncertain as to what to say next, what body language would be appropriate.

'Of course I'm here,' Adam said, almost brusquely, and gave him an all too perfunctory kiss. 'I said I'd be, didn't I? How were the field trips?'

'Oh they were fine. Great in fact. And the tastings…' He smacked his lips. Then his face tensed. 'You didn't call me once. Not even a text message.'

'You didn't call either.'

'I didn't know… I wasn't sure… Did Sylvain come?' His tone was the flat one of somebody who expects bad news.

'Yes he did.' Adam didn't know what to do next. He wanted to hug Stéphane till he squeezed the breath out of him, hug him until everything would be all right. Except it wouldn't be. 'Let's go for a beer,' he said, without much enthusiasm. He wasn't sure how he was going to deal with Stéphane, physically present, alone with him at home. He wanted to delay the moment. 'Spanish bar?'

'Sure,' said Stéphane. 'I don't know why you always call it that. As far as I know it never has been Spanish.'

'Michael started calling it that for some reason when we first went there – the day we all met you. Said it reminded him of a bar he'd been to in Spain. The name sort of stuck.'

'*Et oui*. Michael,' Stéphane replied, without emphasis.

'*Allez, viens alors*. I'll drive us up. Thy rusty steed awaits.'

In his anxiety to put off the moment when he would find himself home and alone with Stéphane, Adam had temporarily forgotten the unpleasantness that had marred his last visit to the Spanish bar, with Sylvain. He suddenly remembered it as they arrived at the door – but by then it was too late not to go in. So he pushed the door open and hoped that René would not be inside. But he was. And with him was a mate of his with whom Adam was also on nodding terms but did not particularly care for either.

Stéphane nodded vaguely to both men and went over to a table. Adam joined him, managing to ignore the two at the bar. But they did not ignore him. '*Bonsoir, mes biches*,' René said. It was about as pointed a greeting as *Hallo sweeties* would have been in English.

'Oh hi,' said Stéphane, slightly startled.

'You're back in favour again, then,' René addressed Stéphane. Then to Adam, 'Your other little friend gone home?' His tone wasn't exactly ill-natured but Adam found it unpleasant enough.

'He's gone back to Burgundy,' Adam said nonchalantly. 'But no doubt he'll be back another time.' Then, to Stéphane, 'Come on, let's go somewhere else.' He stood up. Stéphane awkwardly rose and followed him to the door, with an apologetic shrug in the direction of the *patron*, his onetime boss, who had just emerged from behind the bar to take their order.

'What was all that about?' Stéphane wanted to know as soon as they were outside. 'What's been going on?'

'With those guys? Nothing.'

'I've known that place for years – as a customer and as a barman – and I've never had any bother from anyone in there. No bad feeling ever. Now suddenly everything's changed. Did you go in there with Sylvain?'

'Actually…'

'Don't tell me you've been getting yourselves a reputation, you and this Sylvain character. Not that I should mind – if it was just you and him. But I live round here too, you know. Or had you forgotten?'

'I haven't forgotten,' said Adam crossly. 'And I haven't been doing anything to get any of us a 'reputation'. Neither has Sylvain. The only thing that happened was that I walked in there once with Sylvain, and that *plouc* René started behaving the way he did just now.'

'You must have done something,' Stéphane insisted. They were striding up the steep cobbled Rue Guadet in that purposeful way that arguing couples have.

Adam drew in his breath audibly. 'We didn't do anything, we didn't say anything. Just one gay *mec* walking into a bar with another gay *mec*. All we did was to exist. René took exception to us because we simply existed on the same planet as him and walked into his bar together. You must have led a very sheltered life if that's never happened to you. And you must have been very complacent to think that nothing of that kind could ever happen to you in this remote outpost of pre-enlightenment culture.' He was taken aback to hear himself sounding so vehement all of a sudden.

So was Stéphane. 'Hey, what's got into you?' he protested. 'You don't sound like yourself. You sound like Michael.'

And that really got to Adam. 'Piss off, will you.' But then he immediately came to his senses. He grabbed at Stéphane's coat sleeve and refused to let him shake him off in a reflex gesture of rebuff. '*Merde*, Sté. I'm sorry. I didn't mean that – and you know I didn't. Look, it's our first evening together in nearly three weeks.' They were in the Rue du Clocher and passing the front door of the upmarket wine bar, L'Envers du Décor. Adam nodded towards it. 'If we're going to argue, at least let's have a decent glass of wine in front of us while we do it.'

Stéphane was mollified enough to smile, then his brow furrowed. 'It's expensive there.'

'It's OK, I'm buying. Just this once. To say sorry for being a prick just now.'

'Did you come in here with Sylvain?' Stéphane asked, trying not to sound as if he cared one way or the other.

'No,' said Adam, trying to sound as if it didn't matter.

They each had a glass of Château Fombrauge, velvety and butter-smooth, then Stéphane, not to be outdone in generosity, dipped into his wallet and ordered two glasses of Clos des Jacobins to follow. The spring daylight faded to dusk as they talked about Stéphane's trips to the vineyards of the Médoc and Sauternes, about Adam's progress with the pruning, about meeting Françoise twice, about almost everything, in fact, except the impact of Sylvain's visit on Adam. History was repeating itself. On Sylvain's arrival it had been the subject of Stéphane's existence that Adam had carefully avoided. Now the taboo subject was Sylvain himself. But the wine tasted good.

Perhaps it was the wine, perhaps it was his general state of anxiety, that made Adam put his foot down rather harder than usual during the dark drive back. At any rate, he started up the one biggish hill that their road zigzagged up in the middle of their journey at full enough throttle to cause Stéphane to call out, 'Hey, where are we going, *mec*? Le Mans?' Adam didn't have time to reply. He was just about to change down for the sharp bend halfway up when there was something like a lightning flash outside the windscreen while a heart-arresting bang came from the engine. '*Scheisse*,' said Stéphane, who had a tendency to swear in German in situations of maximum alarm. 'What was that?'

The car juddered but kept going for a second or two, while the beam of the headlights was suddenly clouded with thick blue smoke. Then there was a second doom-laden bang. 'I don't know,' said Adam, 'but there goes another one.' The engine abruptly stopped.

They could see nothing out of place when they peered cautiously in under the bonnet with a torch a minute later. But the wisps of blue smoke still energetically escaping from beneath the rocker cover and an overpowering stench of overheated metal indicated a pretty major rupture of something inside.

'Piston rings? Gaskets?' hazarded Stéphane.

'Something like that, I guess,' said Adam. 'But whatever it was, we're not going to get home in this. The old girl's had it.'

'She was living on borrowed time, rather,' Stéphane admitted.

'And I was rather living on borrowed car,' said Adam. Stéphane managed the ghost of a laugh.

They stood looking at the wreck of Adam's only means of transport for a minute or so. Then Stéphane said, 'I'll phone my dad. He'll come and get us.' Adam thought that sometimes it could be handy to have parents who lived nearby. Especially parents with tractors, trailers and all the mechanical support systems of farm life. Mostly he was glad that his own parents lived hundreds of miles away, but there were moments.

'We're both invited to dinner and you can stay the night if you want,' Stéphane said as he put his phone back in his pocket. Stéphane made life so simple, Adam thought. He'd been smoothing out Adam's life in France for him since day one. This breakdown could so easily have happened when Adam was on his own, and have left him stranded, after dark and miles from home, with no help at hand. He felt himself shiver.

'Of course, we won't be able to sleep together,' Stéphane went on. 'They'll give you the spare room. Still,' he added brightly, 'there's always tomorrow. And after all,' (he did this bit in English), 'tomorrow is another day.'

Adam wondered, as they pushed the car onto the grass at the side of the road, what he would do – how he could possibly manage – without Stéphane. Then he wondered how he was going to tell him that they would never be sleeping together again. He couldn't see how he was going to be able to reconcile the two.

Marc arrived with a tractor and a tow rope and dragged the dead car and its passengers back to Château Beaurepaire. Without fuss, Stéphane's mother switched away from preparing an informal supper for two and into full dinner-for-four mode, fetching frozen steaks from the deepfreeze and slicing tomatoes to have with vinaigrette as an impromptu starter. Meanwhile Marc, as the real owner of Adam's broken-down vehicle, said that he would take full responsibility for disposing of its corpse and that Adam did not need to concern himself with it any further. Adam protested that, as he'd had sole use of the car for the last two months, he ought to see to its disposal at least and bear the cost, but Marc wouldn't hear of it. People were just so nice, Adam thought. Philippe de Martinville, the Leducs, and Stéphane's parents in particular. He thought how easily it might have been otherwise – with himself still alone now at the roadside, an unknown stranger trying to hitch a lift home in the dark. All of this warmth, this support system, this blanket of protection, he owed to Stéphane. But he wondered how quickly this happy situation might change once the penny dropped with everybody, in the way it had clearly done with René in the Spanish bar, and Stéphane's parents realised that their charming young English neighbour had been bedding their son.

But for now concern was everywhere. Adam would need to buy a new car, of course – or at any rate a second-hand one. Marc offered to help Adam read between the lines of the small-ads in the local press. And in the meantime Stéphane volunteered the use of his own small motorbike for Adam to putter around on when he had returned to Bordeaux on Monday morning.

They watched TV and talked, then went to bed – Stéphane to his own room and Adam to the guest room. Stéphane showed him where it was and helped him to make up the bed with aired sheets. The room was spacious and comfortable; arching black beams jutted from white walls like protecting arms. They kissed goodnight before Stéphane left Adam alone there. 'Tomorrow,' he said, and gave Adam's hair and back a goodnight fondle. 'Tomorrow we'll make up for it.' Still all unsuspecting he was, and still Adam hadn't managed to tell him what he had to.

In the morning they went back to the Grand Moulin together, Adam riding pillion behind Stéphane on his protesting bike, his hands clasped lightly round Stéphane's slim waist and thinking, bitterly, that this was a new and rather sexy thing to be doing with his friend but that he couldn't allow himself to follow it up when they finished their journey. Stéphane naturally had other ideas, and wanted to go straight from bike to bedroom. So at last Adam had to come to it. 'I'm sorry, Sté,' he said once they were inside the hall and Stéphane was trying to embrace him – just as he had done in the same place on that first day together, with Adam in tears and the rain falling in torrents outside. 'I'm sorry but I can't. I should have told you earlier but I couldn't find the right moment.'

Stéphane let go of Adam and dropped his hands to his side. 'I see,' he said, taking it on the chin. 'It's Sylvain of course. I should have asked. It's OK though. I'm not stupid and I had been at least half expecting it.' His stoical acceptance made Adam's heart want to burst. Stéphane went on, 'So where does that leave us? Can we still be friends ... or what?'

'I want us to be friends,' Adam said in a voice grown suddenly tremulous and thin. 'If you can deal with that. But if you can't... If you want to tell me to go to hell ... I'd understand.'

'Perhaps we should just see how it goes,' Stéphane said. He said it almost brightly, which made Adam all the more aware of his pain. If Adam was hurting then Stéphane was suffering even more. Adam had the solid bulwark of Sylvain's love and commitment to support him through this moment. Stéphane had only Adam. Or had had until just now.

Being busy kept them both from going mad that day. M. Leduc had reminded Adam that steps needed to be taken to organise the summer letting of the Petit Moulin.

Advertisements had to be placed, website entries to be updated, the building itself needed to be checked for habitability, to be spring-cleaned and aired. There was shopping to do and, later, an evening meal to cook and eat. They both drank rather too much during the evening and then, with a wrenching sensation that they both experienced in equal measure, took themselves off to separate bedrooms for the night.

Adam was woken in the morning by a familiar sound: the sizzle of Stéphane peeing his spectacular grand arc out of the window of the room next door. Adam reached down for his own erection. Two minutes later, mopping his chest and belly, and thinking that Sté was no doubt doing exactly the same thing in the adjoining room, he couldn't help thinking what a waste this was and that there must be a better way to sort things out.

They had Sunday lunch at Château Beaurepaire with Stéphane's parents. Françoise joined them, having driven over from Perigueux. Stéphane took advantage of the safety of the occasion to announce that he would not be around for the following weekend; he had a backlog of work to catch up on and would be staying in Bordeaux. Adam tried not to let his face register any reaction but without success; he realised that Françoise had seen him wince; he didn't know if she understood why. 'But *I*'ll be around next weekend,' she said to Adam. 'Perhaps we could have dinner together.' And Adam, too surprised to think of any excuse, said yes, and what a nice idea, and why not?

Later Stéphane decided that he would have to return to Bordeaux that evening, finding some pretext which he didn't even try to make sound convincing. In the circumstances it was a relief for both of them. Because they had no car now but only a bike between them, they went to the nearer station of St-Laurent-des-Combes, rather than ride the seven kilometres into St-Emilion.

Not so many of the little blue trains stopped at St-Laurent, which was only a hamlet, but they looked in the timetable and managed to find one that did.

'I'll see you in a fortnight,' Stéphane said when they were on the platform. 'I really do have work to catch up on next weekend. It's nothing to do with ... you know. Please believe that.' But his suddenly crumpled-looking face told a different story. 'You're sure you'll be OK on the bike?'

'Yes of course.' Earlier, Stéphane had shown Adam how to handle it and Adam had had a few practice runs on it up and down the drive. Stéphane had said that if you could manage not to fall off it on the rough, stony track up from the Moulin you could probably manage it anywhere. Adam reminded him of this now. He hated to be saying goodbye to Stéphane like this, with both of them churned up inside and hurting. Why did life have to be like this? With all the big bad moments happening on railway stations.

The train came in and Adam kissed his friend goodbye. He wanted to say, *Don't go*. That and, *I love you*. But he managed not to. That Stéphane was fighting an identical battle with himself he had no doubt. Aching inside, he rode Sté's motorbike home alone.

THIRTEEN

Phoning Sylvain wasn't the easiest thing in the world. You had to phone the abbey, leave a message and give a time when you would be available for him to phone you back from the payphone in the guest wing where he lived. Sometimes Sylvain would get the time wrong, or the phone would be busy, and when you did make contact it was never really private at the other end. Next time they were together, Adam thought, he would buy him a mobile. Though perhaps Sylvain, with his six years' seniority, wouldn't like the idea of Adam buying him things. Adam knew he had to be careful there.

He managed to speak to Sylvain twice during the week that followed his departure and the demise of the Renault. He told him about that, and about Stéphane's visit, and explained brightly that their relationship was now transformed into a purely platonic friendship. He didn't say that spending a night in the same house together without having sex had been a major ordeal for both of them, and if Sylvain read it between the lines he didn't let on. Adam was getting on OK without the car, he said. Stéphane's little motorbike was fine for going as far as the supermarket, the café in St-Genès and even the school in Castillon – though of course he couldn't take his own cello with him, but would use his pupils' instruments for demonstrating on.

Concerning the bike, Adam did feel rather wretched about being so indebted to Stéphane and taking advantage of the generosity of someone with whom he was supposed to be splitting up. But it had taken the pressure off him in the matter of buying a car: a big and difficult decision of the kind that just cried out to be put off. Still, it also meant that, when Françoise phoned him to arrange dinner on Saturday, he was obliged to point out a bit awkwardly that any travelling would have to be in her car.

'But I realised that anyway,' Françoise said, unfazed. 'I'll pick you up at half past seven.'

Adam hadn't gone out to dinner *à deux* with a woman for the best part of a year. He spent some time deciding what to wear, eventually settling on his newest pair of denims and an unadorned, roomy white shirt. They drove to the Fil de l'Eau at Porte Ste-Foy, some twelve miles away. The restaurant was, Françoise said, 'smart and a little expensive, but not crazy prices.' Adam was glad the prices would not be crazy. As he was relying on a female to drive him there and back he felt he would be duty bound to cough up the full cost of the meal when the bill came.

The restaurant was perched atop the steep bank of the river Dordogne and commanded an idyllic view across the water of the old town of Ste-Foy la Grande, complete with church spires and old bridges. Below them the first swallows, just arrived from Africa, were skimming the currents and darting between the piers of the nearest bridge. It would be a great place for a romantic dinner for two, Adam thought, and then – with a touch of alarm – wondered if that was what Françoise had in mind.

'There's quite a lot of English customers,' Adam observed after they had been seated for a couple of minutes.

'Then that's fine,' said Françoise. 'We can simply talk French and be as indiscreet as we like. At least when the waiters aren't hovering near.'

And when they were, Adam couldn't help noticing, the waiters were an appealing little coterie. He tried not to let Françoise notice his interest, which in one or two cases he suspected was mutual.

'Have you seen anything more of the strawberry?' Françoise asked him.

'The strawberry?' Adam queried.

'The Leducs' daughter. You remember that dress she was wearing.'

Adam laughed. 'Of course. I could hardly forget. No, not to speak to. She waved to me once out of a car window when I was on my ... your brother's bike. She hasn't moved in among the vines with a brazier yet, if that's what you were wondering. And, by the way, I finished the never-ending pruning yesterday.' 'You were lucky to have Sylvain to help you,' Françoise said. 'Though maybe I should say, lucky to have Sylvain full stop. He's a handsome creature.'

'You noticed,' said Adam. The youngest and blondest of the waiters brought them a plate of *amuse-gueules*.

'I notice a lot.' Françoise smiled. Rather beautifully, Adam thought.

Later on during the meal Adam brought up the subject he had been waiting to ask her about. 'Tell me about the mysterious Alain. Georges Pincemin's son.'

Françoise paused and looked at Adam for a moment before replying. Then she said, 'You wouldn't have expected him to have had a son, I think. I can understand. But actually, well, I don't think Alain was Georges's son. I think he was his young lover.'

'Whatever led you to that conclusion?' Adam asked, genuinely astonished.

'First of all, his name. Alain Pincemin: *aiñ- aiñ- aiñ-aiñ*. Georges was a musician. He wouldn't have allowed any son of his to have such a quacking set of syllables as a name, surely. What do you think? Speaking as a musician yourself, I mean.'

Adam laughed. 'That's an amazingly tenuous bit of deduction. Though I suppose you could just be right.'

'But that's not the only thing. The other thing was – Alain didn't look anything at all like Georges. Just as you don't.'

'You were only a child when Alain died. Are you really saying that you worked all that out back then?'

'No. Certainly not. I didn't even think about it until you arrived.'

'Until I arrived?' Adam was startled.

'You came to dinner with us – you and Georges Pincemin – when you'd just left school. He brought you along to show you off, I imagine. Then several years later he leaves you his house. You shouldn't be surprised that I asked myself why.'

Adam was appalled. 'I went to visit him in hospital when he was ill and dying. That was all. You surely didn't think...'

'I'm sorry if I came to the wrong conclusion. But you see, when I met you again this year I did think that you looked a bit like Alain and it started me wondering. Working as an accountant doesn't exercise the creative, imaginative side of your brain all that much, so I suppose it finds its outlets elsewhere. Perhaps it led me astray on this occasion.'

'You must think me a bit of an idiot,' Adam said slowly, 'or else horribly self-absorbed, but after the first few weeks I never gave much thought to *why* I was left the property. I was so knocked out by the fact of getting it – the astonishing fact of simply being given it – and then the business of trying to build a new life round it, of trying to manage it all – I suppose I had no space in my brain left for wondering about the why. I just put it down as a thank you for some hospital visits.'

Françoise smiled. 'A pretty big thank you.'

An unwelcome thought struck Adam. 'Is everybody in the communes of St-Genès and St-Emilion thinking along the same lines? Was I the subject of ... of gossip before I arrived?'

'No,' said Françoise. 'You needn't worry about that. I never heard anybody mention it. I don't suppose it's crossed anyone's mind.'

'Then why did it cross yours?' Adam couldn't stop himself asking. And thinking, *it crossed René's mind too, though.*

'Only because I had Stéphane for a brother.' She looked at Adam. She clearly knew. She laughed. 'Oh don't worry. You needn't look like that. I've always known about Sté.' She looked around to check that no French-comprehending waiters were at her elbow. Adam was sorry on their behalf that they were not. They were probably about to miss the most interesting bit. 'He used to dress up in my clothes when he was little. It was quite a … a preoccupation with him. My parents caught him once or twice and there was no end of a row.'

Adam gave a snort of surprised laughter. 'I never knew that about him.' Then, 'I never had a sister,' which seemed a non-sequitur until they thought about it and then it became, at first mildly embarrassing, and then ridiculous, and then they both laughed so loudly and unstoppably that everyone in the restaurant turned round for just a second and looked at them.

'Tell me,' Françoise asked, just after the waiter that Adam had by now identified as his favourite had finished serving them from the cheese chariot and was returning with it to the servery, 'when you're with my brother, which one of you is which?' Her voice carried a sheen of mischievous laughter.

'What do you mean? In what sense?'

'I mean sex.'

'I was afraid you did. That tired old question. Neither. Both. It's not like that.'

'Oh really? I suppose I imagined … because of Stéphane…'

'Because he used to dress in your clothes, you mean?'

'I sort of imagined his would be the feminine role – I mean if there is one.'

'No,' said Adam firmly. 'Whatever he may have done as a kid, there's nothing particularly feminine about your brother's behaviour in bed – or out of it. Anyway, we didn't only do that. There were other things...'

'Sucer? Branler?'

'Er – those two in particular.' Adam stopped. The nice blond waiter had re-materialised, apparently from nowhere, to replenish their supply of bread. His eyebrows were most expressively raised. 'Perhaps we should have been talking English after all,' Adam said to him.

'Je vous en prie,' the waiter said, with a half-smile that twinkled.

When Françoise had driven Adam home to the Moulin, Adam invited her in for a coffee or a nightcap, whichever she preferred. It was usually the other way round, he thought wryly – with the boy driving and the girl inviting him in for coffee. Never mind. Couldn't be helped. He wasn't a straight boy anyway. Françoise accepted graciously. Adam poured them both a small cognac.

They sat demurely at opposite ends of the sofa. Adam had had the forethought to lay a small fire before going out. It had kindled at the flick of a match and was now flaming nicely.

'You used the past tense when you were talking about Stéphane earlier,' Françoise said. 'Would that have anything to do with Sylvain?'

'Nothing escapes you. Yes, I suppose that's true.'

'And how has Stéphane taken it?'

'Stoically. He's hurt. I suppose we both are. Does Sté know that you know about him?'

'Possibly not. We've never discussed it. But then, by the same token – I mean the fact we *haven't* talked about it – perhaps he does.'

'And what about Alain and Georges Pincemin? Has he come to the same conclusion about that relationship as you did?'

'I doubt it. He was only five when Alain died. His memory of him would be less clear even than mine.' She stopped and took a very small sip of cognac. 'You know, he still seems very young to me. Younger than his age I mean. I hope he finds someone. Someone who'll cherish him. I'm sorry in a way it hasn't turned out to be you. Sorry for him I mean.' For the first time that evening she gave Adam a look that he wasn't quite sure he understood.

Eventually Françoise said that it was time she went. Adam saw her out to her car, her Renault Five. (Adam was beginning to take an interest in the makes of cars that other people around the neighbourhood were driving.) They kissed each other goodnight, Adam thinking that this too was an odd way round. Normally this would happen on the girl's doorstep – assuming they weren't going to spend the night together – and the boy, not the girl, would go driving off into the night. Then Adam discovered with a shock that this was no mere goodnight peck but the real thing. It wasn't what he'd intended, it had just crept up on him and taken him by surprise; perhaps the same went for Françoise too. Adam hadn't kissed a woman like this for years. Indeed, so long a time was it that he would have called the last one a girl. It was altogether different from kissing with a man: the head so much smoother, less bony and thrusting; the lips and tongue smaller, softer; the female scent a multi-layered, complex thing. With a man you got a maximum of two perfumes only, the scent of the man himself along with – and even this only sometimes

– the perfume of the one thing, whether deodorant or after-shave, that he might have used to mask the first. Adam felt himself getting hard; he didn't think that had ever happened to him while embracing a woman before tonight. Was she aware...? Suddenly, simultaneously, they broke away.

'Well, now I really should go.' Françoise laughed, a little breathlessly, and dabbed at her hair for a second with the tips of her fingers. Adam was too astonished by what had just happened to say a word or move a muscle. He just stood, as if planted in the gravel, while Françoise stepped lightly into her car. Then, with a wave, she was gone. The beams of her headlights continued to wave gently as they retreated up the track.

Adam woke with a slight hangover, partly because he had awarded himself a final, large, glass of cognac after the departure of Françoise into the night – as a sort of cure for the shock of their last minutes together. He'd felt quite elated when he finally climbed into bed, quite *Adam-Coeur-de-Lion*-ish, but the morning found his state of mind quite different. He wondered what on earth he had been playing at, kissing Françoise in such a way – he could no longer tell himself, in the cold light of day, that he hadn't taken the initiative himself – and wondered what misleading signals he might have conveyed to her. Even men took it a little bit seriously if you kissed them like that; it wasn't usually a prelude to nothing. As for women... He sighed as he rummaged in the fridge for breakfast things. As if life wasn't complicated enough already just now with Sylvain and Stéphane. Why did he have to make even more of a mess of things by fooling around with Stéphane's sister? He spent the morning under a cloud of despondency.

Later in the day he did manage to talk to Sylvain. Sylvain's voice always sounded gruff and matter-of-fact on the phone, as well as a bit perplexed, and today was no exception. Yet hearing it today made Adam feel as if the sun had come out. He glanced instinctively out of the window and realised that it had been shining all day, but only now had he noticed it. He told Sylvain about his dinner with Françoise, but carefully omitted the end of the story. Then he found himself way off-script and floundering, heard himself saying things he hadn't even finished thinking through for himself. 'You know how we left it – or didn't leave it. That you'd come back in a few weeks. We never talked about if it would be a visit or…'

'What are you saying?' Sylvain queried, as if he had misheard a date or a number. Talking to him on the phone was even less satisfactory, and even more different from face to face, than it was with most people. Even more reason for Adam to blurt out what came next.

'I want you to come and live with me. I want us to be together. You know, like the two oxen in harness you used to tell me about when I was younger. *Les vieux inséparables.*'

Sylvain's voice did not rise to the occasion. 'I don't know how we'd live. One hectare – you know…'

'I don't know either. I don't even know how I can make ends meet for myself. But I want you anyway. Just come. We'll find a way.'

'I need to think. I'm older now than I was when I said those things. I still love you – I love you even more than back then, but I've got to think things through.'

'Then come down here and think them,' urged Adam. 'We'll sort it out together.'

'And Stéphane? Do we sort him out too?'

'That's already sorted,' Adam said, though he knew it wasn't. 'I told you when we last spoke. I haven't seen him since.' Telephoned though. Texted.

'I can't get away till after Easter. Say in three weeks. Then I'll come. We'll talk.'

'You'll come and live with me?'

'It's what I'd like, but…'

'There isn't a but. Just come.' Their phone-call finished.

Adam realised, when he put the phone down, that he'd made yet another big declaration. He was getting good at those – good at making them at any rate.

Stéphane returned to his home ground at the end of Friday as usual and, as usual, since he was still using Stéphane's only form of mechanical transport, Adam met him off the train. Adam said, as they both prepared to mount the bike with a little uncertainty as to who would take the controls and who would ride pillion, 'Are you staying at my place tonight or at your parents'?' He tried to sound and feel neutral about it. They both knew they would not be sleeping together at any rate.

'At your place, if that's OK,' Stéphane said diffidently.

'That's fine,' Adam said. Then – he didn't know why – he found himself blurting, 'Sylvain's coming back again in three weeks. It may be for good this time.' He was horrified at himself. For Stéphane looked pole-axed. How could he have said such a thing, at such a moment, so directly, so cruelly? And yet, how else was he to have said it at all? But here he was, dumping poor Stéphane, whom Françoise had said needed someone to cherish him, just as Michael had dumped him six months before. '*Merde*, Sté. That came out all wrong.'

'Not if it's true, it didn't,' said Stéphane with irrefutable logic.

'Come on. I'd better buy us a drink at L'Envers du Décor. I think we could do with something expensive. And if the bike won't take the Rue Guadet with the two of us on it then I'll do the walking.'

They had glasses of Château Milou '98, a comforting wine that tasted like cherries, and then a Tour de Beauregard 2000. Stéphane was riveted by Adam's account of his dinner with his sister (though once again he left out the kiss); it was the first time he'd had confirmation of the fact that his sister knew about his being gay and he was relieved to learn that she had no difficulty with it. He was also amused by the story of the waiters overhearing the conversation about what the two of them did in bed. He made Adam describe the waiters and said he thought he might have been at school with one of them. But he was astonished to hear that Françoise believed Georges Pincemin's 'son' Alain to have in fact been his lover. 'It's amazing the lengths people used to have to go to,' he said, 'to hide their true selves in a place like this.'

'As opposed to what you and I do?' Adam couldn't help observing. 'Like we walk bare-chested down the main street of Castillon waving Gay Pride banners?'

'No, but…'

'There is no *but*. We tell ourselves we're so very out and 'in-yer-face' down here, when the reality is that most people, including your own parents, don't recognise what's under their noses. And when people like René do begin to suspect something, somebody not a million miles from here…' he smiled at Stéphane to show he wasn't really attacking him, '…complains that Sylvain and I are getting us all a reputation.'

Stéphane shrugged and made a grimace. '*Ouais*. OK, you win. Life's a bitch, *n'est-ce pas*?'

Adam had no answer to that. It was an untypical remark from the usually sunny Stéphane. But had had a pretty clear idea why his friend might feel that life was treating him shabbily just now.

Back at the Moulin they cooked their evening meal together. Adam had made sure to provide the ingredients for a really good one and he didn't stint on the wine. He wanted Stéphane to have as good an evening as possible in the circumstances. But *entrecôte à la Bordelaise* (cooked exactly as Stéphane had shown him just a few weeks before) and a couple of bottles of Haut Médoc could be no substitute for what Stéphane really wanted from Adam that night, or what Adam wanted from him. They went off finally to their separate rooms, their feelings only slightly anaesthetised by the wine, and both thinking the situation was about as unsatisfactory as could be.

Early the next morning Adam took the motorbike up to the end of the drive to check the letterbox. Along the stream banks thrushes were singing from trees just coming into leaf, and at one point a deer exploded from among the vines beside the track and bounded across his path just a metre or two in front of the bike, a sleek and shining incarnation of antlered energy. There was nothing in the letterbox except for a couple of bills. He was getting used to those badges of adult, householder, status: bills he'd known he'd have to pay; bills for things he'd had no idea about – waste disposal charges, water rates – and failed to budget for. Georges Pincemin's capital outlay account – godsend though it was – was haemorrhaging fast and his only income to date, a cheque for a term's teaching of four cello pupils once a week – had done little to staunch the outflow. Soon there would be cheques from paying guests at the Petit Moulin, it was true, but soon too there would be a car to buy. Something would turn up, he supposed, but he couldn't easily imagine what.

When he had returned from his bumpy ride back down the drive, had switched off the noisy little engine and turned his head to view with a sort of perverse satisfaction the billowing cloud of white dust that his passage had generated all the way between the mill and the distant road, he was surprised to hear the sound of the piano indoors. Stéphane was picking out some tune on it. With more than a little difficulty it appeared. Adam listened more carefully. A sequence of three notes, with long gaps between them, sounded familiar. More followed, like the footfalls of a tortoise. Then Adam realised. Stéphane was trying to find his way through the piano part of one of Beethoven's cello sonatas. It was a challenging piece even for a pianist with a technique. It sounded as though Stéphane might make it to the end of the first movement by about teatime.

Adam smiled. Then slowly the smile faded. It was he who had once suggested that Stéphane might like to help him by playing one or two of his accompaniments for him. But how cruel that suggestion had been. He had asked for something that was way beyond Stéphane's capacity to give. And now Sté was forlornly trying, perhaps had been trying for some time, to do the impossible. For Adam. That wasn't the only cruelty to Stéphane that he'd been guilty of. He'd piled them on, he now saw: torture upon torture. Adam left the bike where it was and walked – no, ran – into the house. He rushed towards Stéphane, who had time only to turn surprised eyes towards him, and threw his arms around his neck, burying his mouth in Stéphane's hair. And this time it was not Adam whose composure was washed away on a flood of tears but Stéphane's.

They made love everywhere, that weekend. In Adam's bed, in Stéphane's. In front of the log fire, out in the warm sunshine, lying among the violets (never mind the occasional nettle) beside the millstream, and, with trousers roughly pulled down, halfway up the stairs. How Adam was going to square this with his conscience – he wondered as he came together with Stéphane for the third, fourth, fifth time, their two hearts and cocks hammering away together in blissful unison – heaven only knew. And leave aside the question of how he would square it with Sylvain.

FOURTEEN

Stéphane said it was a pity that Adam and he had made separate plans to be away over Easter. They had made those plans – Stéphane to visit friends on the Ile d'Oléron and Adam to travel to England – without knowing that their nearly extinguished sexual relationship would be fanned into a new blaze by Adam's guilt-induced embracing of Stéphane as he struggled at the piano. Adam thought, though he did not say, that perhaps it was not a pity at all.

But his visit to England proved disappointing. He didn't manage to see Sean, who was up in Newcastle – so he rather wildly invited him to come across to France in a couple of weeks' time instead. As for Michael, Adam just about managed to meet him over a pint or two in London. Where, in a vast high-ceilinged pub on the Strand they found that they no longer had much to say to each other. And that was all. There was no invitation to Michael's new flat, no arrangement to introduce Adam to … what was her name? Melissa. That was life, though. Old friends grew up and grew apart. His mind went back to a snowy dusk in February and two ships' courses diverging off the Isle of Wight.

He fared little better at his parents' home. His mother fretted the whole time about how he was going to make a living, how he could afford the upkeep of his big house in the Gironde, about how lonely it must be down there. In the end he couldn't wait to get back to France. Life might be complicated there, but he knew now where he wanted to be. At least his visit to England had clarified that.

Adam found his spirits rising during his return journey, even though he was going back to an empty house, to money worries and to a set of personal relationships of which he seemed to be making a total mess. But the weather was working its usual French springtime magic, turning perceptibly warmer after his TGV crossed the Loire; the sun shone on a countryside that had greened noticeably since he'd left it the previous week, and when, just south of Angoulême, they ran past the first village that was all roofed in those red Roman canal tiles that whisper, *south, south, south*, to any traveller who goes in that direction, Adam experienced that feeling, like a playful punch below the diaphragm, that says, *coming home*.

As the train, entering the *vignoble* of the Pomérol, began to slow in readiness for its Libourne stop, Adam saw that another change had come about during his few days away. In all those acres of vineyard, on all those small black vine-stocks protruding from the earth and tied to wires, the buds were opening into fresh green burgeons, all winking away like emeralds in the sun. Arriving by taxi at the Grand Moulin, Adam was gratified to find that his own vines too were putting forth minute rosettes of leaves. But they were not the only things winking like jewels. When he got indoors he found that the light on his answer-phone was doing the same.

There was a message from Gary Blake. When Adam rang back Gary came to the point at once. 'Listen. Something's come up. A bit of an emergency – for me. But a chance for you to do some playing, and help me out at the same time. Can you be in Paris on Monday?'

Adam did a split second's calculation. 'Yes.'

'Good. I'm supposed to be recording some Mozart trios for Radio France Musique. With Nathalie Pujols and Benoît Senseau.' Adam knew the names. Along with Gary they were among the best-known chamber music players in France. 'Benoît's gone sick. He won't be right for Monday. Nathalie can't find another cellist at such short notice. I suggested you. Are you up for it?'

Adam felt giddy. The room seemed to expand and then contract, Gary's voice to echo and fragment. 'Me? What? What are you saying? Make a recording for France Musique? You're winding me up.' Adam mentally checked the date. It was April the twentieth, not the first.

'I'm serious. The concert will be aired at the beginning of June, but the studio slot's booked for Monday. There'll be a reasonably decent fee, by the way, not just expenses.'

'My God,' Adam said, and fell silent. Make a recording for a national radio station, France's number one purveyor of classical music on air. At five days' notice. And Gary had thought of him. Adam, just out of music college and with no experience of the professional concert platform. Gary had thought of him, had thought him up to it.

'Are you still there?' queried Gary.

This is how opportunity comes, Adam thought. Like a ball thrown at you from an unexpected quarter. Like a catch in cricket. You mustn't hesitate, mustn't query. 'I'll do it,' Adam heard himself say. He put his questions to himself. How? How on earth?

'Thank God for that,' said Gary. The relief in his voice was so obvious, so genuine, that Adam felt slightly stronger.

'Yes, but God knows…'

'Now listen to me and don't panic. You know the trios. I remember you sight-read them with me all those years ago, even if you haven't touched them since. You know the cello parts are easy. Tum-ti-tum. The violin and the piano do the hard work.

'Yes I know. But five days' notice… I don't have a copy of the score.'

'Then go into Bordeaux first thing in the morning and buy one. Read them through at the piano till you know them. We're doing the last three: K 542 in E, the C-major 548 and 546 in G.'

'Hang on,' said Adam. 'I'll get a pencil.'

He phoned Sylvain first. Or rather, he telephoned the abbey and left the usual message for Sylvain to call him back. He included in the message the fact that he had some good news to share. Until he heard himself say those words he had not thought of Gary's bombshell in those terms. A shock, a challenge, yes, but good news? Now he saw that of course it was good news. What else did he have to tell Sylvain that was good? That he'd had an unsatisfactory meeting with Michael? That he'd been sleeping with Stéphane?

Later he called Stéphane. He was still on holiday on the Ile d'Oléron and the signal was rather faint. Still, he got the gist of Adam's news and gave him his awed congratulations.

'It's not that the music's all that difficult,' Adam said. 'The cello parts aren't big or demanding – there's no way I could work them up in under a week if they were. But it's the fact of doing it at all, at short notice, for national radio, and with people like Gary and Nathalie Pujols. Have you any idea how important they are in their field? I'll feel like an imposter playing alongside them. It's really scary.'

Stéphane made soothing noises and said that of course everything would be OK. He told Adam where to find the music shop in Bordeaux – the Virgin Megastore in Place Gambetta – and said what a shame it was that he wouldn't be able to meet Adam and go there with him.

'But see you in ten days,' Adam said with conviction.

'What about...?' said Stéphane, but the signal failed at the crucial word.

'What about what?'

'What about Sylvain? Isn't he supposed to be ... you know?'

'*Merde*, you've reminded me of something else. I've invited Sean to come down at the weekend. Look,' Adam said this as much to himself as Stéphane, 'I'll sort something out. Don't worry. But I'll see you in ten days as we said – no matter who else is here.' Separate bedrooms or not. That was a detail that could be ironed out later: there was much else to be lived through first.

'I think you're great,' said Stéphane.

'Take care,' said Adam. 'Keep in touch and see you soon. Love you.'

Oh my God, he thought, putting the phone smartly down as if it had just burnt his fingers, and not hanging about to see if Sté had come back with, 'Love you too.' He had really done it this time. What a knack he had of making tricky situations worse. All the sayings, all the clichés that expressed his new predicament ran through his head. Fat in fire, out of frying pan and into said fire, *les carottes sont cuites*.

Now he had to waste no time in phoning Sean. Perhaps his travel plans were already made, and tickets booked. But luckily they weren't. They decided between them that Sean would come to Paris, subject to Gary's letting him stay a night or two at his flat along with Adam, and then travel back down to the Moulin with him when the recording was over. Adam would check with Gary and ring Sean back.

Five minutes after that his other phone rang and it was Sylvain. Predictable was one thing that Sylvain was not. On hearing Adam's news he announced that he would come to Paris to support him at this big moment in his musical career. He was going to come to Adam that weekend anyway. He'd made up his mind. He was going to leave the abbey for good and had told them so. He had even written to his mother – for the first time in his life –

and told her where he was going to live and who with. 'My God,' said Adam, wondering what the upshot of that would be. There was a court order still notionally in force that forbade Sylvain even to contact Adam again. But Sylvain sounded very sure of himself. There was no more thinking to be done. He'd bring his things to Paris with him. Could Adam ask Gary if he could kindly put him up? If the answer was no, then he'd sleep under a bridge or something.

'Don't be silly,' said Adam, glad to be discussing practical difficulties rather than teasing out the tangle of his relationships with Sylvain and Stéphane. 'Of course you won't have to sleep under a bridge. I'll speak to Gary, and if it's not on we'll go to a hotel. But we won't be entirely alone.'

'You haven't asked Stéphane to come to Paris, have you?' Sylvain said, sounding disgruntled.

'No,' said Adam, relieved that he could say that truthfully, but feeling sick because he'd accidentally told Stéphane that he loved him just ten minutes ago – and how much more than disgruntled Sylvain would be if he knew that. 'On the other hand, I have asked Sean.' And found himself explaining all that instead.

Gary said he thought it a bit perverse of Adam, when he claimed to be racked with nerves about recording a little Mozart for a radio programme, that he should also have to be dashing about Paris, meeting two different lovers at two different railway stations and then having to look after the pair of them. Adam retorted that he liked it that way; coping with the practicalities of playing host to one past and one present lover would be just the thing to take his mind off his pre-performance nervousness. 'And who'll actually be playing the host?' Gary wanted to know. 'I can see my apartment turning into a youth hostel – or the YMCA.' But he couldn't feel too cross about it. Adam had made his diffident request to be allowed to bring the other two very politely – the circumstances were rather exceptional after all – and had thanked Gary so warmly when he said yes, that he was not left with any feeling that his hospitality was being abused, or himself taken for granted. Besides, he had enjoyed meeting Sylvain a couple of months before – and had been treated to the unexpected sight of him frolicking naked with Adam in his salon. Sean too he remembered meeting, when their visits to Adam's home on the Plateau de Langres had overlapped all those years ago. Gary remembered Sean as a rather over-polite but almost impossibly handsome teenager, and found himself wondering how he had turned out.

The next morning Adam was waiting on the doorstep of the Virgin Megastore when it opened. He was back at the Moulin before midday, and spent the rest of Wednesday and the next two days learning his notes: playing the trios through at the piano (albeit rather approximately – he was glad there was nobody there to hear him) and working on the cello parts till the sweat was running off his face. Adam remembered his teachers quoting the pianist, Schnabel: 'Mozart is given to children to play because of the quantity of the notes; adults are afraid to play him because of the quality of the notes.' Quite right, he thought now, wiping sweat out of his eyes. Many people heard only delicacy and elegance in Mozart, but for Adam there was grandeur and glory too. At least it was chamber music and you weren't expected to play from memory; he would have the dots in front of him when the moment came.

He travelled up to Paris on Saturday and spent most of the afternoon, and the whole of Sunday morning rehearsing the trios with Gary and Nathalie Pujols. (No, call me Nathalie, she had said at once, laughing, when Adam had begun by addressing her as Madame.)

Nathalie was a striking-looking woman of about forty with piercing brown eyes, a very straight nose and a determined manner. Adam thought immediately of pictures he had seen of Ida Haendel when young, and of Augustus John's portrait of the formidable Madame Suggia. She was married, Gary had told him, to an insurance broker and they had two teenage children. She brought a practical, no-nonsense approach to the business of music making, for which Adam was grateful. In view both of his inexperience and of the time factor, he needed that, rather than having to spend time in abstract speculation about Mozart's soul or what the music *meant*. By Sunday afternoon he was exhausted, but, for the first time, confident that he would at least manage to play the right notes at the next morning's recording and not let down his senior partners, even if he wouldn't be delivering the most stunning piece of cello playing that listeners to France Musique had ever heard.

He took the familiar bus number thirty to the Gare du Nord to meet Sean. And soon there he was, striding towards him down the apparently endless platform alongside the carriages of the Eurostar, looking just the same as when Adam had last seen him at Christmas. His blond hair was a bit longer now than it was then, which looked nice. (Encouraged by each other, Adam and Stéphane had both been letting their hair grow longer too, while Sylvain, untroubled by the changing demands of fashion, had kept his mop of shining black curls just the same over the years.) But hair length apart, Sean really didn't even look much different from the way he'd looked six years ago when, aged seventeen, he'd come with Michael to visit Adam in France, hopping off a coach in Chaumont with a backpack. Adam thought it was probably the same backpack now. The cornflower blue eyes were certainly the same ones, and they'd lost none of their light.

Seeing him after a gap of four whole months, Adam experienced that same sensation in head and stomach that he had used to feel when he was younger. Pheromones, or what? It was as if he were going to fall in love with him all over again. Adam told himself not to be silly. It was far too late for that now, and life had already got much too complicated. But there was nothing half-hearted about the hug they exchanged on the platform.

Adam had told Sean, during their two or three phone calls of the last few days, a little about recent developments with both Sylvain and Stéphane. So Sean was not entirely surprised to learn that their next stop was the Gare de Lyon, where they would be meeting Sylvain off another train. 'But let's get a beer first,' Adam said. 'We've got about an hour.'

They sat in the sun outside the Hotel Terminus Nord, and Adam poured out his troubles with the urgency of someone who has been balked of the opportunity to do so before and now has only an hour in which to get everything off his chest. He explained about being in love with Sylvain, and trying to be faithful to him, and about not sleeping with Stéphane, and then sleeping with him after all…

Sean gave Adam one of his heartbreaking smiles. 'We've been here before, don't you think? Though I was part of the jigsaw once myself and now I'm not. But that doesn't seem to have made any difference. Do you remember what Michael used to say about you? "Same old Adam". For once I'd have to agree.' Sean always agreed with people 'just for once'.

'What I want to know,' said Adam, 'and I need to know within about the next forty-five minutes, is whether you think I should tell Sylvain about sleeping with Stéphane again or not.'

'First,' said Sean, 'tell me which of the two of them you're more in love with. I know you love them both, that's clear. It usually is the case with you. You've not yet got the habit of just loving one person at a time.' Adam thought this was deeply unfair, coming from Sean, who had never even managed to make his mind up about whether he was in love with even one person or whether he wasn't, but he held his tongue. Sean went on. 'But between the two of them there must be a front runner. Even if you can't work out which of the two it is when you're with one of them – well, right now, neither of them's here. So, tell me.'

Adam looked down at the table. 'Sylvain. Obviously Sylvain. You didn't need to ask.'

'Maybe not,' said Sean. 'But perhaps you needed to answer. And if that's the case, then maybe you need to make that a little bit more clear to Stéphane, don't you think? Like, instead of just making it clear sometimes, try making it clear all the time.'

'Thank you for the lecture,' said Adam a bit huffily.

'You wanted to know what I thought,' said Sean reasonably. 'Now your first question. Should you tell Sylvain about what happened or not? I think that ought to depend on whether you plan to go on having sex with Stéphane or not. If you decide that that last weekend was a one-off, then maybe you shouldn't tell him. Put it behind you and let go of it. But if you're going to go hopping into bed with Stéphane every time Sylvain's away for a few days – either because you plan it that way or because you can't help yourself – then perhaps you ought to be a gentleman and explain to Sylvain that that's the way you are and he's just got to accept it.'

Adam stared gloomily at his glass of Heineken. 'He might not accept it. And I'd lose him.'

'That's the risk you'd have to take. And at the risk of sounding a bit cold-blooded, at least you'd still have Stéphane as a consolation prize.'

'I suppose you're right,' Adam said slowly. 'I guess I've been telling myself the same thing, only not listening properly. I've tried to put Sté behind me, but I can't manage to do it. I am like that, as you say. I can't pretend to Sylvain that I'm some sort of paragon that I'm not. I'll just have to come clean with him, as you say, and take the consequences.'

Sean took a swig of beer. 'Then comes the harder question of how and when.'

Adam looked at his watch. 'I think it's time to hit the metro.'

Half an hour later they both stood on a second railway platform, waiting for an orange-coloured TGV and another young man with a backpack. Adam was nervous and tense. He had no idea how Sylvain and Sean would react to each other. They came from such different regions of his own world – from opposite ends of his kingdom – as well as from social backgrounds that were poles apart. He thought, without taking any pleasure in the comparison, that it would be like placing two newly discovered chemical elements in a test tube together for the first time.

The train arrived, disgorged its crowds, and then suddenly there was Sylvain, striding along the platform in the middle of the throng, just as Sean had been. In contrast to Sean he was weather-tanned and raven-haired, but he looked just as bright of eye and radiant. Like Sean he carried an old backpack; unlike him he carried a large and shabby hold-all as well. Unlike Sean, he was bringing all his worldly goods; unlike him, his all fitted into a hold-all. And unlike Sean, he was going to stay with Adam for good. Well, that was what he and Adam hoped.

Blue Sky Adam

They met halfway along the platform. Sylvain embraced Adam fiercely, full of pent-up longing. Then he disengaged himself and turned to Sean. 'I remember you,' he said in French. And Sean managed to reply, 'Me too,' in the same language. Adam had quite forgotten that they had once come upon each other at close quarters, though they hadn't spoken, near a lake on the Plateau de Langres six years before. Later, both men had commented on the good looks of the other. And Sylvain did now. He looked searchingly into Sean's face, then cracked a brilliant smile and said, *'T'es toujours beau.'*

And Sean laughed in surprise and said, *'Toi aussi.'* Then the two young men gave each other an unscripted hug, and Adam felt a sudden sense of elation, relief and astonishment all together, at the realisation that at least one thing in his life of anxieties and self-inflicted troubles might be going to turn out well.

Sylvain was someone who, faced with any 'social situation' (that meant any situation involving any person besides himself and Adam) either said very little, or a lot. Adam had fully expected him to be tongue-tied, faced with Sean and then Gary together, and with Adam all preoccupied and geared up for concert giving. But, presumably because his own encounter with Sean had gone so well – and he must have been feeling as nervous about this as Adam had – his tongue was loosened and he talked in the metro all the way back to the Place de Clichy. In French, obviously, which made it a bit hard for Sean – though not impossible. Sean had had some opportunity to scrape the rust of his own school French last summer, during his first, eventful, visit to Adam's new home.

Back at Gary's flat, once he had confidently placed his luggage alongside Adam's in the spare bedroom that they had shared a few weeks before, Sylvain was asking to see Adam's music, wanting to know what he would be playing the following day. Adam knew that Sylvain was always excited by the thought of him as a musician, remembered that even in the very first days when their relationship had consisted entirely of sex, it was the first 'other' subject that had captured Sylvain's interest: he had soon been demanding to hear Adam play. So Adam showed Sylvain the score of the Mozart trios and ran his fingers along bits of the cello parts while humming snatches of melody under his breath to bring them to life.

'Why is the cello part written above the piano part, with the violin, when it's actually lower?' Sylvain wanted to know.

Adam was floored. Gary answered. 'It's a very good question. Perhaps it should be written right through the middle of the piano part, since they overlap. But actually it's simply to make it easier for the pianist to read.' And he sat down at the piano and strummed a few bars for Sylvain to hear.

Gary swept them off to the Coq Hardi for an evening meal. He told Adam that this was to bring him luck and explained to the others (Adam didn't need reminding) that the last time he'd taken Adam there it had been his seventeenth birthday, and he had met Georges Pincemin ... and come to inherit the Moulin de Pressac in consequence.

Sylvain continued in talkative mood. Perhaps, thought Adam, it was the natural reaction of anyone who'd just left a Trappist monastery. He told them about spending Easter there and how, out of curiosity, he'd attended some of the services that marked that high point in the Church's year. He described the atmospheric *Tenebrae*, the matins service that the monks sang in choir just before dawn on the three days leading up to Easter. '*C'était quelque chose, eh ben oui.* Quite something.

The first day, Thursday, the only light in the whole church comes from a huge, branched, wrought-iron candlestick in front of the altar. It has fifteen candles on it, one at the top and the others,' he demonstrated their position with his hands, 'you know, like flying geese. Fifteen flames flying bravely through the darkness, *parmi les ténèbres*. As each psalm is sung one candle is snuffed out at the end, so on Friday morning the church is that much darker, there's only about ten candles left. By the end of Saturday's service there's only the one top candle left. And then that goes, too, leaving total dark. It's meant to show the death of ... you know.' He told them how the church remained unlit all day until, late in the evening, during the Easter Vigil, the abbot lit the Paschal Candle, a small spark in the gloom, and then candle after candle was lit from it until the whole church was ablaze. 'The Resurrection, of course,' he added, in case anyone had missed the point.

Adam was not surprised that Sylvain had been moved by the experience, though whether it had been the religious or the theatrical, musical side that had captured his imagination he couldn't guess. He would ask him at some point, but not just now. So much was piling up for *some point but not just now*.

It did feel rather weird to be going off to Gary's spare room to sleep with Sylvain, and leaving Sean to be offered the put-u-up in the salon by Gary, but everything seemed weird just now. Adam would make love with Sylvain half the night. They were both equally hungry for each other. They would fall asleep seeing ranks of *Tenebrae* candles blazing against the dark. Grandeur and glory. In the morning Adam would get up and record Mozart for Radio France. In the morning he would wake and find that everything had been a dream.

When Adam and Sylvain had finally shut their bedroom door behind them, Gary offered Sean a nightcap. 'Just a small one, mind. At any rate for me. Adam's not the only one who has to play Mozart in the morning. But you have whatever you want.'

Sean accepted a malt whisky but, taking Gary's hint, said 'when' at a fairly early stage in the pouring.

'Tell me,' Gary asked, sitting across the salon at a decorous distance from him. 'What's going to happen to those two? They seem very smitten with each other. But didn't I gather that there's some other young Frenchman in Adam's life?'

'Stéphane,' said Sean, and told him what he knew. 'Stéphane's very sweet and lovely. I met him on holiday last year.' He had to look down to hide an involuntary smirk. 'We all got to know each other rather well.'

'I'm sure you did,' said Gary with a straight face. 'But if Adam's inviting Sylvain to go and live with him and not giving this Stéphane character his marching orders first, then I can't see any possible outcome other than the whole thing blowing up in all their faces.'

'I did tell Adam,' said Sean, 'this afternoon, but only because he asked me, that he ought to either finish with Stéphane or come clean with Sylvain about him.'

'And what did he say to that?'

'Oh, he agreed entirely. But then he would. He always thinks the right things. That's the easy part.' Sean looked across at Gary and gave him a smile of such beauty that it made him ache.

'Well,' said Gary when he'd recovered, 'if he's going to do a *mea maxima culpa* with Sylvain, he'd just better hold it off till after tomorrow morning. Not just for our sakes but for Mozart's.'

FIFTEEN

'I know you love me, and I love you too, but you'll have to accept me the way I am. However fully I commit myself to you, I can't do it to the exclusion of sex with other people. I tried not having sex with Stéphane while you were away but I simply couldn't hack it. It's the way I'm made. Sorry, but you have to take it or leave it – I mean, take me or leave me.'

This, or something like it, was the speech Adam was going to have to make to Sylvain. Or would perhaps have to. He hadn't even considered making it last night. They had not been alone together until bedtime and then their time had been too valuable, too occupied with sex and all the other intimacies that reaffirmed their togetherness. This morning had been hectic. His phone, and Gary's, had rung nearly non-stop while Sean and Sylvain had tried, like surrogate parents, to get him to eat a croissant and drink fruit juice. His real parents phoned in their good-luck wishes, Even Michael too, and Stéphane – 'I'm on the bus' – on the way to college for the start of his new term. Benoît Senseau, the cellist whose indisposition was responsible for Adam's opportunity and present state of nerves, had phoned Gary and asked to be passed to Adam too. The French don't say 'Break a Leg' to wish each other luck in these situations, they just say *'Merde'*, and that's what Benoît said to Adam.

Adam had brought his dark suit and silver-grey tie; he'd given the suit a press the day before. He asked Gary, should he wear it? Gary said, yes of course. But now in the metro he wondered that Gary, dressed in open-necked shirt and chinos, hadn't kindly stopped him from so unnecessarily overdressing. Perhaps Gary had been preoccupied and nervous himself. You felt your own nerves keenly, yet you were often unaware of other people's – especially when they were older and inhabited a far higher artistic plane than your own. There was not much conversation among the four of them in the metro. Sean and Sylvain had caught the mood of subdued tension from the two performers and were more or less silent.

'However fully I commit myself to you... That's the way I'm made... Take me or leave me...' Adam kept running the speech through in his head. It sounded cheesy. And he could guess only too easily, gloomily, what Sylvain's response to it would be. 'I want all of you, Adam,' he'd say. 'I'm not going to share you with this Stéphane, phoning you from 'on the bus' to muscle in on your big moment, nor with Sean, nor Michael or anyone else.' Then he'd continue... But Adam couldn't bring himself to go on conjuring Sylvain's injured voice in his head – Sylvain who now stood strap-hanging a few inches away 'on the train', sharing this Gethsemane moment with him. Adam couldn't bear to imagine Sylvain telling him the last thing in the world he would ever want to hear.

'Come on, look sharp.' Gary's voice, taking charge. The underground train had rolled out into daylight at Passy station and the doors had brusquely opened with their familiar, slightly threatening, clunk and whoosh. Adam had made no move to pick up his cello. He grabbed it now, almost in panic. 'I'm sorry, I was...' Amidst a surge of alighting passengers they all tumbled off the crowded train.

Arriving at the studios, Adam looked wistfully at the Seine running serenely by, and at the Eiffel Tower rearing beyond tower blocks on the far side, before they passed in through the doors and signed for security. They had to go separate ways at this point: Sean and Sylvain (*invités*) were ushered one way and Gary and Adam (*artistes*) another. In the band room, which was vast, capable of accommodating an entire orchestra, the three of them (Nathalie had arrived a few minutes before) seemed pathetically few: three peas in a drum. Nathalie was in sensible slacks and a lightweight jumper; Adam felt even more keenly that he was overdressed; why on earth hadn't Gary spared him this and told him not to bother when he had asked? But it was too late now for such preoccupations. He opened his score and peered at it, turned pages. He saw only a blur of notes, falling like black snow flurries across the pages. Was this the slow movement he was looking at? Or the final allegro? Sharps or flats? What key was the bloody thing in?

They were called, then taken to the studio. Facing them sat a small invited audience of about forty people, among them – the lights were up and they were not hard to spot – Sylvain and Sean side by side. Before the last few days Adam would not have permitted himself to imagine such a scenario in his wildest fantasies. But now everything had an unreal quality. Mikes were positioned, sound levels checked; but it was as if it were all happening to someone else. He was an actor in a play about three musicians; he didn't really play the cello. They were going to do the C-major first. Gary was striking the tuning triad. Adam checked his strings, retuned the C. He glanced round at Nathalie, seated behind her own music stand, finely tuning her violin. He must have been looking apprehensive; she gave him a smile that was almost motherly. A light went on. They were on air. Two bows were raised above two sets of strings. Gary's hands were motionless, poised above the keys. Simultaneously three heads nodded. Uncompromising unison and octave Cs. Played forte. They had begun.

Even when the first trio ended, Adam still felt that he was in a dream. The sound of applause, as if coming from far away, astonished him. They had a short break and played the second trio. They had a coffee then played the third, Mozart's last, in G. Only towards the end did Adam begin to feel the situation was ordinary, normal. Day in the Life of an *Artiste*. The last trio ended. Applause again, not from a distant galaxy this time but near at hand, appreciative, a warm nugget that you could reach out to, clasp and hold. The 'on air' light went out. The producer came down from his box, walked across and asked the musicians to stay put. 'Just one little moment to do again, if you would. In the G-major, movement one. Bar fifty-one, fifty-two.'

'I fluffed my semis,' said Nathalie.

'No,' said Gary, 'it was me. Late entry.'

'Would you like to lead in to it from bar forty-two, the double-bar?'

Adam picked up his bow again with a feeling of elation. He was floating above the earth like a balloon. He felt nothing in life could ever go wrong for him again.

They walked to a nearby café, sat down at a table outside and looked down the hillside of Passy to the Seine flowing below. Gary ordered a bottle of champagne. Everything was surreal again. Adam had never had champagne at a pavement café before. With the foil-topped bottle on the table in front of him and a glass of its contents in his hand he no longer felt incorrectly dressed in his smart suit. Other people looked in their direction from time to time and benignly smiled. Nathalie clearly enjoyed the presence of the two extra young men. 'You and your boys,' she teased Gary. 'But you've certainly collected a handsome trio this time.'

She turned to Adam. 'You and I must make music together again some day.' In his state of post-performance euphoria he was already high above Paris, viewing the city from above like a bird that has sipped champagne; Nathalie's words propelled him into the stratosphere. She quizzed him about the repertoire he had learnt at the Academy. The Elgar Concerto had been his warhorse, he said; she could understand that. He'd done the Brahms double concerto for violin and cello; interesting, she said. For his final recital he'd played one of the Beethoven sonatas. 'And one of the Bach suites, I suppose?' she had queried. 'Of course,' Adam said.

Sean and Sylvain were competing to identify landmarks on the Paris skyline, Sean working at his French as he did so like a blacksmith effortfully working iron. It was so good, so unexpected but so right that they had taken to each other, Adam thought. Perhaps they too were finding the experience of that morning surreal and beyond the ordinary reach of things.

Adam had tentatively planned to spend a couple of days in Paris with Sean before returning with him to the mill. That was before Sylvain's sudden decision to come to Paris himself. But in the event that changed nothing. Gary had no objection to his flat continuing to serve as a youth hostel for a few more nights, and Sylvain was delighted at the prospect of a couple of days' sightseeing. So Adam found himself, bizarrely, playing tour guide to the two great loves of his life. Those two seemed, equally bizarrely to Adam, quite unfazed by the situation. Sylvain was secure in the knowledge, which his own observation confirmed, that Sean, though the great love of Adam's past, was now simply a best friend. He had quickly ceased to treat Sean as a new person, and behaved towards him as if he were simply an extension of Adam himself – albeit an extension that expressed itself in rather rickety French. Sean for his part had such a trusting and generous nature that he tended to like the people he met, until and unless some negative experience happened to change his mind. He took Sylvain exactly as he found him. Where other people, educated French people, would have heard Sylvain speak and perceived a half-educated yokel from the back of beyond, Sean simply heard without prejudice a young Frenchman speaking French and struggled to catch the drift. Sean was also keenly determined to enjoy the moment – and that all three of them should. He was convinced that everything would go wrong as soon as Sylvain found himself sharing Adam's home patch with Stéphane. He might as well make the most of the present sunny calm while it lasted.

The three young men climbed the Eiffel Tower, they visited the Quartier Latin and the Place du Tertre, they lunched at street-corner cafés, took a boat trip on the Seine. With Gary they even visited a gay club in the Marais. 'Even', because Adam had some doubts about taking Sylvain to such a place. Sylvain had no experience of clubs or urban gay life, had never before seen gay men *en masse* before, and Adam had no idea what his reaction might be and was a little afraid in advance. But he deferred to the wisdom of Gary who selected a place that was, 'only a little bit gay, more a music and cabaret bar than anything else,' so as to break Sylvain in gently. In the event it all turned out fine. Adam was relieved and gratified to find that, after an initial few minutes during which Sylvain's eyes were on stalks, those eyes came back to rest on him for the remainder of the evening. He was then anxious, briefly, that that might be a bit of a pain for the other two, but whenever he looked in their direction he was reassured to find that they were also getting on very well together and seemed to be finding plenty of things to say.

For the second time in ten days Adam found himself returning by TGV and taxi to his watermill home. This time he was with Sean and Sylvain, not alone. Again the countryside had ratcheted up the green factor by a notch or two; the emeralds that had studded the vine-branches everywhere were reinventing themselves as translucent miniature tentacles and plumes. Again various messages waited on the answer-phone.

The first was from Philippe Martinville. It told him that Adam's neighbour on the other side, M. Ducros from Château La Carelle, was wanting to lop some trees that grew near the property boundary and needed access to Adam's land to do it. Philippe had explained that Adam was now managing the land attached to the Moulin himself and that M.Ducros should talk to him direct. He'd taken the liberty of giving Adam's phone number to M. Ducros. The second message was, predictably, from M. Ducros – or at any rate from his son – explaining what he wanted to do and when, and inviting Adam over for a drink with himself and his wife, 'in order to get to know a new neighbour'.

Adam phoned back, assured his neighbour that he had no problem with his coming to cut a few trees, though he asked if the social drink could be put off for a few days as he had friends staying. But Ducros junior said cheerfully, bring the friends, and they arranged a time for the following day. Adam asked if they might walk across through the vineyard, which must have sounded a bit odd, since everyone drove from château to château by car and Ducros was not to know that Adam was temporarily without one. It was only at that moment that it dawned on Adam that transport over the next few days was going to be a problem. The three of them would not be able to ride around all together on Stéphane's bike. Shopping trips would be lonely affairs – perhaps they should have a roster – while trips to neighbourhood bars would be out of the question. Never mind, though. The weather was good, the outdoors beckoned and the cellar had not run dry – not quite yet.

But that very afternoon a phone-call came from Stéphane's father. He had seen a car for sale at the garage at St-Christophe-des-Bardes, just a couple of miles away on the road to St-Emilion. It was a Peugeot 309, only three years old and, in Marc's opinion, very reasonably priced. If Adam wanted to go and look at it, he would be happy to drive him there. Adam said yes, and went to look for his chequebook.

He had been pondering what kind of car he ought to get. While he cared little about cars as status symbols himself he was uncomfortably aware that your car did say something about you to other people, whether it was the down-at-heel Peugeot 205 that the typical Côtes de Castillon *vigneron*'s wife drove to the supermarket, or the Porsche or Audi that usually graced the driveways of the St-Emilion châteaux – alongside the inescapable four-by-four. But now it seemed that he didn't even have to make the decision. A three-year-old, silver-grey Peugeot 309 would do very nicely.

Ten minutes later Marc had arrived (in his Peugeot 307 Estate) and, despite Adam's protestations that his friends could be left behind, insisted that all three of them climb aboard. Marc remembered Sean from the previous summer but was meeting Sylvain for the first time. If he thought this rather rustic-sounding lad from France's far east an odd choice of companion for someone like Adam, at least he gave no sign of it.

Turning left out of the top of the driveway, and passing the top of the driveway down to Château La Carelle where they were bid to drinks tomorrow, they overtook a ragged old man pushing a bicycle. 'Is that M. Ducros?' Sean asked in fun.

'It's Pépin the Mad,' answered Marc, and Adam, repeating what Stéphane had told him right back at the beginning, added, 'Have nothing to do with him.' Everybody laughed.

'Are you sure you're going to survive down here?' Sean asked Adam quietly while Sylvain chatted away amiably to Marc in French. 'I mean money. I know you're well endowed with bricks and mortar but you can't eat those.'

'I'll get by,' said Adam. 'At least I hope I will. I'm living on Georges's capital at the moment. And although my fee for Monday will pay for half of the new car (thank God) the other half will make another big dent. The cheque for the first holiday let should arrive any day now and there'll be more of those. But I've got to wait till autumn for the cash from the grapes – like last year. I'll need to get some more cello pupils if I can.'

'Or play some more concerts.'

'That's a daydream. It was pure fluke I got the one I did.'

'Well I hope you've told your pupils about it. Told the school when it's going out and all that. That should net you a few more classical babes dead keen to learn the cello.'

'Actually, I haven't told them yet. It's still holiday time. Anyway, it was only the bass line in a few Mozart trios. Any real cellist would know it wasn't all that much to write home about.'

'You know,' said Sean, 'considering how many faults and vices you do have, your modesty always comes as something of a surprise.' Adam gave him a mock punch, just as the car drew up outside the garage in St-Christophe.

Fifteen minutes later, his confidence bolstered by the supporting presence of Marc, Sylvain and Sean, who had all nodded gravely as they peered under the bonnet and examined the tyres, and had waved to him as he took it out onto the road for a short test drive, Adam was filling in insurance documents and other papers and signing the biggest cheque he had written in his life.

So it was that they were able to arrive at La Carelle the following day, with a degree of château-cred, in a reasonably decent vehicle and not have to march up through the fields like the Von Trapp Family, or step absurdly – given that they were visiting a next-door neighbour – out of a taxi.

Château La Carelle was a medium to large house, built of the same honey-coloured stone as Adam's mill house but in the classical Bordeaux style, with two windows equally spaced on either side of the front door and a symmetrical five on the floor above. Having been ushered in through the front door, though, they were ushered straight out again through French windows at the side onto a broad paved terrace above the lawn, where a table was laid with half a dozen glasses. Adam noticed with some pride that, looking down the slope of vines, he could see the picturesque roofs of his own property a little way below. But he also noticed that you couldn't actually see into his garden because of the line of trees that grew along the stream. Remembering the naked antics that the garden had witnessed the summer before, he was reassured – and not only for the past but for the future.

'Young' M. Ducros *(Apelle-moi Robert)* was about forty, tall and big-boned, and just about making it into the category of ruggedly handsome, provided you put the accent on the ruggedly. His wife was a handsome, shapely woman of same age. They had two boys, aged seven and nine, who were briefly introduced and who then returned to playing war games in the garden.

'I'm sorry my father isn't here to welcome you himself,' Robert apologised. 'He's had to go into Castillon.'

Blue Sky Adam

Adam did know old M. Ducros by sight: a hunched figure in a cloth cap at the wheel of an Alpha Romeo that had seen better days. He didn't have the air of a man who inhabited a gold mine, yet with nine hectares of the precious St-Emilion vignoble under his feet, his family could look forward to a fairly untroubled financial future.

Then came the ritual that Adam was getting pleasantly familiar with: the pouring of a glass for everyone from a bottle of one of the château's better recent vintages. In this case it was far from recent – it was a bottle of the great vintage of '85. All sipped slowly and carefully, and looked grave, out of respect for its seniority. It did taste truly magnificent, though Adam had previously sampled the '85 from his own, or rather Philippe's, Château L'Orangerie, and from Stéphane's Château Beaurepaire and found that they compared not unfavourably, despite being 'mere' Côtes de Castillon.

'Not that your own wine isn't in pretty much the same class,' Robert Ducros said generously to Adam when everyone had made appropriate appreciative comments. 'Philippe tells me you're doing all the cultivation yourself now.'

'I need to,' said Adam. 'With that place to keep up. But I get a lot of help from Stéphane from Beaurepaire.' Stéphane who would be arriving at the weekend, with his father's plough and tractor. He had yet to bring this detail to Sylvain's attention, though he hadn't tried to hide the fact that they exchanged phone-calls from day to day.

'Ah yes, Stéphane. It's nice to have good friends.' Robert looked round at Sean, whom his wife had engaged in conversation in effortless English, and at Sylvain, who had descended from the terrace and was helping the two boys to construct a wigwam out of bamboo canes and fertiliser sacks under the big cedar

195

tree on the lawn. 'No doubt we'll be seeing you with a girlfriend before too long.'

Adam hated it when small-talky conversations took that turn. What were you supposed to answer? 'Ha.' He managed a non-committal laugh. 'Believe that when you see it.' Which might have meant anything. He changed the subject. 'I suppose you knew Georges Pincemin, who died, and his son Alain.'

'Georges, yes. He was a friendly enough neighbour. Though he lived in a different world from the rest of us. Jetting around Europe playing a spinet or whatever. As for Alain, that was a bit strange. He'd have been about my age, but there was no sign of him around the place when I was a kid. Georges lived there alone after his parents died – not that I really remember them. We never heard of Georges getting married or anything. My parents never saw him with a woman. Then ten years later this fellow Alain turns up, aged about seventeen, I suppose. Wasn't around very often, though, and didn't mix with us when he was. Maybe there was a divorce, or maybe his mother wasn't someone Georges had wanted his parents to know about.' Robert looked away for a moment with a frown. 'Maybe. But we were never told and we never asked. Then we learned Alain had died. About fifteen years ago.' A thought struck him. 'Did you know Alain? Maybe I shouldn't be talking about him like this – if he's part of your family.'

Adam reassured his host that there was no family connection – that Georges Pincemin had simply been a professor at his music college.

'Bit of a stroke of luck, that, *hein?* Him leaving you the Moulin de Pressac.'

'Yes,' Adam agreed. 'A big stroke of luck. Like being born in a St-Emilion Grand-Cru Château.' And, luckily, Robert laughed. But then it was his turn to change the subject.

'You know,' he said, 'here's a strange story. A funny thing happened to me the other day.' And Adam felt a strange shiver run down his spine, as if a part of him already knew that he wasn't going to enjoy this one.

'At the market in Libourne, there's this bloke comes up to me. Big hulking chap, and I recognise him. It's someone I haven't seen since I was at school with him. And do you know what he does? He throws his arms around me and gives me a bloody great hug as if I was a woman. Kisses me and all.' Robert gave a mirthless laugh. 'Couldn't shake him off. I remember him as a great rugby player, captain of the St-Magne team, and he was still a lot stronger than me even now.' He must have been built like a real barn door, Adam thought, since Robert himself had the kind of muscular frame that you wouldn't want to make an enemy of. 'And do you know what? He'd turned into one of those bloody ... what do you call 'em?'

'Pédale?' suggested Adam, tight-lipped. *'Gai, dans le sens anglo-saxon?* '

'Yes. Well, he said how well he remembered me and how he wanted us to go and have a beer together. But I got out of it and said – some other time. You see, the thing is...' he looked almost beseechingly at Adam as if he needed his support in this, 'I can't be doing with people like that. They make my stomach go in a knot. I know we're supposed to be broad-minded and all that these days. Live and let live. Well that's fine, but let them keep themselves to themselves and not come near me.'

As it happened, people like Robert made Adam's stomach also 'go in a knot'. He could feel the prick of sweat on his forehead and under his arms, while his mouth had gone so dry that he didn't know if he would even be able to speak – once he'd decided what to say. This was the moment, of course, for standing up, throwing the precious glass of Château La Carelle '85 in Robert's face and saying, 'That's me and my friends you're talking about,' calling to the others, 'Come on, we're getting out of here,' and driving off never to return.

In a pub in London, or a Paris club, it would have been easy. But here? Adam glanced round him: at Sean getting on so well with nice Madame Ducros – Sean, still apparently believing he wasn't gay, so why should Adam embroil him in a row that didn't strictly concern him? There was Sylvain, innocently playing with Robert's two young boys. Perhaps Robert would want to make a big deal out of that if he knew more about Sylvain. At the foot of the vineyard slope the roofs of Adam's new home glowed in the evening sun. Robert was his neighbour. They would need to work together often: agreeing on the chopping of trees, the clearing of streams, the maintenance of fencing. Adam at last understood the full implications of Stéphane's predicament: growing up gay on the *vignoble*, his future tied up in the immoveable *terroir* of a wine estate. It had been easy for him, Adam, to tell Sté to come out to his parents; he had judged him unfairly. And Stéphane's 'château-cred', his status on the *vignoble*, was also at stake in this moment. It wasn't up to Adam to out him to his neighbours in a moment of justifiable rage. He wished Michael could be there to help him right now. He'd have known what to say. But Michael wasn't there.

'Takes all sorts to make a world,' Adam heard himself say, none too cheerfully. He only just managed to get the words out.

'Well, that's very broad-minded of you,' Robert said, as if he had just come out himself – which in a sense he had. 'And I suppose it's a question of the generations. You youngsters are more – well, more exposed to different things than we were twenty years ago. Tell me, do any of you three play rugby? Your friend Sean looks a particularly well-built fellow.'

With twin feelings of relief at this deliverance by change of subject, and shame at his failure to stand up and be counted, Adam allowed the conversation to continue on its course.

Adam told the other two about his conversation with Robert as soon as they were safely in the car and on their short journey home. Neither Sylvain nor Sean was critical of him for not boldly confronting Robert with the truth about his sexual orientation. Sylvain said, 'If you were brave about everything and in every situation you'd soon end up dead.' And Adam understood for the first time that that was the savage reality behind the genteel expression, *Discretion is the better part of valour*. Sylvain knew what it was like to grow up homosexual in a rural community, and Adam knew how brutal and wounding his eventual exposure had been.

'But what I don't understand,' Adam said, 'is why someone should come out with a story like that when they hardly know us. Did he make an assumption about the three of us that was, maybe, unconscious? Had he made the same unconscious assumption about Georges and Alain, and did my raising the subject trigger something? Because it was as if he was simply bursting to get this story out. As if he had some great compulsion to talk about it that he couldn't control.'

'Some people are like that,' said Sean. 'They have a problem with it at a deep level. I don't mean they're all latent gays,' he added quickly, 'or that Robert Ducros is. But some people do still seem to have a problem with it. Like those people who're always telling you they can spot a poofter a mile off – and they never can.'

This was not the moment to pick holes in Sean's analysis of his own sexuality. Adam was simply grateful for his presence and support. In fact it was great to have these two particular people with him right now: the great love of his past together with his lover of now, and the two of them getting on so well together. How this dynamic would change when Stéphane arrived at the weekend with the tractor and plough was impossible to foresee, and Adam was not without his apprehensions about it. But for now Adam could not have felt luckier in life and love if he had wanted to. The likes of René and Robert Ducros could go and boil their heads for all he cared.

SIXTEEN

The following day Philippe Martinville arrived with a
vanload of wine: eighteen dozen bottles of Château
L'Orangerie 2006, recently bottled, after eighteen
months in oak casks. Adam had forgotten that this
personal entitlement would be due to him each year, and
had begun looking a little uneasily at his wine cellar.
Even conscientious replenishment from the supermarket
and the Maison de Vin in St-Emilion were failing to
keep pace with the inroads he and his friends had been
making into his stock since he had first got his hands on
it. Now the damage could be more than repaired:
eighteen dozen, he calculated with a bit of an effort,
came to a healthy-sounding two hundred and sixteen
bottles.

Stéphane's father, who had been bottling his own 2006
Château Beaurepaire, also delivered a dozen bottles by
way of a gift, and Adam was delighted to be able to
return the compliment by presenting him with a dozen
bottles of his own. Marc told Adam that he had nearly
finished his first vineyard ploughing of the season and
that, if he liked, Stéphane could bring the tractor over on
Saturday morning. 'Let you have a go at ploughing.
Show you how it's done.'

'I'll be here,' interrupted Sylvain with some emphasis.
'I can show him. I know how to plough a vineyard.'

Adam caught the sulky annoyance in his tone but Marc
took no message from it. 'Well that's good,' he said.
'And you might like to know that Françoise'll be here at
the weekend.' He still had no problem imagining that his
daughter would automatically be a magnet for all three
boys.

Françoise. Oh dear. Adam hadn't seen or phoned her
since their dinner together a month ago. Neither had she
phoned him. But sooner or later their paths would

inevitably cross and it was going to be, at least momentarily, embarrassing for both of them. 'I tell you what,' he said boldly. 'Why don't you all come to lunch on Sunday?' Sylvain and Sean both looked startled but Adam reckoned that the invitation, if taken up, would kill a number of birds with a single stone and, anyway, Stéphane would be there to help with the cooking.

'You didn't tell us Stéphane was coming for the weekend,' Sylvain said when Marc had accepted the lunch invitation with pleasure and departed. 'Like, is he staying here, at the Moulin?'

'He usually does. But if it's a problem for you...' Adam spoke directly to Sylvain. He dared not look at Sean's face.

'I guess not,' Sylvain conceded. 'There's enough bedrooms.'

Exactly. Adam would not now be sleeping with Stéphane ever again. And Sean had advised him that in that case it would be better not to make that speech he'd been practising: the one that began, *I know you love me*, and ended, *...take me or leave me*. Better. Safer. Easier. They'd start with a clean slate.

Now Sean came to the rescue again. 'Have you ever cooked for seven, mostly French, people before?' he asked Adam.

'You should do something traditionally English,' suggested Sylvain. Perhaps he was glad not to have to go on talking about Stéphane. 'What do English people eat?'

'Mostly the same as you,' said Adam. 'What do you think you've been eating when Sean or I cook for us?'

'I've sometimes wondered.'

Somehow you never threw mock punches at Sylvain or groaned aloud when he made his occasional jokes; there was an air of solemnity that still clung to him even then.

Sean suggested roast beef and Yorkshire pudding, but none of them had actually made a Yorkshire pudding before. Adam remembered that they sometimes didn't work out: it was either because the oven was too hot or not hot enough but he couldn't remember which. So it might be a bit risky, and roast beef without the Yorkshire pudding would simply be French: no doubt everyone would agree that Stéphane's mother did it better.

'At the monastery,' volunteered Sylvain, 'they sometimes do a dish with chicken and potatoes on a Sunday. An Italian monk brought the recipe. You put chicken joints and potato slices with olive oil, white wine, parsley, grated Parmesan and salt and pepper. Oh, and a bay leaf. Mix it all together and leave it an hour. Then bake it in the oven for an hour and a half, till the potatoes on top go crunchy. It's dead simple. You could say it was an English speciality.'

'Actually,' said Sean thoughtfully, 'it is a sort of Lancashire hotpot, only with different ingredients.'

'If it's got different ingredients then it's not a Lancashire hotpot, you stupid sausage,' said Adam. ('*Quel andouille*,' he translated the sausage for Sylvain's benefit.) 'You might as well say it's a *cassoulet de Carcassonne* with different ingredients.'

But whatever they chose to call it, it seemed fairly foolproof. Adam thanked Sylvain for the idea, and it was agreed that it should form Sunday's main course, with a green salad to follow. Sean said he'd seen smoked trout in the supermarket, which would do for a starter, and Adam said that Stéphane could be relied upon to do a *tarte tatin* for afters. He'd seen him do one several times and they'd always turned out of the pan in one piece.

Any worries that Adam might have had that the blossoming friendship between Sean and Sylvain could turn into something else – that they might start to find each other sexually attractive to an inconvenient degree – had proved unfounded. Sylvain was too preoccupied with Adam to get over-excited about Sean's undeniable physical charms while Sean had always had a take it or leave it attitude to sex anyway, as far as Adam was aware. Perhaps he was less libidinous than Adam, or at any rate had a different kind of libido. If you imagined that everyone else's sexuality was exactly like your own, Adam was beginning to realise, you were only making the same mistake as those imagination-deprived heterosexuals, such as Robert Ducros, who thought that anyone who didn't do exactly the same in bed as they themselves did must have something wrong with them.

Besides, there were two other things about Sean that had to be taken into consideration. One was that he belonged in the league of the extremely beautiful and, like most others who belong there, was inoculated to some degree against beauty in others. The other was that he was the perfect gentleman and would not have abused Adam's hospitality by trying to get off with Sylvain any more than he would have done by trying to restart old intimacies with Adam behind his new lover's back. And if all that should have made Adam feel even more guilty about his behaviour with Stéphane during Sylvain's absence three weeks ago, well, yes, it did.

It was that time in mid-spring when all of nature is at its most beautiful, the trees in fresh robes of translucent green, the copses acting like magnets for arriving migrant birds – cuckoos and hoopoes, blackcaps and turtle doves; the garden an oasis of birdsong. Adam had never seen his watermill in early May before, had never seen his garden so closely approximating to an image of the Garden of Eden. He wondered, as the three of them set off that Friday end-of-afternoon to go and collect Stéphane from the station, how long it would remain so after the four of them got back.

Stéphane embraced Sean like the old friend he was, but was careful not to be any more demonstrative than that when he hugged Adam in his turn, in front of Sylvain. Then Stéphane and Sylvain shook hands formally, warily, looking searchingly into each other's eyes as they did so.

Adam at once decided that they should head up the hill for a beer at the Spanish bar. For folk with a car rather than an underpowered motorbike the Rue Guadet presented no challenge. Besides, Adam was still feeling bruised after his encounter with Rober Ducros and was in the mood for putting on a public show of strength. Stéphane was dubious about the idea but the other two, who had been to the Spanish bar with Adam the previous day, had no misgivings. René had not been propping up the bar yesterday, and Sylvain seemed to have dismissed his previous encounter with him from his memory, while Sean had never met him at all. But he was there today, as they all saw when Adam pushed open the door, and as Adam had secretly rather hoped he would be. He felt vindicated when René paid them no attention at all, beyond an initial neutral glance in their direction. That was exactly what Adam had guessed would happen.

Later, arriving back at the Grand Moulin, Stéphane took Adam aside and said, 'Are you sure you want me around? I can always go back to my parents to sleep the night. You've got quite a full house already.'

'I want you to stay,' Adam said. 'But it's up to you. If you don't feel comfortable with the idea of sleeping here when I'm with Sylvain…'

Stéphane looked at him quizzically. 'I don't think I have a problem with that. But it's you I'm wondering about. Are you quite sure you're not just using me to make a point with?'

'I promise you I'm not,' said Adam in tones of the utmost conviction, while somewhere deep inside him a chasm opened and he felt giddy at the realisation that Stéphane might have got it right.

But the evening passed off harmoniously and there was no awkwardness when it came to bedtime. And nobody was so crass as to suggest that Sean and Stéphane might like to try getting it together.

Early the next morning Stéphane set off on his motorbike for Château Beaurepaire and returned, not much more slowly, at the wheel of a vineyard tractor which trailed a plough behind it and had iron counterweights bolted onto its front to prevent the front wheels rearing up, mustang fashion, every time he hit a pothole. There were different ways of ploughing vineyards. Most people on the *vignobles* of Côtes de Castillon and St-Emilion ploughed between alternate rows of vines in alternate years, leaving the other alleys undisturbed except to mow the grass that grew there. This allowed half of each vine's roots to grow undisturbed for a full year while manure and fertiliser could be incorporated into the soil on the ploughed-up side.

Sylvain lost no time in telling Stéphane that they used a different system in Burgundy, but Adam firmly insisted that his own plot should be ploughed in the standard local manner. He didn't want to give Philippe Martinville the smallest excuse to refuse to buy his crop when autumn came.

'You've got it on far too deep a setting,' Sylvain admonished Stéphane when he had completed his first demonstration furrow between the rows. 'You hack the roots about far too much and it's no good for them.'

'*Couilles*,' answered Stéphane. 'You're talking bollocks. This method of ploughing prunes the roots. That's what it's supposed to do. That's why we leave the alternate alleys unploughed till next year.'

'In Burgundy we set the blades like this.' Sylvain made a grab for the hydraulic lever and would have changed the depth setting himself had not Stéphane quickly thwarted him by switching off the engine. Then he jumped down from his perch and faced Sylvain, eyeball to eyeball, on the ground.

'In Burgundy you work for a band of monks who grow grapes in their back garden. I'm using the setting that my father uses at Château Beaurepaire – which happens to be the same one they recommend us at the Institute of Viticulture and Oenology where I'm a student and you are not.'

'Then you should know that the monks of Cîteaux were responsible for modern red wine making in the first place – at Clos-de-Vougeot. Grapes in their back garden, *leche mon cul.*'

All this was said in very rapid French: so rapid that even Adam could only just follow the words; he had never heard either Stéphane or Sylvain sound so angry. Sean couldn't catch the words at all but the undercurrent of jealousy was as clear as anything. Sean caught Adam's eye and did something expressive and rather French with his shoulders and eyebrows. Adam waded up over the loose, turned-up soil. 'Cool it,' he said. 'It doesn't matter who's the expert. It matters who brought the tractor. And since that was Stéphane I think we should go on doing it his way.' He squeezed the back of Sylvain's neck. 'Please, Sylvain. If we upset Stéphane so much that he takes his tractor away we're not going to be able to get another one. We can't turn over three acres with a garden fork.' And he was surprised as well as relieved when Sylvain turned to the younger man and said, albeit with a bit of a growl,

'Sorry, Stéphane. We'll do it your way.'

With four of them taking turns to drive the tractor, they got it all done in one day. Stéphane and Sylvain manoeuvred the equipment with a confidence born of some years' experience; Adam and Sean were slower and more cautious and had to be shown how to manage the tractor and steer straight between the rows. Brushing the heavy machinery up against the vine-stocks would not leave many survivors. In their anxiety Adam and Sean both gave themselves cricks in the neck from trying to look ahead to steer, and behind to see if the plough was still avoiding the vines in the tractor's wake. Stéphane told them cheerfully that, since the process – together with that of mowing the alternate alleys – would need to be repeated two or three times over the summer, they – or at least Adam – would have plenty of opportunity to make practice perfect. And, although the rivalry between Sylvain and Stéphane did come back up to the surface from time to time ('Look, *connard*, you've missed a bit.' 'You nearly took the post and wire with you on that last turn.'), by the end of the afternoon sufficient harmony prevailed as to allow Adam's suggestion that they all drive into Castillon for a few drinks and a pizza supper to be met with unanimous agreement.

Harmony lasted well into the evening. But it was the pizza that, surprisingly, proved the next source of discord. Or rather, Stéphane's choice of pizza: *Quattro Staggioni*. Stéphane started hacking away at it much as the others were doing with theirs, indiscriminately going in from different points around the rim, but Sylvain, after watching him intently for a minute or so, felt compelled to protest. 'That's not the way you're supposed to do it. *Tu sais?*'

Stéphane stopped chiselling. 'What do you mean?'

'I mean you're supposed to go round clockwise in the order of the four seasons. Doesn't matter where you start – winter, spring, whatever – but get the order right.'

'Are you winding me up?' Stéphane asked cautiously, remembering their arguments over the plough.

'No. It's just that that's the way it's supposed to be eaten. An Italian told me.'

'OK,' said Stéphane. 'So that's very interesting, but we're not in Italy. I'll eat my pizza the way I want to. You can eat yours how you like.'

'It's probably bad luck or something,' Sylvain muttered.

'Oh don't be so ... ridiculous.' It had been on the tip of Stéphane's tongue to say, childish.

Then Sean spoke up, doing his best to make his stilted French equal to the situation. 'My friends. What is this? Let us eat without ... without ... er ... disputation. Sylvain, if you can be a friend to one of Adam's friends – to me, then you can be a friend to another one, Stéphane, who is my friend too.'

'Yes, but you don't sleep with Adam,' said Sylvain matter-of-factly. 'Not now.'

'Stéphane doesn't sleep with Adam,' Sean said, with the heavy emphasis of someone unsure if he is correctly conjugating a foreign verb. 'Not now. Not since you came back into his life. It's the same thing with Stéphane as it is with me. All in the past. So let him eat his pizza the way he wants to. For me.' He treated Sylvain to one of his trademark smiles and, after a moment's indecision on Sylvain's part, was rewarded with quite a nice one in return.

Sylvain turned to Stéphane. *'Bon appétit,'* he said. 'Forget what I said. And it probably isn't bad luck at all.'

Stéphane looked unsure how to react for a moment. Then he said what was probably the only sensible thing in the circumstances. 'Thanks. It's OK.'

Later that evening, Sean took advantage of a few seconds in which he was alone with Adam in the kitchen to tell him, 'I told half a lie for you earlier. You'd better bloody deserve it.'

In the morning Stéphane took the tractor home, dumped the plough and came back with a mower attachment instead. Mowing was a piece of cake compared to ploughing, he said, and gave a thirty-second demonstration. Adam and Sylvain could cut the grass in the unploughed alleys between the vines on Monday and then return the tractor to Château Beaurepaire.

'We could do the lawns too while we're at it,' suggested Sylvain, but Adam vetoed the idea: he foresaw problems with M. Leduc, who took a fierce pride in his grass-cutting – as well as appreciating the cash-in-hand that he received for doing it.

Then it was time to prepare for lunch. Sylvain and Stéphane now seemed able to share a kitchen without bickering – to the relief of the other two. Stéphane's parents and sister arrived just after midday – together, to Adam's further relief. Meeting Françoise again among a group of family and friends was less awkward than if they'd been alone together. Stéphane's mother seemed both astonished and delighted that four young men – two of them actually English – could bake a dish of chicken and potatoes. And Stéphane managed to turn out his *tarte tatin* without it breaking.

There was one small surprise. Françoise announced that she was going to England in about a month's time to do a short training course. She wasn't looking forward to it, she said. She was worried that her English wouldn't be up to the demands the course would make on it. Adam and Sean assured her she'd have no problem, and whereabouts in England was she going? Newcastle, she said. It seemed a very long way north and she knew nobody there.

'But you do,' said Sean. 'Newcastle is where I am.' They swapped phone numbers and wrote down dates and places, and Sean promised gallantly that he would look after Françoise for as long as she remained a guest in his university city.

Sunday lunch lasted most of the afternoon and no-one did very much afterwards. After Stéphane's parents had finally taken their leave and the washing-up had been thrown rather haphazardly into the dishwasher, the young people spent the early evening lazing about on the lawn, talking about nothing special, and the boys drinking more than Françoise thought was appropriate. 'You English don't know when to stop,' she told them, adding with feigned affrontedness that her brother and Sylvain seemed to be catching English habits. Sylvain was taking it upon himself to help Sean improve his French and was lying on the grass beside him, making him repeat whole strings of phrases whose usefulness was questionable, and teaching him the names of all the weeds that grew in the lawn and that could be reached without standing up. At least he was insisting on an exactly correct pronunciation. Adam would not have dared to correct Sean's French in this way, but Sean seemed to be enjoying his lesson, laughing as he tried to contort the muscles of his lips and vocal apparatus into unfamiliar positions. Then the phone rang inside the house. '*Merde*,' said Adam. 'Who's that on a Sunday?' Grumbling, he got up and loped indoors barefoot to answer it.

It was Gary. He had Adam's mobile number but never used it. He didn't seem to believe in mobiles. 'News for you,' he said. 'You'd better make sure you're sitting down and, if you've got a glass in your hand, don't drop it. But it's good news at least, not bad.'

'I'll brace myself,' said Adam. 'What is it this time, a date at the Albert Hall?'

'That's not as funny as you might think. Nor as wide of the mark. Nathalie's agent's lining up a series of concerts for her: to do the Brahms Double at some pretty good venues around France over the next year or so. She wants to know if you'd like to be the cellist.'

Adam had left his glass outside on the lawn. He dropped the phone instead.

'Are you still there?' Gary was enquiring when Adam had recovered it.

'Yes. I dropped the phone. Are you joking this time?'

'No, I'm serious. Nathalie's been saying for some time that she'd like to do the piece but that all the cellists she knows are either grumpy old men or else young women who're more glamorous than she is. She's attracted by the idea of having a nice young male partner. And don't worry – she only means a partner in music.'

'But she doesn't know if I'm any good,' Adam objected. 'She's only heard me do a few notes in the bass of some trios. Even I don't know if I'm good enough for this.'

'Come on, Adam. It's what you've been trained for. It's what all the people you were at college with have been trained for but that most of them will never have the chance to do. Now you've been offered it. And by the way, *I'm* quite sure you can do it. You mentioned to her that you'd already done the Brahms Double at the Academy.'

'Yes I did. I was showing off to her, I suppose. But it was a student performance, with a student orchestra and a student audience.'

'We're all students,' said Gary patiently. 'All of us musicians, we're students for life. But it's by playing public concerts that some of us get the chance to become better students. You've been lucky. Nathalie liked the suit you were wearing. She said afterwards how nice she thought you'd look in white tie and tails.'

'Jesus, Gary, you did that on purpose.'

'Did what on purpose?'

'Set me up to go to the recording studio all dressed up – *tiré à quatre épingles.* Just so that she'd take notice.'

'Nonsense. You brought your suit halfway across France, I didn't tell you to do that. It seemed a shame to let your effort go to waste. Anyway, would it matter if I had? Look, just say yes now and we can talk details later.'

Adam heard himself say yes in a whisper. He put the phone down and moved from the cool darkness of the hallway out into the bright garden as if in a dream. The faces of the others looked up at him expectantly from their various positions on the lawn where they seemed oddly fixed and motionless, like pinned butterflies.

'You look very white,' said Stéphane. 'Are you sure you're OK?'

'I've got some concerts,' Adam said quietly. 'Big dates coming up over the next year. The Brahms double concerto with Nathalie Pujols.'

There was a second's silence while this sank in, then Sylvain climbed to his feet, took hold of Adam's two hands and danced him across the grass like a bear, upsetting a half empty wine bottle, to the protests of the others, and stopping only when they knocked over a garden table.

Later in the evening Adam spoke again to Gary. The big concerts would be in the following year. It was hoped the dates would include the Grand Théâtre in Bordeaux and find a big-scale climax at the Salle Pleyel in Paris. Meanwhile there were some tryouts in smaller venues at various local festivals during this summer. Beginning in the cathedral at St-Malo in Brittany some time at the end of June. Then at Angers. Even those venues didn't sound all that small to Adam. 'Surely those summer programmes must have been fixed months ago,' Adam queried. 'How has she…?'

'Dates fixed, but programmes can be altered I suppose,' said Gary. 'I think she'd been booked to do the Brahms violin concerto, but it's become a very old warhorse for her and she wanted a change. Anyway, don't look a gift-warhorse in the mouth.'

'It'll take me every minute of every day to learn the thing. And we're just getting busy, what with paying guests arriving next weekend and there's ploughing to be done…'

'You're not to go driving tractors when you've got concerts to play,' Gary said sternly. 'Be serious. You could break your thumbs going over rough ground.' Adam knew that tractor steering wheels were notorious breakers of thumbs if held incorrectly; he was surprised that Gary knew that too. 'But you've got Sylvain with you now, haven't you?'

'Yes.'

'Well, that's what he's for. So bloody well make sure you keep him now. No fooling around with Stéphane. …Or with Sean,' he added after a short pause.

Stéphane would normally have set off by train for Bordeaux alone, early on Monday morning, and Adam would have taken Sean to catch his train back to England later in the day. But all plans were now changed by Adam's urgent need to buy music and so all four of them piled into Adam's Peugeot and headed into Bordeaux together. They drove first to Stéphane's college, and dropped him off. As he got out of the car he said, 'See you at the weekend?'

The question in his voice tugged at Adam's heart. He turned to Sylvain. 'He can come and stay over again, can't he? We'll need all the help we can get around the place. With PGs coming and stuff.'

Blue Sky Adam

Sylvain was amused and surprised by the intensity in Adam's own voice, but still more was he reassured by being deferred to in this way: finding himself the arbiter of who should or should not be a guest in Adam's house. 'Yes of course,' he said. And Stéphane, relieved, kissed all three of them goodbye – a bit clumsily because they were all still inside the car while he had already stepped out of it – and went into college.

Back in the city centre they made for the Place Gambetta where Adam needed to buy his music. He wanted not only the solo parts of the concerto but also the full orchestral score and, in addition, the piano 'reduction' – of the orchestral score, so that he could re-familiarise himself with it at the piano. And then perhaps, if he asked nicely, Gary would be prepared to run through it with him once or twice in Paris. The Virgin Megastore had the solo parts and the piano reduction in stock, but not the full score. They promised to order that from Paris and to phone him as soon as it arrived.

It was Sylvain's first visit to Bordeaux so they spent the middle part of the day doing a quick tour of the city's sights, including, of course the classical, colonnaded Grand Théâtre, which Adam approached with a mixture of awe and incredulity, hardly able to imagine that next year he might be sitting on its stage with Nathalie Pujols and some famous orchestra, playing Brahms to an audience of two thousand. Dressed today in old shorts and T-shirt, and thinking that back at home was a tractor-mower waiting for him to cut the grass between his vines, he touched the honey-coloured stones of the portico as if to convince himself that they and he really existed in the same world. Or maybe just for luck.

Sean took his own opportunity to wish Adam luck just before his TGV arrived in Bordeaux station later that afternoon – taking advantage of Sylvain's briefly disappearing to answer a call of nature. Though he approached his fond farewell by a rather roundabout route. 'I suppose it would be convenient for everyone if Stéphane and I had got it together over the last few days and then gone on and fallen in love with each other. But I'm afraid that was never on the cards. I don't think I'm quite Stéphane's type. I've started to get to know myself a bit better over the last few days.'

'What do you mean by that?' Adam asked. Sean did not usually do enigmatic.

Sean laughed. 'Did I say that? I'm not sure I know what I meant. Forget it, anyway. Seriously, though, I wish you all the luck in the world. You're going to need it. I can see all three of you – Stéphane, Sylvain and yourself – getting really badly hurt, and no-one coming out the winner.'

'Oh thanks, Sean. I really needed to hear that. And I thought today was going quite nicely.' An announcement echoed around the glass vaults of the station to the effect that the TGV for Lille and Brussels would shortly be approaching the platform.

'Sorry, but I worry about you. You wouldn't expect me to care so little about you that I didn't do that. For one thing, how do you know Sylvain's going to be up to doing all this work that you're assuming he will while you're being a concert performer in training? I remember how hard you used to practise when you were a student. You didn't have an estate to run back then.'

'He buckled down to doing all that pruning with me back in March,' Adam said defensively. 'He's not the same as he was all those years ago. His head's been sorted out. Shrinks, doctors, the right medicines. Learning about responsibility from his time at Cîteaux. He's completely OK now.'

'I hope so,' said Sean.

'I tell you what worries me more than that,' said Adam, trying not to let the conversation be dragged back to his relationship with Stéphane. 'It's the society we're going to have to live in. We've learned what Robert Ducros thinks about having gay neighbours – even before he's quite realised he's got any. Supposing it turns out that Philippe Martinville thinks the same way, or Sté's parents – who haven't yet twigged they've got a gay son? We've been telling ourselves that they're enlightened and tolerant people, or at least that they aren't interested in what *the folks that live at the mill* get up to in bed. But maybe they're not.' Adam was silent for a second. 'Maybe they're just monumentally unseeing and ignorant, and may wake up one day to a massive surprise. Life's going to turn into one hell of a bitch if that's the case.'

Sylvain came striding back along the platform just as the TGV shimmered into view, cautiously rounding a tight curve in the distance behind him. 'I've bought you something to take back to England,' he said to Sean. It was a jar of local, Landais honey. 'If you don't like it you can use it to wash your hair with.'

Sean took the gift with a laugh of surprise, called Sylvain his comedian friend, and then hugged and kissed him. Adam was surprised to see that Sean had tears in his eyes. Then he turned back to Adam. 'Make sure you tell those dumbos at the lycée what a famous musician they've got as a cello teacher. Or if you don't, I will.'

The train was now rolling slowly alongside them, purring like a huge grey cat. It came, infinitely gradually, to a stop. Sean and his baggage disappeared inside it. La Gare de St-Jean, Bordeaux. Railway stations. Adam was collecting them.

SEVENTEEN

They had sex together as soon as they got home from the station, as soon as they crossed the threshold, just as they had done the first time they'd crossed it together, standing in the hall, letting their semen rain among their dropped shorts and on the flagstones. Adam thought it was as good a housewarming as any. Perhaps in time it would become a regular rite of homecoming.

As soon as they'd pulled their shorts back up Sylvain announced that it was his turn to cook and went off to the kitchen in search of the ingredients for mushroom omelettes while Adam made for the living room to start looking through his music at the piano.

So began a new phase in Adam's life, and in Sylvain's too. Living with someone. Not simply sharing a flat and having sex together as Adam had done in the past, but sharing a home and a life with the person you loved most. Being married, to all intents and purposes. It was both scary and wonderful. Scary because the territory was so uncharted. During the first period of their relationship, six years ago on the Plateau de Langres, they'd scarcely been indoors together. They had only been into a shop together for the first time within the last few weeks. Now there was a whole domestic routine to sort out. The last few days hardly counted. That had been a sort of holiday, shared with other people, with Sean and Stéphane. And when Sylvain had been at the Grand Moulin in March, helping Adam with the pruning, that time had been in the nature of a honeymoon – a magical period, but one that belonged in parenthesis, profoundly separate from the ongoing prose of everyday life. Back then, if Adam had loaded the washing machine or if Sylvain had astonished Adam by ironing a couple of his shirts rather well, or if Adam had had a bash at cooking *bavettes aux échalotes*, then it had been in the nature of a love game, a Marie Antoinette fantasy of home making. But now all these things had to be done for real as part of the flow of life.

And if that life had been busy before the recording session in Paris it was going to be vastly more so now. The first paying guests were due to arrive at the Petit Moulin in a few days' time; the gardens as well as the vines needed constant attention; the new school term had started and Adam's cello teaching would recommence. Except for that last, all those responsibilities would have to fall largely upon the shoulders of Sylvain. For Adam had the monumental tasks ahead of him of committing to memory the whole structure of a Brahms concerto, and drilling his fingers as rigorously as any band of soldiers who would need to perform their task unflinchingly under the stress of combat. Adam was a competent musician, but he was not in the league of Stravinsky and others who had famously memorised all of Bach's forty-eight preludes and fugues by the age of twelve, nor of Rostropovitch who once played thirty cello concertos in the space of a few days. He would need all the time at his disposal between now and the end of June if he were going to be equal to the challenge thrown down to him by Nathalie Pujols and Johannes Brahms.

Adam still didn't know how Sylvain would cope with full-time work. Sean's misgivings had sown doubts in his mind. Sylvain hadn't been able to do a full day's work when he first knew him. Yet the monks of Cîteaux had seen fit to put him in a position of trust. And there was the evidence of his pruning work back in March.

As the days passed, though Adam hardly dared to believe it, Sylvain began to prove his doubts, and Sean's, unfounded. He took control of the day to day running of the estate, liaising with M. Leduc and giving polite instructions to him about the various garden and maintenance jobs that needed to be done. He dealt with telephone enquiries from prospective paying guests and the agencies that handled the lettings – except the ones from people who only spoke English, and then he had to call for Adam, which was fair enough. Then, once Adam had shown him the way a couple of times, he learnt to deal with emails. If his spelling on the replies was a bit original, well, provided the message got through, who cared? Adam was surprised by this at first but then realised that he shouldn't have been. Why should Sylvain not be able to learn new skills just because he had been brought up on a small holding and had had fragile mental health when young? He was stronger and more stable now in every respect and anyway, he was still not quite twenty-nine.

By contrast with Sylvain's rapid mastery of new tasks and technologies Adam felt his progress with the Brahms concerto to be slow and laborious. But, bar by bar, movement by movement, he worked at it, assimilating and internalising it slowly but conclusively like a very small caterpillar munching its way through an enormous leaf. Time and again he would refer back to the old copy of the score that he had used as a student, and which he'd had his parents send over, to see what fingerings, what bowings, he had used back then and whether he would want to use the same ones now or whether, with experience and hindsight, he could find a better way.

Sylvain took to asking him to play for a few minutes each evening what he had been working on in the daytime. Then, to Adam's surprise, he would find things to say about it. Quite simple things at first. 'You played that bit faster yesterday,' or, 'You're making that louder.' But as the days passed his comments became bolder, more curious. 'Why do you make that bit sound so angry?' or, 'That's nice – like bees round a fruit tree.' Adam explained how the piece was a dialogue, with the violin and the orchestra also contributing to the conversation, and how each voice had to react to what the other ones were saying. He went over to the piano to strum a bit of the orchestral part to illustrate the point, and was then astonished to hear Sylvain unselfconsciously sing the phrase from the cello part that was due to come next. So he had not just been listening politely, but learning the piece along with Adam, internalising it just as Adam was. The impact that this made on Adam could hardly have been greater. The additional discovery that Sylvain was the possessor of a clear, tuneful baritone was just a bonus.

For the first time ever, Adam went off to the lycée in Castillon neither in an old banger of a Renault that had to be hidden away and parked in a side street, nor on an underpowered motorbike, but in a proper car: one that he was not ashamed to park in the row of spaces reserved for teachers. Another novelty was that on entering the staff room he was greeted not with blank stares or curt nods but with an array of smiles that seemed warm and – was he imagining this? – almost admiring. The head of music came up to him, beaming. 'Congratulations, I think, Adam. Your recording at Radio France Musique. We're all going to listen when it's broadcast next month. And to record it too.' She looked at him with a mock frown. 'You've been far too modest. Hiding your talents like that.'

Adam was startled. 'How did you know about it?'

'Your agent phoned from England and told me. He said you'd be too shy to mention it yourself.'

'My agent?' Adam wondered if he had heard correctly.

'A very charming man, Sean Oliver. He asked me if I'd mind his speaking English because his French wasn't very good. Most English speakers don't do that, they just launch into it, but he spoke very carefully and clearly. Very considerate.'

How lovely Sean was, Adam thought. Being considerate was only a part of it.

Stéphane was back on Friday and on his best behaviour, like any guest who is visiting an ex plus new partner, meekly accepting his place, as he had done the previous weekend, in one of the spare bedrooms.

'Why does he always piss out of his window first thing in the morning?' Sylvain asked Adam, and Adam explained the reason.

'What about tomorrow, when we have paying guests?'

Adam told him Stéphane's usual alternatives: the shower or the bathtub. 'Or else he could have a room with a different aspect – where the window isn't visible from the garden of the Petit Moulin.'

Sylvain chuckled and sleepily nudged his own wet-nosed morning erection between Adam's thighs.

It was Sylvain's idea to put vases of flowers, fresh-picked from the gardens, in all the rooms of the Petit Moulin. It was an inspired idea, and today especially so because it was this day of all days that, as the three young men awaited the arrival of the first PGs with some degree of nervousness, the drains chose to back up and overflow. It didn't happen inside either half of the mill house, which was something, but it did happen in the middle of the parking area into which the visitors' car would turn as soon as it arrived at the bottom of the drive. It happened when the washing machine emptied itself on the last rinse of its cycle with the week's washing, creating a dark grey lake about three inches deep and fifteen feet across.

There was no time to do anything about it before the guests arrived, so that when they did round the corner that brought them in sight of the mill they were greeted by the sight of three young men clad in T-shirts and shorts, their feet planted wide apart and their heads held high, standing in a straight line the way cabin crew stand when they want you not to walk beneath an aircraft's wing as you make your way to the rear steps: a human *cordon sanitaire* between the new arrivals and the evil-smelling swamp behind them. Keeping his gaze higher than the horizon and thereby almost forcing the new arrivals to do the same, Adam marched them purposefully in through the door of the Petit Moulin and showed them – a French couple and their teenage daughter – their accommodation. He warned them that the supermarket was better visited early rather than late and was delighted when they took the hint and drove off again towards St-Magne almost at once.

Adam fetched drain rods from one of the outhouses and the three of them removed shoes and T-shirts and got down to the business of clearing the flood: locating the manhole cover beneath the murky waters, then rodding the pipes in all directions, competing as they got into the spirit of the enterprise to assemble the greatest number of rods and drive them hardest and furthest into the blocked channels. At last – and the breakthrough came with a satisfying suddenness and an eruption of foul black bubbles – the effluent began to slide away into the underground septic tank.

'Now look at us,' said Stéphane. Without comment, Sylvain stripped off his shorts, the only garment that he still had on, and walked and waded into the lower millpond. Adam and Stéphane followed his example, jumping naked into the lively water. They cleaned themselves and swam and splashed each other, and they were still in the water, still naked and laughing and splashing, when the paying guests returned from the supermarket half an hour later.

The gardens were filling with colour. Roses were flowering in places where nobody had ever thought there might be a rose. Mock-orange blossom crowded the trees and its scent rolled across the lawns, overlaying the fragrance of fresh-mown grass. At the bottom end of the garden, where the two millstreams reunited below the mill, the lawn narrowed to a point like the bow of a ship, surrounded by water. Here the three young men sat for a while, still naked after their swim. They sat close together but without speaking, each lost in private thoughts as they gazed ahead. From here they saw at first a solid curtain of green that hung over, and was reflected in, the water. But when they looked longer, as if into a hologram, the vista acquired depth upon depth and they found themselves in a tunnel of green – of dangling willow and branching lime, of white thickets of moon daisies and red blurs of ragged robin glimpsed along the banks, and all the time the water glided limpidly away, with only an occasional ripple to shiver and spangle in the sun where a stone or half-submerged stick broke the smooth surface.

'Your friend Stéphane looks cute without his clothes on,' said Sylvain to Adam when they were getting into bed that night. He said it as matter-of-factly as if remarking on the colour of the walls.

'Sté said the same about you,' Adam replied. He smiled. He hadn't intended to tell Sylvain that, but what the hell.

Two weeks later the PGs departed, expressing their total satisfaction with their accommodation and welcome. 'Like the Garden of Eden,' the wife remarked. 'And the nude bathing sequence only served to enhance the impression. We'll tell all our friends.' There was a hectic scramble after they had gone: to clean and tidy, put out new sheets and towels, refill the vases with fresh flowers before the second wave of guests arrived midafternoon. Again there were three of them to do it; Stéphane's weekend visits had become accepted by Sylvain as routine, which was more than Adam had previously dared hope. A thought began to take shape in his mind – he dated it from the occasion of the naked bathe: it writhed and shimmered temptingly among the undergrowth. He banished it.

The foliage was darkening on the trees and summer was setting in. Sylvain bought Bordeaux mixture for the vines, which were now sporting leaves and tendrils two feet long; then Stéphane attached a spraying machine to the back of one of his father's tractors and within two days they had turned the whole vineyard a garish but necessary blue. Adam took to doing some of his cello practice out of doors, in a partly shaded area of the garden. He was not alone. In addition to the blackbirds, thrushes, warblers and wrens, a new voice was making itself heard high among the trees. It belonged to a golden oriole, a bird that Adam had never come across before. The size of a large blackbird and its colour a brilliant lemon yellow, it was nevertheless almost impossible to spot, being perfectly camouflaged high up among the never-still poplar leaves, where it lurked in dappled sun and shade. But it signalled its presence by a repeated liquid four-note call – like a flautist endlessly practising a tricky ornament in a baroque air. Years ago Adam had tried to coax nightingales to sing along with his cello, playing outdoors after dusk in imitation of Beatrice Harrison. But golden orioles, he thought, were just as good. If there were serpents too, he would ignore them.

Towards the end of May Gary telephoned to ask if Adam would like to do a run-through of the piece with Gary playing the orchestral part on the piano – the offer that Adam had been hoping he would make. He remembered with gratitude how Gary had made him practise concertos with him at his Paris flat in the Eurostar days. Adam could come up to Paris. Or… They made a date for the following week.

Just two days before Gary was due to arrive, a card came for Sylvain in the post. No post had ever arrived for him before. It had a picture of a brimming champagne glass on it and said – in French, of course – *Happy Birthday, son. With all our love. Maman.* Underneath, another hand had scrawled – and Adam could see Sylvain's mother holding the card under her husband's nose until he signed – *Papa.* Two twenty-euro notes fell out of the card. There was also a short letter from Sylvain's mother which Sylvain read but did not share with Adam.

The pathos of the single card, placed by Sylvain carefully in the centre of the mantelpiece, was greater than if there had been none. Adam was both upset and infuriated. 'Why didn't you tell anyone? You make me look uncaring and stupid.'

'I just didn't think about it,' was Sylvain's curt reply.

Sylvain of the solitary birthday card, the boy whom nobody loved except his mother – and Adam. He told him so, with a vehemence that was stronger even than usual. Adam did at least have a circle of friends, even if they were mostly in England – there would be perhaps a dozen birthday cards for him when his own birthday came round. But Sylvain had come into Adam's life with no network of relationships trailing behind him. In an odd way that was something Adam, as an only child, identified with. Sylvain had been the loner in a vast family. Perhaps that was why Sylvain had been so ready to be friends with Sean; the reason his initial hostility towards Stéphane had melted so quickly. He needed friends more than rivals.

'We have to do something,' Adam said. 'No work today. But no card, no present from the man who loves you... I've got to make that up to you, like now.'

They drove up the Dordogne, saw the low hills that framed the river valley rise into cliffs, and the river writhe and thrash between them like a snake in a shoebox. They made love on the forested cliffs of Trémolat under the dark pine trees, above the sunlit view. And late in the afternoon they came to Sarlat, the sleeping beauty of the oak and walnut woods, its fairytale houses with their turrets and clambering limestone roofs a-slumber in the sun.

Returning, they stopped for dinner by the riverside at Ste-Foy where Adam had been taken by Françoise. The waiters remembered Adam and greeted him with smiles. No reference was made to overheard conversations of the previous time. They sat on the terrace in the fading day, watching the swallows and swifts that skimmed the current relinquish the air, as dusk thickened, to the evening's bats.

'Marry me?' asked Adam with a laugh.

'I already have,' said Sylvain. 'Long ago.' They left it at that.

Gary arrived by train at Libourne. Having been assured by Adam that he now had a relatively new and reliable car, he decided not to bring his own on the very long drive down. 'At least it does look like a car,' he sniffed when he first saw Adam's new transport, 'even if it is silver-grey. Most of the new ones have come to look so much like mobile phones, and mobile phones to look so much like cars that it's only by their size that you can tell them apart.'

Gary was a perfect house guest. He didn't seem to feel at all awkward at being the older visitor *chez* two younger men who were very obviously still in the first flush of love. Still, Adam thought, age differences didn't seem to matter so much as you got older. Gary joined in with the cooking, the shopping and the washing-up; they would drive out to a bar in the evening. Adam had become aware recently that people like René had stopped taking notice of him and his friends. Now when they went into the Spanish bar one night and René and his mates were there they didn't even look up as they walked in. Adam was fine with that.

In the daytime Sylvain was busy trimming and tidying among the vines, pulling off unwanted growth, replacing the odd rotten fence post. He even managed to carry out an effective repair on the washing machine in the Petit Moulin without having to call in an expensive repair man. Meanwhile Adam and Gary worked together on the Brahms. Gary played the orchestral part on the piano, adding in the solo violin line with a spare finger whenever he had one and humming it when he didn't. In the evening – before heading out to a bar, not after – they played the fruit of their labours through to Sylvain – though as much for Adam's benefit as for his.

'How well did you know Georges Pincemin?' Adam asked Gary one evening.

'Your benefactor. Not all that well. I actually think I had more to do with him after you first met him than I ever did before.'

'But you seemed... When I first met Georges, you seemed like very old friends.'

'Yes and no. Remember he was twenty years older than me. We hadn't been students together and we were neither competitors nor colleagues on the concert circuit. He was a harpsichordist and I play the piano. Different worlds in some ways. But of course we knew of each other. We both had high profiles in the small world of concert giving. We'd seen each other's photos on CD covers and in the press. I'd read reviews of his work, seen interviews with him, and no doubt he'd read about me too. We first met, I suppose, at some reception or other, perhaps a CD launch or after a concert, and we met a few more times after that. Then years went by without our seeing anything of each other and then suddenly there he was in the restaurant that night – and so, by happy chance, were you.'

'How did you know he was gay?' Adam asked.

Sylvain came in. 'How does anyone?'

'Quite so,' said Gary. 'Maybe I heard it from somebody. Maybe not.'

'Did you know Alain? His... Some people say he was Georges's son, others...'

'That they were lovers? They got it right. I met Alain once. I might not have remembered that, or the fact that his name was Alain, except that in the last few years – and I mean after Georges met you – he talked about him once or twice. He told me how he'd felt obliged to pass him off as his son when he was down in... down here. There was a very big age difference. He didn't think his neighbours were ready for ... well, you know what I mean. But Alain died of Aids. It was in the late eighties, a time when lots of people did die of Aids. Then when Georges met you... But you already know what I'm going to say. He was struck by your resemblance to Alain. At a physical level I suppose I can see what he meant. Beyond that, well, I don't know. I only met Alain once.'

'Was he ... a musician?' Adam asked.

'Didn't I say that?' Gary smiled. 'He was, of course. He was a cellist.'

EIGHTEEN

Adam found it hard to remember when it had started. It was some time before Gary's visit, but it was such an insignificant thing in itself that he had no cause to remember the date or the day. A flat tyre, that was all it was, discovered after leaving the supermarket at St-Magne. And Sylvain had been with him to share the minor hassles that go with changing a wheel on a new vehicle: finding the spare, locating jack points, working an unfamiliar wheel spanner. It was two days before Adam remembered to take the punctured wheel to the garage at St-Christophe-des-Bardes and a couple more before he remembered to go and collect it. When they handed it back to him and said they had found no trace of a puncture – they'd pumped it up and it had stayed at pressure for two days – even then his suspicions were not aroused. He had too many other things to think about.

When it happened the second time, a few days after Gary returned to Paris, and this time in St-Emilion, the penny still didn't drop until he was halfway through changing the wheel; he was on his own this time. 'Kids,' he said to himself. 'Pains in the *cul*.' And it must be becoming some sort of a local craze if they were doing it both here and at St-Magne, eight miles away. He looked along the row of cars parked under the long wall of the Clos Fourtet estate. Nobody else's vehicle had been tampered with as far as he could tell, nor was there any sign of kids playing nearby or watchfully lurking. This time he didn't bother to present the flat tyre to the garage for inspection but simply filled the wheel at the air line and threw it into the boot. It was Sylvain who rang Adam's alarm bell. 'Are you sure it's kids?' he said.

'What do you mean?'

Blue Sky Adam

'Just that,' said Sylvain and would not be drawn further. But Adam noticed that his lover held him more tightly than usual as they sat together before bedtime, listening for the sound of the last train down the valley to echo in the chimney.

Perhaps it was a week later, perhaps not so long, when things moved up a notch. This time it was in the centre of Castillon. Adam had parked near the river while he went to look for some ironmongery that Sylvain needed for a repair job. And meanwhile someone had come along and slashed two of his tyres, on the same side of the car, using something efficient like a Stanley knife. The job had been done thoroughly and must have cost whoever did it a certain amount of time and effort. The two tyres would need replacing, not just repair. Adam had to walk nearly a mile to the nearest garage to arrange for the car to be picked up by a breakdown truck and taken back to have new tyres fitted. That did not come cheap and it also used up half a day that Adam should have spent practising Brahms. He had to telephone a concerned Sylvain back at home to let him know where he was.

Home again himself, Adam telephoned Stéphane's father. It was good to have parents sometimes, even if they weren't your own. Perhaps especially if they weren't. What did Marc think he should do? Go to the police? Marc had never heard of such a thing happening in this peaceful neighbourhood. People round here all knew each other and looked out for each other. Of course there were rows sometimes between neighbours and between families, even petty feuds, but … tyres getting slashed? He was deeply sympathetic. He seemed to take it as a personal affront that one of his fellow Castillonais had let the side down by such unwelcoming behaviour towards a newcomer. He hated having to say so but, yes, he did think Adam should go to the police.

'To the local gendarmes in St-Genès,' Adam asked, 'or the police in Castillon?'

'Start local,' Marc advised, 'and take it from there.' Meanwhile he would make a few discreet enquiries of his own: see if anybody knew anything. Had Adam made any enemies since he'd arrived? Marc thought it hardly likely but he had to ask.

No, Adam said. Not that he was aware of. He thought of René in the bar at St-Emilion and his semi-hostile behaviour a couple of months before, then of Robert Ducros, his self-confessedly homophobic neighbour, but he wasn't going to mention them to Marc. Anyway, Robert Ducros, family man and heir to a *Grand Cru Classé* St-Emilion château, was hardly likely to go slashing tyres in a public street however homophobic he might be, and as for René, Adam couldn't imagine him having the energy or the will.

Adam telephoned the local gendarmerie. He was not surprised to be told that, since the vandalism had taken place in the town of Castillon, it should be reported to the police there. But Adam persevered, mentioned Stéphane's father by name, and added that his tyres had also been interfered with at St-Magne and in St-Emilion. It didn't seem to be an exclusively Castillonais problem. His persistence was rewarded. He was promised a visit later that day.

The gendarme who arrived was a dour-faced man with iron-grey hair and manner. He took a statement from Adam, which he wrote down with a rather abstracted air; to Adam's surprise he appeared more interested in the presence in the household of Sylvain. He seemed to find it odd that a British expatriate (of whom there were many on his patch) should have a young Frenchman staying – or living – with him. And which was it, he wanted to know: staying or living? Adam looked the gendarme straight in the eye and said, 'He lives here. He lives with me.' It was a small step, he thought, towards redeeming the pusillanimity he had shown when confronted with the attitudes of Robert Ducros.

'I see,' said the gendarme in a neutral voice. Then he too asked Adam if he had made any enemies.

'No,' Adam said. 'There are one or two people who don't seem to like me very much – which is probably only natural since I'm a foreigner – but there's nobody I can imagine doing that.'

The gendarme wanted to know more. Names? Adam said vaguely, one or two people who hung out in the bars of St-Emilion but he didn't know any names. He tried not to catch Sylvain's eye as he said this. He didn't really suspect René and he couldn't imagine that giving his name to the police would do anything except make matters worse.

The gendarme put his notebook away to signal that the interview was at an end and stood up. He couldn't be very optimistic about catching anyone. It was difficult to solve a crime against a person when there was no apparent motive. But if the tyre slashing or anything like it happened again, Adam was to let him know. Then he turned to Sylvain and asked him what he did for a living.

Adam didn't give Sylvain time to answer. 'We plan to live off the income from the vines, plus what we get from letting the other half of the building, the Petit Moulin. And I'm a musician. I make some money from that. We shan't starve.'

'I see,' said the gendarme. 'Everything shared. Well I hope you've got all that in writing somewhere.' He turned to Sylvain again. 'Otherwise you'd be in a bit of a hole if your friend ever met with a more serious accident.'

The Mozart trios were broadcast later that week, during the early evening. Adam and Sylvain listened together in awed silence. *(Me doing that? Really me?)* *(C'est vraiment lui. Mon copain, mon p'tit-loup.)* Sylvain put his arm around his lover and squeezed him till he could hardly breathe. 'I'm proud of you,' he said when the music was finished. Adam still felt dazed. He thought Gary and Nathalie had played beautifully. But himself? He couldn't judge. Perhaps it was enough to know that he had played. In any case you could never play beautifully enough for Mozart. It hardly mattered that your own contribution appeared to vanish against his blazing light. He thought of the golden oriole, fluting its mordents and cadences high in the poplars, almost invisible as the sun shimmered and sparkled among the leaves. In a few weeks he would be playing a concerto with Nathalie Pujols in cathedrals and concert halls. He still found it hard to believe. But he'd found the Mozart radio recording difficult to believe before he'd done it.

The head of music at the Castillon lycée phoned a few minutes later, full of congratulations, and then the principal piano teacher phoned also – he was someone Adam had hardly spoken to, which made it the more surprising. Would Adam like to do some chamber music and sonatas with him and other local musicians some time? Adam might have been sniffy and said no, that he was far too busy practising the Brahms. But in the euphoria of this particular moment he said yes. Why not, after all?

At school a few days later he found that a great thaw had taken place. The music department had recorded the broadcast and played part of it to the teachers in the *salle des profs* that morning. Some of the more musical pupils had actually listened to it on the radio and a number of youngsters who barely knew Adam by sight came up to him with mumbled, half-embarrassed congratulations. The head of music told him he could probably expect at least another four cello students when the new school year began in September. Adam left the school with an unprecedented spring in his step. Until he reached his car and saw that all four tyres had been let down. The head of science, full of apology and commiseration, found an electric pump and helped him to blow them up.

The school made its own internal enquiries. They had a visit from the police too, whom Adam contacted a second time. The gendarme revisited Adam. He had nothing to report, he said; he hoped Adam wasn't too surprised. But was he aware, he asked him, that his companion Sylvain had a police record? That six years ago he had been involved in something that might have been an abduction, but wasn't quite, as the boy in question, the victim, had already turned sixteen? Apprehended, he had produced a shotgun...

'I know,' said Adam 'I was there. I was the boy of sixteen.'

'I see,' said the gendarme. 'Then no doubt you need no advice from me. And no doubt you don't need reminding that there was a court order, still in effect, forbidding the young man ever to contact you again. Well, I don't think anyone's going to do anything about enforcing that, provided none of the parties decides to make any kind of complaint. But you may need to be more careful than other people when it comes to keeping your affairs in order.'

'What do you mean by that?' Adam said sharply.

'I meant your business affairs,' said the gendarme. 'No offence intended.' He might have smiled then, as he took his leave, but he didn't. Adam noticed that.

Stéphane had listened to Adam's broadcast and phoned in his congratulations. He would see Adam at the weekend. CD copies of the broadcast were sent off to Adam's parents and to Michael and Sean. Adam phoned Marc to tell him about the latest tyre-deflating episode –

he had been so helpful and supportive before – but was surprised to find him sounding rather distant and preoccupied. He agreed that Adam had done the right thing in alerting the police a second time, but Adam missed that tone of warm concern that he had displayed previously.

Stéphane arrived on Friday evening in good spirits. Some of his friends were going clubbing in Bordeaux the next night. Why didn't they all go along together? Sylvain had seen Bordeaux but only in the daytime; Adam was curious to know what he would make of Le Key-West or Le Grand Polux – and what their habitués would make of him. On the other hand, Adam was worried about his car but, as Stéphane said, if Adam's phantom tyre-slasher decided to tail them forty-five kilometres into Bordeaux city centre he would have to be not just paranoid but terminally short of better things to do. Sylvain thought it an odd thing for Stéphane to do: leave Bordeaux for a weekend in the country only to drive back to the city for a Saturday night in the middle of it. Adam told him to stop behaving like a reasonable adult, and he actually laughed and said he kept forgetting he was keeping company with a pair of kids.

Meanwhile Stéphane had had a phone call from his father, who wanted him to go and see him about something: he didn't know what. His motorbike was in one of the outhouses at the Moulin. He'd go on that – if no-one had slashed the tyres on it – and wouldn't be long. Adam said, take the car instead. And so he did.

But he was a long a time. Adam and Sylvain didn't notice at first. They were planning to have a barbecue that evening, the first of the year, and what with getting it going and collecting up vine prunings to throw on the embers to give the authentic regional flavour to the smoke, they quite lost track of time. Only when they'd opened a couple of cans of beer and then found that they'd emptied them did they notice that Stéphane had been gone an hour and a half. But then, a few minutes later, they saw the car come bouncing down the track in the usual cloud of white dust. It pulled up by the millstream bridge and disgorged Stéphane.

But it was a different looking, different walking Stéphane from the one who had driven off. He was white-faced and tense and came towards them as if picking his way among tall nettles. Adam and Sylvain had been ready to tease him about his lateness; instead they walked towards him and asked him what was up.

'I think I've just lost my inheritance,' he said. 'I think that's what's up.'

'*Merde,* Sté,' said Adam. 'What happened?' And Sylvain, without saying anything, pulled the ring off the can of Amstel he was carrying and handed it to Stéphane, who took a swig before replying.

'I wasn't prepared or anything,' Stéphane said. 'My father said he needed to talk to me. That he'd been talking to people round about – trying to get some idea who might be behind this tyre-slashing business – and he'd discovered there was talk going around about the Moulin – about the 'boy' who owned it and all his friends. Including me. He was very angry. More angry than I'd seen him since the time I... Well, anyway, he demanded to know what my relationship was with you, Adam.' Stéphane had spoken strongly up till now, looking Adam and Sylvain alternately straight in the eye. But now his eyes dipped down and his voice faltered. 'I said you were my lover.'

'My God.'

'He did his pieces. He wanted to know what your relationship was with Sylvain here – and with Sean of course. It was at the front of his mind that Françoise was in Newcastle and seeing Sean there. He didn't mention Michael. Perhaps he'd forgotten about him.'

'Perhaps that's one good thing at least,' said Adam. 'Then what?'

'He said if that was the case I'd better leave – with the car I'd borrowed from my ... from you ... and go and join you. Not to go home till I'd come to my senses. And even then he'd think hard before letting me back.'

Sylvain spoke for the first time. 'And your mother?'

'He wouldn't let her get a word in edgeways. She was crying by the end. She wanted to...'

'I know,' said Sylvain. 'I know she did.' In one movement he took the beer can out of Stéphane's hand and held it in his own, behind Stéphane's back, as he embraced him. Then he talked to him softly, like someone comforting a child, using phrases Adam had never heard before: little words plucked from somewhere deep in their memories of their French childhoods – something they shared but which Adam, with a sudden pang of want, realised he did not and never could. Of course Sylvain did know, he must know – just as Adam did – about Stéphane and his mother. Sylvain had been returned to his family eventually, after prison, after the psychiatric unit, after his first stay at Cîteaux Abbey. It had been a long time after Adam had been sent back to confront his own parents, but Sylvain must have had to go through it just the same. It was something they had never talked about, Adam realised now, something that he and Sylvain had not yet shared. Maybe, even after six years it was still too raw to touch on; maybe they would never be able to, long as they might live.

'I'm sorry, Sylvain.' Stéphane was still managing not to cry. 'I'm sorry I said what I said about being Adam's lover. When I'm not now. And you are.'

'*C'est pas grave, P'tit-Loup,*' Sylvain said, moving his head just far enough away from Stéphane's to be able to look into his eyes. 'It's us three now. The three of us against the world.'

There was silence for quite a time after that. The three of them stood together, holding on to each other as closely as they could, given that two of them were also clasping beer cans. Then Stéphane said, a bit diffidently, 'Wasn't there some talk of a barbecue?'

It is a myth that people who have been deeply upset by some major event in their lives – accident, bereavement or other crisis – are not interested, in the immediate aftermath, in such mundane things as eating or drinking. All three of them had excellent appetites for their outdoor meal when they eventually got round to cooking it. They drank – perhaps rather excessively – and no-one went to bed. They sat talking, out on the night-smelling lawn, and only when it was beginning to get light did they fall asleep, one by one, close together and almost touching, under the dimming stars.

NINETEEN

The first concert, the one in the cathedral at St-Malo, was only ten days away. For Stéphane the next two weeks would be occupied with end of course exams; after that his college days and his tenancy of the room in the student flat in Bordeaux would both be at an end. With no job to go to and no parental home to fall back on it looked as if he would have to become a fixture, at least for the short term, at the Grand Moulin. Fortunately Sylvain raised no objection when Adam tentatively brought the subject up; the rejection of Stéphane by his father had put the seal on Sylvain's growing acceptance of the younger man.

Adam had told Stéphane time and again that he would have to confront his parents with his homosexuality at some point. Now that he had at last done this it would hardly have been reasonable for Adam to complain about the outcome – or the timing. Still... Adam remembered wryly that he had once worried that if he made too clean a break with Stéphane he would lose all the backup from Château Beaurepaire – the ploughs and tractor-mowers, the support from his father Marc – that came along with the alliance. Now he had lost all those things anyway, and instead had gained Stéphane as a dowerless house guest, very much dependent on him. As a household they would now be three, trying to scratch a living where there wasn't even a living for one. If he chose to think of it in those terms. But of course he didn't choose to. He cared too much for Stéphane for that. Instead he had to think of the new situation as simply another twist in the surprising path that life was laying out for him.

The first weekend of their ... *ménage à trois* didn't seem quite the right expression so they took pains to avoid it, even though they were naturally speaking the whole time in French together ... the first weekend of their *new arrangement* passed without incident. There was no sign of a change of heart on Marc's part. Midweek, Adam went to Paris for a rehearsal with Nathalie at Gary's flat, with Gary once again generously agreeing to play the orchestral part – this time on his own Steinway. Sylvain drove Adam to Libourne to catch the early train and would meet him there when he returned late that evening. In the meantime he had strict instructions not to leave the car out of his sight long enough, if he went shopping, for anyone to slash the tyres.

'You have a very natural way with Brahms,' Nathalie said encouragingly. They were taking a break from rehearsal and drinking coffee on the pavement outside the Bar Florence. 'What do you know of him – of Brahms the man, I mean?'

'I know that he wasn't born with a beard and a beer belly. Though that's how we always think of him – because of the photographs of him after he became famous, I suppose. He was considered quite a pretty boy in his teens. Slim, blond, long-haired. He used to play the piano in a brothel in Hamburg. Some of the sailors used to sit him on their laps and, how shall I say...?'

'Fondled him, I think would do,' said Gary. 'Not to put too fine a point on it.'

'Men were very drawn to him anyway,' Adam went on. 'Joseph Joachim wanted the two of them to go to bed together. But it was never reciprocated. Brahms was exclusively attracted to women. One in particular. Clara Wieck – who was married to Robert Schumann.'

'Well done,' said Nathalie, her carefully plucked eyebrows slightly raised. 'You've done your homework. It was the classic love triangle. Brahms couldn't, or rather wouldn't, run off with the woman he loved, because she was married to his best friend.'

'That doesn't stop most people these days,' said Gary.

'I don't expect it stopped most people back then,' returned Nathalie. 'But in the case of Brahms and the Schumanns it did. Causing no end of heartache.'

'Which left its footprints all over Brahms' music,' said Adam. 'We're the lucky ones. We get the emotional highs when we listen to Brahms or play the music; we feel the pain but without getting hurt ourselves.' Adam was beginning to think of himself as something of an expert in the field of triangular relationships but was not going to say this to two people who were nearly twenty years older than he was. Adam was well aware of his very junior role in his musical partnership with Nathalie. When she made suggestions about the music and the way he played it he took them on board without argument. She was the one who had made her concert début in Paris at the age of fifteen, not he.

Gary also had some advice for him. 'Have you ever played in a cathedral before?'

'No, of course not.'

'Only asking. But a church maybe?'

Yes, Adam remembered, he had done that. Once when he was part of a youth orchestra while at school, then once or twice while he was at the Academy.

'Well then, you probably have some idea of how beautiful the acoustic will make your tone sound when you first draw your bow across the strings. Don't let the beauty of the acoustic become a siren song. Don't be beguiled into playing too slowly. Especially in that first recitative. Keep your tempo up. Remember the conductor has to follow you, not you the conductor.' It gave Adam an even more frightening sense of his responsibility.

It was decided that Sylvain would accompany Adam to St-Malo. Stéphane could go to the next concert, which would be in Angers, at a weekend. Gary would be coming to that one, and also Nathalie's concert agent, wanting to hear Adam and needing to decide whether the large-scale concerts would go ahead in a year's time. A lot would be riding on that second date at Angers. As for the St-Malo concert, Adam thought it would be quite enough just to get through it. He was glad that Sylvain would be with him, glad that only Sylvain would be.

There was the question of Adam's concert wardrobe. Nathalie and the promoters had insisted on full tails and white tie. Adam foresaw his entire fee disappearing in expenses if he were to fork out for a whole new outfit. He decided he would try and hire one. If the big-scale concerts went ahead next year he could think again about investing in tails of his own. But in the end Stéphane provided the solution. He reminded Adam that last year they had discovered some old suits of Georges Pincemin's hanging forgotten in a bedroom cupboard – Stéphane was an inveterate poker-around in wardrobes – and now, checking again, he rediscovered what they had seen first time round: the full set of tailcoat, dress shirt and white tie. When Adam tried the things on they fitted almost perfectly, which was a big surprise: Adam remembered Georges being both shorter and considerably thicker round the waist than he was; so perhaps they dated back to when Georges was a younger man. But whatever the case, after he had taken them to the dry-cleaner's in Castillon they looked as good as new.

A thought struck Adam as the final preparations for the trip were being made. He asked Sylvain, 'Have you ever seen the sea?'

'No,' said Sylvain. 'Not yet.'

If, like Adam, you came from any part of the British Isles, where no place on the map stood at more than about seventy miles from the surrounding ocean, it was an experience that you took for granted. Yet for many people in other parts of the world it was by no means an ordinary thing. And Sylvain, born in the landlocked uplands of eastern France, was going to have his first sight of it in a few days' time.

Adam remembered passing through the ferry port of St-Malo en route for childhood holidays in France and Spain. He remembered an impressive fortress of a town jutting into the sea: Flaubert's *couronne de pierre, posée sur les flots*. Crown of stone, resting on the waves. Now they studied the map. It was five hundred kilometres away. The train would provide a restful but expensive way of getting there, but there remained the problem of where the car could be left without being vandalised. They decided to drive. It was motorway most of the way. They could share the driving and, provided they set off really early, would arrive in time for a bite of lunch before the run-through with the orchestra in the afternoon.

In the event the drive took much longer than they had allowed. There was heavy traffic, and Adam's nerves were playing him up so much that they had to take frequent stops for him to empty his bladder. Then they went wrong twice: first at a motorway junction near Nantes, and then again on the outskirts of Rennes. When they arrived at the walled citadel of St-Malo, driving up to the arched gateway through the forest of sailing boats' masts that filled the basins on both sides of the roadway, it was already two fifteen. The rehearsal of the concerto was due to start at two thirty. It wasn't difficult to find the cathedral of St. Vincent – you could see its spire pointing up above the town as you approached – but a parking space was another matter. Adam was not yet in the league of soloists who could keep an orchestra waiting with impunity. In the end Sylvain had to drop Adam off at the cathedral, with his music and cello, and go on alone to find the hotel that had been reserved for them, park, check in and deposit their overnight things.

'Mon Dieu,' said Nathalie, when Adam found her, 'you youngsters do like to cut things fine. This conductor doesn't mess about. He's almost finished taking them through the overture. We'll be on in about five minutes.'

And they were. There was the orchestra, filling the central space of the cathedral, the crossing, under the spire. There was he, Adam, taking his place, then coming in on cue. The sound of the full orchestra was reassuringly familiar, just as he remembered it from when he'd done the piece at college. He was grateful for Gary's advice not to fall in love with the sound he made in the building's rich acoustic, was careful not to dawdle.

Nathalie was right: this conductor did not mess about. They only stopped a couple of times. The whole process seemed to last just five minutes. Adam checked the time; they'd been working for an hour and a quarter. The conductor would now take the orchestra through the Beethoven symphony that formed the second half of the programme. But for the next three hours or so Adam was free. He was almost surprised to find Sylvain sitting waiting for him at the back of the cathedral, yet where else would he be?

'I've seen it,' Sylvain began as they walked out into the sunshine together.

'Seen what?'

'I've seen the sea.' His eyes were shining. 'Nothing prepares you for it. Not photos in books or in travel brochures, not the cinema, not the TV. I saw it from the ramparts, right next to the hotel. You go through a great arch then up some steps. First the smell of it, of the wind blowing off it, like the biggest, freshest tray of oysters you could imagine. Then there it is. *V'là.* So full, so full.

It made me feel my balls up in my throat. There's islands dotted around the bay, some with little castles on like in a fairytale, others like caps of green among the blue. And the movement of the water, different currents, different colours, racing between the islands like tight-packed herds of horses with wild white manes. Then in the distance...' He stopped. 'Sorry. You know all this. You've seen it a thousand times.'

'Go on.'

Sylvain continued, but in a more measured, less excited tone. 'Beyond the islands with their fringes of white spume, there's such a deep blue – like the sky, only like no sky I've ever seen – but pricked with lights, like there are diamonds in it. One will flash suddenly, bright as the sun. You turn your eye to it, it's gone. Another one sparks into life somewhere else, you try to catch that one too. You can't. And on and on. And do you know what came into my mind? That somewhere beyond those sparkles and all that blue is the place you come from, your green England. I screwed up my eyes and tried to see it. Of course I know it's too far from here. Even on a day like this. You told me you can only see it from the Pas de Calais. But I still tried to see it, just in my head.'

'You'll see it one day,' Adam said. 'Promise.' He thought that if even one person in his audience this evening could get half as much out of his performance as Sylvain had got from his first sight of the sea, he would have won.

Sylvain took Adam's cello from him. 'I'll carry that. And I'll show you the way to the hotel. Show you the sea on the way.'

'The hotel, of course. You found it OK? And it's all right?'

'It's fine. Only...'

'Only what?'

'They'd only booked you a single room – with one small bed in it. I didn't know that until I'd got the key and gone inside and seen for myself.'

'So did you ask them to change it for a double? We can simply pay the difference.'

'No I didn't.' Sylvain looked a bit sheepish. 'Things got into a bit of a tangle. They sort of assumed I was you as soon as I pointed to your name in the register. Then I couldn't think quickly enough to say there were two of us – and who you were supposed to be.'

'So you've checked in as me and if I'm to get into the hotel that's been booked for me I have to pretend to be someone else, is that it?'

'I suppose it is. I'm sorry. But I'd never checked into a hotel before. I didn't know quite what to expect.'

'They must have thought it odd, a bloke who looks and sounds as French as you do having a name like Adam Wheeler.'

'Maybe you could pretend to be my agent or something,' suggested Sylvain.

'That's going to look bloody funny when we set out for the concert later with me in white tie and you in jeans.'

'Well, maybe I could wear the tie and tails and then we could swap clothes in the vestry or wherever when we get there.'

'Are you crazy? Look, I haven't eaten since last night. Do you think we could...?' They stopped at a café, had crêpes and tea. Nothing too heavy before a concert. Especially no booze.

At the hotel Adam dealt masterfully with the double room question, offered to pay the extra and, when told that the only available double room had a double bed in it, managed to keep a straight face while he said, yes, OK, that would be no problem. But having got that far he felt unable to go on and undermine Sylvain by explaining that he, Adam, was the soloist and that Sylvain was ... was what? His agent? No French concert agent spoke with Sylvain's rustic Haute-Marne accent. It was marginally less improbable that he might be the cellist.

Their new room had not only a double bed, on which they spent most of the next two hours lying prostrate, exhausted – and, in Adam's case, apprehensive as well – it also boasted a fine view across the ramparts to the bay with its islands and other splendours, just as Sylvain had described. There might be worse places in which to suffer pre-performance nerves. At last it was time to dress and go, and then they really did follow Sylvain's idiotic plan, dressing in each other's clothes. Adam caught sight of Sylvain admiring his own reflection in the mirror, dressed in unaccustomed brief finery, when he thought Adam wasn't looking. He was glad then that he hadn't vetoed the idea, guessing that for Sylvain to see himself so attired had been an unconscious aspect of the strategy all along.

Nobody commented on their appearance as they left the hotel. Why should they? Nor did anybody take much notice of them as they walked back through the grid of narrow streets towards the cathedral. Except for just two people whom neither Adam nor Sylvain, fortunately, saw. But those two people, seeing them, nearly fainted with the shock. They were Hugh and Jennifer, Adam's parents, who had taken the ferry across from Portsmouth to give their son a surprise.

'What are you playing at now?' Nathalie greeted them when they had made their way in through the north door (*Entrée d'Artistes* for the evening). They explained why they were wearing each other's clothes. She laughed. 'At least you're in good time. But there's nowhere private to change.' She was already resplendent in blue chiffon. 'It's not like backstage at the Salle Pleyel, I'm afraid.'

The orchestra were filling, over-filling, the north transept which had been curtained off with heavy black drapes from the rest of the cathedral. It was like a nest of bumblebees, Adam thought. And with all the tuning up and trying out of difficult passages that was going on, it sounded like one as well. Fortunately everyone was far too preoccupied to give more than a passing glance to the two young men stripping and exchanging clothing in their midst. Fortunately because, as Adam noticed halfway through the process, Sylvain had not thought it worth the bother to put on any underwear.

Sylvain departed, after an encouraging handclasp and a kiss, to take his seat among the audience in the nave. The orchestra trooped out through the black drapes, the conductor followed, and a moment later Adam, left alone now with Nathalie, heard the opening notes of the first piece on the programme, an overture by Glück.

Nathalie only said a few words during this final period of waiting. 'Try and hear what is in the composer's heart. The rest will follow.' They were the ones that he would remember later.

The overture was finished in a flash, like the journey to school on your first day. The conductor reappeared through the drapes, perspiring lightly. Applause could be heard behind him. He gave Nathalie a peck on the cheek and Adam a tweak on the shoulder. Then the three of them filed out together around and in front of the seated orchestra. Adam tried not to look at the audience but he couldn't help seeing them: a mass of expectancy filling the nave and south transept. Where had they all come from? He had no idea how many they might be. He was not yet at the stage of being able to estimate the number of an audience, multiply by the average ticket price and calculate his percentage of the take during the first orchestral *tutti*. Some old pros could do that. Perhaps Nathalie did.

He sat. They checked their tuning. The conductor's baton went up, the orchestra dived in. To Adam's delight the sound was not remote and far away but near and familiar. He knew the piece. He'd played it with these sixty or so professional musicians only this afternoon and they had beamed their encouragement at him. He'd played the piece at college. He knew exactly what he was doing. All he had to do was... After only a few bars the moment came for his first entry, his unaccompanied recitative. Eye contact with the conductor. With Nathalie. He drew his first bow across the strings and knew it was going to go well.

Adam knew that old hands on the concerto circuit would leave the building at the end of the first half of the programme, directly after their own contribution, and be halfway down the motorway by the time the concert ended. But he was not an old hand. This was his big night and he wanted to be part of all of it. He checked with Sylvain first. Would he want to stay and sit through a Beethoven symphony? That was quite a different matter from sitting through a concerto in which your lover was making his début as a soloist. But Sylvain thought, why not? He'd been exposed to Mozart and Brahms in the past few months and had no problem with them. Beethoven was a name he had heard of; no doubt he'd be OK too. They agreed that they'd sit at the very back of the cathedral together, in the shadows, hopefully unseen by the rest of the audience.

In the interval there were nice words for Adam from everyone. Sylvain came bounding through the drapes like a boisterous puppy. *'C'était extra. T'étais super. Tout était...'* His words were extinguished by the hug he gave his lover. *'Mon Dieu*, but you're sweating,' he said next. ('Why are you surprised?' said Adam. 'It goes with the job.') Nathalie said she would be dining at the Porte

St-Pierre in a couple of hours' time along with the conductor. Adam and Sylvain were welcome to join them if they wanted. They said they would. The Porte St-Pierre was right opposite their hotel. Nathalie would go back to her own hotel to change first. She smiled when Adam explained that he wanted to stay for the Beethoven, thinking nostalgically of her younger days when sitting through a symphony after playing a concerto could still seem more of a treat than going home to a hot bath.

Adam and Sylvain left the cathedral by the north door and went round to the west front, hoping to slide in unnoticed on the tail end of the audience returning to their seats for the second half. Then Adam caught sight of two other people who appeared to be doing the same, though they also had the air of people who are waiting for someone and not being quite sure from which direction they will appear. They were Hugh and Jennifer.

'I'll catch you up,' Adam told Sylvain quickly. 'Go on in. There's some people I need to see.'

Sylvain obeyed and Adam walked up to his parents. They seemed unsure how to greet him. 'Good to see you, son,' Hugh said, and shook his hand. Jennifer pecked him on the cheek a bit nervously. 'You played very well.'

'We didn't tell you we were coming,' said Hugh. 'We thought a surprise might be more welcome. Only I'm afraid we've had a rather unwelcome surprise ourselves.'

'How do you mean?'

Jennifer answered. She grabbed her son's hand and held it tightly. 'You're with that Maury boy. Sylvain Maury. We saw you before the concert. Him dressed in your concert clothes. The two of you laughing together.'

'There's no law against laughing,' said Adam ill-advisedly.

'You make a mockery of everything,' said his mother. 'Of your aspiration to be taken seriously as a musician. Parading him through the town dressed in your concert things. A mockery of the court order. Of French law. He was never supposed to see you again. A mockery of our feelings – your father's and mine. A mockery of our love. And I'm saying nothing of the religion you were supposed to be brought up in.'

'Mother…' Adam squirmed. He was hot, still running with sweat after his solo. You can shower backstage in a concert hall but if you're playing in a cathedral you have to wait till later. 'Mummy…' A few stragglers were looking at him with curiosity, perhaps sympathy. The young soloist they had just applauded, still in his white tie and tails, being berated by a middle-aged woman. This was supposed to be his big moment, his big day, his début on the professional concert platform. And his mother had taken the trouble to cross the Channel and turn the whole experience to ashes. Making him feel like a child. Making him look like a child in front of … his public. 'The Beethoven. Don't you want to hear the Beethoven? I want to hear it.' (Sylvain wants to hear it, sitting beside me; we've never sat together at a concert… But he was wise enough not to say this.)

'Darling.' Hugh put a hand on his wife's arm. 'Let's go in. We can talk afterwards.'

'We're having dinner with Nathalie,' said Adam. 'And the conductor.' It came out a bit rudely. 'At the Porte St-Pierre. Join us.' He wasn't sure if he meant this to be conciliatory or challenging. Then he thought, what did it matter what he meant, whether one thing or another? Today wasn't supposed to be about all this.

'I don't think so,' Jennifer said. Adam could see how much it was hurting her to say it. 'But can we talk – for a few minutes – before you go off … to your dinner? And I mean talk with you, without young Monsieur Maury.'

Blue Sky Adam

The sound of expectant applause came billowing from inside the cathedral. 'Let's go in,' said Hugh.

'I'll be at the back,' Adam said quietly as they shuffled awkwardly in. 'I can't sit in the middle of the audience dressed like this.' He let them pass in front of him.

Sylvain put his hand on Adam's knee as soon as he sat down beside him, then forced it like a wedge between his rigidly compressed thighs. *'Désolé pour toi,'* he said. 'I'm sorry for you. I know who those people were.' Adam leaned his head on Sylvain's shoulder without a word.

Listening to a Beethoven symphony in between the first and second rounds of a row with your parents offers interesting insights into both the music and your feelings. Perhaps it should have been the Pastoral, or the gentle Symphony Number Eight. But it was the Eroica, celebrating Napoleon in his world-his-oyster, pre-Imperial days: heroism of the most uncompromising sort.

Sylvain wanted to be with Adam for round two but Adam insisted so vehemently that he deal with his parents alone that Sylvain eventually gave way. 'In ten minutes. At the hotel,' Adam told him. 'I promise. Then I take a shower. We go and eat. We drink till dawn, then we fuck for the rest of our lives. It's a deal?'

'It's a deal.' They shook hands and Sylvain left the cathedral ahead of the rush. They would be arriving back at the hotel in the opposite sets of clothes to the ones they had set out in. It couldn't matter less. How could they possibly have thought it would?

Adam waited for his parents at the west door. Hugh spoke first. 'I think we'll go back to our own hotel and get something to eat there. Sorry, old feller.'

Jennifer said, 'Don't think we're not proud of you – for tonight. For what you've achieved. For the way you played. And don't think we don't love you. But we did think – you let us believe – you were down in the Gironde on your own. You had a friend in Stéphane, of course, but... Please don't be too angry if we tell you we won't be able to visit you down there if you keep the Maury boy with you. I have to accept that you're gay, whether I like it or not – you're an adult after all. But you have to accept that I have my feelings too. Sylvain is further than I can go. You're welcome at home always and forever. Please don't stay away. But don't bring him. And if things go wrong for you in the Gironde, financially I mean, you can just come back and we won't say a word in blame. But you won't expect any help ... I'm sure you've realised that ... if you choose to stay with him.'

'I think I have to go now,' Adam said a bit unsteadily. 'I need to shower, then eat. I haven't eaten since last night.' The last was only a slight exaggeration.

'We'll be in touch,' said Hugh. He rolled his eyes in the direction of his wife. 'When things are calmer.'

Adam strode off, elegant but uncomfortable in his splendid clothes, resisting all urges to shake hands, offer a kiss, turn back and wave, or even cry.

Sylvain was standing over by the window when Adam came in to the bedroom. 'Don't try talking,' he said. 'Come and share this.' The midsummer sun was about to go down. It had manoeuvred itself cunningly behind one of the islands on which there was a ruined fort, and was shining through an archway in what was left of the fort's façade, like an orange torch. Adam thought of pictures he had seen of midsummer at Stonehenge. But the declining sun was not the only thing to have transformed the view. Sylvain might already have seen the sea six hours ago but nobody had told him about the mystery of the tides, or that St-Malo, with its forty-five-foot range, presented one of the extremest changes of landscape between high and low water anywhere in the world.

Blue Sky Adam

Now the sea had almost drained away. The islands were no longer flattish caps of green but pinnacles of rock emerging from a rocky basement sea floor. The remains of the great high tide were reduced to frothy rivulets that came and went between the islands. The sinking light was giving them silver, black and liquid gold. 'Fuck parents,' Sylvain said. 'Fuck the world. This should be good enough for us. Today's been the best day of my life. So far. Now shower.' Carefully he began to undo Adam's bow tie.

They were rather late for dinner. Nathalie and the conductor took that in their stride. They had spider crabs to begin with. You tackled those with a set of silver tools that reminded Adam of scaffolders' keys or the equipment that very serious pipe smokers carry with them. Sylvain handled them with instinctive mastery: dealing with advanced food runs deep in French genes. After that they had halibut in a seafood sauce. Nathalie said champagne was a must, and the conductor seconded that. It was Adam's baptism as professional soloist after all.

'Where is the third musketeer?' Nathalie asked, after the second glass. 'The blond blue-eyed one. Or am I being indiscreet?'

'He's in England,' volunteered Sylvain. 'With a young woman friend of ours.' Then, rather to Adam's surprise and very much to that of the others, he added, 'I don't think he's sure if he prefers girls or boys. Perhaps this'll be his chance to find out for sure.'

'I see,' said Nathalie, who hadn't thought she'd wanted to know so much but found she did.

After dinner and polite goodnights the two young men found themselves a bench seat on the ramparts. They were a couple among many couples, gay and straight, each pair intent on exploring that newly-discovered thing, their couple-self, and oblivious to every other pair.

Adam and Sylvain remained there for an hour or uncountable two, their trousers open only for each other in the midsummer half dark. Beyond the parapet the tide heaved and gave off comforting sounds and smells. Lighthouses on distant headlands played a rhythmic dance of flashes and at one point a ship appeared, a floating constellation of stars that threaded its way among the black islands and then disappeared around the corner of the ramparts on its way to the port behind the town.

Next day Sylvain didn't want to leave. They rebooked their hotel for a second night and telephoned the PGs at the Petit Moulin – a Dutch couple this time – to let them know their change of plan. Then they did all the familiar seaside things that Adam had done a hundred times but Sylvain never had before. They ate ice creams, lazing on the sand. They drank Breton cider and ate galettes. They swam in the sea. Sylvain was all for rushing in naked, insisting that the families with their kids would never notice, but Adam was sure they would. He walked to a beachside stall and bought two pairs of cheap and scratchy trunks. It turned out that they were made for children and in the end their extreme smallness and tightness caused nearly as much of a stir as Sylvain's original suggestion would have done. They took a boat trip across the bay, breathed the oystery, crabby smell of brine, felt the waves beneath them and looked back at St-Malo from the sea. *Couronne de pierre, posée sur les flots.*

And the day after, the long drive home. The tenants of the Petit Moulin issued from their front door as soon as they got out of the car. *'Oop-là,'* said Adam once he was near enough to see their faces. 'This looks like two people with a complaint to make.'

But it wasn't a complaint exactly. 'I thought I should warn you,' said the Dutchman. 'Someone's done something to your front door. It isn't very nice. Last night it wasn't there, this morning it was. My wife thought I should get rid of it, but I'm afraid I thought you'd better see it first.' As they walked across the millstream bridge, and as the door of the Grand Moulin came in sight, they could see that someone had attached something to it. It might have been a bunch of withered flowers – or Luther's theses. But it wasn't. It was a dead owl, transfixed with a six-inch nail.

TWENTY

Tyto alba. Barn owl, white owl or screech owl in English. Sylvain called it an *effraie.* He sounded quite *effrayé* himself. 'Witches do that,' he said. 'That's witchcraft we're up against now.'

'You don't believe in witches,' said Adam tersely. He dismissed the Dutch couple with a polite thank you.

'No, not really,' Sylvain admitted.

'Then why say it? It's an ordinary flesh-and-blood person who's done this. Some malicious...' his vocabulary failed him 'Some malicious idiot.'

'But you have no idea who. You can't begin to imagine who.'

'No,' said Adam.

'Then what's so unreasonable about saying it was a witch?'

They pulled out the nail and the bird fell at their feet. The face and under-parts, even the feet, were clothed in white feathers so deep and soft that you could have buried your face in them. The back was a sandy colour with pepper flecks of lavender, white and black. Congealed blood in a few places beneath the feathers showed where the body had been penetrated with shot. Its great eyes were closed, slanted slits. 'Whoever shoots owls?' Adam asked. Sylvain shrugged. A foreign country could be a frightening, unfathomable place.

They buried the dead bird, and the nail, at the extreme downstream end of the garden where the lawn narrowed to a point and the two streams raced to join each other in the tunnel of overhanging green. They hadn't needed to discuss the choice of place. It was as if the rushing waters would draw the evil and the magic out of the owl-corpse as it decomposed, dissipating them harmlessly down the river valley, washing them away from the house they'd made their home. So Adam vaguely thought. He who didn't believe in witches either.

Stéphane, when they met him off the train a few hours later, pursed his lips and shook his head. He had heard of such things happening. They'd happened in the past to people one's grandparents knew, or to people who knew them. He had never imagined something like this happening so close to home. Happening *at* home. For this was his home too now, he had nowhere else at all. On Sunday they were going to drive to Bordeaux to empty his old room and pick up his remaining things: sound-system, computer, books. Expelled from his family home yet still only a mile away from it by road, he had in that sense the worst of both worlds. He was liable to find his parents coming towards him in the car every time he set foot or wheel along the narrow country roads. They might come face to face in the supermarket checkout queue. Stéphane's wiry limbs turned to jelly whenever he thought about it. And as if that wasn't enough, now someone had come along in the night and nailed an owl to his new home's front door.

The three-way goodnight hug, before Stéphane made his separate way to bed, had already become an institution. Tonight it lasted longer, was tighter and stronger than before. Adam felt his cock beginning to thicken. He knew without needing to check with his fingers that the same went for the others too. He knew that they knew. And he knew also, without asking, that they shared another secret: the knowledge that the next step for the three of them lay only a little way ahead; it was now only a matter of time. The thought both titillated and appalled him. Three comrades in arms, they were marching as one towards – what? Sunlit uplands? The abyss?

They had some second thoughts, the three of them, about the wisdom of burying the owl so soon. Shouldn't they perhaps have left it in situ, as evidence, to let the police have a look at?

'Screw the police,' said Sylvain. 'They don't take notice of witch work. And even if they did they wouldn't turn out till Monday now. We've got new PGs coming. What would they be thinking if we'd left a thing like that on the front door?'

They had to agree he had a point. Adam did tentatively raise the issue of fingerprints, only to be reminded that you couldn't get them off feathers, that you'd be lucky to get much off a cylindrical galvanised nail, and as for the door, dozens of people used it – the Dutch PGs, the previous ones who had now returned to their native Germany... 'Anyway,' Stéphane wrapped the matter up, 'there won't be a file on people who make a habit of this, and they're not going to go round house to house, fingerprinting everyone just because somebody's hexed us with a bird.'

So they didn't go to the police over the weekend: there was the Petit Moulin to be got ready, the new guests to be welcomed, and Stéphane's things to be fetched from Bordeaux. They were still undecided about the police on Monday, but on that day the police came to them.

'Sorry to trouble you.' By now Adam was as familiar with the grey-faced, grey-mannered gendarme as he was with the dark blue saloon car from which he emerged. 'But a complaint has been received.'

'About what?' Adam asked. He invited the gendarme into the hall.

'You may think it a bit of a technicality, but we do take the *Appellation Contrôlée* laws rather seriously around here.'

'I'm quite well aware of that. Go on.'

Blue Sky Adam

'Monsieur Ducros from Château La Carelle has made a claim to the effect that one of you...' With a little ballet of hand and head movements he managed to include Adam and Sylvain in the *one of you* and at the same time exclude Stéphane. '...That one of you had offered to sell him the grape crop from your property here.' He paused and looked at Adam, then at Sylvain. They both looked back in mute astonishment. 'You don't need me to tell you,' the gendarme went on, 'that the use of grapes grown in the *vignoble* of Côtes de Castillon for the production of St-Emilion *appellation* wine would be in contravention of the laws of origin.'

'I know that,' said Adam. 'We all do. But I'm happy to be able to tell you that no such offer was made. When is this offer – this conversation – supposed to have taken place?'

'Last Thursday, it would appear.'

'Then M. Ducros has made a mistake,' Sylvain said. 'Both of us were in St-Malo all day on Thursday. Staff at our hotel would confirm that if you asked them.'

'I was playing at a concert there on Wednesday night,' Adam said, 'which was the reason for the visit. You'll see my name in *La Voix Malouine* when it comes out later this week – if you care to look. And, actually, neither of us has ever met M. Ducros. We've only met his son Robert.'

'Well,' said the gendarme, 'as a matter of fact it was Robert Ducros who brought the matter to our attention. A dark-haired man of medium height had apparently tried to sell his father grapes from here.'

'A dark-haired man with an English accent or a French one?' Adam asked. 'Old M. Ducros can only ever have glimpsed us out of a car window. If he can't say which of the two of us he thinks it was, that doesn't seem a very positive identification. Did he have anything else to say?'

'I haven't spoken to him about the incident yet. I'm on my way there now.'

'So you came to accuse us first,' said Sylvain, 'before you'd even heard the complaint from the horse's mouth.'

'I'm not accusing anyone,' said the gendarme, his mouth somehow narrowing to a coin slot as he spoke. 'It simply happens that one reaches your driveway before the Ducros's if one's coming from the St-Genès direction.'

'Well, when you do speak to him,' Adam said, 'you can tell him where we were on Thursday. It's perfectly clear that somebody's got their wires crossed.'

'Fair point,' said the policeman. 'I'll see what M. Ducros senior has to say, check his story, and with any luck I won't have to trouble you again.'

'Before you go,' said Adam as the policeman was turning to leave, 'can I ask you if there's been any progress with finding who slashed my tyres?' Of course there hadn't. 'Well you might like to know, for what it's worth, that someone nailed a dead owl to our front door. And that did happen on Thursday.'

'You'd think,' said Stéphane as soon as the gendarme had gone, 'that they'd have checked the story with old Ducros first, before coming bothering us. *C'est chiant.* Bloody cheek. To come accusing us without even getting their facts straight.'

'Welcome to the minorities,' said Adam.

It was the next day that it finally happened. There was not too much work to do. The next concert was not till Saturday, and though the concerto still needed to be practised – Adam had to keep his ears and fingers in trim and his memory sharp – it no longer required to be studied, learnt. The vineyard too was more or less taking care of itself now; the vines had flowered and the subsequent bunches of green pinheads would take their own time about transforming themselves into luscious purple grapes.

The paying guests were out in their car. Their hosts had all learnt by now to look out for the tell-tale cloud of dust a quarter of a mile away that heralded the approach of anyone on wheels. Now, for only the second time, they took an afternoon swim in the lower pond. When they felt sufficiently cooled they hauled themselves out to dry their naked bodies in the sunshine on the grass. Eyes still occasionally checked the distance for the signal puff of dust but none came. Then, which of them was it that started the tomfoolery: the sprinkling of dry grass on someone else's chest, the mock protest, the grabbing of an arm? None of them could ever be sure. But soon a gentle three-way tussle was getting under way. Three sleepy appendages that had caused no comment, attracted scant attention, nestled in fur since they'd stripped off for their bathe, now began to stir, to blossom and grow hard. It was Sylvain in the end who, kneeling over the unprotesting Stéphane, whom Adam had lightly pinioned by an arm, drew one finger along the underside, the long curved ridge, of Stéphane's slender bow. It jerked and bobbed about in Stéphane's spasm of delight: thrilled with the attention, wanting more. *'Je peux?'* Sylvain asked, a movement of his head including Adam in this request for permission to proceed. Almost imperceptibly Adam nodded, wondering what he was unleashing by assenting; wondering who, this time, was betraying what or whom.

Angers was not much more than half the distance of St-Malo and in the same general direction. They knew their way by now but took the precaution of setting out early all the same. Sean met them there. He'd flown to Nantes and travelled the last bit of the way by train. 'Left your sister in Newcastle,' he told Stéphane. Which spoke volumes, Adam thought. Françoise would be back in France for good in five more days and could catch Adam's playing, assuming she wanted to, at a later date. In the circumstances there hadn't seemed much point in her rushing expensively to Angers for a short weekend. In the circumstances. Had she and Sean become any kind of an item in the last few weeks the circumstances would probably have guaranteed her being here.

Even without Françoise there would be quite a crowd of them at the Hotel Ibis. Adam, Sylvain, Stéphane and Sean. Then Nathalie, Gary, and Nathalie's concert agent, Luc, whose promise to attend was, this time, the main source of Adam's pre-concert nerves.

They walked together briefly in the streets of the small, attractive town. Saw the castle where the Plantaganet dynasty had been spawned: Henry II, Richard the Lion-heart, King John. Angevin meant 'coming from Angers'. Adam had never made the connection before. They were amused to find themselves standing at one moment outside a venerable fifteenth-century house called *La Maison d'Adam*. Its timbered walls and gables were carved with an eye-popping gallery of gargoyles and monsters-in-wood. 'My house,' said Adam. 'For when I'm in residence in Angers.'

'I'd have thought you'd got enough sagging roof-beams and slipping tiles already,' said Sean, and then wished he hadn't. Adam didn't seem to think it was a very good joke.

They drove Adam and his cello to his afternoon rehearsal at the Centre des Congrès, then they – Sylvain, Stéphane and Sean – whiled away an hour or so by the riverside till he was finished. Sean was immediately aware of a change in the rapport between the other two. The last time he'd seen the two Frenchmen together they'd been spiky and belligerent, their rivalry for Adam's regard only too apparent, though they were beginning to become friends by the end of that weekend. Now, however, they were extremely matey with each other, joshing each other in a French that Sean couldn't begin to follow. Yet at the same time there was a wariness between them; they were cautious with each other, closing in on each other in conversation and in physical movement only to shy away at the last moment. With his experience of the previous summer to draw on, Sean was fairly sure he knew what had taken place to effect this change. When they all met Adam again after the rehearsal Sean took him on one side. 'What's going on?' Sean asked him. 'Are you all – the three of you...?'

'Sort of,' said Adam. *'Avant-garde, n'est-ce pas?'*

'I hope you know what you're doing, then,' said Sean. He wasn't sure in his own mind if he was disappointed by his friends or merely jealous of them. Adam heard the note of ambivalence in his voice. Sean went on. 'You know Françoise wants to put an end to the rift between Stéphane and his father. She's tried to sort things out over the phone but it sort of didn't take. When she's back in France next week she'll get it sorted properly, she says. But...' Sean shook his head. '...I can't help thinking that Stéphane being part of a *ménage à trois* now isn't going to make her task a whole lot easier. If she, and if her parents, get to know about it, that is.' Then curiosity got the better of him. 'Do you... do you do the whole ... gamut, the three of you?'

'Pretty much,' admitted Adam.

'Well I hope you all still...'

'Yeah, yeah, Sean, we wear those things when appropriate,' Adam said.

Lovely, considerate Sean. Always concerned for Adam's welfare. Sometimes he seemed too good for this world: too fair of face and form, too beautiful by nature and physique. Was he perhaps an angel? The guardian angel that Adam's mother's religion promised had been

given him at birth – but, by reason of some celestial
cock-up in Adam's particular case, accidentally given
fleshly form? 'Do you do the whole gamut with
Françoise?' Adam wanted to ask him. 'And do you wear
a thingy too?' He found he couldn't. Not today at least.
Perhaps there were some questions you just didn't ask an
angel. But Sean had told a lie for him a few weeks back.
A real angel perhaps would not do that.

A purpose-built concert-hall this time, not a church.
Adam felt ready and prepared. Lulled by the benign
presence of the orchestra, and with Nathalie beside him,
he forgot the existence of the agent. Perhaps he was
feeling too secure, because he also forgot his music. It
happened in the middle of the final movement. One
moment he was securely dancing along the stepping
stones that Brahms had provided for him in his path
across the universe, the next he had missed his footing
and was floundering in the infinite void of space. Terror
seized him, the abyss yawned. The flash of surprise on
Nathalie's face. Then Nathalie's expression changing
immediately to relief, smiling a nanosecond of
encouragement, and he knew he'd made it back. The
whole episode had lasted no longer than two seconds.
But they had been seconds of the cosmic kind. Nobody
in the audience would have noticed anything amiss
unless they also played the piece themselves, but for
Adam it was a lapse of memory never to be forgotten.

A late supper at the hotel. For Adam it was a working
supper of sorts. Luc, the concert agent, sat next to him.
'How well you play,' he said.

'I had a memory lapse,' said Adam.

'Never mind about that. I didn't clock it and neither
did anyone else. Beautiful tone, secure technique, and
you do some special magic with the audience. I can't put
a finger on what it is, but perhaps that's in the nature of

magic. Can't put a price on it either. Have you seen the *Voix Malouine*?'

'Not yet.' Adam had ordered a copy from a newsagent's in Castillon. The girl had been perplexed at anyone wanting to read a paper from such a far-off place as Brittany.

'I have a copy here.' Luc produced a photocopy of a review from an inside pocket. Adam was surprised at how easy it was to find the bit about himself.

Ce jeune anglais, he read, *plein de talent, a su capté l'esprit fugitif de cet œuvre majestueuse…* It was almost too good to be true. It was like reading a prayer or an incantation. Adam read on with trepidation, awaiting the sting in the tail, the big 'but', the big *'mais'*. But it never came. All was praise. He found it difficult to believe they were talking about him. Perhaps when he'd read it a few more dozen times. Meanwhile Luc was speaking. Adam swung his attention back with an effort. '…Happy to let you do the concert series next year with Nathalie. I was unsure, to tell the truth, when she mentioned it. But now I've heard you. Seen the hold you had on that audience. Though what about you? Nine big dates over three months, including the Salle Pleyel. Think you can handle it?'

Never say no. However scared you might be feeling. Never say no. Never say no. 'I'll handle it OK.'

'You realise that wouldn't necessarily be the end. If all went well. Even without Nathalie. There'd be the possibility of recitals around the country. Find a young pianist to match you. A bright young girl maybe. On second thoughts, though, perhaps another boy. Something special about your platform personality. Chemistry might be even better with a man.' Involuntarily he glanced around the table, peopled, with the exception of Nathalie, entirely with males. 'Then solo concertos with an orchestra. Nathalie tells me

267

you've played the Elgar. That might go well, a young Englishman doing Elgar. What else do you have for repertoire?'

Trooping backstage earlier, Stéphane had hardly known what to say to Adam. He'd been blown away by the whole experience – a classical concert in which his lover (for Adam was his lover again now, returned to him with the bonus of the husky nature-boy Sylvain as lover number two) ...in which his lover had played one of the solo parts, under the bright lights in his white tie and tails, adored by the audience. He hugged him, cuddled him, tasting on his lips the sweet sweat of Adam's cheeks. Sean had embraced him too. 'You were wonderful, my darling,' he said, mocking his own words as he spoke them, yet meaning them at the same time. The brightness in his cornflower eyes showed Adam how sincerely he meant what he said – not just the 'wonderful' but also the 'my darling', and just for a moment Adam almost wished the clock turned back a year. But only almost. And only for a moment. Secure in his possession of Adam, Sylvain came up to embrace him third. *'Pas mal, P'tit-Loup,'* he said. *'Pas mal, quoi?'*

Luc and Nathalie had both retired for the night. Gary, Adam, Sylvain, Stéphane and Sean still lingered in the hotel bar, around a low table, seated in comfortable leather chairs. 'Take Luc with a pinch of salt,' Gary was cautioning Adam. 'Don't be too beguiled by his long-term dreams. Those things may happen, they may not. Oh dear, but don't let me dishearten you.' Gary had seen exactly that look on Adam's face. 'The concerts next year are going to happen, that's for certain now. And once you've played them they will never go away. Just as nobody can take away from you the success of the two you've already played. At the very least, any orchestra – any orchestra at all – would be pleased to hear you play. A music college would take an approach from you most seriously. If you wanted to teach, that is. And anyway, who knows? Perhaps Luc will be proved right and a full-scale career as a concert soloist will open up: the concert halls of the world will be at your disposal, their audiences at your feet.' (As they were at Gary's, Adam thought.) 'If that's what you really want, of course,' Gary added with a searching look at Adam's face. (And is it? Adam thought. Is that what I really want?)

An awkwardness had been hanging in the air for the past few minutes: a question mark over the timing and the order of their going to bed. It was Stéphane who had the nerve to say it in the end. 'Time for bed, *mes copains, quoi*?' He stood up, then Adam and Sylvain followed suit. Stood up as if to be counted. *Un, deux, trois.* Then they said and kissed their goodnights like children with their parents, though infinitely more self-consciously. Each of them in turn glanced back. A private look at the other two that mutely said: this is the way it is now; sorry if we've surprised you or given any offence. Finally they jostled their way out of the door together, each one trying not to be either first or last.

Gary looked at Sean, sitting across the table from him. 'Have I interpreted that correctly or am I making a great mistake?' he asked.

'I think you've got it right,' said Sean soberly. 'Adam told me about it this afternoon.' He was leaning back in his armchair, looking very relaxed, Gary thought, his legs spread almost impolitely wide. And yet not as relaxed as all that. One of his knees was drumming rapidly up and down as if he'd left an engine running. His thigh muscles filled his chinos, Gary noticed, in the way that athletes' do – in a way that Adam's and

Sylvain's didn't quite aspire to, and that Stéphane's never would. The taut fabric was forced into little inch-long parallel pleats only just before it came to meet the even tauter seam of the inside leg. 'And what did you make of it?' Gary asked. 'Oh by the way – one for the road?'

'No thanks. I mean, thank you very much but no. But don't let me…'

'No, it's OK,' Gary said. 'I don't need one either.'

'What I thought,' said Sean slowly, fixing steady blue eyes on Gary, 'was… I remember reading, when the Concorde crashed all those years ago, one of the eye-witnesses said as he watched it leave the runway at Charles de Gaulle with flames pouring out the back of it, 'Christ, this shouldn't be happening.' The outcome was hardly difficult to foresee. Well, when Adam told me … I'm afraid I felt exactly the same.'

'I see.' Gary left it at that. He didn't have anything more apt to say.

'I once had a threesome with Adam,' Sean said next, much to Gary's surprise. He smiled that smile. 'Fun while it lasted, I suppose.'

'But it lasted…?' Gary could not help but be curious.

'Oh, just one night. It was on holiday at the Grand Moulin last year. Stéphane turned up a day later and saved the situation by getting off with Michael within the hour. We became two couples for the duration. Stéphane with Michael, Adam with me. It was just a holiday arrangement, nothing more.' Sean leaned forward, put his hands on his still outspread knees. The movements of someone who is about to stand up but then isn't sure. He was less than relaxed now. Sod the position of that table, Gary thought. Then Sean did stand up. *But he isn't sure*, thought Gary.

Somehow the table wasn't an obstacle any more. To his dying day Gary would never know how he managed it but suddenly he was standing at Sean's side. He touched him gently underneath his smooth-skinned chin. Kept his hand there. 'Or am I making a great mistake?' he said.

Sean looked straight back into his eyes. Beyond his face no other muscles moved. 'No,' he said quietly. Very slowly. 'No, I don't think you are.'

TWENTY-ONE

You were never entirely alone, working in a vineyard. When you were out pruning, so were your neighbours, even if they could only be glimpsed as specks in the landscape a mile away. When you were ploughing, so were they, and when it came to the harvest in two months' time there would be the scene, for hundreds of square kilometres all around, of bowed heads and bobbing baskets among the vines – the scene that had been enacted and witnessed here in the Bordelais for nearly two millennia, and looking much the same today as it did in the sumptuous illustrations of the medieval Psalters.

Right now the ongoing task was the removal of suckers: unwanted shoots from the base of the vines that would sap their strength, drawing precious resources away from the slowly swelling bunches of grapes. Sylvain and Stéphane were engaged in this the morning after their return from Angers. The distant sound of Adam's cello practice came humming up from the garden below. The next concert was in eight days' time. *Les deux S*, as Adam called them now, were not surprised, this morning, to see Philippe Martinville wading towards them down the rows of vines.

'I saw you last week – spraying by hand. No tractor. Are you boys OK?'

'We got some backpack cylinders from the second-hand shop,' volunteered Sylvain brightly. 'They work OK.' He hadn't wanted to embarrass his friend.

But Stéphane said it anyway. 'I had a kind of falling-out with my father. That's why no tractor.'

'Yes, I'd sort of heard about that,' said Philippe carefully. 'But you don't have to do everything in the hardest possible way, like monks enjoying a penance. You can always ask me if you want to borrow things.

When I can help you out I will, and when I can't I'll simply say so.' He paused, inspected a bunch of green, ball-bearing-sized grapes. 'I don't bite, you know. I'm an old softie, like my dog. Look, why don't the three of you come up for an aperitif this evening? Say six o'clock. There's something else I want to propose, but it concerns Adam especially so it had better wait till then.'

They sat under the cool of sunshades in Philippe's garden. At six o'clock the July sun was still fierce. Philippe opened a bottle of the '86; his three guests were conscious of the honour. Madame Martinville pushed a plate of *amuse-gueules* towards them. She wanted to hear all about Adam's concerts. When would he be playing at the Grand Théâtre in Bordeaux? In eighteen months' time, Adam thought. It seemed a long way off.

Had the police got any further in their hunt for whoever had interfered with Adam's car? Philippe had heard about that. A horrible way to behave towards an incomer, he said. Until the culprit was caught it tarnished the honour of the whole community. Stéphane told them about the owl. *'Mon Dieu,'* said Madame. 'I haven't heard of anything like that happening around here since before I was born. Since before the war even. What are things coming to?'

'Listen,' said Philippe. 'This rather brings us to what I wanted to talk to you about. We'd heard about the unpleasantness you'd been experiencing. And I can't possibly say that this would put a stop to it – but, you never know. I'm going to put you forward for membership of the Winegrowers' Association of the Côtes de Castillon. I know you don't own a château exactly, but you do own part of one.' He looked at Adam. 'You'd come to meetings, to the annual dinner and so forth. Take your place among the community.'

Adam said, 'I'd stick out like a sore thumb. Not only am I English but...' This was the moment he'd dreaded, but it had to come. 'I'm not like all the rest of you. I don't have a wife. No girlfriend.'

'No.' Philippe glanced at his wife, then looked back at Adam. 'You have two young friends instead. So I'm going to propose your membership of the Association in the name of the Moulin de Pressac, to be represented by all or any of the three partners who work it: Adam, Sylvain and Stéphane here. With your permissions of course. See what they say.'

Stéphane broke in. 'My father...'

Philippe cut him off. 'What will your father say? I don't know. We'll have to see. He's just one vote among many. Meeting his son as a fellow *vigneron*, as an equal at the AGM or across the dinner table might do him a power of good. Who knows?' Philippe looked at his wife again. 'I'd better, hadn't I?' She nodded assent. 'Listen,' he said to the three young men. 'If we go to one of these Association bashes and we meet Monsieur and Madame Machin-Truc, we don't ask ourselves about the state of their marriage. Do they still sleep together in a double bed, or is their relationship now just what amounts to being business partners? Or if Monsieur Machin-Truc is in fact sleeping with Madame Clique-Claque in town, or doing something in an outhouse with his *régisseur*.'

'Philippe!' his wife protested.

'Sorry, but you know what I mean. No, we don't ask those questions. And if we did, the answers would be none of our damn business. Are you with me? And if other people think, yes this *is* my business, then that's their problem.'

'Yes, but in the case of my father...' Stéphane tried again.

'Fathers are special cases,' said Philippe. 'I'm one myself and I know. In the case of *your* father I can't help at all, so let's not talk about him. The only person I'm telling you about is me – is us.' He nodded towards his wife. 'And I only wanted to tell you that I – that we – don't have a problem with the three of you.' He looked at the three business partners in turn and noticed that they had all rather rapidly drained their glasses. 'Adam,' he said. 'You'll find a second bottle in the kitchen. Be a friend and fetch it. And then top us all up.'

Françoise came to see them almost as soon as she was back in France. The course in Newcastle had gone well: she had actually enjoyed herself much more than she was expecting to. Forced to use her English, she found it was better than she'd realised, and that it quickly improved with use. Thanks to Sean she'd met a whole new crowd of people and discovered, to her great surprise, a real liking for Indian food. But she had more important things than that to talk about, especially with Stéphane, as they all sat together on the lawn between the millstream and the house.

'I've done my best with Papa but he won't budge,' she told her brother. 'At least not yet, though I'm sure he'll soften in time. But I warn you, it might be months or even years. It might have been easier for me if you didn't happen to be shacked up with two young men right on his doorstep and under the nose of everybody he's known since school. If it were simply a question of him having a gay son in Bordeaux or in Paris, that might be easier for him somehow but as it is… And since even I can't help wondering sometimes who gets up to what and who with, now that there's three of you living here together – though I promise I'm not going to ask – you can hardly expect him not to wonder about it too.'

'Philippe Martinville said he never gave a thought to what we might or might not do in bed,' said Adam. 'I thought that was highly commendable of him.'

'Philippe Martinville,' retorted Françoise, 'has the luxury of not having any of you three for a son.'

'What about Maman?' Stéphane wanted to know.

'I'm coming to that. She's unhappy of course. Divided, torn. I really don't think she cares if you're gay or not or who you sleep with or don't. But she won't say that to Papa, and if he doesn't want you back in the house just yet she's not going to go against that. Classic case of Stand by Your Man. On the other hand she asked me to arrange with you to have lunch with her, in Castillon or St-Emilion, in the next couple of days. Neutral territory and all that.'

'Oh God,' said Stéphane. 'What will she want to say?'

'I don't think it's a question of saying anything at all,' said his sister. 'Neither her nor you. She just wants to see you, hear your voice, and be with you for an hour or so. That's the way mothers are.'

'Exactly so,' said Sylvain.

'Some of them,' said Adam. 'I've got the same problem with my parents, only in their case it's rather the other way round. But then I have a mother who's a Catholic.'

'Shouldn't make any difference,' said Françoise. 'In France everyone has one of those.' She changed the subject. 'Anyway. I don't know what you all did to Sean last weekend. He came back in an extraordinary state.'

The three men exchanged glances. 'In what way extraordinary?' asked Adam, pretending, not very convincingly, not to know what she meant.

'Abstracted, *distrait*... He only just about remembered I was going back to France. We met for a drink to say goodbye. He said to tell you he'd see you soon in France: that he'd be back in a few weeks' time.'

'Interesting,' said Stéphane.

'Very,' said Adam. 'And it's nice to have some news from him at last. He hasn't been responding to any of my calls or texts since last weekend.'

'He was pretty undecided about things when he left us,' said Sylvain, without explaining what those things were. They all had vivid recollections of last Sunday morning: the morning after the concert in Angers. Gary and Sean had arrived together for breakfast quite unable to disguise, even if they'd wanted to, what had happened between them the previous night. But they both looked happy – and more. There was no trace of that soggy-cornflake atmosphere that pervades the shared breakfasts of people who made the wrong decision at bedtime the night before.

Gary had left soon after that (the boys had tactfully withdrawn while he said his goodbyes to Sean); he was catching the train back to Paris with Nathalie and Luc. The four musketeers, as Nathalie now called them (she was finding it a little hard to keep up) killed a little time together and then drove Sean to the airport at Nantes. Adam insisted it was not very far out of their way. But Sean clearly didn't want to talk about the new turn his life had taken – and especially not in French. Adam found himself experiencing a curious sense of loss, though he knew he hardly had the right to. It was not as if Sean belonged to him these days. Arguably he never had. But Sean did say, when they finally said their goodbyes at the departure gate (and was ever the name of an aperture in a wall more surely programmed to lend poignancy to farewells?), 'Looks like I've got some pretty big thinking to do.' When it came to Adam's turn to give him a final hug he squeezed Sean tight and didn't know how he would ever manage to let go.

'Of course he may have been preoccupied with Michael.' Françoise's next words bursting into Adam's reverie gave him an almighty jolt.

'Preoccupied with Michael?' His astonishment was plain.

'You mean you hadn't heard?' Françoise said.

'I told you,' Adam said. 'Nothing from Sean since Sunday. So do please tell us, if you wouldn't mind, just what is going on.'

Françoise made an *I'm-not-too-comfortable-saying-this* kind of face. 'I'm hardly the one to be telling you Michael's news. I've never met the guy, remember, and he's such a close friend of all of yours.'

'Count me out there,' said Sylvain, calmly brushing away a hornet that was taking too much of an interest in his wine glass. 'I've never met the bloke either. Not that that makes much difference. I sometimes feel I've been living with him for years.' Everybody laughed, though even Adam was unsure whether Sylvain was joking or giving expression to a real, if minor, irritation.

'The only thing I can tell you,' said Françoise, 'is that he's split up from his girlfriend. That's literally all I know. An older woman, have I got that right? The expression Sean used was, *chucked him out.*'

'She chucked him out?' queried Stéphane.

'That's what Sean said.'

'Well that'll be a bit of a first,' said Stéphane. 'From what I know of him it's usually he that does the chucking.' You could hardly blame him for the faint glow of *schadenfreude* with which his voice was tinged.

Not even Adam felt he could phone Michael directly and say, 'I hear Melissa's chucked you out.' In days gone by, when they'd been close, he would have done exactly that (though when they'd been close there had been no Melissa to do any chucking) but a different situation existed between them now. They hadn't made contact with each other at all since Easter, and they hadn't exactly had a meeting of hearts and minds even then.

With Sean playing hard to reach, Adam decided he might as well try to get whatever information there might be from Gary. He needed to phone Gary anyway. Tuesday's concert was going to be at St-Germain-en-Laye, effectively in Paris, and it had already been arranged that Adam would stay the night at Gary's flat. He only needed to confirm a few details like his arrival time. He made it clear that this time he would be coming on his own, without an entourage. Then he asked, pretend-casually, if Gary had had any news from Sean.

'Yes of course,' Gary said, as if it were the most natural thing. 'Haven't you? I am surprised. And not returning calls? Most unlike him. I'll have a word. But you'll be able to talk to him yourself on Tuesday night.'

'Do you mean face to face?' Adam asked him.

'Yes,' said Gary without so much as a flicker of coyness in his voice. 'When you come to Paris he'll be here.'

The more of it you had, the readier you were for more. As Adam already knew. Not only in the set of your mind but in your glands as well. Springs eternal in the human dick. After the first couple of days they no longer spent whole nights three to a bed. Such cosiness might have proved anaphrodisiac in time. It was also, in mid-July, extremely tickly and hot. Instead, Stéphane would arrive at dawn to join the other two, or else the two would get up early and, like panthers, go hunt Stéphane in his bed. Find him, one to fuck him and one to fondle him and then be fucked by him in turn. All this after Sylvain and Adam had already made love together during the night. Then sometimes in the garden, in the sunshine, after swimming, keeping half a watchful eye for the distant cloud of dust that betokened visitors or returning paying guests, it would be all hands to the pump and, *thar they blows*, and three fountain plumes of white.

Only two more concerts to go. School had finished and the labour in the vineyard was reducing down. The three of them had, if not much money, then at least, at last, a cornucopia of time.

Adam had time on Saturday to be helping Stéphane with the bedrooms in the Petit Moulin, between outgoing and incoming paying guests. Sylvain was busy somewhere else. Crossing and re-crossing each other's paths and brushing against each other as they unfolded sheets together and sorted towels. Stéphane, like Adam, was wearing nothing but a T-shirt and a skimpy pair of shorts. There was no hiding what lay underneath the latter when Stéphane's excitement began to take visible shape: that unmistakeable long curved ridge. It drew further attention to itself when a coin-sized patch of damp innocently blossomed in the tautened fabric, highlighting the tip. 'I think the shorts had better come off,' Adam said.

It was the first time in months that they had allowed themselves to share such a pleasure – just the two of them – without the benediction of Sylvain's participation, the first time since they'd become a trio that they hadn't played as a full team. Except of course for what Adam and Sylvain did in bed together, but that was something sacrosanct and not subject to team rules. There was a first time for everything, however. In his current upbeat state of mind Adam began to think that perhaps the whole of life could be seen as one glorious compendium of first times. And he decided that, in any case, Sylvain wouldn't mind about what he was just now doing with Stéphane. Even if he knew.

Later that day, beside the millstream, Adam found a frog among the grass. Beneath its dark camouflage blotches it was mainly copper-brown in colour where, Adam seemed to remember, British ones were olive green. He caught it in his hands and held it for a minute or two, gazing into its liquid dark brown eyes. A strange feeling came over him as the frog unblinkingly looked back: an unearthly feeling, as if he were making contact with another world. He showed it to the others then let it go. It hopped without undue haste down the bank towards the stream.

Adam arrived at Gary's flat around midday. There was no sign of Sean yet. Gary said he would be arriving later in the afternoon.

Adam went to St-Germain-en-Laye on his own. It was only about half an hour by metro and RER, and you couldn't easily miss the concert venue when you got there. For the performance was to be in the castle, and the castle stood right at the top of the metro steps. It enjoyed a splendid situation: something that Adam was able to appreciate only after the end of his rehearsal, when he had time to take a walk with Nathalie in the grounds. The extensive gardens were perched on the edge of a miniature cliff. Below lay a loop of the River Seine and in the distance was the whole roofscape of central Paris: the Grande Arche and glass towers of La Défense, and beyond those the Eiffel Tower, Montmartre, and more church spires than you could name.

The castle of St-Germain had a colourful past. It had been loaned by Louis XIV to James II of England when the latter had lost his throne in 1688. The loan turned out to be a very extended one, as first King James' son and then his grandson, Bonnie Prince Charlie, both dismally failed to get their kingdom back. It took nearly sixty years for the Jacobite cause to wither finally and die, and by that time the end of the French monarchy itself – a more abrupt end thanks to the invention of the guillotine – lay only a few years in the future. Adam felt unaccountably chilled discussing this turbulent history with Nathalie. A kingdom, he thought, was a hideously easy thing to lose.

Adam was still feeling slightly melancholy as he changed into his concert attire. For the first time he had no supporters to cheer him on. No Sylvain, no Stéphane. Stéphane himself was having quite a big day today; it was the day scheduled for his lunchtime reunion with his mother. But there were no Sean and Gary either. Adam supposed that, understandably, they would want some time by themselves, and in any case they would hardly want to hear him play the same piece of music a second time in a mere ten days. He pulled himself together as he tied his bow tie. He was a big boy and a professional now; he couldn't expect always to take his mates with him when he went to work.

There was a minor commotion at the door of the improvised band room: a little exchange of *No you can'ts* and *Yes we musts*. Then in came Gary with Sean – and Michael. 'Change of plan,' said Gary. 'We weren't going to come, but then Sean arrived with Michael in tow. Michael insisted that he had to hear you play ... and so we thought we'd better come along as well.'

'Counting on you to be good,' said Michael. It wasn't the moment, ten minutes before a concert and surrounded by seventy-odd musicians fussing with trumpet-mutes and rosin, for going into things.

That came later, as far as Adam and Michael were concerned. After dinner, back in Paris, at Le Coq Hardi. ('We came here on your seventeenth birthday. I remember,' Michael said. 'It hasn't changed at all. Even the menu's just the same.') And after Gary and Sean had gone to bed. (This time it was they who went first and looked a mite self-conscious as they did so.) Michael and Adam had been left alone with Gary's malt whisky bottle and the strict injunction that if they finished it they would have to replace it in the morning.

Blue Sky Adam

'Incredible,' said Adam, meaning Gary and Sean. 'Of all the things I might have expected to happen to Sean…'

'I don't know,' said Michael. 'He lost his father a few years ago. Older man. Read your Freud. And anyway, people do change, you know.' He shot a mischievous look at Adam as he said this. Once, when they were about fifteen, they had spent nearly a whole afternoon arguing whether people changed or merely developed. Michael had said *changed* and Adam had said *developed* – and they'd stuck it out for gruelling hours, till tears were shed and they'd nearly come to blows.

'Or develop,' said Adam, returning the mischievous look but very quickly moving on. 'Anyway, what of you?'

'Sean's heard the whole story now, of course. On the train coming over. Or should one say under when it's the Eurostar? And I heard all about you too, of course. I think you've gone completely off your rostrum if you must know, but then, who am I to criticise?' Michael's tale was simple and quickly told. Melissa had found a man – a while ago now – who, unlike Michael, was the same age as she was, lived on a salary rather than a student loan and had the even greater advantage of being unequivocally straight. Over a period of some months they had fallen in love. It was obvious really, Michael said, when you looked back. An accident waiting to happen.

Michael talked lightly of his misfortunes but Adam was not deceived – he who knew him better than any one. His friend had clearly been hurt by the experience. Bruised, battered and bewildered could be read in the depths of his eyes. And if not changed, well certainly… developed?

They talked till late. The whisky bottle was all but empty. Then it was Adam who said laconically, 'Well, do we?'

Michael thought before replying. Then he said, 'Meaning that if you're playing with fire already you might as well pour petrol on?'

'I suppose you're right.' Adam accepted the point, although reluctantly. Memories of their past physical closeness were coming back to him in warm and lovely waves. Absence did that. 'Perhaps another time.' Without further argument, and with only the briefest of goodnight kisses, Adam went off to bed in the spare room as usual, leaving Michael to pinch his fingers in the hinges as he turned the sofa into a put-u-up bed in the salon.

The following afternoon found Adam and Michael on a train together, bound for the Gironde. Michael had been very unsure about this idea when Adam had first mooted it the previous evening. He didn't much relish the prospect of seeing Stéphane again. But Adam reassured him that he wouldn't be left with Stéphane on his own and reminded him of something he already knew: that Stéphane was the most amenable and forgiving of mortal men. Adam had thought – as Sean had done a few days before – that it would be good for Michael to have a break from life in England; it wouldn't exactly speed his recovery from the injuries he'd suffered in his break-up with Melissa, but it might take his mind off them a little. And whereas Sean had generously suggested Michael might like to stay on with him and Gary in Paris, Michael himself was not so sure. Gary and Sean seemed to be in the throes of falling very much in love, and Michael felt that in hanging around with them at this precise time he would be in danger of becoming a *groseille à maquereau*. Adam corrected him. In this context, he said, the French for being a gooseberry was *tenir la chandelle*. So in the end Michael had let himself be persuaded by Adam to travel south with him.

Adam tried repeatedly to phone *les deux S* to warn them to expect the unexpected guest but the fixed line at the Moulin was permanently in answer-phone mode and there seemed to be something wrong with Stéphane's mobile. 'I'm going to have to get Sylvain a mobile of his own whether he likes it or not,' Adam said in eventual exasperation. 'We can't go on like this. Just hope they remember to meet us off the right train.'

Michael asked Adam how the three of them were managing for money, and noticed that Adam looked a little sheepish as he replied, 'Well, it's only a temporary arrangement of course, but what we do at the moment is – I cash the cheques the PGs give us and we split the cash three ways.'

Michael was appalled and said so. 'You can't go on like that. What about tax? What about...?' He stopped. A thought had struck him. 'And your concert fees?'

'They go straight into my account. With my teaching money. I do keep hold of those.'

'Thank God for that at least. But that's no way to run a business. Did you draw up a business plan before you started? No. Worked out a simple budget at the beginning of the year? (That means estimated expenditure and income by the way, just in case you didn't know.) I see. Same old Adam. But you could be missing out on all sorts of things.'

'Like what?'

'Oh, I don't know. But you're an EU farmer now. There may be grants for things like capital equipment. Refurbishing the buildings. Renewing roofs. Who knows? You could at least have looked into it.'

'Stéphane...'

'Have you got yourself an accountant yet?'

'I snogged an accountant a couple of months ago.'

'Oh get real!' Michael paused. Then curiosity got the better of him. 'Who was he then?'

'She, actually. Françoise. Stéphane's sister, who you haven't met.'

'Oh for fuck's sake. You go from bad to worse. Madame Bovary in trousers, you are. Though more often out of them it seems. Thank God I didn't agree to climb into the sack with you last night. Adam Bovary. I'd probably have ended up with an owl nailed to my head.'

They were relieved to see Stéphane standing in the booking hall when they finally alighted at Libourne. But Stéphane's face dropped a mile when he saw Michael. *'Scheisse,'* he said, which wasn't a very promising start. In fact he looked a great deal more upset than the unexpected appearance of Michael might reasonably have accounted for.

Adam began to wonder if perhaps something else was wrong. 'Why weren't you picking up the phone? Where's Sylvain?'

'Sylvain's gone,' said Sté.

All that you could do in this situation, Adam now discovered, was to recite the clichés – like a litany. In English or, as now, in French, it was just the same. 'Gone?' he heard himself say. 'What do you mean, gone?'

'Gone. Left. Walked out.' Stéphane's antiphonal answer.

'Why? What the hell has…?'

'Get in the car. We can't talk here.' Miserably the three of them shambled across the car park, trailing cello and overnight bags. They stuffed them into the boot. Once they were all inside, 'We slept together,' said Stéphane in a leaden voice.

'Meaning what?' Adam wanted to know.

'Meaning...? What do you think it means when one adult person tells you that they've slept with another?'

'You had sex.'

'Right. We had sex.'

'And what ... and what exactly did you do?' Adam couldn't have even found names for the storms of feelings, the hurricanes of hurt and anger that blew through his fragile kingdom and engulfed him then. They were too wild and dangerous to be corralled and classified, analysed and named. He only knew that he'd never experienced anything worse than this in adult life. The abyss had finally opened and he had been plunged into it.

'We... Look, you don't need to know all the details...' But Adam did. 'He fucked me. I came in his hand. Simple as that. And just the once. We slept the night.' In answer to the look that Adam gave him, Stéphane said, 'No, in my bed, not in yours.' As if that mattered, Stéphane thought.

It couldn't matter more, thought Adam. 'And you didn't fuck him?' He wanted to be absolutely sure.

'No. I've told you exactly what did happen. That's the truth. Look, can we move on now?'

Sté had not fucked Sylvain. A small mercy. Lazarus' moistened finger for Dives to lick for a brief instant as he burned.

Adam was just able to think clearly enough to notice this: it was not the fact of Stéphane's having sex with his other lover in his absence that had hurt him, it was the fact of Sylvain's doing so. There was no equivalence between the two facts, because there was none between the relationships he had with the two men. Much as he loved Stéphane – and he still did, even in his anger now – that was as nothing compared to what bound him to Sylvain. Sylvain and he had been put on this earth for no

other reason than to meet and then belong together. So
why, oh why...?

'Look,' Michael said. 'Do you think we could drive
somewhere and have the windows down? It's about a
million degrees in here.'

Stéphane drove. And told the remainder of his tale.
'He knew I'd had a difficult day. Meeting my mother
and so on. He just, I guess, wanted to comfort me, that
was all. But in the morning he felt really bad. OK, so did
I. But he was worse. *Inconsolable*, we say in French.'

'In English too,' said Michael.

'I told him about last weekend,' Stéphane went on.
'About you and me and what happened in the Petit
Moulin. And about that other weekend back in the
spring. Thinking it would make him feel better. Ease his
conscience. But it didn't. I see now...'

'That wasn't very bright of you,' said Michael.

'Look, stay out, can you?' said Adam. 'Please?'

'Michael's right,' said Stéphane. 'I wasn't being
clever. He went berserk. I tried to phone you. He
grabbed my mobile, threw it against the wall then
stamped on it. Broke it in smithereens.'

'And then he left?' The anger had departed. Blown
through like a hurricane and gone. Only the desolation of
its wake remained. An infinity of emptiness. They'd told
you when you were little what Hell was like. Well now
you knew. They'd had it right.

'I went with him to the station in the end,' said
Stéphane flatly.

'You did what?'

'It wasn't quite like that. He packed a bag. Two bags.
You know – that old hold-all of his and his backpack,
and set off walking.'

'His medication,' said Adam. 'Did he...?'

'He packed all those. After a few minutes I followed
him in the car, drove alongside, wound the window

down, tried to reason with him, get him to come back, make him change his mind, wait till you came this evening – anything. Finally he said he would. Got into the car, but insisted he should drive. Well, of course you can guess what happened next. In no time at all we were at the little station at St-Laurent-des-Combes. You'd be hard put to it to find a train that stopped there if you waited six hours. But as luck – ill-luck – would have it, one came in almost straightaway.'

'Going in which direction?' Adam wanted to know.

'Towards Libourne and Bordeaux. Change for Paris, change for London, Brussels or Madrid.'

'You don't know where he went?'

'There's no ticket office at St-Laurent, you remember. He'd have had to get his ticket on the train. I tried to get on the train with him. We struggled a bit on the steps. He pushed me – not that hard – and I fell. He'd been at the top of the steps, you see. Me at the bottom.' Poor Stéphane. It wasn't only Adam who had his big bad moments on railway platforms. 'By then the door had shut.'

'You let him go,' said Adam.

'Oh come on,' objected Michael. 'He hardly had a lot of choice.'

They arrived at the Grand Moulin. Adam and Stéphane continued to argue in the garden. Michael left them to it and went off into the kitchen. Whatever anybody else was in need of, he at any rate felt he could do with a drink.

Adam was all for driving straight off again and trying to follow Sylvain's tracks. The other two practically had to hold him down. There was no point, they argued, until they had some idea of where he might have gone. London, Brussels and Madrid, mentioned earlier, could be ruled out: there was no earthly reason why Sylvain should want to go to any of them. They narrowed the logical probabilities down to four: St-Malo, where he had first seen and fallen in love with the sea; Paris, where he knew Gary Blake – and could perhaps have guessed that Sean, whom he'd grown so fond of, might be there too; third was the monastery at Cîteaux; and fourth, his parents' home.

Stéphane volunteered to phone the hotel at St-Malo: it was he, after all, who had the native-standard French. Michael took it on himself to phone Gary and Sean; he understood how painful a call it would have been for Adam. They both drew blanks. Adam had no phone number for the small holding in the Haute-Marne. He phoned the Abbey of Cîteaux instead. And received an instructive reply. The speaker, the guest master as he called himself, knew who Sylvain was, he said, but was not at liberty to say whether Sylvain was actually there at that time or not. Which Adam interpreted as meaning that he was. If he hadn't been, the man would have told him so. Adam thanked him, a touch sarcastically, and put the phone down.

'He's arrived there,' he said. 'I'm going. Now.'

They talked him out of that. It was evening already and Cîteaux was the other side of France – about as far away as you could go without finding yourself in Switzerland. And Stéphane even brought up another thing, which seemed monstrously trivial at the present time. The *notaire* in St-Emilion had phoned the previous day. Stéphane, not knowing what the next twenty-four hours had in store for everyone, had made an appointment for Adam to go and see him at eleven the following morning. This bit of nonsense did nothing to help Adam change his mind, but the other arguments did. He didn't really think it wise to try and cross France by unknown roads alone and in the dark. Twelve hours might bring

Sylvain to his senses. He might be returning by train even now. He might phone them.

Stéphane said he'd see about some supper. Nobody felt very hungry but still, one always ate. He disappeared into the kitchen and Michael, alone with Adam in the garden, at last let rip.

'Adam, this time you've really fucked it up. I don't know how you've got the nerve to blame Stéphane.' He looked around him. 'Everything just falls into your lap. You're the luckiest man on the planet, the luckiest man I know. You found the great love of your life after six years apart and found that he still wanted you. That almost never happens. But what do you do? You play around with Stéphane on the side and then let the whole thing degenerate into a three-handed farce. And you lose Sylvain.'

Adam was stung. '*We* had a threesome, if you remember. You and me and Sean. Right here last summer. Didn't seem to do us any harm. And if that's not exactly what you meant, do you remember all those years when I was sleeping alternately with Sean and you? I did have precedents – reasons for thinking that it wouldn't have to all go wrong this time. Of course it has done, but don't make me out to be such a big fool as that.'

'It was different then. We were only kids.'

'Kids last summer? Hardly!'

'Well I've grown up a lot since then. And if your relationship with Sylvain is as deep and meaningful as you always say, then you should have done some growing up too.' Michael looked up and round him at the old house behind them. 'And take this place. Someone leaves you a beautiful gaff like this and makes you a paper millionaire. Why so? Because you were a pretty boy and he fancied you, nothing more. You should be thanking your lucky stars. But you're going to lose this too. Going on as if you were still a child. No business plans, no sense. You'll be bankrupt in a year.'

'I won't be,' said Adam, though there was doubt as well as hurt in his voice. 'There's my concerts coming up. I've got a future as a soloist. The concert agent said a big one.'

'My arse,' said Michael, getting into his stride. 'You even think you're a real big-shot cellist now. You're nothing of the sort. You're a competent college graduate, that's all. Not that you didn't play well last night, but you did just the same at college, you played just as well as school. You just got lucky because yet two more people fancied you. One of the leading pianists of his generation lets you live in his flat in Paris, coaches you and plays your bloody accompaniments, and then a middle-aged lady violinist thinks you'd look nice beside her in a dicky bow.'

Stéphane had re-emerged and stopped in his tracks beside the door, surprised to hear Michael in mid-tirade. But then he came startlingly to life. '*Ta gueule*, Michael. Shut the fuck up. What's happened to you?' His face twisted up. He was half shouting, half crying. 'You don't have the right any more to talk to Adam like that. If you ever did. He doesn't belong to you. He belongs to all of us.'

Adam felt that hurricane-force anger once again. 'I do not belong to all of you.' It came out like a roar. *Coeur de Lion.* 'Time we all fucking realised.' He was shouting at himself mainly. He pushed past the unhappy Stéphane and stamped his way indoors and up to his room.

The emptiness of his bed that night. An Arctic desolation of white sheets. Ice-sheets that stretched to infinity beside him. And the worst of it was that there was no part of this disaster that had not been caused by himself. It was hardly the point that Sylvain had gone to bed with Stéphane. Hardly the point that Sylvain had been the one to initiate a three-way on the lawn. It was he, Adam, who had insisted on keeping Stéphane in his life after Sylvain had returned, he who had brought the other two together, he who had not given Sylvain and himself the chance to grow back into the special thing that they had once been – and now might not be again.

Had he been asleep? He didn't think he had. But all was dark and someone was trying to lie on the bed beside him, half on top of him: not trying to get into bed with him, just lying on the empty duvet cover – the only cover you needed on these summer nights. Adam knew the touch of those knees and arms, the sound of that breathing, the faint, pleasing scent of his skin. He knew the comforting physicality of this visitor as well as he knew his own. It could be only Michael.

'Darling,' Michael said. Michael had never called him that before. Maybe this was a dream. He pinched himself. Yes, people really do.

'Darling, I'm sorry. Those awful things I said. None of them are true. You need to know that.'

'You said them.' Adam's voice came in a whisper. 'You meant them at the time.'

'I was hurting and angry too – for reasons of my own. …Go into that another day. I was jealous of you. Always had been, I suppose. Your having so much. This place. Two lovers always, not just one. A promising career in music.'

'So you didn't mean the things you said. That's good to know. But it doesn't matter anyway, does it?'

'Why?'

'Because all of them happen to be true. You're right. I don't deserve the luck I've had. And yes, I have lost it all. No, worse than that: thrown it away; out of the window with both hands.'

'Adam, don't think like that. Sylvain will come back. Tomorrow we'll make a plan.'

'You sound unjustifiably optimistic.'

'Justifiably – in the light of experience, I think.'

They lay together for a few minutes, the duvet cover still between them, Michael making no attempt to climb beneath and Adam not offering to invite him in. Though he did begin gently to stroke Michael's hair. Then a thought came to him. It was obvious really. 'You know,' he said, 'there's someone else you could try saying sorry to if you wanted to. And maybe, just maybe, with more profitable results.'

'I know,' said Michael. 'I've just come from there. It was Sté who wanted me to come here now to talk to you.'

TWENTY-TWO

This day would be like no other in his life. Adam knew that when it dawned. To say that he awoke would hardly be correct; he had barely slept, either before or after Michael's nocturnal visit. And yet he must have slept a bit, or dozed, because he was able to recall a dream. It was about the frog he had caught and held in his hand a few days ago. Only, in the dream there were two frogs, one in each hand, and he had stood for some time contemplating both. Then one had hopped from his grasp into the stream and swum away. On the rare occasions when dreams told you something, he thought, it was usually the supremely obvious.

Michael and Stéphane wanted to come with him, but he refused to let them, though he was grateful when Stéphane made a list of road numbers, motorway exits and town names and blue-tacked them to his windscreen. Anyway, he was going via St-Emilion to keep his appointment with the *notaire* first. The import of anything the *notaire* might have to tell him would pale into insignificance beside the burning imperative to find Sylvain and get him back. But there was other business that he wanted to set in train with the lawyer – if he hadn't already left it too late.

He arrived for his appointment on the dot. 'I owe you a bit of an apology,' the *notaire* said. 'I should have contacted you last week. On the anniversary of Monsieur Pincemin's death. I hope, though, that it won't make too much difference in practice. He didn't know the exact date of his death when he wrote his instructions. When he wrote this.' He handed Adam a letter. The envelope, addressed to Mr Adam Wheeler, bore the message: *To be handed to the addressee on the first anniversary of my death.* Adam tore it open with some apprehension. He read:

Dear Adam

I wonder if you will ever read this letter. A year is a long time to look ahead. Who knows if even you will still be alive one year from now? I can not guess what you will have done with my mill house and scrap of vineyard in France. Sold it? Or kept it and tried to make it work for you? Naturally I hope the latter, but ... well, you'll have discovered by now that turning a big house into an asset is not as easy as finding it has become a liability. So, if you have sold up already in order to use the money for something else, you're forgiven, though something in my heart tells me you won't have done.

I have to tell you, before you read any further, that no additional funds accompany this letter. If I had them they would be yours – however I don't. I hope you will go on reading anyway.

The reason for this final communication (and don't worry – there will be no more in future years) is that I didn't want to overwhelm you with too much to think about all at once. You may by now have discovered that I used to share my life, and the Moulin de Pressac, with a young man whom I loved, called Alain. Like you he played the cello, like you ... I only write this in the safe certainty that you will read these words long after I am dead ... he was charming and beautiful. You will not need me to tell you now that, meeting you for the first time in Paris, and then again in London, you reminded me of him very much. I felt as if, in a strange way, I had been given Alain back. Though not as a lover, obviously; I hasten to reassure you I have never imagined that! And then you came to visit me in hospital – to see an ailing, rapidly ageing man whom you knew only slightly. We've talked only of small things during your visits, though you've occasionally let slip your anxieties about your end of year exams, your recital at the Academy – the Beethoven, the Bach. Just as Alain used to, of course.

Blue Sky Adam

And you've been visiting me, week after week, without any expectation of anything in return – just as I would have hoped Alain would, had he still been alive. Had Alain still been alive he would have the Moulin de Pressac – our Eden in the Gironde he called it – to take on into the future. Suddenly I saw how it made sense to pass that on to you instead. (Have you found Alain's concert clothes, by the way? You'll have thrown them out, no doubt, though sentimentally I would like to imagine you wearing them if or when you play concert solos yourself.) It made sense, as I say, not only for your benefit but for mine. Because now, at the end of my life, I have a future to think about once again: your future with what – little or great, however you see it – I am able to give you. Perhaps by now you will have found someone to share that future with. Allow me to hope so. I remember you telling me about your early love on the Plateau de Langres, Sylvain. I also remember introducing you to my neighbours' son, Stéphane – with startlingly immediate results. And of course I'm not forgetting your English friends, Michael and the handsome Sean. But if none of them fits the bill – and I'm not laying odds on any favourite – your sea will remain a wide one for a long while yet.

I wish you luck. Thank you for giving me this final opportunity to imagine a future in which I have some small part.

And allow me to express, for the first and last time,

My Love.

Georges

Adam read the letter a second time. Then he handed it to the lawyer. 'You may as well read it yourself. There's nothing in it needs to be a secret any more. And, by the way, there'll be no reply.' The lawyer smiled at that. It was he, after all, who had made the joke about dead men's lawns going on growing after their deaths along with their fingernails.

'I see,' the lawyer said, after he'd read the letter and was handing it back. 'I think that probably concludes our business for the present. But should you need any help or advice in the future…'

'As a matter of fact I do,' Adam said. 'I want to talk to you about making a will. And about changing the title to the property. But not today. Other things have to happen first. I'll phone you in a day or two – I hope.'

Adam walked down the Rue Guadet, towards the Spanish bar. Georges's letter had given him many things: a new dispensation of courage not least of all. Of course there was no reason why René should be in the bar, it was barely midday. But when Adam pushed the door open, there he was, standing at the counter with a beer in front of him, dressed in combat trousers – which seemed appropriate – and a T-shirt celebrating a *Fête du Vélo*, sponsored by Lipton's Ice Tea back in 1999, which softened the effect somewhat. But he was substantially bigger and more solid than Adam was. Were it to come to a fight. Adam had no idea what that would feel like. The last person he'd ever had a fistfight with had been a scrawny Michael when both of them were just thirteen years old. With René he couldn't be very hopeful of his chances. He told himself it wouldn't come to that. 'Hallo, René,' he said at once. 'I want to talk to you.'

'Ah bon?'

'To ask you a question.' He was in now. 'Was it you went slashing my tyres? Letting them down and that? Nailing a dead owl to my door?'

René looked at him steadily for a minute. The muscle-filled T-shirt inflated a couple of times as if for practice. Then René said, 'No, it wasn't me. What reason would I have to do that?'

'I formed the strong impression you didn't like me.'

'I don't like you all that much, tell you the truth. Cocky little English fucker. You're a bit girly for my taste. Poncing around the place like you think you're the *Caïd du quartier*. Cock of the rock. With any number of little boyfriends in tow. *Copains comme cochons*. One, two, three, four, five is it? I hope you'll forgive me if I haven't managed to keep count.'

'Well, thank you for that,' said Adam, feeling himself shaking slightly. 'It's good to know where we stand.' He turned and prepared to depart.

'Don't you want to know who did do it, then?' René's voice, quieter, behind him.

Adam spun round again. 'You know?'

'Course I know.'

'Then tell me.'

'Pépin le Fou.'

'Pépin the Mad?' Adam was astounded. 'But I've had nothing to do with him.'

'Maybe that was the trouble then. You had the chance to put a bit of money his way. You blew it.'

'Yeah, but... Other people, French people, say no to his offers of faulty goods, things off the backs of lorries. They don't all get their tyres slashed.'

'That's because they're not jumped-up little English...'

'OK, OK. We've been through that bit.' Adam paused, wondering what, if anything, he could say next. Then he thought of a new question. 'Since you're turning into such a mine of information suddenly, do you know who it was that pretended to offer my grapes for sale to old Ducros at La Carelle and has got me questioned by the gendarmes about it?'

René looked genuinely surprised for a moment. 'Get away,' he said. 'You're having me on.'

Adam shook his head.

'Well, sorry. Can't help you there. Course I can tell you who it was set the police after me in connection with his tyres being slashed.'

'I did not, René. I was asked if there was anyone living round here who had taken a dislike to me. I said I thought I wasn't too popular in this particular bar. Which happens, as you've just confirmed, to be the truth. But I named no names. I accused nobody. I swear.'

'Hmm,' said René.

'Anyway,' Adam went on. 'Any suggestions what I do about Pépin? Go to the gendarmes again?'

'That'll get you nowhere pretty fast. If I were you I'd make a point of buying something off him quite soon. Don't matter what. Load of ballast. Half-rotted fence posts. That'd keep him off your back for a year, I'd say.'

'Well, thanks for the information, I suppose. Better late than never. And for the advice.' Adam was about to go, but René had one more tip for him.

'If you go round imagining enemies everywhere you look, you may find that's the best way to make yourself some. So don't look for them in the wrong place – and especially don't make too many assumptions about the reasons people might take against you. Messy old world, *hein*?'

Adam turned towards the door again, but looked back just before he went through it to deliver a parting shot. 'By the way, I have never tried to pretend to be any kind of *Caïd du quartier*. My sort usually don't.'

'Ah well,' René answered slowly, 'maybe it was just an impression.' He took a long slow draught from his glass of beer.

Outside, Adam phoned the Grand Moulin at once. 'Sté?' At least someone had picked up. An improvement on yesterday.

'Yes?'

Blue Sky Adam

'Any news of Sylvain by any chance? No? Now listen. I need you to do something for us. Urgently.'

'What? Where are you phoning from?'

'Still in St-Emilion. I'm just about to head off up the motorway. But there's something you must do and it had better not wait till I come back.'

'You sound kind of...'

'Get hold of Pépin the Mad and book him to do a job for us. Doesn't matter what. Fill the puddles in the drive with broken brick, buy a load of old railway sleepers... Anything, but do it soon.'

'Are you OK? This sounds crazy. Can you tell me why this is so important all of a sudden?'

'Best if you don't know, actually. It'll all go more smoothly. 'Bye now. Gotta go.'

Adam threaded his way through vineyards and then turned east onto the E-70 *autoroute*. He would have to be both driver and navigator today. He had mixed feelings about refusing the offer of the others to come with him. True, a navigator would have been useful and he did feel a bit daunted about driving four hundred miles, from one side of France to the other, all alone, but on this particular mission he had not wanted company.

He didn't listen to radio or other music either. He had no need to. He had an enormous reservoir of music in his head which, in moments of heightened tension sometimes came pouring out unbidden, like Stéphane's German swearwords. First came the Eroica symphony, the one he'd recently listened to, sitting beside Sylvain in the cathedral at St-Malo – their first live concert together. He'd had no idea he knew the piece so well. Yet now here it was, unwinding in his head in an unbroken tapestry of sound: almost every note of it – strings, woodwind, brass – all four movements in their immutable order, unhurrying as the stars in their heavenly courses. By the time it had finished he was past Périgueux and well on the way to Brive.

Next came a modest keyboard piece, *Les Niais de Sologne*, the Simpletons: first as Sté had strummed the beginning of it unpretentiously on the piano; then that was overtaken by George Pincemin's rendition of it on the Taskin harpsichord, at the Moulin all those years ago when it had made him think of Sylvain suddenly and nearly made him cry. First the frilled and formal dance steps of the theme, next the counter-rhythm joining – more village-maypole hop now than courtly gavotte – and finally the fanning out of the opening theme like a peacock's tail into a kaleidoscope of sound. Back then it had made him think of Sylvain – he thought – because of its simplicity. How blind and stupid – how young – he had been. To have preserved a memory of Sylvain as someone simple. It was the richness, the complexity of the beauty that had brought Sylvain to his mind. He saw that clearly now.

He stocked up with bottled water at a service area. The day was hot. He hadn't felt like anything to eat. His route began to skirt the northern flank of the Massif Central and as those distant hills rose steadily higher to his right, Mahler's Symphony Number One came to him, though less perfectly remembered than the Beethoven. There were hazy bits, and cuts. It was Mahler One, the abridged version.

By the time he forsook the motorways for the ordinary road system somewhere to the north of Clermont-Ferrand he had found himself hearing, by some trick of the mind, a Schubert symphony, the Elgar Cello Concerto and Holst's Planets Suite. And then, as he headed more directly north (Sibelius in the background now), the road signs began to turn themselves into wine lists once again. The hair on the back of his neck rose slightly as he passed a turning to Givry: Givry where he

had drunk his last glass of wine with Sylvain before the
police apprehended them at the remote farmhouse … a
lifetime ago. Meursault, Beaune, Nuits-St-Georges. He
was exhausted and numbed by the drive, as well as by
the crisis in his life that had made it necessary, but he
recognised just in time the turning in Nuits-St-Georges
that led to Cîteaux, and still had enough of a grip on
reality to marvel at the fact that he'd got this far without
accident, mechanical mishap or getting lost.

The last leg. Through the village where he had
glimpsed Sylvain through a line of traffic back in March.
The last unfamiliar mile or two. (Back then they'd taken
a short cut across fields.) Finally turning up the driveway
into the monastery grounds. It was still day but before
long, here in the east, dusk would be spreading its grey
wings.

The gift shop and the tourist welcome centre were both
closed. No-one was in sight; no sound came from
anywhere around. From the Abbey Church no echo of
plainsong could be heard. Adam walked up to the door
he remembered as belonging to the guest wing, where
Sylvain had lodged and now maybe did again. He rang
the bell. Waited long. No answer. Rang again. Then
knocked. Waited. Wake Duncan with thy knocking.
Rang and knocked again.

Adam was reluctant to believe what he was hearing
when sounds finally came from behind the door, such an
age had he been knocking. Then there was a movement:
a small wood panel behind a little grill that he had hardly
noticed moved an inch. Then bolts pulled back. The door
opened. Adam stood facing a grey-haired man in the
white habit – tunic and scapular – of a Cistercian monk.
The collar of his striped pyjamas showed at his neck
above the folds of his thrown-back hood, and the cuffs
of the pyjama trousers were visible, five feet below,
resting on the instep of his sandaled feet. 'You make

enough noise to raise the dead,' he said. 'What's up with you? The brothers have to rise at four.'

'I'm looking for a friend. Sylvain Maury.'

'Compline is finished. You break the *Grand Silence* to ask after a friend?' He stopped and looked Adam up and down – a young man clad in only shirt and shorts. He peered beyond him at the drawn-up car. 'Are you alone?'

'Very,' said Adam. 'I've just driven from Bordeaux.'

'I think I know your voice. You telephoned for Sylvain yesterday.'

'I did.'

'Come in then.' He turned and led the way, pointed Adam towards a door, then re-bolted the outside door behind them.

'Come in' does not immediately take you very far inside a monastery. Adam found himself inside the plainest reception room he'd ever seen. One polished round table. Four polished wooden chairs. One polished parquet floor. White walls. Plain crucifix.

'Asseyez-vous maintenant.' Adam sat. 'I'm sorry to tell you,' said the monk, 'after you've driven all this way, that Sylvain is not here.'

'But…'

'He's been here, yes. He came last night. He left again today at noon.'

'You could have told me on the phone that he was here.'

'I could have, yes. But I did not. At that time I judged that my first duty lay towards him rather than you. You will perhaps not appreciate that judgement just now. I hope that in due time you may.'

'And where has he gone now?'

'He chose, after some thought, to return to his parents' farm. Perhaps you know…'

'Thank you. I know exactly where that is.' Adam moved to stand up. The monk laid a hand gently on his sleeve. 'Are you sure you're in a fit state to be driving another hundred and more kilometres after the journey you've already had? It'll be the middle of the night when you get there. You are welcome to stay the night here. I can offer you a bed – and a sandwich and a hot drink.' He smiled for the first time. 'Not the Ritz perhaps, but we monks are not allowed to be choosy. Leave as early as you like in the morning but for your safety's sake, rest a little first.'

'You're very kind ... Father.'

'Brother. Brother Placid. Guest master.'

'Adam Wheeler.'

'Yes, I know.'

'But I must go. I'll drive carefully, I promise.'

'Then, if you won't stay the night, can I prevail upon you to accept the sandwich and the hot drink?'

Adam was won over. He ate the sandwich, straight from the fridge, and the hot drink, already waiting in a Thermos, standing in the cavernous kitchen while the brother watched. Then his host escorted him to the door. 'Can I ask one thing?' Adam asked him. 'May I step inside the church one moment before I go?'

Adam knew what he would find in the church. The darkness. For night had truly fallen now. The silence. The *Great Silence* of the conventual night. And the one small quiet flame, steady inside its little red glass. You didn't need to be a believer to feel the resonance of that, to understand what it was meant to say.

In the still darkness a thought came to him. It was like the answer to a question he hadn't asked, to a prayer he didn't know he'd made. And perhaps the answers to prayers were, after all – like the information supplied by dreams – simply the blindingly obvious. For what he realised, as he stood here quietly, briefly, was that he didn't simply need to persuade Sylvain, convince him to come back with him and that they could start again. He would have to say sorry to him first.

It was a technicality that it had been Sylvain who had made the first move towards Stéphane, transforming their potentially three-way sexual relationship into a physical reality. Sylvain was hardly wise in the ways of the world; Adam could not expect to hide behind the excuse that he had merely followed Sylvain's lead. And Sylvain's ending up in bed with Stéphane was only another inevitable step along the same path: one that he, Adam, had led the three of them along over the months. Sylvain had simply gone along, perhaps reluctantly at first, with what he sensed Adam had wanted deep down. And he had wanted that. At the time. Though now there was nothing that he wanted less.

He drove back to the motorway near Nuits-St-Georges. Joined it. Skirting Dijon, headed north. At last the familiar Junction Six. Pierrefontaine, the highest point on the Plateau de Langres. He turned off. He drove through silent, shuttered Perrogney and then stopped the car where the flint track led downhill from the lane. It was just gone one o'clock. Were Sylvain down there alone he would have no hesitation in driving straight down and waking him with knocking on the doors, stones at the window, whatever it might take. But, mindful of his initial reception at the abbey a few hours earlier he decided against waking up the whole, potentially hostile Maury family – adults, children, cats and dogs. They might not have matins to get up for, but like the monks they were farmers; had early nights and early starts. They would be up and abroad at daybreak, and in this eastern corner of France, in July, that would come soon enough. Everything needed to go right, now. This would be his last ever chance with Sylvain. As he well knew. Either that or he'd had that last chance already – and blown it.

Slowly Adam drove on again. Into the village of Courcelles. Past the house where he had lived. (Who slept in that front bedroom now?) Down the wooded hill towards the lake. He dawdled along the lakeside road. Might Sylvain be, not asleep in bed at all, but wandering his old walks by night? By bicycle? On foot? Adam kept his tired eyes peeled. He was having difficulty keeping them open at all. But to knock the object of his quest down by accident with his car would hardly be the outcome he desired. Adam turned onto the road that led across the dam. The dam whose need for repair some seven years ago had brought Adam's father – and himself – to France in the first place. Halfway across he stopped. Parked up in one of the passing places. Allowed himself to close his eyes.

He was woken abruptly by a flash of light in the rear-view mirror. The sun had stolen up behind him and was blinking through the trees that crowned the hills to the east. He must have been asleep for a couple of hours. He started the engine, drove on across the dam and turned the car round on the far side, in front of the bar where, years ago, the *patron* would serve him and his school-friends with nothing stronger than shandies. Then he re-crossed the dam and retraced his route in the now bright day. In Courcelles someone was rounding up cows to be herded in to be milked. One of the Lepage family perhaps, whose dairy had once supplied his family with milk and cheese. Other people were astir. Shutters were opening. He overtook someone on a bicycle. Not Sylvain. He made sure.

His heart was pounding as he took the right turn down the rutted cart track and he was struggling with his breath by the time he got out of the car in the farm yard, between the low house and the three great barns.

Surrounding him were dogs of all shapes and sizes, barking and jumping up. A face he didn't recognise stared expressionlessly at him from the gloom of an outhouse doorway: one of the younger children perhaps, now a big teenager. Then coming towards him was the dumpy little woman with the long unkempt hair – looking older now, and the hair an uncompromised grey – whom he recognised as Sylvain's mother. He stood by the car, waiting for her to approach him, waiting for her to find her words first. He himself had none.

'It's you,' she said. She called him *vous*. 'At last you've come.'

'I came as quickly as I could,' said Adam. 'I've driven through the night.'

'I didn't mean that,' she said 'I meant the years. Those long years when he was unhappy and you never came.'

Adam felt something welling up inside him, punching upwards through the diaphragm; it found expression in a sound: an animal howl of pain that at first he could hardly believe was coming from inside him. Then he got a grip on himself. Stop that. Frighten the dogs. He felt giddy. 'I'm sorry,' he said. It was almost impossible to speak. 'I'm sorry.'

Estelle Maury took her son's lover in her arms.

Adam climbed the back wall of the largest barn towards the high loading door under the slate roof, using as a ladder the familiar great iron staples cemented into the stone wall. For a second he thought of his concert audience of two nights ago. Were they asked to guess what he might be doing now, they might more easily imagine three-in-a-bed sex than this. Sylvain hadn't slept in his bed last night, his mother had told Adam. He was almost certain to be here, at the top of the barn, the old retreat of his troubled teenage years. The top of the barn, that cathedral-like roof-space that held big memories of

Blue Sky Adam

Adam's too. Up here he had first called Sylvain by his name, first told Sylvain his, and had first kissed another man. There had been a bottle of damson brandy hidden under the floorboards, under the straw. Up here, a few weeks afterwards, Adam had been fucked by Sylvain for the first time and as they writhed together he had hit his chin on a beam half-hidden in the hay and chipped his top front teeth. Memories.

Arriving at the weathered wooden door above the topmost of the staples, Adam was unsurprised to find it unfastened and opening easily. What did surprise him was the discovery that the roof-space was filled solid with bales of straw. His memories were of a wide open loft full of angled beams and posts, with only here and there a few residual stacks of straw and hay. But that had been springtime. Now, following the haymaking and early harvests, the place was crammed from floor to roof. There hardly seemed room for a litter of cats to sleep. But after a moment Adam realised that an empty corridor ran between the wall of bales and the stone wall of the barn. Light poured into it through the familiar slits that were like the loopholes in a medieval castle. And looking left along the straw corridor, Adam saw that at its end it widened slightly. And there, sitting bolt upright on the end of some bales that had been laid together to form a sort of divan, was Sylvain. Bolt upright, presumably because he'd heard Adam's scramble up the wall and his push at the half-open door.

Sylvain was wearing shorts and a shirt – the same ones Adam had last seen him in two days ago – both unbuttoned. Sleeping naked on straw bales was clearly not a practical option. Apart from his inscrutable face and his brown legs with their weightless fuzz of dark fur, the only visible part of him was his navel and the little curl of hair that spiralled round it, the tapering tip of the Van Gogh cypress tree that bushed around his sex. It was part of, and gateway to, the most hallowed territory of Adam's kingdom, but as Adam's eyes were drawn to it now he was bitterly conscious that he was looking at something that no longer belonged to him; it had been withdrawn from his legitimate touch; the territory had seceded. Dear God, I love him, Adam thought.

'You,' said Sylvain. He sounded genuinely surprised. 'How come?'

'I drove,' said Adam.

'To take me back?' Adam nodded. 'And was that you in the yard?' Adam nodded again. 'I thought it was one of the dogs. Then I heard something in the sound that ... well. You're pretty determined, *quoi?* Mind you, you always were. Coming all the way here. But I can't possibly come back with you. You must know that.' Sylvain had made no move towards Adam, no gesture of the hand even, nor a smile. That wounded Adam like a knife, but he had hardly dared to hope for a friendly reception, let alone supposed that he deserved one.

About six paces separated Adam from where Sylvain sat. Adam now took two of them. 'I'm sorry,' he said. 'That's the first thing. And I don't just mean for sleeping with Stéphane. There's more to it than the advisability or otherwise of threesomes, more than simply having sex with the wrong person at the wrong time.'

'You're right,' said Sylvain. 'If it's just about sex then I have to say sorry too. I shouldn't have fucked Sté when you weren't there. *Ce n'était pas tout à fait le cricket, hein?* So I'm saying sorry too. And maybe you'll manage to forgive me for that one day far from now. But sometimes a little thing in life tells you a bigger thing. Fucking the wrong person one time, discovering one little lie – they're not such big things in themselves. The biggest thing I've discovered in all this is that ... I don't belong. I don't belong with you.' He delivered this in a reasonable, unimpassioned tone as if he had been practising it.

'Don't say that. You can't say that.' Adam discovered that he had taken the remaining four paces towards Sylvain and had somehow fallen to his knees in front of where he sat. 'I look you in the eye and tell you from the depths of my being that it isn't true. You're wrong.'

Sylvain still made no move towards Adam. 'I see you with Stéphane, with Sean. Nice boys both, beautiful both in body and in *esprit* – in Sean's case exceptionally so. But they live, and you live, in a world that isn't mine. Of money, education – class, if you like. I can't come near to that. This is where I belong.' He patted the straw bale he was sitting on. Not emphatically. Just a reflex. 'Where I should have stayed.'

'You don't believe that,' said Adam, surprising himself with his sudden calmness. 'I know you don't. You're inventing an excuse, that's all. Something you've heard people say in films and on TV. Coming from different backgrounds is neither here nor there. You're only saying that because you're hurt. Because I've hurt you.'

Sylvain would not be deflected. 'You've got a concert career coming to you. You'll be off, travelling Europe, travelling the world.'

'I won't travel anywhere without taking you with me.' Adam's voice was low and rough-edged, almost a growl. 'And if you don't want to come then I'll stay at home with you. Screw concert careers. What do they matter compared to having you? And anyway, that's still not the thing that's upset you, turned your whole heart inside out, made you bleed. Sex isn't a small thing with you. It's big. It was you who said, years ago, 'All I ever want, and everything I've ever wanted, is you.' And I threw that away – can you imagine? – I didn't understand what it meant. Or else I was frightened by it. Being only

311

sixteen. But then I didn't grow into the idea as I got older either. I tried to have everything both ways: to have one special relationship but also to screw around with friends. But – but I've started to grow up quickly since two nights ago. Can you believe that?'

Sylvain leaned forward on his seat. They were near enough now to touch each other but neither of them made that move. Sylvain spoke. 'I tried to fit in with your way. You know, sex among good friends. Did my best. And it wasn't difficult to enjoy sex with Sté. As you know. But in the end, *tu sais*, it's not for me. I wanted you on my own terms. I didn't get that. So I withdraw. If that's being selfish then so be it.'

'It isn't selfish,' Adam protested, 'it's being you. Being the person I really want, and should have known I really wanted all along. Can't explain that. It's you and me that belong together. You know what Montaigne said when they asked him about the great big friendship of his life? *'Parce-que c'était moi, parce-que cétait lui.'* Same goes for us. You don't have the same thing with Stéphane as you do with me. You will admit that, won't you?'

Sylvain gave a faint reluctant nod.

'Well, it's just like that for me. I don't have with Stéphane what I have with you. Never have had. And the other thing is this: that I can change. About relationships, I mean. Learn to be exclusive, faithful. Learn to be like you.'

'But you won't.' Sylvain shook his head. 'You never do. That's why Sean turned you down when you offered to share your life and home with him last year. He told me.'

'Sean told you that?' Adam felt for a second as if the floor was giving way.

'You tell me you don't feel for Stéphane what you feel for me.' Sylvain still spoke softly, measuring out his words. 'But it was different with Sean, *n'est-ce pas*? You did have those feelings, that love for another, with Sean.'

Adam struggled to get his thoughts and feelings back into order. 'In the past, yes. I admit that. But past is past and doesn't come again. Except for you and me. Our past – yours and mine – came back, became our present for a while. Please, please, Sylvain, let it be our future too.' He tried another tack. 'And by the way, don't think that Sean will ever be part of the equation again where I'm concerned. Sean's in love. He's fallen in love with an older man.'

'With Gary?' For the first time Sylvain showed a spark of interest in something beyond his immediate misery. A light appeared in his eyes that might almost have been the beginning of a laugh, though the laugh itself did not ignite.

'Yes,' Adam confirmed. 'It wasn't just a flash in the pan, that night in Angers. You see, we're growing up, we youngsters. If Sean can do it, so can I. Nothing's more important to me than us, than you and me. Let other people have their open marriages and their *ménages à trois* if that's what they want, and if those things work for other people then that's fine for them and fine by me. But I don't want that now. I've changed. Believe me, Sylvain. You must.'

'And Stéphane? We're still at square one while Stéphane's still around.'

'Fuck Stéphane,' Adam said irritably. But then their eyes exchanged a look. For the first time that morning. A look of complicity in a shared, unspoken joke, the *we both did* repartee that in less dire circumstances might have heralded a giggle. Instead, Adam went on, 'I wasn't going to tell you this. I thought I could convince you – make you believe I really would change – without bringing this in, but it seems I can't. So listen up. I haven't got Stéphane. Sean once said that Stéphane would be my consolation prize if ever I lost you. But he wouldn't have been any kind of consolation. I'm really fond of him, I know, but he just isn't you. I'll say it again. *Il n'est pas toi.* And the other thing – the reason I said 'wouldn't have been', not 'wouldn't be', is because Stéphane is no longer in the equation any more than Sean is. Don't dare come back to me with, 'You've only come to look for me because you've lost Stéphane,' when I tell you that I left him at the mill with Michael. They're picking up the fragments of the thing that Michael so heartlessly let drop a year ago and, with any luck, they're piecing them together.' He hadn't wanted to tell Sylvain that, to play his almost trump card. It was the move of someone who has already almost lost. Now he only had one card left up his sleeve: his intention to give Sylvain joint title to the Moulin de Pressac. But if he had to play that card – he knew – the game would be well and truly over, and the loss irretrievable for both.

'Michael? With Stéphane? Now you tell me!' Again Sylvain's face nearly kindled into a smile. Nearly but not quite. 'How did Michael come to be down at the Moulin?'

Adam told him. 'He spent half the evening telling me what a fool I was for risking losing you. He was right.' Adam smiled ruefully to himself. 'Everything he said was right. He spent the other half of the evening telling me how much luck had landed on my plate and how I'd just thrown everything away. Told me I was just a run of the mill musician who got lucky because Nathalie fancied me. That I played no better than any other college student, no better than I'd done as a school kid. It's true, of course.'

Sylvain reached forward and took hold of Adam's hands. 'He said that? That you played no better than any other college student? *Couilles.* I heard you play years ago. You were good then, but the difference now is – well, you can't measure it. I can hear the difference if he can't. So don't go believing him over me. If he thinks that... Well, he doesn't know your music like I do. He doesn't know you like I do. You do believe that, don't you?'

'Thank you. But he was right about the music. I'm not in the big league and never will be. That might not be easy for you to understand...'

'What do you mean, me not understand...?'

'What I mean...'

'You're going to tell me about some Russian geezer who played thirty concertos in five minutes...'

'Five days, I think. Rostropovitch...'

'Sod Moscopovitch. When people listen to you they're not asking themselves, can he play this or that? Ten concertos or only one, or did he master five hundred five-finger exercises or whatever at the age of six or not till he was seventeen? That Gary went to music school at twelve and you not till eighteen? Because none of that matters. People hear you, and it's magic. Real witch-work stuff. I know that. Michael doesn't. Because... Because...' Sylvain's voice faltered. 'Because,' he went on brokenly, 'nobody loves you like I do. Nobody ever will or can. *Putain, connard*, bastard – you're all of those things. But who else could love you, except for me? Only me.'

'Then why,' said Adam, feeling his hands trembling as he spoke, 'do you want to stay away from me, holed up here? If you stay here and I stay there in the Gironde, what do our futures hold? You continuing to pick up the occasional adventurous teenager in the woods – as you did me – until you get too old to attract them, and then somebody reports you and ... well, you know the rest. And me, trawling the Bordeaux bars and clubs until I'm past that too. Then what? A lonely old age for both of us, five hundred miles apart? I promise you, look as hard and as long in those woods as you like, you won't find another me.'

Sylvain stared at him almost angrily for a second. Then he said gruffly, 'And maybe you wouldn't find another me in Bordeaux either, come to that.'

'So?' Adam asked. *'Et maintenant?'* He looked around him. 'There used to be damson brandy in a bottle under the floor.'

Sylvain was surprised into a laugh. 'Damson brandy? At this hour of the morning? It's only half past five!' He peered at Adam's face as if he hadn't focused on it before, and perhaps this morning he hadn't. 'You're tired. You look all washed out. It's not brandy you want, it's sleep.'

'I drove half the night and half of yesterday.' Adam was beginning to feel faint.

'Some host I am then,' Sylvain said, trying to be more brusque than tender. 'Come here.' He pulled Adam towards him and onto the straw bales at his side. 'Lie there. Sleep a little. Later I'll get you some coffee. Before you go on your way.'

'On my way?' Adam felt another animal howl arising from the depths. He choked it off. 'Jesus, Sylvain, you can't mean that. I can't go without you. Can't go anywhere without...'

'*Chut*. Close your eyes and sleep now. Then we'll see.'

'Stay with me now anyway? Just don't leave me now.'

Sylvain looked at Adam, curled up now against him and trying with hands in spasm to hold onto him tight; observed the silent rivers of his cheeks. He tried to think: to make sense of the situation in which he found himself – or, more honestly, into which he'd got himself. Two things that Adam had said were true. There was no future for him here, living out an empty life on the Plateau de Langres with no Adam beside him. And he had, as Adam said, only been casting round for excuses when he'd said he didn't belong in Adam's world. Because he absolutely did. Adam had shown him the very world in which he did belong: a world of beautiful friendships and beautiful friends, of beautiful places and beautiful sounds. He'd heard Adam play Mozart in a recording studio in Paris, and Brahms in a cathedral. He had opinions now about the way he played Elgar and Beethoven too. He'd discovered a voice in himself – and in more ways than one: Adam had told him he could sing.

He'd seen the sea.

Then Adam had said that he could change. Sylvain was less sure about this. He suspected that people didn't change all that much. And the male sex had always had a fatal tendency to roam. He'd learned that for himself during the last years. There was no doubt that Adam had meant it when he said he'd changed, protesting it with tears in his eyes. But people didn't always live up to their promises of amendment. *Et alors?* The seeds the farmers sowed did not always germinate, the eggs they set under hens did not all come good. But that didn't stop them sowing seed and setting eggs to hatch.

He'd started on a journey with Adam once, six years before. It had been cruelly interrupted. This year they had started out again. There was no knowing where it would lead, and whether it would be a happy one or not was beyond any power to foretell. But why had he decided to abandon it so soon?

What he'd said to Adam, that he wouldn't go home with him, that their time together was at an end, was simply cruel. He'd wanted to hurt Adam because of his own hurt: the shame of betraying Adam, in Stéphane's bed; the pain of Adam's betrayal of him, time and time, in the very same place. And beneath that still lay the residual pain from the cruelty of Adam's disappearance for six whole years. But hurting Adam now, as he clearly had, had done nothing to assuage his own suffering. In fact the opposite was true. He couldn't hurt Adam, he discovered, without hurting himself.

He wanted to write a book about blue sky, he'd once told Adam. He hadn't known why. But now he thought he knew. The blue sky was his lover's heart or soul. It had in some mysterious way been shared with him, the way the sky shares its blue with the sea. It was revealed in the music that he played. And it was the mirror also of Sylvain's own soul. Even the distress they now suffered was a hurt that mirrored between them, making the two of them one.

He knew now what he hadn't admitted even to himself two minutes before. He wouldn't be leaving Adam. Not even for as long as it would take to make him coffee. Not ever now. He lay down beside him, cradled his young man's head in his arms.

The last thing Adam heard as he drifted into unconsciousness was the voice of Sylvain in his ear, half-singing some song that must have come to him from the depths of his childhood: a cradle song of strange music and unfamiliar words.

VALEDICTORY

July – August

The golden oriole ceased its fluting in the poplar tops
and left only the breeze to rustle the shimmering leaves.
The cuckoo's call changed, and darkened: three notes
instead of two. Then silence and the bird flew south.
Stéphane and Michael also left the mill, once Adam and
Sylvain had returned together from the Haute-Marne, but
migrated no further than the nearest bit of coast. They
would be back for the grape harvest. So Adam and
Sylvain were alone together when Robert Ducros's men
arrived a couple of weeks later to lop the trees that
overhung the millstream. As the arrangement to do this
had been made back in April, and nothing more said –
after that unhappy meeting with Robert at which he'd
told the story of the gay rugby player – Adam and
Sylvain had reached the conclusion that the plan had
been shelved indefinitely or even forgotten altogether.

But now that it was happening, Adam and Sylvain
both turned out to join in the work. Adam had no reason
now to worry about damaging his fingers. He had played
the last of his summer concerts with Nathalie, not so far
away, at Arcachon, and now there were no more
concerto dates for five months. Besides, the Moulin de
Pressac, not only Château La Carelle, would be
benefiting from the clearance of superfluous
overhanging boughs. Soon the two of them were
clambering about among the branches, fixing ropes and,
back on the ground again, helping to haul the sawn-off
timber out of the way.

Robert Ducros arrived in the course of the morning to
see how the work was progressing. He showed signs of
surprise at the discovery of his two young neighbours
climbing trees, bare-chested in the sunshine. Sylvain

explained that, since they were going to share the benefits of extra light and general trim, they had felt it only fair to put in a bit of work themselves.

'Well, that's very … hmm,' Robert said, and stopped. Then, 'Look, I think I owe you a bit of an apology. There've been a few misunderstandings. There was that silly business last month of my father remembering someone offering him grapes for sale – your grapes. Or rather, thinking that he remembered. When the police asked him about it directly it turned out that he was remembering something that had happened more than twenty years ago. He gets a bit … anyway. So then it was case dismissed. And I realise I should have phoned you then and there to make an apology – the police troubling you for nothing and all that – but, to tell the truth there was a bit of bad feeling about you in the neighbourhood around that time. People were saying things … well, untrue things of course.' He stopped a second time.

Sylvain, from the branches above his head, volunteered to finish his sentence. 'Saying that we were – how did they put it – *gais dans le sens anglo-saxon*?'

'Yes, more or less. I shouldn't have taken any notice of course. I realise…' He looked up at the two young men, tanned, lean and muscled, and sweating slightly from the effort of hauling logs.

'You don't need to apologise,' Adam said, 'The rumours were right. And that would go for most of the friends who visit us here too.' Somehow it was easier to say all this leaning out of a tree a couple of metres above Robert on the ground.

'Oh,' said Robert. He thought a moment. 'Does that include young Stéphane from Beaurepaire as well?' Adam nodded. 'So that was what all that falling out with his father was in aid of. I see.'

'We're planning to be your neighbours for a very long time,' said Sylvain, off at a slight tangent. 'In fact no plans ever to be anywhere else – either of us.' He didn't say, *like it or lump it*. He knew when a point had been made.

'I see,' said Robert. 'Looks like you go in for surprises rather. I was about to say that I'd just seen the *Sud-Ouest* and there was a picture of Adam here, playing professional cello at Arcachon. I'd heard him practising in the garden sometimes. Very nice it sounded in fact but I never knew…'

'He's far too modest,' Sylvain said. 'He's got an international career ahead of him. Next year the Grand Théâtre in Bordeaux and the Salle Pleyel in Paris.'

'*Mon Dieu*, then he is too modest. And maybe that scuppers the next thing I was going to say. It was about the St-Magne rugby team. They're short of players for the opening match in September. I'd been wondering… Though maybe…'

Adam and Sylvain looked at each other in mute surprise. Then Adam said, 'We're hardly rugby-playing size, are we? Anyway I haven't played since I was fourteen. I don't know if Sylvain…'

'Think about it anyway. St-Magne isn't exactly Six Nations standard. They're not all built like barn doors. Just think it over, that's all. Unless…'

'Cellists usually don't play rugby,' Adam said. 'They're afraid they'll get their fingers broken. But it was good of you to ask. We'll talk it over.'

Robert nodded and started to move off. But then he changed his mind, turned and looked up at Adam again. 'Uh… It looks as if I made a bit of a gaffe, didn't I, when I spoke to you back in the spring. I told you I thought you were broad-minded, which you must have thought was a bit rich, but I spoke without knowing what the real situation was. Perhaps I'll have to be a bit broad-minded myself with you two as my neighbours. If you're broad-minded enough to live with a neighbour like me.'

Sylvain answered. 'We can live with that, I reckon. How about now you come drink a bottle or two with us later? Bring the missus and the kids.'

Robert was rendered speechless for a moment, staring at him out of wide grey eyes. Then, 'OK,' he said. *'Et pourquoi pas?'*

September

The rugby match was still fresh in everyone's memory when the *vendange*, the grape harvest, began at the end of the month. Adam and Sylvain regaled their houseguests – their workforce – with the story of it. After much hesitation they had agreed to play – just that once – for the St-Magne team, as part of their drive to integrate – ingratiate? – themselves into the local community. They had both been full of trepidation in advance of the game and their fears proved well founded. Adam, having last played at the age of fourteen, had no idea what it felt like to play against adults who had been playing as adults for years. He just made it through to the end of the game without giving up, and had spent the following two days barely able to walk. Sylvain proved more physically resilient, prepared to play aggressively when need be, and was a fast runner into the bargain. But he proved to have no idea of what it meant to play as part of a team and also to have only the haziest grasp of the rules. It was not entirely the fault of the two new players that the St-Magne team was soundly thrashed by the neighbouring commune of Gardegan-et-Tourtirac, but they certainly played quite a major role in the débâcle.

'But at least you did it. Said yes and had a go,' Sean said. 'People will remember that and respect you for it, long after the disastrous score is forgotten. I'm proud of you both anyway.'

The vines of the Moulin de Pressac were being picked by hand: by Adam's and Sylvain's hands, by Michael's and Stéphane's, by Sean's and by those of two local lads – those last were the only ones that had to be paid for. For the first time Adam began to see the advantage of owning a house with a large number of bedrooms.

Most of the other vineyards of the Côtes de Castillon, including Beaurepaire and L'Orangerie proper, were machine picked. Only the grander vineyards of St-Emilion employed human hands – mostly eastern European ones these days – to gather the harvest. On the Côtes de Castillon Adam and Sylvain's vineyard was something of an anomaly. But next year it would be less anomalous. A more professional system would be in place, thanks to Françoise who was starting to take over the accounts, and maybe involving the use of Philippe Martinville's picking machine in return for some physical graft on the part of Sylvain and Adam: the details had yet to be sorted.

But this year, although the harvest wouldn't be as big as in 2007, and the resulting wine not be expected to rival the superb vintage of 2005, it looked promising enough. Despite storms and torrential rains in August that had sent the Dordogne backing up the river Lacaret and into the millstream, turning the gardens into a lake and the mill house into a moated castle for half a day, little damage had been done to the crop, beyond a small proportion of split fruit. The wholesale sliding of soil and vines down the slopes that some had feared did not happen; the indications remained good.

The pickers worked long days, bending and stretching, with ordinary secateurs. Sylvain had equipped everyone with knives too, for dealing with the tougher vine stalks, and PVC capes with waterproof hoods. These were needed not only on the odd rainy day that inevitably came along but even on the fine ones when, in these early autumn mornings, the pickers wrestled with the vines' foliage in drenching dew. Sylvain had had nagging doubts as to how waterproof the capes would be: they had been bought at a knockdown price from Pépin the Mad. But in the event they proved equal to what was required of them, given the general kindness of the weather.

Sean had to return to university before the end of the *récolte*, the others stayed to the end. Despite the fact that Stéphane was now driving a hired tractor only metres away from the boundary of his parents' property where picking was also under way, there was no contact between him and them. Michael's suggestion that he might boldly turn up on the doorstep of Château Beaurepaire and introduce himself – effectively ask for the hand of the son of the house – was firmly knocked on the head by Adam and Sylvain, though they did admit that it had a certain chivalrous charm. But it would have been certain only to make matters in that quarter worse. So Stéphane returned with Michael to London at the end of the harvest. There was a similar lack of reconciliation between Adam and his parents. No word, no 'Good luck with the harvest', had come from them. In a reversal of the way things had been a few months ago, it was now Sylvain who regularly phoned his parents on Sunday nights.

There came one moment of revealing candour on Sean's part towards the end of his last evening, after champagne had been drunk, out on the lawn, the trees softly illuminated by flickering garden lamps. He sat himself down on the bench on which Adam was, just at that moment, sitting alone and placed an arm round his shoulder in that lovely – yet irritating, because teasing – way he had. He hadn't told his mother yet that he'd finally decided he was gay. Mindful of the bad reception that Adam's mother and Stéphane's father had given to similar news he was going to bide his time. But it was not about that that he had come to talk to Adam. 'You'd better not lose him again, that's all I can say,' was what he said.

'Thank you, Sean,' said Adam, half mocking him. 'I'll let you be my example. In constancy as in everything else. Ten whole weeks is it now?'

'Very funny. Seriously though, don't ever think of me as an example in anything. That was always the problem between us. You saw me always as the older and wiser one – and you even made me look at myself that way. But that was like looking at me through the wrong end of a telescope, do you see? I always knew I wasn't really looking for a relationship with another boy. Even though I loved you. But it wasn't till after you and I split up that I began to realise that I might have been looking for something else. I had a few flings in Newcastle – experimenting if you like…'

'Jesus Christ, Sean!' Adam's head was spinning and the champagne had only a small responsibility to bear for that. 'You are the darkest of dark horses. Or at any rate the blondest.' Not only the disclosure about Sean's sex life. Adam was also trying to deal with Sean's extraordinary phrase: *after you and I split up*. After we split up? How differently two people could remember the same key event in their two lives. As far as Adam was aware they had never been an item – and that had not been for lack of trying on Adam's part. *After we split up?* Sean's take on events left Adam temporarily speechless.

'Like you, I suppose,' Sean went on, 'I was unconsciously looking for someone more grownup than me. I saw you together with Sylvain in Paris, saw how happy you were, how you fitted together. I even told half a lie for you – remember? – to try and stop the Stéphane thing tearing you apart.' He darted a quick look around, hoping that Stéphane himself hadn't been in earshot of his last remark. He wasn't. 'And – anyway, you know the rest. So ... look. Don't lose it. Don't do anything to lose it.' He gave Adam one of his smiles. He was quite profligate with those these days. For obvious reasons. And besides, they cost little to give.

'I'll bear that in mind,' said Adam. 'And by the way, I still love you, fuck it.'

'Me too,' said Sean. 'I mean I love you too. But we won't unbutton our trousers for each other any longer. That'll be the only difference.'

Dear, dearest Sean. Off to Paris in the morning to spend Gary's forty-first birthday with him, before jetting back to Newcastle – and then presumably Gary would be spending his own life's savings jetting to Newcastle and back himself. But Sean did like to spell things out with plonking clumsiness sometimes. Still, Adam thought, that was hardly going to disconcert Gary as he contemplated the blue-eyed best birthday present of his life.

October

The annual dinner of the Winegrowers Association took place a couple of weeks after the end of the vintage. Adam and Sylvain went along in almost matching dark suits and white shirts. Though while Adam wore his hallmark silver-grey tie, Sylvain sported a new crimson silk number which had recently caught his eye in Bordeaux. Matching ties, they felt, would have been a step too far: you could make a point more charmingly without double exclamation marks.

The rugby-playing exploits of the two newest members were still a hot topic, though evincing good-natured teasing rather than scorn. It was as Sean had predicted. Nobody really cared that the English classical cellist and his slightly other-worldly French boyfriend with the cornstalk-chewing accent were rubbish – *nuls* – at rugby. Instead they were heartened that they had taken the invitation to play seriously and had had the guts to expose their sporting inadequacies on the field. And nobody minded too much when they said that they wouldn't be doing it again. It had done no harm to their social credibility that they were known to be on visiting terms with Robert Ducros of Château La Carelle.

Stéphane's parents were at the association dinner, though they managed to avoid Adam and Sylvain until quite late on. Even then it was not Marc who came over and offered his hand to the two young owners of the Moulin de Pressac, but his wife, who left his side to do so. Her previously unlined face now carried its fair share of furrows, the decorations that the world awards to the survivors of its nasty shocks. 'When you speak to my son, next time, please – you must – tell him he's much missed. Working as a waiter in London.' She shook her head in a mixture of incredulity and pain.

Adam nodded. 'Smithfield. La Table Gasconne.' He added, sugaring the pill, 'Smart French place.'

She managed a half-smile, half-grimace. 'His inheritance isn't in jeopardy, you know. You can tell him it never was. But things take time.' Her eyes jerked involuntarily towards her husband, busy in conversation on the other side of the room. 'How long I don't know. Maybe it depends in part on you.' Adam and Sylvain both frowned. 'I mean, the way you live your lives among us here. The messages we take, unconsciously maybe, about what people like yourselves – like Sté – are like.' With that she walked away. It was only the first hint of a thaw, but even the end of the Arctic winter is heralded by a single water drop.

They talked to Philippe Martinville, their sponsor as members of the association and thus their reason for being at the dinner in the first place. They told him about their exchange with Stéphane's mother and, while on that subject, mentioned their improving relations with Robert Ducros. They hadn't told Philippe the story of old Monsieur Ducros and the offer he was supposed to have received in connection with the Moulin's grape crop. They related it now.

'Turned out it was twenty years ago,' Sylvain said. 'When he eventually remembered his story correctly. God knows what that was all about. The old *connard* must be hallucinating things.'

'Well', said Philippe, looking suddenly a mite uncomfortable, 'there might have been an occasion – I don't remember too well – when the Orangerie vineyard had a bit of a surplus and Lacarelle was short. I seem to remember talking about it with young Alain Pincemin – you know, Georges's son. I never imagined he'd have done anything about it, but then, you never know. He'd only have been about seventeen at the time.' Philippe chuckled involuntarily, like someone taken by surprise by a naughty memory. 'It was a long time ago. Long before I was married.' He paused and Sylvain and Adam exchanged glances. Then Philippe recollected himself and finished, 'I suppose we all do a few stupid things when we're young.' He smiled then, in a way they hadn't seen before.

...And Then...

And then – and now – it is November. The wind is blowing up from the Dordogne valley and chasing the yellowing leaves of the vines high into the air where they get mixed up with the orange and lemon leaf-fall from the poplars sailing down. At the mill are only

Blue Sky Adam

Adam and Sylvain. *Les vieux inséparables*, as Sylvain had wished them to become all those years ago, the two oxen harnessed together for as long as the future might hold for them.

Sylvain has recently astonished Adam, after hearing some songs by Reynaldo Hahn on the radio, by announcing that he wants to learn to sing them. Today they have been to the Virgin Megastore in Bordeaux to buy the music – which Adam will have to learn to accompany on the piano. This marks another new departure: yet another casting of them both in new roles. It still isn't entirely sure that they'll be able to make enough money, from all their various activities, to keep the Moulin de Pressac going. But they're determined to try. Right now though, it is the end of the day and they are sitting on the floor together in front of the big fire, resting their backs against the front of the sofa. Each can feel the animal warmth of the other through their clothes where they rub at the shoulder, and where their legs press together from hip to knee. The sound of the last evening train, clattering along the valley, begins to funnel down the chimney.

THE END

****

About the Author

Anthony McDonald is the author of more than twenty novels. He studied modern history at Durham University, then worked briefly as a musical instrument maker and as a farmhand before moving into the theatre, where he has worked in every capacity except director and electrician. He has also spent several years teaching English in Paris and London. He now lives in rural East Sussex.

Novels by Anthony McDonald

THE DOG IN THE CHAPEL

TOM & CHRISTOPHER AND THEIR KIND

THE RAVEN AND THE JACKDAW

SILVER CITY

RALPH: DIARY OF A GAY TEEN

IVOR'S GHOSTS

ADAM

BLUE SKY ADAM

GETTING ORLANDO

ORANGE BITTER, ORANGE SWEET

ALONG THE STARS

WOODCOCK FLIGHT

MATCHES IN THE   **DARK: 13 Tales of Gay**

Blue Sky Adam

Men

Gay Romance Series:

Gay Romance: A Novel

Gay Romance on Garda

Gay Romance in Majorca

The Paris Novel

Gay Romance at Oxford

Gay Romance at Cambridge

The Van Gogh Window

Gay Romance in Tartan

Tibidabo

Spring Sonata

Touching Fifty

Romance on the Orient Express

All titles are available as Kindle ebooks and as paperbacks from Amazon.

www.anthonymcdonald.co.uk

70646357R00186

Made in the USA
Middletown, DE
15 April 2018